CHAPTER 1

The man's name was Hood. Like a germ on a pellet of city dung, he stood on the peak of a mighty skyscraper, now laid down sideways in the debris of the explosion that had demolished it, and scanned his horizons with an intent expression and a small black telescope. In all directions around him, for as far as he could see, there stretched a landscape of the discarded and disused. He was searching for good quality junk. In the language of recycling, he looked for the reusable, like steel girders and bricks, and the function transferable: the steering wheel of a crushed Mercedes, for example, which could, with mere polish and packaging, become a collectible piece, or the cornice of this very skyscraper which could be sold on as garden sculpture. The world was rich enough to treat rubbish as art. The world was rich enough to cover the abandoned slums with all of last year's models while in another part of the country unattended machinery hummed as it built next year's, but right now Hood was not concerned with all that. He was the finder, and other people paid him for his findings, and that was all he did. He saw the potential in the object. And right now, he saw the potential of large quantities of copper in an object sticking out of the shimmering ground in the distance. A substation transformer, unless he missed his guess, which he almost never did. Copper was expensive, and like the millions of other workers who had been rendered obsolete by technology, Hood was on the SHA - the Self-Help Allowance. The world might be rich, but not everyone in it.

"Don't move a millimetre," he shook his finger at the transformer. "Just you stay there." He snorted out a guttural laugh and climbed carefully down to the ground, although it was not the ground except in as much as he could walk around on it. From this lower altitude he could no longer see the shard of folded metal, projecting a metre above the irregular surface of broken glass and dead petrol pumps and old PCs, but he had the direction and set off towards it.

He got lost a few minutes later and regained his bearings by getting up on the bonnet of an antique, Bedford truck, itself worthy of attention. He was off target by a good fifty metres. He redoubled his pace, mumbling a variety of curses and imprecations. To his considerable relief, because rushing around in a pile of junk is no fun, when he climbed out of the bowl of an aluminium can lake and took his next sighting, he was right over the spot. He looked down on the steel canister from almost spitting distance.

"Heh," Hood grunted. He climbed down. With satisfaction, he noted that the bolts holding the casing together were all in place, paint unchipped, edges dull. No tomb-robbers before him, then. He reached into his bag for his spanner and penetrating oil and quickly pulled off a side panel.

Even before he had it off, he was beginning to puzzle over an unfamiliar smell that seemed to come from inside the transformer. As he removed the last bolt, he realised that the transformer casing, untouched since no-one knew when, smelled slightly of heat and hot varnish. The sun was hot, damned hot, but not enough to melt varnish.

"Shit!" he cried as the heavy steel side with a resale value of $2.50 crashed down. The transformer was gutted. Not a scrap of copper remained on the armatures, which were just empty metal arms sitting naked in their cupboard. Hood looked pointlessly into the carcass, then sat down slowly on his heels and shut his eyes and sighed.

"There just ain't no fucking Santa Claus," he said after a minute. "Now, how'd the bastards get into this thing?" Chang Hood had always wanted to be a member of the Secret Society for Getting the Insides Out of Things Without Opening Them, and this might be his chance. He looked the transformer all over, studying it from each side and sticking his head into it and making sure that the bottom was as intact as the rest of it. How'd they do that? He gave up. The transformer was made empty. That's why it was here instead of up some pole somewhere. The man who designed it, he lost his job, and - what's this? As he stepped back over the panel he had removed, he saw in the bottom left corner a hole. Perfectly round. Probably an access patch of some kind, Hood decided, but he was already eyeball to hole by that time so he might as well make sure. Round hole. No burrs or other indications. But the edges shone like the sides of bright new coins. Hood frowned so deep that his upper lip met a drop of sweat from his nose.

"Ah! What's fifty bucks worth of copper?" he said at length. "Plenty more stuff where that came from." Straightening up, he stashed his tools back in his bag, pulled out his telescope and began to climb the nearest observation point.

Weeks later, he came to the realisation that that day had been the start of a gradual decline in his luck. The sort of stuff he usually picked up in the wasteland was not as abundant as he liked: pure metals, unfractured ceramics, functional electronics, retro artworks, were becoming hard to find. And there were little round holes, always the same size, appearing in things. He had come to realise that if there was a hole, there was no point in him opening up the whatever it might be, because it would sure as damn it be empty of anything useful or valuable. He took to crawling around under the surface, in the complex tunnelways made from the uncoordinated collapse of the underworld, where he hoped to locate the good shit. He had several entry points, the best being the open top of an elevator shaft. The rest of the building had been decapitated at the third floor long ago and since then the accumulation of rubbish had brought ground level up to the collar of what remained. Hood didn't even have to climb to reach it. He lowered himself by rope into the dark, and then out the side of the shaft into a way formed at first from a large sewer pipe, along which he crawled.

'What for am I doing this?' he wondered. 'Shitloads of crap above me, shitloads of crap below me, concrete and girders sticking out all round me. Even if I find something down here I'll never be able to get it out. Unless it's small. So I'm looking for, say, handguns. Or PDAs. Or car parts, there's always someone who needs a stub axle for an '03 Toyota. Or, shit, anything at all, it doesn't really matter what it is, so long as I find something and get that little buzz that says hey!, you found something no-one else would ever have found. And the money, of course'.

He was on his hands and knees. Ahead of him there was an aeroplane carcass, of all things. He felt slightly lifted. He'd tell the guys, there's a goddamned aeroplane under there. They'd all act like they didn't care what was down anywhere, but they really wished they had the guts to actually get down here in the danger and the dirt and see it themselves. Or so Hood liked to believe.

He crawled towards the aeroplane propelled by visions of chrome-plated aeronautical instruments and collectible airsickness bags. The object that was the roof of his crawlspace he now saw to be a wing, twisted and incomplete. The body of the plane was likewise broken, and there were only gaps where the portholes had been. Out of one of these gaps something suddenly jumped.

"Jesus!" said Hood, banging his head on the underside of the wing. The thing ran past him and into a gap in the debris. A rat. Dusty clouds of decayed paper and wood fell from the disturbed wing, getting in Hood's eyes. He blinked out tears. Through the now uncertain air between himself and the nearest porthole he saw another small creature moving. Another rat, he thought, but when a moment later his sight cleared he saw that it was not a rat. It was not anything he had seen before. It was something like a large crab or an impossibly large scorpion, with fewer legs than either, and it was made of metal. While he stared at it with his mouth framing an unsaid what-the-fuck-is-that, it calmly jumped off the porthole edge, out of his sight, into the aeroplane. Hood moved as fast as his awkward position would allow to the side of the plane and stuck his head in the hole.

He could see the scorpion-like machine, as he guessed it to be, walking towards the cockpit end of the craft. It reached an obstacle: a bulkhead door, which was shut. As Hood watched with increasing excitement, the scorpion placed it's two front limbs against the door and began to rotate them rapidly anticlockwise. Hood didn't dare to move. He sat with his head sticking into the plane at an angle of seventy degrees to his body for several painful seconds while the scorpion completed the full circle. Then a disc of metal fell out of the door and the scorpion stepped through the perfectly round hole it had just created.

"Man!" Hood breathed. "It's the hole maker!" He tried to squeeze himself through the porthole space, but after ripping his shirt and drawing blood from his thin shoulders, he gave up and withdrew to look for the door. 'Up the front. There's usually a door up the front'. His face was bright and blank with concentration as he wriggled over a series of crushed metal cases towards the cockpit.

"Got to catch this thing," he muttered to himself. "It's got to be worth a fucking fortune. It's probably a military robot or something. Something pretty expensive, anyway." He didn't know much about the technology that made his world what it was and by implication made him what he was. It was just magic stuff that people could do if they knew how, but he had a good appreciation of what all that magic could do and what it couldn't. It could put computers on Pluto and cities in the sea, but he knew perfectly well it couldn't make robots the size of rats that could find their way around the Wasteland cutting holes in sheet metal and making everything worth a damn disappear. So whatever the scorpion was, it was valuable. He found a door and, good luck at last, it was open enough that he could squeeze through into the plane itself.

"Whoo. That's more like it," he breathed in relief. Inside, he could straighten up and actually stand. He looked slowly around in the gloom of a tin can buried under fifteen metres of junk. He could hardly see a thing in here. He rustled around in his toolbag and brought out a torch and shone it down the length of the plane. It was clean and clear. It had never been used as a rubbish container, so he immediately caught sight of the scorpion, marching with a weird smooth gait up towards him. It seemed to have no reaction at all to either him or the light. One leg sprung up and forward while the other three were motionless, then the opposite leg, then the rear adjoining, and so on. It didn't make much sense that it should be moving at all.

"Got you, you little sucker," Hood said. "Your ass is mine." He took from his bag a pair of tongs that he usually used to pull small objects out of difficult places and advanced on the scorpion with the tongs raised up by his face. The light of his torch reflected slightly off the interior metal: the scorpion marching, him advancing.

Hood's arm shot out and grasped the scorpion securely in the tongs. Hood rotated it this way and that, studying it. It had four legs. It had a kind of shell or exoskeleton that seemed to be folded out of a single piece of metal. It's tail, curved up in the back, had a little pod on the end that might have been where the eyes were, if it had eyes, which he wasn't sure of. At the front was a slot arrangement from which the cutting tool must be extended. But in addition to all that, it had a feeling of irregularity about it, as if it had been designed with little regard for symmetry or finish. It bore no resemblance to any machine he had ever seen. Hood, standing there shaking his head very slightly from side to side, had a bad feeling, quickly put aside, that whatever this machine was, it was big trouble.

He found a sturdy metal box in the plane, that by the look of it had at one time been a document file, and stuffed the little robot into it. Then he pulled it under the wing and through the sewer pipe until he reached the surface. Lugging the box along back to his home, he met a friend at the big crossing from the bus depot to his street, who said "Whatchagotheah?"

"Found it," Hood said. "It's... it's a box." He realised halfway through his reply that if what was in the box was worth some money, he didn't want to share it with anybody. Not at all. "I'm going to keep magazines in it."

"Awesome notion. From the Wasteland?"

"Yeah."

"You're a real scavenger. That's a good thing. All this production and no scavenging. It's not the way it works in Nature, you know. In Nature, everything fits into the great design, you know, or else it just dies out, like the panda. You're like, fungus. You understand?"

"I know all your shit about Nature, man. This isn't Nature. This is the fucking century 21."

"Well, excu-u-use me!" This was an old argument, which wasn't about to be settled on the pedwalk, so with diminishing conversation shouted over their shoulders as they separated, they went on their own ways: Hood to what he grandly called his apartment, the other onto the next bus.

Hood was thinking hard about what he should do next. The robot was bound to be a government or military thing. So, when he got in his door he immediately made a phone call to the only government agency he knew the number for, the Department of Self-Help.

"DSH," said the receptionist, after he had finally navigated his way through the voice mail system.

"I want to talk to somebody about something I've found," Hood told him.

"Like what?"

"Like something important."

"Important?" The voice at the other end echoed blankly. "To whom?"

"I don't know! Somebody! It's important! I want to talk to somebody about it!"

"Name please."

"Chang Hood."

"One moment."

Hood heard the soft sound of a stylus on a screen. 'He's looking me up', he thought. 'The bastard's looking me up. To see if I'm a nutcase. Well, I'm not a nutcase'.

"Chang Hood of B-168 level 1 Chert St?"

"That's me."

"You have failed to appear for a retraining appointment. Do you realise the penalty for non-attendance?"

"Shit, look, I didn't know. The mailbox gets raided by kids." Hood was instantly afraid of losing his SHA. "But I've got to talk to somebody about this thing I've found. Please."

"One moment."

Hood waited while ten minutes of radio talkback chattered in his ear before he hung up. He looked at the metal box in the corner of his ugly little room. He could touch either wall by standing centrally and leaning slightly in each direction, first this way, then that way, like a man pretending to be a tree swaying in the wind. As he watched, a small circle appeared in one side of the box.

"What the blue Christ," Hood muttered, stepping forward. As he stepped, the centre of the circle fell out, and the robotic scorpion shot out at the high speed. He jumped out of the way - if it could cut through metal there was no telling what it might do to him - but the prospect of losing his ticket to somewhere, not here, was too much for him. He stretched out like a cat and grabbed the thing up in his hand, fully expecting to be drilled full of holes, but instead the scorpion stopped moving and sat in his hand, immobile. After a minute he put it down again and it took off, running rapidly around the room until it found the TV. He picked it up again as it was starting to drill a hole in the side of the plasticised metal case. Instantly, it stopped moving again.

"Crazy little machine. Back in the box with you, but first I'm going to wrap you up in something. Like sticky tape. That should slow you down a bit." Hood rummaged in his cupboard, found masking tape, and wrapped the scorpion up in about fifty layers. While he was doing this, he had an idea. TV. So the government wouldn't listen? No problem, TV listened to everyone. And everyone listened to TV. He found a telephone directory under his bed and rang the newsroom of the channel he watched most out of the forty-five available, Eighteen.

"Eighteen Newsroom."

"Hi, I'm uh, look I've got something I think will make good news."

"Uh-huh." The female voice did not seem very enthusiastic.

"I've found a robot."

"Yeah, so?"

"It's a little robot, like big as a rat, and it moves around by itself. It's something really different."

"We have a Science show. Would you like me to put you through to the science editor?"

"Yeah."

Dum-de-dum-de-dum.

"Hello, Science Editor."

Hook was beginning to get the picture. All these people talked nice. He copied the science voice: "Hello. My name is Chang Hood. I have found a small robot which I think you might want on the Science show."

The man at the other end was amused. "Why are you talking like that?"

"Shit! Look, I've found this thing and I think it's some kind of gotaway military prototype or something and I think you guys will want to show it on TV!"

"Hmm." There was the sound of keys being pressed and then, "Well, we're a bit short for next week's show. If you bring this thing in we could have a look see whether it's an item. Chang Hood, yes? Do you know where we are?"

"Yeah!"

"Ask for Dr Huster at reception, tomorrow at ten ay-em." Click/brrrrr.

"Well, shit." Hood threw the phone down. "Okay, then, ten ay-em. You got it." He looked on his bed, where the ball of sticky tape was just as he'd left it. "Better put you back in your box," he told it, and having done so, he secured it further by putting it in the fridge. There wasn't much else in the fridge, so there was plenty of room. SHA day still two weeks away, Hood thought glumly as he took a cold sausage from the door, and there had been little extra money from the Wasteland since this robot thing showed. Well, this Dr Huster would cough up some readies when he saw the scorpion, or no show.

"I am for sure the best finder on the planet," he assured himself, "and I am going to be rich."

The sensation of hope was a little overpowering. He sat around thinking about it for a long time.

CHAPTER 2

The next morning, Hood rolled out of his slightly smelly bed and groped, by habit, for the TV remote. Good reruns on channel six in the mornings. His hand went through all the motions of finding and pointing the remote, but he noticed with some surprise that it was empty. He put a fraction more of his early-morning brain to work on the problem of finding the TV control, and soon enough he did find it, next to the fridge, part of it, anyway, the empty case. And then he noticed a hole, neat and round, in the fridge door.

"Oh Christ," said Hood, looking rapidly left and right.

A two-minute frantic search of his room discovered no scorpion, and Hood felt the anguish of loss, or perhaps it was unrealised gain. Either way, dreams of fame and money became suddenly distant.

"Well, maybe there's another one in the Wasteland somewheres," he tried to comfort himself. Never having had much, he accepted his loss as no more than his due. "I need a sood." Sood was awful but it was cheap and it did the jolt. He tried to boil water on his tiny two-element stove, but it failed to get hot, or even warm. He fiddled with it for a while, took the back off it finally, and found bits of the rheostat missing. And a perfectly round hole in the backplate. Aargh. Fucking little bastard scorpion screwed my stove. Punched holes in my fridge. Ate my TV control. What the hell hasn't it got into? What does it do with all that shit? With this litany echoing in his otherwise empty mind, he looked in the fridge for something, anything, to consume.

Sitting where he had put it the previous night was the metal document box. Like everything else in his room, it had a hole in the side of it. Not really expecting anything to be there, he looked inside it and there was the ball of sticky tape. Beside it, the scorpion. Yo! And beside that was... another scorpion. Hood bent close and stared at it. Not the same. Not the same colour or finish. Not even complete. It had no tail. It's back was not completely closed, and he could see a grey silicon substrate casing through the gap, and little gold connections, and hairlike filaments. There was a small neat pile of metal fragments, remote control buttons, and wire coils behind the original scorpion, which continued to sit quietly. Hood picked it up. It remained dormant.

"Tired out, huh?" he said to it, shaking it in front of his face. "Tired out after a long hard night of wrecking the joint? Huh?" The scorpion did not reply. So Hood snatched up the other, incomplete one. "Looks like the only way to keep you in one place is to hang onto you!" Then he noticed that he was still wearing his underpants and that the time was - well, he didn't know what the time was, because now he looked at it, his clock wasn't working. Time to go, probably. He managed, with enormous difficulty, to put on clothes without opening his hands; including his totally inappropriate, heavy, dead man's overcoat which he selected only because it had large, deep pockets. Buttonless fashions. Zipless fucks. With his hands still clutched around the two robots, invisible at his sides, he hit the street.

It was a long walk to the studio, but Hood made it on time. The building had one of those wallscreen TVs mounted on the side of it, forty metres up, and in between showing shorts of whatever was upcoming on Channel 18 and Coke commercials, it took it's place in history as the world's biggest clock face. *09:57:21. 09:57:22. 09:57:23. Always... Coca-Cola. 09:57:46. And next up on Eighteen...*

Hood ignored it. He went up the entrance steps and through the glass doors and was almost immediately stopped by a polite gentleman wearing a uniform.

"Good morning, Mr?"

"Hood."

"Might I ask what your business is at Eighteen today?"

"Seeing Dr Huster. Science Program. At ten o'clock," Hood replied, doing his best to control a snarl. In his experience, anyone wearing a shoulder holster who asked questions was not just his enemy but an inhabitant of an alien universe with which he could barely communicate, in which he didn't understand the rules, and where he had to bristle with hostility in pure self-defence. "You got a problem with that?"

"Not at all, Mr Hood. Please step over here to reception and we'll make sure that your appointment is verified." The shoulder holster man, who wore a name plate which Hood didn't look at, guided him to an island in the centre of the foyer where a beautiful woman did the usual shit with pens and computer screens before she handed him a disk that went ping every time he walked near a door. Sometimes the door opened, and sometimes it didn't. He wandered all over the floor they sent him to, looking for doors that opened, and at last he got to another reception, looking just like the one downstairs, except this one was the Science reception.

"I'm here to see Dr Huster." Jesus. This was like the time he had to get a jab for the hep.

"How nice. One moment pleeeease."

One moment went by.

"Mr Hood!" Dr Huster was a big guy in a woolly jumper. He seemed to take Hood in with a single glance and wave of his arm. He didn't offer to shake hands. "Let's see this robot you say you've found." Hood guessed from his tone of voice that he wasn't sure about the use of the word found in this context.

"What, here?"

"Sure, why not? Sit down." There were a couple of two-seaters and a coffee table in the corner. Dr Huster sat down so that they faced each other. "Well?"

Hood took his hands out his pockets and placed the two scorpions on the table. The complete one immediately began to walk, fairly quickly, towards Dr Huster, whose eyes grew round. He reached out to pick it up, but Hood's hand was there first.

"Ah-ah. You've seen it for free. Now I'll be going."

"Okay, okay." Dr Huster wasted no time. "Let me have a good look at these things and I'll tell you how much I think they're worth to us."

"Nah. You tell me how much you think they're worth and I'll let you have a good look at them."

"All right," Dr Huster sighed. "Give me two minutes and I'll pay you two hundred bucks."

Hood thought that was not bad for starters, but he was too skilled a bargainer to show any reaction. "Two minutes. Then you better be ready to name a number."

"Of course."

Hood put the mobile scorpion back on the table. It walked. Dr Huster picked it up and looked at it very closely, top, bottom, sides. He wiggled a leg joint and studied the tail assembly, all the time making hmm and hunh noises to himself. Then he put it down again, (Hood immediately picked it up), and said,

"Where'd you get this?"

"Name a number."

"Look, this is a very peculiar little machine. It's been assembled in the strangest way. All the joints are molecular welded, seamless. I can't figure out who would want to spend so much effort on making what is essentially just a toy. I think it's a good item, but if it's been stolen I need to know before we go to air."

"It's not stolen."

"We protect our sources. We won't tell anyone what you tell me now."

"It's not stolen. I found it."

"Let me think for a minute."

Hood let him think. After a lot less than a minute, Dr Huster suggested they move to another room. This room was enclosed entirely in grey glass and had a huge table in the centre.

"Would you place them on the table, please?"

"OK, but don't let this one get out of reach. It can move when it wants to."

Huster chuckled. "I would guess, Mr Hood, that you're not an educated man, so you probably don't realise that a gadget this size can have only a limited amount of computing power onboard. It will have a very small number of modes of operation. It can probably walk, climb over obstacles, change direction at random, that sort of thing. I doubt that it can 'escape' from us in this room."

"Shit, smartass. It damn near escaped from me in my own box!"

"Well, it doesn't seem to be trying to escape now."

In fact the scorpion was motionless, except for it's tail, which drifted backwards and forwards in a manner reminiscent of the head of a hunting cobra. Then Dr Huster reached out for it, Hood opened his mouth to protest, and the scorpion moved with the speed of a disturbed rock crab. It went straight off the end of the table, hit the floor two metres further on, paused at the glass wall just long enough for Hood to say 'fuck', and disappeared.

In the glass was a perfectly round hole.

Dr Huster gaped. Hood snatched up the incomplete scorpion.

"I told you, didn't I?" he said.

"How the hell are we going to get that one back?" Dr Huster paid no attention to Hood's remark. "It could be anywhere! I had no idea it could move that fast. And cut through glass!" He got down on his knees and stared at the hole, shaking his head. "We'll have to wait until it's batteries run out. Although where it'll be by then is anyone's guess." He chewed his lip. "It does take batteries, doesn't it?"

"I don't know."

"There must be a hidden panel somewhere." Dr Huster came back to the table and peered at the other scorpion, still in Hood's hand. "Can't see one. Well, Jesus, it has to run on batteries. How are we going to catch it if it's got some superdooper power supply?"

"It went to a lot of trouble to build this other one," Hood pointed out. "So it'll probably come back to finish it, I betcha."

"You're telling me it built this other one?"

"Yeah. In my fridge."

"You're certain of that."

"Fuck yes."

"But, how? Out of what?"

"Out of every damned thing I own that used to work and now don't, that's how. It cut up my stove, my clock, my TV control, my..."

"Oh my god. It's a Von Neumann machine. Holy Jesus Christ. No-one can build Von Neumann machines. They're only theoretical. A Von Neumann machine. Where did this thing come from?" Dr Huster's expression was comical.

Hood listened carefully to all these new words and weighed Huster's reaction up in the only way that mattered. "Name a number," he said. "A big one."

Eventually, Dr Huster recaptured the mobile scorpion, by following a suggestion of Hood's. They sat up most of the night, in the dark, with Hood cheerfully swigging from a bottle of rum, and when the clitter-clatter of metal feet sounded in the glass room the two men only waited until Dr Huster had evidence that the first scorpion was actually completing the second before they wrapped it up in nine hundred layers of polyethylene sandwich wrap.

"This'll only hold it a while," Hood said when they had finished.

"Von Neumann machines," Dr Huster muttered. "Self-replicating machines. My god."

The scorpions were to appear on TV the following week. Before then, Dr Huster made the most of his notoriety in the circles of academia. While he and Hood stood poised like presidential bodyguards for the slightest sign of mechanical movement, a train of theorists from well-funded and not so well-funded institutes and laboratories came into the Science studio. The door pingers made it a frog dawn chorus, and many bulging eyes made it altogether too lifelike to be pleasant.

Dr Huster, to give him credit, was solicitous of Hood's part in the discovery of self-replicating machines. "SRMs," he told him. "I've decided to call them SRMs. Short and snappy, easy to remember. Apologies to Johnny Von Neumann, but face it, no one's ever heard of him. You and I, though! You're going to be famous, Chang."

Hood hated being called Chang, and said so.

"Hood, then. You'll be famous." Dr Huster's eyes glittered with excitement.

"And rich?"

"I don't know about that. But think of the benefit for mankind! These things are utterly new! They must incorporate more new engineering principles than you've had hot dinners! It's on a par with finding an alien's spaceship parked in a pay-and-display, working interstellar drive and all. I tell you, Hood, the world is going to change, thanks to you."

"Yay for me." Hood didn't look very impressed. In fact, he was shaking his head.

"What's the matter?" asked Dr Huster.

"Change," Hood told him, "isn't usually for the best. In my experience."

"Dr Huster to reception, please," droned the comms system. Huster looked irritated, either at this call on his time when he would far rather be presiding over the covey of esteemed scientists and professors that he had brought into being, or at Hood for lacking starry eyes. Whichever, he pointed at the table in the centre of the room, which was now enclosed on all sides by two-centimetre armoured glass and littered with mechanical debris - defunct computer parts, mainly. The two scorpions prowled around the table under the scrutiny of two ceiling video cameras and five academics. So far they had failed to commence upon construction of a third.

"Don't let them - " he meant the academics, not the scorpions, " - do anything while I'm not here," he said. "I'll be back in five minutes."

"No problem."

In fact, he was gone for fifteen or longer. He returned at last with a beaten expression and four new faces, blank ones appearing at the end of necks protruding from expensively plain woollen suits. Hood instantly recognised them as police, of some variety he knew not which, but police for sure. Between here and back, Dr Huster's eyes had lost the glitter of excitement and now looked flat, tired and dead.

"Gentlemen," he said quietly as he came back into the room, "these men are from the Government Security Organisation, and I'm afraid that the party's over."

The five academics got shooed like so many chickens. The GSO men placed the two SRMs into solid-looking metal cases, ignoring Hood's warnings about their chances of getting to the ground floor without losing them both. Without so much a issuing a receipt, the grey-suited men departed. Hood and Dr Huster stood side by side looking out the glass walls, watching them go.

"I wonder what project spawned those little babies," Dr Huster said with a sigh. "I'd sure like to be on it. There go the two most amazing machines in the damned universe."

Hood shook his head.

"If you find one cockroach, it might be the only one, but when you find two cockroaches, chances are there's a million of the fuckers."

CHAPTER 3

Voiceover: Coming up on Eighteen, the Science Show! Tonight, the Science team will be giving you the story of the hottest scientific discovery of the decade, made right here by the Channel Eighteen Science Show technical editor Dr Albert Huster! So stay tuned to Eighteen, the channel with more advertising revenue than the others!

Three minutes of advertisements

Science Show startup sequence

Three minutes of advertisements

Rolling long distance zoom-in through studio ending on main presenter, diagonal aspect.

Presenter: Welcome to the Eighteen Science Show, sponsored by Continuous Loop! We've got a feature-packed show for you tonight! Let's -

Flash animation of angler fish and a sulphur vent

Presenter: - take a look at the new bacterial life-form discovered in the ocean depths that may hold the secret to longer lives, and -

Rotating view of a shaved male head with a metal implant mounted above the left ear

Presenter: - find out whether database connection implants really do cause epilepsy. We are also going to show you a sneak preview of the Io lander videos. But first,

Aerial shot of the Wasteland, spinning slowly counter-clockwise and drilling in to an off-vertical upper body shot of Hood, hand across brow shading the sun

Presenter: who is this man, and what does he have to do with Science? For the answer, we now speak to our Technical Editor, Dr Alfredo Huster! *(wild applause as Dr Huster seems to materialise in the guest seat, starting with his head and proceeding downwards).* Dr Huster - may I call you Alfresco?

Dr Huster: Damn it Vengo, you know my name isn't Alfresco. Is this a take?

Vengo: A take? This is live! *(walks from the centre spot to the presenter's desk and sits on the edge furthest from Dr Huster)* Ha ha ha. That's Dr Huster! Our Technical Editor is a stickler for correctitude in every way. It's thanks to this man that Eighteen's Science Show brings you nothing but serious science.

Half the screen starts to fill with water and enormously enlarged protozoa, through which Dr Huster is visible, looking resigned. Vengo hands him a snorkel set and motions him to put it on, but he shakes his head

Vengo: See? Now, Dr Huster, tell us, who is this man (flash face shot of Hood, looking inscrutably oriental/black) and what has he done to astound and amaze the scientific community? *(the water drains away with faint gurglings and the protozoa thrash about around Huster's feet)*

Dr Huster: This man is Chang Hood, and he has discovered what I think can justifiably be called a new life-form.

Vengo: Like the new sea-bottom - ooh, I love that word, don't you? Sea-bottom. Sea-bottom. The new sea-bottom bacteria? Sea-bottom bacteria right after the third ad segment, audience.

Dr Huster: The bacteria just discovered living near a single deep-sea sulphur vent are extraordinary, because they have a type of DNA which has markedly lower cross-linking and replication defect rates than our own. That is very exciting for biochemists and geneticists all over the world and may have radical implications for our future. *(He gets to his feet and walks to a large flat screen display which becomes visible off left screen. Vengo has somehow changed his clothes and is there already with a near-naked female hanging on his arm, game-show style).*

Dr Huster: But what Chang Hood has found is something even further removed from normal biology than that. In fact, it isn't biology at all.

Vengo: Ad break time, Dr Huster. So you just dissolve quietly while we tell the audience why THEY should SUCK TOOTHTUBES!

Right-to-left slide in of the Science Show logo, accompanied by a cacophony of voices shouting, 'Toothtubes! Toothtubes!' while Vengo and Dr Huster appear to turn into viscous liquid and drain upwards out of view.

Toothtube advert

Two more minutes of advertisements

Science Show interim startup sequence

One minute of advertisements

Sudden close-up of the Scorpion, with voiceover by Dr Huster. As he speaks, a small cartoon figure of Vengo floats around the Scorpion, pointing at leg joints, tail pod, and body armour.

Dr Huster: This is what we have called the Scorpion. (draw back to Dr Huster standing before the display panel, Vengo now beside him, wearing a rumpled suit and looking a little like Neils Bohr) It is a machine, quite obviously, but it is a machine with some amazing characteristics. It can reproduce, for example! (display panel draws back to show the other scorpion beside the first) This second scorpion was constructed by the first, under controlled conditions, from pieces of equipment and other materials it located within this very building. You may notice that the second scorpion is slightly different from the first. I am afraid that fidelity of replication is very much less than even our own DNA, not to mention the sea-bottom bacteria that Vengo is so fond of. This machine species is therefore going to mutate very rapidly, probably into a degenerative state where it can no longer reproduce or even function.

Vengo: Wow.

Dr Huster: Indeed. It gets even more interesting than that. We have simply no idea how this self-replicating machine functions at all. What it's power supply is, how it processes information, what it's sensory equipment is - although I believe that this is it in the tail - we just can't understand how it is made or what makes it tick. And there is the question of where it comes from.

The screen fills with tiny people running everywhere, carrying insanely shaped tools and parts, climbing over each others shoulders, bolting and welding, lining up and racing to be first, constructing a bulky metal letter S, others lowering girders into place within the framework of an R, large springs bend into the double curve of an M.

Voiceover: Do the SRMs, self-replicating machines, if that's what they are, come from the secret laboratories of the military? Or from another country? Or another planet? What are they for? What do they mean? What are they designed to do?

Screen slap. Left half, Vengo, right half, Dr Huster, slam together at screen centre and bounce around. When the picture stabilises, Dr Huster, looking agitated, talks to the air above his head which is where the viewpoint slowly swings to.

Dr Huster: Two days ago, this studio was visited by your government and the two scorpions which we were researching were confiscated 'for the security of the nation'.

(obviously pre-recorded crowd murmur)

Dr Huster: We have been able, however, to obtain one further specimen, although we cannot reveal our source at this time.

Vengo: All you rating units out there, here is LIVE video of the only SRM remaining in private hands at this time!

The picture dissolves to side view of the armoured glass table, in the opposite corner of which is a scorpion, busily cutting into the unidentifiable carcass of some piece of consumer electronics. The viewpoint zooms in to the cutting mechanism swiftly moving from point to point, snipping, and moving on. Then it shaves the surface from a grey package, exposing an integrated circuit. The viewpoint withdraws and moves to front. Out of the tail sensor pod extends a long, invisibly fine piece of wire. Moving above, the viewpoint reveals that there is a postage-stamp sized piece of plastic next to the scorpion, to which it is transferring sections of the wafer. The wire touches them with a minute spark and welds them together. Leaving the plastic smoking slightly, the scorpion starts bending a thin piece of aluminium casing in apparently random ways.

AD BREAK

Science Show start-up sequence

Instantaneous focus on Dr Huster's face

Dr Huster: We have a group of experts online tonight, all of whom have visited the Science studio during the last week and seen the SRMs firsthand. They will now put forward some conjectures about the origin and construction of SRMs. On behalf of these four distinguished scientists, Channel Eighteen hereby makes a formal protest to this government which tramples on the scientific community's right to unrestricted research into any subject. Gentlemen!

The display panel splits into four quarters, each containing a talking head.

Vengo: (walking in front of the display panel and thwacking each face smartly across the nose with a riding crop as he speaks their names). Professor Acton, Department of Applied Evolution, Pittsburgh University. Dr Feshala, Chairman of the Combined Technologies Panel. Professor Ewonkle wonkle wonk. Shit! What is happening to my cognitive subroutines? (He disappears with a flash of red smoke. The display panel crackles and flashes, then stabilises.)

Dr Huster: Vengo? Vengo? Ah, audience, it looks like we have a slight technical hitch with our presenter systems. I'm sure

Vengo will be back with us shortly - *(his eyes track something happening off screen)* - or at least tomorrow. Gentlemen, can we start off with some discussion of what a full understanding of the SRMs might gain us? Professor Ewonkle wonkle wonk? *(looks surprised)*

Head #2: It is Professor Wood, actually. Is everything all right there? *(streaks of colour fill the screen)*

Voiceover: Channel Eighteen is currently experiencing some systems failures. Do not be alarmed. Relax and watch the Science Show and everything will be attended to shortly. We return you to the Science Show. *(picture returns)*

Dr Huster: Professor Ewonkle wonkle wonk, what is there to learn from SRMs?

Head #2: Well, clearly the method of construction is fantastically advanced, as is the sophistication of whatever passes for instruction processing equipment. I... *(his head catches fire and burns)* Is everything all right?

Head #1: Listen to me! I didn't agree to come on this show to talk about mere technology! There are more important aspects to this!

Dr Huster: Vengo! Where the hell are you when we need you? Ah, Professor...

Head #3: Why hasn't anybody admitted to being responsible for making these things?

Dr Huster: Well, I suppose that the government is responsible for them. After all, they came and confiscated them.

Head #3: If the government confiscates a ton of cocaine it doesn't automatically follow that they were responsible for making it in the first place. Where did SRMs come from?

Head #2: They might be a spontaneous assemblage. From a coincidental juxtaposition of parts.

Head #4: Dr Wood, get a grip. Entropy runs things down, not up. The laws of physics would have to be different at a macro level for such a thing to happen. Your suggestion is ludicrous. It's obvious that SRMs are made by someone, or something.

Head #3: Something? What are you suggesting? Extraterrestrials?

Head #2: *(still on fire)* I think it's very clear that no one on Earth could have made them. They're either a statistical accident - and that's all entropy is, you know, a statistical expression of the expansion of the universe - or they're something completely out of our ken. I'm open to the possibility of life from other star systems. Are any of you?

Head #4: There you are. Extraterrestrials.

Head #3: Good God.

Head #1: Yes, God indeed. That is something which, as men of science and truth, we should also consider. The possibility that our knowledge falls short of the everything-there-is. As we understand more, so we realise that there is more to understand. Every great thinker has realised that there is something greater than ourselves which may, on occasion, reach into our mundane lives.

Head #3: Spare us. Do you have to invoke the unknowable every time you encounter something that orthodox science can't explain?

Head #1: It may be unknowable to you, but that's because you have no spiritual side whatsoever. Listen! The millennium might be running a little late! These machines are a new life form. Under what circumstances could they have come into being? This isn't a primitive planet with ammonia atmosphere and high temperatures, and even if it was, I'd expect amino acids to form, not silicon circuits! How do you explain it?

Head #3: It's still not impossible that somebody has made them.

Head #2: Why are you all looking at me like that? (his eyes move upwards and focus on what must be an overhead monitor) Jesus! I'm on fire!

Head #3: The image is not the object, Dr Wood.

Head #2: (calming down) What's wrong with the system down there? (viewpoint draws back to disclose Dr Huster talking in rapid whispers with a technician) Dr Huster!

Dr Huster: Oh, yes, yes, ah, Dr Wood. Very interesting. We seem to be having some serious problems here with the presentation system, but the technician assures me that he'll have found the problem shortly. So, we can only conjecture as to the origin of the SRMs at this point, isn't that right?

Head #3: They're either a made thing, or they're a physical impossibility, and I use the word physical in it's technical sense. Laws of physics.

Head #4: They're a physical impossibility anyway. I've done some calculations on their energy output. They radiate more energy in the microwave spectrum than a cellphone, and they've been doing so continuously since I first examined them. There's no battery system that size that can produce that much energy continuously for such a long period without any reduction in output. And they move as well! Short of taking one apart, I can't begin to explain their energy supply.

Head #3: Now you're talking. You're all acting like a bunch of children with a Christmas parcel. You're guessing what might be in it, when the only way to be sure is to open the damn thing. Schroedinger's cat. We should have dismantled them while we had them.

Head #1: We should observe them carefully, as we would any other new species. Not rush the only specimen not in government hands into the dissection room!

Dr Huster: We believe there may be more where these came from.

Head #4: Nonsense. You said it yourself: the SRMs have terrible reproductive fidelity. They'd degenerate in three generations if they were left in the, ah, wild I suppose you'd call it.

Head #2: If they're a physical impossibility, then perhaps the laws of physics are wrong. Because there they are. Maybe entropy doesn't always run down. Perhaps spontaneous assembly is possible.

Head #3: Now you're redefining the basic laws of the universe. Almost anything is more likely than spontaneous assembly of inanimate matter, including a hoax. How do you explain four billion years of spontaneous disassembly?

Head #2: I have no explanation at present. Things might have changed recently.

Dr Huster: Gentlemen, your contribution to this show is much appreciated, but now our time on the SRM phenomena is nearly up. We will be having a Science Special later in the week recapping all this and further examining SRMs: where, what, and by whom? I expect Vengo will be working again any minute now, but until then, let's have an ad break.

(the display panel clears and the Science Show logo starts to fade in, rotating counter-clockwise, while Dr Huster watches, wiping his forehead with his sleeve)

Voiceover: Next on Eighteen, the Science Show and the sea-bottom bacteria! Sponsored by Continuous Loop Limited, the artificial intelligence business you can trust!

Fifteen seconds of advertisements

Darkness

CHAPTER 4

How does a man become a poet? In the case of Whak Puihare, it must have been something to do with his name. There had been a time, nearly fifty years ago, when the fad was for baby names that made political statements. Parents always name their children according to how they see themselves: it's even more expressive than the car you drive or the clothes you wear. Naming your child Earth Flower Magnifica or PnP CyberKing says a lot less about the child than it does about the parent. To demonstrate their solidarity with people with whom they had absolutely nothing in common except the land they lived in at the time, Whak Puihare's parents had adopted a Polynesian-sounding surname, and given their only son a cognomen to match.

Whak Puihare. Because Polynesian culture was politically correct in those times, he was obliged to pronounce his inappropriate name with the proper Polynesian fricative: F-aa-k Puee-har-i. He was white, and blue-eyed. But he'd become used to it. In fact, he even took a kind of satisfaction out of it, now that he was old enough and wise enough to preclude embarrassment. There comes an age where you just say, fuck everybody. But his parents, John and Sandra Puihare nee Cooke, well, to be frank he was glad they were living at the top of the Andes, looking for yak eggs, or whatever it was they were doing.

Of course it takes more than a funny name to write poetry. He knew in his gut that the world as it had become, desperately wanting authority and control whilst wracked with chaos, was silently crying out from it's crushed heart for poetry. Beliefs like that came easy to Whak. Unfortunately, the need for poetic insight into the shape of things did not translate into mainstream appreciation. There was a world to put in order, and a handful of irregular rhymes, while clever, did not contribute to the important task of figuring out just what had happened in the previous ten years to cause odd bits of inanimate objects to spontaneously assemble into motile, reproductive constructions. Self replicating machines. SRMs. All different sorts of the buggers. The effect of these creatures on the economy had been devastating. The high-tech industries of the previous decade had been eaten alive, their plants reduced to empty concrete shells, their products incorporated into the bodies of a billion impossibilities that seemed to have no other objective than to make more of the same. It was all so pointless.

Whak remembered very well the early days, when there were only scorpions, primitive and harmless things that basically only wrecked television sets, computers, and TV studios. Now there were teddy bears, pocket calculators, hosenoses, welders, buzzsaws, caterpillars, wagglers, uncountable minor weirdies, and crocs, which were large, fast, and equipped to render down the best part of a car, if that was on the menu today. No-one knew exactly where the menu was written, but it was a fact that larger SRMs like crocs were fond of hydraulic leads, which meant that you had to check your brakes carefully every morning unless you wanted to end up wrapped around the across-road neighbour's gateposts.

With the natural order going crazy, poetry was a matter of little concern. It might have been a reaction to the unhinging of nature, but it seemed that when people need poetry the most, they want poetry the least. Luckily, Whak was incapable of dismay. He chose to put his work in the face of society by going out and spraying it in giant letters onto the fabric of the city itself. And slowly, he began to attract attention. The sporadic appearance of Whak's handwriting, in fluorescent green and red, across the eighth floor of a hulking collapsicle or on the pillars of the central motorway, was taken to be either the visible sign of decay and cultural decadence, or a the emergence of a new post-industrial art, depending upon the point of view.

Whak didn't know which point of view was the truth, in fact he doubted the existence of truth. But over several years, he had attained notoriety, which was enough. Now, his graffiti poems were, if not critically acclaimed, at least analysed for their connection with the urban subconscious, and whenever a new Puihare piece was found painted on whatever cancerous masonry, it was sure to be quoted wisely by the street. He had almost single-handedly revived interest in a nearly dead art. You might have said that Whak Puihare, graffiti poet, was content. A bad thing to be.

At the moment, Whak was watching a flower. He had time for this sort of pursuit, because he had no Job. His wife, Jelli, had a Job. She had a Very Good Job. So Whak could watch a flower without guilt. He had plenty of other things to feel guilty about, though. He could get guilty about not writing. His hands were actually resting on the keyboard, but the sunflower was framed so beautifully by his window that his fingers just refused to move. He could feel guilty about the pile of coffee cups in various evolutionary stages piled on the corner of his desk. He turned his eyes back to his computer screen - thanks to Jelli he had the luxury of a computer screen - and scanned his latest work.

the white plastic sky reminds me of the side
of my fridge
the stars are flecks in the paintjob
of my sportscar
and the sun is eclipsed
by my fine black shades
it's only half an inch on the map
but perspective cheats when I look across the water
and see only the ends
of ocular imperfection

Poetry, thought Whak, is supposed to be an instantaneous flash of the common dream. It should happen quickly, but he had been working on this for days, and it had a long way to go. He wondered if his patience was going to hold out. He was reading it over again when Jelli appeared at the door, just home from work, which brought him up short with the irregular pace of the forward movement of time.

"Hi," he said.

"Hello," said Jelli. She was small, dark, and suited the Puihare name far better than he, having a mix of blood which plainly included at least one tropical island. This might have explained why she wore it, for keeping your birth name in a marriage was more common than not. She was in her business clothes, a jump-suit straight out of Star Trek which would have shown every undergarment seam, if they had any or she wore any, and she had a briefcase three centimetres thick hanging at the end of her left arm, which Whak knew from experience would explode from internal pressure if unlocked. Since Whak wore exclusively loud shirts and baggy cotton trousers, they failed miserably as a matched power couple, but that's not what they were. Truth was, they were an ambitious and successful woman supporting her offbeat husband's compulsion to make words, for even though Whak had achieved a reputation as a voice of the folk, he couldn't even afford his spray paints without Jelli's financial backing. She thought that for a grown man to go out and embellish every available surface with poetry was a poor substitute for real work, but she could understand that Whak needed to be noticed. Everyone wants to be noticed. Jelli, too. She had differentiated herself from the herd, long ago now, by marrying a poet.

"Coffee?" Whak asked, getting up.

"Thanks," Jelli replied, turning back into the hall and heading for the main bedroom. Whak, leaving his study behind her, saw her glance at the doorway opposite their bedroom. Lino's room.

"Lino in?" she called out. There was no point in asking the door. If Lino was behind it or not, she would not answer.

"I don't think so," Whak answered. "There are no dark clouds over the house, are there?"

"Whak! Please!"

"Try to laugh, Jelli." He gave a rue, hopeful smile.

"I think making fun of your own daughter is not something to laugh about," Jelli said sternly.

"Jesus, you can be so serious sometimes."

"That's why I'm the chief executive at PushRight Creative Media, and you're a poet, Whak." Jelli was kind enough not to remind him that he was only barely a poet, more by comparison than by absolute right.

Whak immediately struck an exaggerated pose right there in the hall and declaimed

"Be the company that owns you
There's no consequence too evil for a pat on the head
If you flourish from it.
Commitment's the paradigm, influence the measure,
May I help you, sir?
May I give you pleasure?"
Jelli glared at him.

"Shut up, Whak," she snapped.

"Too close to the bone, is it?"

"It's outright bullshit."

"Your are in advertising, are you not?" She was in a lot more than advertising, as he well knew. She was, to all intents, the propaganda minister of the government, the Correct Management Consortium Party as they called themselves. The corpse of democracy, Whak thought a more suitable description.

"Get the coffee!" Jelli said.

"At once, my love."

Whak made a right to the kitchen and became involved with a percolator. He was not famous for his easy relationship with machinery of any type, and anything that jetted compressed steam around at 1500kpa was certain to cause trouble. So it did. He blew a faceful of coffee grounds straight into his face and reeled around the kitchen with tears streaming out of one eye for long enough that when Jelli, changed now into her at-home wear of leggings and absurdly puffed-out shirt, finally came barging through the door he had only just recovered sufficiently to pour two espressos.

"Thanks," Jelli said when he pushed her cup at her. "What did you do to your eye?"

"Blew coffee grounds in it."

"Oh, Whak. You should be in the entertainment business."

"It hurts."

"I'm sure it does. Have you finished your poem?"

"No, I bloody well haven't."

"Lost the muse?"

"No, I bloody well haven't."

"I'm meeting with someone from the DeptConServe, tomorrow. They want us to arrange some kind of public relations campaign to encourage burial at sea, or something."

"The Department of the Environment are the new face of Adolph Hitler."

"Who?" Jelli pretended ignorance.

Whak knew when he was beaten. He silently pointed his finger in the direction of the lounge. Jelli followed him down the hall, both hands full of coffee cup, and they were passing the front door when it flew open. Whak jumped, and Jelli frowned at the familiar crash. "Lino is here."

Lino appeared, following the sound of her entrance, dressed in a black dress, eyes to match, hair to match, lips to match.

"Coffee?" Jelli offered.

Lino without pausing lifted one cup from Jelli's outstretched hand and proceeded towards her bedroom. Whak wasn't sure, but it seemed that she mumbled something, her voice floating back over her shoulder, something like

"Fucking crocodiles are out again." Then she was gone.

"That was my coffee," Whak snapped.

"I'll get you another," Jelli shrugged.

Later that evening, when the sky had darkened, Whak returned to his study. He had feelings to express, and now, when the house was quiet and he was alone and the crocodiles were about, was always a good time. Whilst the universe reminds us that our cosy little world is a statistical fluctuation in an infinite void of chaos by letting impossible things walk the streets after sundown, then let me too remind myself that all this is caused by chance and my life is random. He stood by the window and clicked down the venetian blind, opening a gap through which his soft blue eyes could peer.

The Puihare house, like most in this suburb, was a giant edifice perched on the side of the hill that overlooked the broad and flat expanse of Coolio Park. The house had more rooms than Whak knew quite what to do with, spreading out from the grand hallway like the crenellations of a snowflake, or the intestines of a square. A short, but gracefully curved driveway reached from the cast iron gates by the street to the garage, which once would have housed a few Ferraris or Aston Martins, but now held no more than Jelli's company car and Whak's lonely survivor of the Japanese invasion. Since the day when Japan succumbed rather more quickly than anyone believed possible to anarchy, a Mazda was now an almost retro piece from the car-age. Whak liked that.

Beyond the garden wall, the few, operational street lamps cast their violent wavelengths onto the ground. The street was empty.

"Damn. Fucking crocodiles are not out," he whispered.

"What?" said Jelli from the doorway. "Come and catch some TV."

"I've got to write," he replied doubtfully.

"You wrote all day. You must have done, you certainly didn't do any housework." Jelli was joking. The Puihare household was regularly visited by cleaning and maid services. If Whak heard them knocking on the door and let them in.

"Maybe I can train pocket calculators to wash dishes. Since the dishwasher has never worked since the little bastards got in and removed all the logic circuits from it."

"Life's hard being the fully supported spouse of a media mogul, isn't it, Whak?" Jelli's voice was just a trifle acidic. Whak took a careful look at her face before he answered, a tactic he knew pissed her off thoroughly, although he could never understand why. He wondered idly, whether she had some problem with her own appearance. This didn't seem like the right time to ask.

"Okay, GOV1 it is," he said. "Let's go watch your handiwork."

"It's brain work, as a matter of fact."

"Har har."

Whak was about to turn from the window, when, in the shadows that lay where the street lamps had lost their innards to teddy bears, he caught a glimpse of red. It flicked back and forth for a second or two, then settled and as his eyes adjusted separated into two distinct spots. Binocular spots, perhaps, and up his favourite tree, by the dim silhouette.

"Jelli," Whak said, beckoning. "There's someone up the slippery elm."

"Oh yes?"

"Really! With night binoculars, I think."

"It's probably just another blue suit." Jelli did not approach the window. Whak stepped back and to the side. Jelli continued, "They watch anyone suspicious."

"We're not suspicious, are we? You're practically a Consortium member yourself, aren't you? Why would they watch you?"

"Well, as a matter of fact, I had lunch with the head of Blue Suit last week, and I asked him just that."

"You had lunch with the head of Blue Suit? What's his name?" Whak was interested, because to understand why people elect governments which then turn upon them is to gain some insight into what is human. When the technological power of civilisation began to wane, since the appearance of SRMs, society had been showing it's dark side. So, civilisation is falling apart and the masses are restless without internet access, microwave ovens, and self-tuning internal combustion engines? The Blue Suit Social Management Agency was contracted to deal with that, by a system of observation, reporting, and internment that was, by government fiat, horrifyingly legal. Blue Suit was charged with preventing the breakdown of acceptable behaviour patterns, and once a government believes that such a thing is within it's power, mass executions cannot be far away. Whak was also acutely aware that Jelli, chief executive of PushRight Creative Media Incorporated, was charged with exactly the same objective.

The Correct Management Consortium Party was made up of the same people as the last government, which had called itself the Public Interest Group. Politics was dead. Whak had always thought that the world would be a better place when the human race finally outgrew politics, along with diplomacy and other forms of lying, but now he was not so sure. The Consortium was quite a small organisation in absolute size, and in these straitened

times even their vast tax spending power was under pressure.
With efficiency uppermost and accountability lowest in their
collective mind, they out-sourced almost everything to specialists.
Hence, propaganda: PushRight Media. Security: Blue Suit. It
was not uncommon, either, for some of the Consortium's service
providers to have overlapping responsibilities. It kept them on
their toes.

Whak wanted to learn more about Blue Suit's mouthpiece.
"Does he have horns?" he went on.   "Is he humanoid in
appearance?"

Jelli looked blank for a second. She might have been wishing
that she had never mentioned her acquaintance with the man.

"His name," she said carefully, "is Blue Suit, believe it or not.
That's what they call him. Blue Suit."

"Of course.   That makes sense.   The organisation is an
extension of it's master. What they see, he sees.   Good
psychology." Whak glanced out the window again. "So why is he
watching you?"

"He isn't," said Jelli. "He's watching you."

CHAPTER 5

Although she didn't want Whak to know it, Jelli had been having meetings with Blue Suit for some time, months, in fact. They were both important and powerful figures, and sometimes it was possible to delegate Consortium-mandatory inter-outsourcer dialogues to the second ranks, so they did, but at other times it was necessary to be there in person, so they were. Freedom, as Whak sometimes said, is believing that it's you that is making the choice, though at other times he would say with equal certainty that freedom was not making any choices at all. In Jelli's opinion, he certainly fell into that second category, but she didn't exactly fit in the first. She made decisions, but they really were her decisions. She didn't believe that her every choice was dictated by the irresistible tide of events. Who does?

She remembered clearly the first one of the meetings she had bothered to attend. It had been held at PushRight's executive conferencing centre, which was on the same floor as her office. There were eight glass-walled rooms with board table or lecture room layouts, projectors, multimedia systems, and so forth, and PushRight guarded them jealously. The main reason that the conference rooms were on the same floor as Jelli's office and the other senior executives was the hopeful idea that SRMs were less likely to find them way up there, sixty metres from street level, and eat all that hard-to-replace computer stuff. So far, that idea, and the efforts of a dedicated team of SRM sweepers on the lower floors, were holding them at bay.

The room for the PushRight-Blue Suit meeting was just a boardroom, however, holding nothing more sophisticated than a large table and twenty chairs. Jelli liked punctuality and was pleased to see that Blue Suit did the same. At less than a minute before the appointed hour two of the lift indicators bonged and out marched a small army of men in blue suits, some obviously wearing guns, and a single tall man wearing light grey. Handsome, youthful yet mature, and legally entitled to sentence to death without trial.

Jelli widened her eyes slightly. He was gorgeous. She suppressed an unseemly urge to lick her lips. While she was watching him enter the room, he was also observing her. His gaze flicked over the small group of PushRight people attending, rumple-shirted producers, over-painted assistants to assistants who reeked of insecticide number 5, and the man named Dukker who had been the mouthpiece of authority at the last session. All nobodies. Instead, he settled his attention on the petite, short-haired woman towards whom every other person in the room was slightly turned, and whose feral eyes were looking him up and down.

He was disturbed by her gaze. He was the sort of man who becomes sexually aroused when stroking a cat, or brushing past a woman in the corridor. He considered that this was his greatest flaw, although some other people might have thought his indifference to misery and pain to be a strong contender. When Jelli ran her eyes over him his skin reacted as if brushed with her fingers. He was displeased, especially since he let some of his reaction show, however briefly, in his face. He did not like to show weakness. Quickly, he sat down at the opposite end of the table to Jelli. His protective bodyguard took their positions. His offensive bodyguard remained outside.

The meeting began.

Jelli sat through the session with her eyes firmly on Blue Suit, at the opposite end of the table. It started with Jelli's personal assistant, Allynn, reading the agenda. Allynn was a quiet, attractive woman who combined a charming naivety in some matters with ruthless efficiency in others and a facility for being overlooked when things went wrong and heads were rolling. She read out the agenda in a voice of newsreaderish anonymity. Jelli didn't bother to listen. She continued to watch Blue Suit out of the corner of her eyes.

The convention for these meetings was to only allow topics of no interest to anyone, but this time the PushRight team had prepared a presentation by PushRight on the Law and Order Project. Jelli had to control a quite uncharacteristic giggle when Dukker, who was her most senior veep, tried to explain what the project was.

"PushRight has decided that in order to direct social behaviour into channels acceptable to society, we must obtain a complete understanding of what Law and Order actually mean. This is a complex social issue and not at all as simple as you might think." He looked around the table for people who might think it simple, then turned back to the projection screen on which a colourful bunch of arrows and boxes suddenly pinged into being. He pointed at a large blue rectangle labelled 'Law'.

"As we all know, laws are the formal expressions of social mores and standards, which inevitably lag behind the actual behaviour patterns occurring in the real world. In times of rapid change and severe social dislocation, such as now, the lag factor can be severe and can affect such important context factors as respect for law enforcement and government, individual life plan visualisation, and so forth. We have put together a project team with the aim of both quantifying these indicators and codifying the relationship between social administration and the underlying culture." He tapped a button and the picture became a layered stack of social components, criss-crossed with lines and labels.

Appreciative murmurs from the PushRight side of the table. Blank stares from the other. "This project will, in time, provide us with tools for safe, non-invasive social management."

That was the point at which Jelli had to cough to disguise her chuckle. What Dukker said was partly true, but the Law and Order Project was more than that. It was only a small shining thing of hope, but the objective was, in her opinion, vastly important.   The project aimed to learn how to control the increasingly violent and factional swings in society that, like the pendulum of a demented clock, would sooner or later tear apart this country and all the others in the world. The impact of SRMs on communication technology, mainly, was to blame. Ways of wiping the creatures out were not abundant any more, since all the ideas to date had failed. Tribalism was ascendant. The cohesive substrata of common beliefs and behaviours that could have been taken for granted ten years ago was losing it's grip. The cogs were grinding. Jelli hoped, no, wished fervently that sooner rather than later the Law and Order Project would come up with some answers.

"Have you had any success in this laudable aim?" Blue Suit asked dryly. Jelli sensed at once that the idea that human society was a complex mechanism rather than a fishbowl of opportunity was anathema to him. Like her, Blue Suit probably believed in freedom - his own, not other people's. "Have you any results?" he went on.

"Not yet," Dukker said, shrugging his shoulders. He was under instructions not to reveal anything important, which was easy, because so far the project had come up with close enough to zero. "It's a research project. We don't expect anything this early. But eventually we may get metrics for population management."

He made a false smile. "And put you out of a job," he finished with a clear note of relish.

Jelli saw Blue Suit make a note, or rather, indicate to the creature on his right that a note should be taken. He didn't look very concerned that the Law and Order Project would affect his job security in the near future. She wondered whether the same was true of Dukker.

Later, Jelli sent Allynn out of her office to fetch coffee while she burrowed through a pile of weekly reports. She turned over the news team facial expressions summary and lifted the Law and Order progress report. Although it was thick and every page thrilled with possibilities and projections, in fact there was no progress. The problem with the Law and Order Project was the reams of experimental evidence, or rather the lack of reams of experimental evidence. The lack of any evidence, statistics, or facts. Jelli was presently disposed to believe that there really might be something in what Dukker and his team said, that it might really be possible to predict social behaviour with a precision not now imagined. There were hints of predictability coming through in the trivial amounts of data that the team had collected by correlating soap viewer surveys with defacement of public works by district, enough to tantalise with promise. The manipulation of the public mood was an art, an art that Jelli was a skilled exponent of, but shoring up a collapsing civilisation, (Did she say that aloud? She looked around guiltily), could not rest on the shoulders of intuition. Mass psychology had to become a science, and quickly, or PushRight would lose the war for people's minds, which meant the Consortium would lose control of the populace, which would mean at the very least that the strong arm of suppression would fall, and people would die. Jelli didn't want that. She wanted to succeed in holding the centre.

She dropped the folder and gave birth to a thought. There was one organisation that might have population behaviour data in the volumes required. It was said that Blue Suit had one of the largest remaining computer centres left in the world buried under their architecturally obscene offices right here in this city. Jelli doubted most things, but this happened to be true, and it was the reason why a relationship with the Blue Suit Social Management Agency might be of immense benefit to PushRight. If she could access those enormous quantities of population behaviour data, then the Law and Order Project could come up with ways to bend the public mind in any direction she chose. She could become the

Consortium's single most powerful subcontractor, if Blue Suit's data could be hers. She could keep the ship of civilisation afloat and save the world, a strange but satisfying thought. What's more, she could have fun doing it.

Over the next few days, she did some digging - well, Allynn had it done - and found that Blue Suit had some history. Not a lot, because his very existence prior to his present position as head of the Blue Suit Social Management Agency was not to be taken for granted, but apparently he was fascinated to the point of unbalance by anything with tits. When she read this, Jelli smiled widely.

"What are you so happy about?" Allynn asked her.

"I have found a weakness," Jelli proclaimed grandly. "I have a plan."

"Very nice," her PA said, unenthusiastically.

Blue Suit had commissioned the same sort of investigation into Jelli as she had into him, and the results were in front of him, neatly bound in a dark blue cover. He opened it and noted from her date of birth that she was the same age as him, and by the look of her weight and measurements she looked after her body as well as he did his own. Not that he was looking through this dossier solely because he was interested in her body, although that was a factor. He was also interested in her organisation.

Organisations share many of the characteristics of individuals. The Consortium was a body concerned mainly with self-preservation. The ministers of state thought it wise to keep everything strictly under control. But at the same time, for they were not stupid men, they realised that suppression alone is like chemotherapy: it damages the whole organism. It affects the cells that are not part of the cancer. The world was ravaged by disease: SRMs, tearing civilisation into ever more digestible chunks, and with that came the secondary infection which was the collapse of the economy and unsurprisingly, of education, employment, and the social order. SRMs might be fatal to civilisation, but it was the secondary infection that was really going to do it down. So much money had to be poured down the social welfare drain that there wasn't much left for finding an answer to SRMs, or repairing the industrial base, or locking people up for being bad, or maintaining a credible military force.

So the second string of the 'keep-a-lid-on-it until we die' policy was the appointment of PushRight Creative Media Inc to guide this disintegrating society in to a soft landing. Whak likened this to increasing the morphine dosage, patting the patient consolingly on the shoulder and saying that everything was going to be fine, but Jelli took a less pessimistic view. She believed that, while things were getting steadily worse in almost every respect, that there must be a bottom somewhere, and somebody had to keep the population cheerful. Everyone likes a smiling corpse.

Blue Suit, however, had never liked this dilution of his responsibilities. PushRight impinged on his task of keeping the laws of society, as he saw them, intact. How could he maintain order when PushRight periodically redefined the basic standards of behaviour - in ever more loose and fuzzy terms? When the Inter-Outsourcer Communication Act was proclaimed, demanding regular communication between government service providers, he could have vomited with disgust, although such displays of feeling were not his way. It had affected him badly. Statistics showed that more people disappeared forever on that day than was the norm. As time passed, though, he was beginning to appreciate the exposure to PushRight, if not the other piddling service providers that were in feeding frenzy around the public purse. PushRight had strengths. PushRight was adroit at mass communication and manipulating people's minds. Blue Suit had an increasing need for those skills. And Jelli, the powerful woman who headed it, was someone with whom he could surely find common ground. He found himself wondering whether she was faithful to her husband, who was a graffiti poet for God's sake, in the absence of being anything else, and surely a weak point.

For that reason alone, he ordered the man with the peculiar name of Whak Puihare put on the observation list.

Observing Whak was difficult. It was not a choice assignment. It required sleeping the day and shadowing the night. The pay was no better than more exciting assignments, such as watching, through Blue Suit-provided telescopic lenses, the Ambassador from Ecuador sniff coke off the many breasts of his mistresses. Worst of all, unless you were an avid fan of the pop medium, it involved watching this clown of a man deface half the walls in the city with words of dim wisdom and worse wit.

The man assigned to watch Whak's every move was deliberately chosen for his lack of artistic appreciation. Blue Suit was not going to allow any rapport between watched and watching. This was not a lion hunt, this was the tedious but necessary business of finding out everything there was to know about everybody, and since most people lead lives commensurate with their insignificant expectations, everything was usually not much.

The watcher knew this. He muttered it to himself sarcastically as he stood enclosed by the moon shadows, wondering what Whak Puihare was doing. In the half-light he could see Whak, at the foot of a deserted building, jumping in the air and grabbing at something above him, flailing his arms and springing his body in energetic fashion, leaping up and floating down. The watcher brought out his pad and pencil and made a brief note describing the situation. He added no comments of the rightness or normality of what he was seeing, because that was not procedure, but he thought that this was more evidence that Puihare was seriously deranged. About then, Whak managed to catch whatever it was he was jumping for, and his watcher saw him draw it down with long hand-over-hand motions. Perhaps he was doing a street mime. At three o'clock in the morning. But no, a rare hole on the cloud cover and an instant of full moon's rays showed that he was pulling on a rope. Turning upon a pulley, lowering from way above his head a creaking wooden platform, a window-washer's cradle. Someone who had space in this building of few unbroken windows must have wanted their view of the filth and grime of the streets unobscured by window smut. While the watcher grew concerned, Whak got the thing all the way to the ground, climbed into it, and hoisted himself into the unobservable sky.

Much later, he came down again, singing a stupid nursery ditty to himself sotto voce, went back to his Mazda, and drove home. The blue suit assigned to him went and looked at the cradle, then up the wall into the darkness. There was no way he was going up there. Shaking his head, he went to his car and followed Puihare back to his home.

Blue Suit put a call through to Jelli in her office. Jelli was delighted. Gaining confidence is so much easier when the victim initiates the conversation. Both PushRight and Blue Suit had phones that worked, unlike ninety-five percent of the population. They had to endure much clicking and static as their respective switchboard systems did their dumb best to find them a line that worked, but at last they could speak and be heard.

"Mrs Puihare," Blue Suit addressed her. "I would like to meet you."

"Jelli, please," Jelli was interested in a closer relationship than that. "We have met, at the inter-outsourcer communication forum."

She noticed that Blue Suit always spoke with unnatural exactitude, in perfectly measured sentences. His voice was deep, smooth, atonal. She would have liked to have known what would break that self-control.

"Yes. However, we should meet again. I think that we should develop a culture of co-operation between our two organisations. These weekly inter-outsourcer meetings are not achieving what could be achieved."

"I'm sure you're right. And I'd like to meet without the hordes of bodyguards and other superfluities," Jelli said airily, thus dismissing her entire senior staff as insignificant. "I suppose you have this line recorded."

"Yes."

"Then let's have a private follow-on after the next meeting." The line crackled while Blue Suit thought about it.

"Where is the next meeting?" he asked.

"At PushRight. They're all at PushRight. We have the conferencing facilities." Jelli's smile was visible in her voice. She enjoyed playing host to all the other service agencies, not least because she had all the conference rooms on video. But Blue Suit hesitated. He did not like others to set the scene, but he did have a desire to see Jelli, alone.

"Very well," he agreed. There was the sound of him flicking pages in a diary. "That's Friday at ten, isn't it?"

"See you there." Jelli put the phone down. She let the feeling of anticipation intensify a bit. "Hmmm," she murmured to herself. "I'm glad he's not gay." She had risen to the top of PushRight by virtue of a lot of qualities, but being fastidious about who she had sex with was not one of them. The driving force of the human species, the exploration of the unknown, came down to this: a man, erect cock in hand, looking for another female to impregnate. Jelli smiled at the thought.

That Friday when the meeting closed, she and Blue Suit stayed behind while all the non-security people in the room made their way out of the room. Blue Suit's protectors remained in their positions of carefully chosen readiness. Jelli looked at them pointedly, and then at the door.

Blue Suit signalled that they should leave. His senior protector glanced up and down Jelli's tightly clad body, looking for hidden weapons no doubt, and took a step towards her, but Blue Suit stopped him.

"Jelli can be trusted," he said.

The protectors' entire lives were predicated on the assumption that no one can be trusted, but they managed to lurch reluctantly out the door. Blue Suit closed it behind them.

"You start," Jelli suggested. She stood up and moved over to where Blue Suit was standing with his arms forward, leaning on the table, poised to say important things, and parked her behind (her sexy behind, she emphasised with a settling shiver) two millimetres from his left hand. His mouth already open to begin his speech, Blue Suit stopped and took his hands from the table, but he did not move away. He spoke almost directly into her face, but quietly.

"I do not like PushRight Creative Media's role in public affairs," he stated. "You are an alternative influence that I do not always agree with."

"I can see that," Jelli agreed. "I don't like your role, either."

Blue Suit nodded as if he had expected no other response. "So," he said. "Since we are in agreement, we should be able to come to some partitioning of responsibilities."

"Or we could go on making life as difficult for each other as possible." Jelli glanced out the window at the derelict concrete behemoth opposite, and felt a slight shock. Words of Whak were painted across it in letters half a metre tall. It had not been there last time she was on this side of the building. He must have written it there specifically to attract her attention. By the standards of graffiti, it was a long piece, the words crossing the entire side of the building twice:

Difficult times and difficult people
Are asking me to be this way and I am doing it
I am doing it there isn't any way
That I can not do it
Without changing into someone else
Entering a personality transmitter and being
Torn into pieces of myself
Put back together looking the same but
The real me is dead

Was the real her dead?
Jelli looked away, back to Blue Suit.
"We should co-operate," he said.

"Compare notes before we speak," agreed Jelli, thinking 'damn that Whak for fucking with my mind'.

"Speak with a united voice."

"Have sex together occasionally." Jelli suddenly tired of all this mutual co-operation shit. She got out of her chair, wiggled up to Blue Suit, and stood very close, making provocative body movements. Without any change in expression, he radiated an intoxicating mixture of alarm and desire.

"You're very attractive, Jelli," he said with obviously forced calm, "but I prefer to keep our relationship on a business level."

"You do not." Jelli replied sweetly and accurately. "You want to fuck me right now." She ran a finger up the side of his face. He did not move away. Jelli felt a knot of pleasure form somewhere near her solar plexus.

"Perhaps I do, but that would not make Blue Suit a more effective force for order." His voice remained level and controlled.

"Will co-operating, speaking with one voice, comparing notes and agreeing responsibilities do that?"

"Certainly."

"Well, let me tell you what I think." Jelli went back to her chair again and resumed the businesslike approach, partly to keep him off-balance, and partly so that she had some time to rebalance herself. "I think that any co-operation between PushRight and Blue Suit is going to be to PushRight's detriment. We are persuaders, and you are enforcers, so we always want to use the least possible change approach, and you will always want to use the lock everybody up and throw away the key approach. Our two cultures couldn't be more different. Didn't you see in that meeting how all my people talked about influencing behaviour and all your people talked about manpower and surveillance?"

He thought about what Jelli had said and shook his head in disagreement.

"That is simply two ends of a spectrum. We live together in a broad church. We both want a controlled, predictable social environment, because that will be both economically and culturally more profitable - and I use the word in the most abstract sense - than what we have now."

"Of course that's what we want." Jelli pretended to be undecided. "All right then. Why don't we start out by agreeing to share some information. We'd be interested in any data your surveillance people have collected. We could do some image remake work for you in return."

"Surveillance data is classified," Blue Suit said flatly.

"See?" Jelli sighed. "We have no points of contact. But I'm willing to try and develop some."

Blue Suit's peripheral vision roved over her with visible signs of self-irritation as he considered this. "How?" he asked at last.

"We'll have to get to know each other better. We might end up being friends." She got up and went to the door. "Let's discuss this again, soon." She went out.

Blue Suit came after her out of the boardroom, and his eyes could not help but follow her legs as she walked away. He thought that Jelli would probably sleep with a snake in order to further her own interests. He respected that. It made her even more interesting and attractive. Her finger on his face. But at the same time, he was Blue Suit. He should be able to disregard sexual games. Apart from her role as CEO of PushRight, she was only a woman, and not the most beautiful woman he would have enjoyed, either. He would have to remind himself of that, as frequently as possible, because she was clearly a master of getting inside skin.

A week later, they began to have sex together. When two intelligent and willing adults both have the morals of a ferret, it doesn't take long for attraction to become penetration. They became regulars at the inter-outsourcer meetings. For appearances, Jelli even put her face in, from time to time, at meetings with the Transvation Corporation (transport) and the Sickness Co-operative (health), but she made sure she was always present when Blue Suit attended. They scheduled a regular discussion that took place after each meeting, in Jelli's office, during which they talked business as they pulled each other out of their clothes. Blue Suit was not a great giver of emotional feedback, but he possessed a lust that poured through Jelli's body, glands, and mind like a stormfall through a leaky roof. Her own excitement did the rest.

It was exciting and fun, but as yet Jelli had nothing to show for it in return, except the knowledge, carelessly disclosed, that Blue Suit had Whak under surveillance. She worried about that. She never could be sure what her husband might say or do without warning. As she lay in bed next to Whak, sleepless as she often was at four in the morning, she wondered what was going to happen next.

CHAPTER 6

John Firely had his cock in his hand, but only because he was peeing through it. He gave it a good shake when he was finished and stowed it back where it belonged, under clothes, out of his sight. As he washed his hands, he reviewed in his head a number of experiments that were in progress back in the lab. It was only right that he should be the director of this establishment, but it did carry a lot of responsibility, especially since he also had to fill the role of chief theoretician. He envied some of his correspondents, one or two of whom were also naturally brilliant, but not dependent upon the bureaucracy of a giant corporation like this one. He wasn't even sure that he had the benefit of bigger budgets. Since SRMs appeared a few years ago, budgets had tended to shrink, but not the paperwork and reporting that went with them. Paperwork and reporting not only cost money, they stifle the creative instinct.

There was one man in particular, running the Smalltech project, who had proposed function models so convincing that all the other projects around the world, including this one, were using one or another variant of his originals for functional typing. Academic rivalry aside, John often ran his thoughts past him for peer review before he soaked up any increasingly difficult to obtain funds in actual experiments. He was sure that Smalltech would go under before this place, but they had a reputation for collecting unwashed genii and giving them their head. A false reputation, for John Firely was the ultimate unwashed genius, in his opinion.

John Firely ran the largest nanotech research centre in the country. He had a passion for it, and life is good to a man with a passion. A passion or an obsession. As John left the toilet and started walking back to his office, he passed a few of his staff in the corridor. They made nervous obeisance: John Firely was not a man to get chummy with, he was a man who was always right and not to be contradicted, a dancing insect of certainty that paralysed the humble workers with his incisive sting. It was why he was called the Firefly. It was only due to his brilliance that he could be forgiven his constant berating and rudeness.

"That's the Firefly. He's an absolute asshole," one of the simulation programmers told a new colleague quietly as they watched him walk away with short twitchy steps. "Keeping out of his way is good for your blood pressure. But he's also one of the top two theorists in the field, so sticking around him is good for your career. Spends a lot of time in the men's. He dreamed the F-tool configuration up over a leak. The Fuck-tool, the designers call it. It's a real step forward in monad replication."

"I wondered why it looked like a penis."

There was an alert on the Firefly's screen, telling him that his three o'clock appointment was cancelled. He had no idea that he had ever had a three o'clock appointment, and he didn't recognise the name. He clicked on his schedule, and was informed by a cheerfully patterned dialog box that the network schedule file was currently unavailable, possibly due to a change of network address, and that he should contact his network administrator. He grunted. More likely due to one of those self-replicating machines taking the server SIMMs for baby food. There was a lot of that going on, these days. So his appointment, whoever it was, was cancelled. Good. He would spend the next couple of hours going over his proof of derivable, vibrational energy maximums. He pulled a sheaf of papers out of his drawer and began to leaf through them.

Then there was a knock at the door.

"Damn!" John said with more irritation that the event deserved. He hated to be interrupted when he was head full of symbolic logic. He stood up, put his hands forward on his desk in a threatening posture, and shouted at the door in a rather thin, high voice.

"What is it?"

The door opened. There was a stranger there. He was wearing a suit that was too expensive for the average academic, and behind him stood two more of the same model. The Firefly made the instant assumption that these were visitors from the corporate offices. Accountants, or project managers, or marketing. He sat back down and waved at the chairs on the other side of his desk.

"Come in," he said ungraciously. "I thought you'd cancelled."

"We haven't cancelled."

The Firefly's eyes danced angrily.

"I can see that," he replied with uncontained venom. "What do you want? If you're looking for a tour of the complex then you'll have to come back another day. If you're auditors or some other corporate bottom feeders then you'll have to make an appointment. I have important work to do." Firely chose to forget that they already had an appointment, and began to compose arguments as to whether they ever really did. If he had come back to an alert that his three o'clock appointment was waiting for him, of course he would have dealt with them, however grudgingly. But he had thought the afternoon was free and was already five pages deep in his own paper on powering nanos by random atmospheric kinetic energy. Life was short enough without one of the infrequent jewels of free time being plucked from his fingers like this.

The three men came into his office without seeming to be distressed by John Firely's rudeness, and shut the door behind them. The first one, slimmer and younger than the other two but clearly in charge, sat down opposite him and crossed his ankles comfortably.

"We're not here for any of those reasons."

If they weren't here for the corporate tour and they weren't here to audit the admittedly improbable paperwork, then why were they here? John could only think of one other reason.

"You're not here to..." he stopped. Of course they weren't. "Of course you're not." Not now when results were starting to come through. They were a long way from sustainability, as he liked to call it: the level of stability and consistency at which a nanomachine population could remain viable. But he was sure that he knew how to get there. There was no chance that the corporation would close the project at this stage.

"We're not here to shut you down, Dr Firely. We don't even work for your company. We're the competition. We're here to offer you a job." He said 'job' in a long, supercilious kind of way, as if Firely was a person without work and meaning in his life. It might as well have been designed to make Firely bridle, and he did.

"I have a perfectly satisfactory position here as Project Director," he said, getting to his feet and leaning across the desk in his most intimidating manner. "I have a team on the verge of some of the most exciting breakthroughs in engineering and physics since Enrico Fermi. If you think I'm going to walk away from this for a few dollars then you can go and hunt for heads in the Salvation Army car park. The trouble with you people is that you think everyone can be had for a bigger pay check. There are more important things in my life than whether I get a bigger laboratory or a new house, thank you very much, and the years I have spent gathering together the fine set of minds I have working for me here is NOT FOR SALE!" He straightened up with a satisfied sigh. It was always a pleasure to bollock complete strangers and have no fear of the consequences. He eyed his visitors, waiting for them to slink from his sight, but instead, the slim young guy uncrossed his ankles and nodded understandingly.

"To be perfectly frank, Dr Firely, we expected that response from you. Which is why we brought this." He nodded to the man on his right, who brought into view a thin briefcase which John had not noticed before. While John watched, puzzled, the man opened the briefcase and took out a small hypodermic. The other man went and stood by the closed office door. John looked at the younger man with asymptotically increasing panic.

"What's that for?" he demanded.

"Well, Dr Firely, knowing your reputation, we thought you would refuse to listen to our very generous and career-enhancing offer. Our client is not a man who likes to be refused. And he doesn't want any competition. So, if you're not willing to be tempted, I'm afraid this is the alternative."

The man with the hypodermic was coming around the side of the desk, holding the little syringe delicately in his large-knuckled hand.

"But wait!" John shouted. "Don't do this! You don't need to drug me! Let's discuss this further!"

"Oh, Dr Firely," the young man smiled. "We know you to be a man of principles. Don't try to pretend that we could talk an historic figure like you into anything with the mere threat of violence."

"But you can! I'll compromise! I -" John Firely looked down, startled, at his hand. There was a thin trickle of blood running down onto it from his forearm, where the syringe was hanging. While he stared at it, the large-knuckled man removed it and dabbed efficiently at the spot with a piece of cotton wool. "What was that?" he whispered.

"Quite undetectable," the young man assured him.

He felt a hideous pain in his chest.

CHAPTER 7

Whak was not sure whether he should be pleased at being considered a dangerous dissident, but rightly or wrongly he was smiling. And weeping, but that was because there still seemed to be coffee grounds in his left eye and it was hurting like hell. He rolled over to the side of the bed which was by now cold with the absence of Jelli and slid out onto the floor.

"Damn, my eye hurts," he said as he pulled on his clothes. In the bathroom he pulled his eyelids this way and that as he tried to find and remove the elusive grounds, but after he found himself considering popping his eyeball out as he had heard could be done with a dessert spoon he stopped with a blink - ouch - and a grunt of despair.

"Doctor," he muttered. "Who's our doctor?"

On the side of the kitchen fridge was a magnetic notebook with all kinds of telephone numbers in it. Whak found the phone, a bulky affair designed mainly with SRM resistance in mind, on the dining table with the remains of Jelli's breakfast. He dialled the doctor with one hand while he poured coffee with the other.

"You have reached the appointment service of Doctors Imbruck and Stellman. Please indicate your answers to the following questions by pressing keypad 1 for yes and keypad 2 for no. Press keypad 3 to continue," said a voice that was artificially melodic. Whak was surprised, because SRMs were particularly partial to some forms of technology, voice mail systems being high on their list. He was also disappointed. His lips turned down with the knowledge that he would now have to conform to a series of binary options. He pressed keypad 3.

"Thank you. Doctors Imbruck and Stellman hereby give assurance that no information received by this voice message management system will be released without the written consent of the patient, that is, you. Please press keypad 9 to proceed."

Whak pushed keypad 9.

"Thank you. Please indicate your ailment by pressing keypad 1 for yes or keypad 2 for no. Do you have a respiratory infection complaint?"

Whak pushed keypad 2.

"Do you have internal bleeding?"

"No, I do not have internal bleeding!" Whak pressed keypad 2.

"Do you have pain while urinating?"

"Oh for Christ's sake," Whak said. He pressed keypad 4, 5, asterisk, and redial, and whistled into the mouthpiece.

"One moment please." said the appointment system. After a length of time measured in mouthfuls of coffee, another voice spoke.

"Hello? Do you want to send a fax?"

Whak was pleasantly surprised at this knowledge that he could imitate a fax machine, especially since he had not heard the sound of one for several years.

"Hello, my name is Whak Puihare, and I have something in my eye."

"Oh, I'll put you onto the appointment system, shall I?"

"I think it's broken," Whak lied.

"Not again! We just had it fixed!"

"It'll be pocket calculators, most likely," he elaborated. "Always getting into appointment systems, those little bastards."

"Well, yes, I'm sure. What did you say your name was?"

"Whak Puihare."

"I beg your pardon."

"Whak Puihare. W-h-a-k Puihare."

"Oh, I'm sorry. I thought you said, ah, here we are. You haven't visited us for a check-up for quite some time, Mr Puihare."

"I haven't been sick," Whak replied. "Can you make me an appointment?"

After a pause, indicating that being not sick was no excuse for not visiting the doctor: "Well, I suppose so. How about at nine-thirty?"

Whak looked at the clock over the stove. "In ten minutes? I'll be late," he warned the voice.

"That's fine," it replied. "The nine-thirty appointment won't be seen today until eleven o'clock. Please arrive punctually. Good day."

Whak slumped over Jelli's breakfast tray and held his head, which was aching sympathetically with his eye, in his hands. Was he to arrive at nine-thirty? Or at eleven? Should he be late for an appointment which was scheduled to be late, or should he be early for an appointment that was already past? He was still sitting there, but now taking an interest in the view out of the kitchen window when Lino crashed out of her bedroom and into the light. He waved his finger vaguely at the scene, which involved a car parked, or broken down more likely, in the middle of the street and a tailback extending into the distance like the ouroboros. Lino glanced at it without interest.

"I'm bored," she told Whak. This was her normal morning greeting.

"Must have been a bad night for cars," he mused as one by one people started getting out of their vehicles. With briefcases and handbags hanging from their arms they walked, stick figures moving in directions that were only random if you didn't know where they were going.

"Are you listening to me?" Lino demanded. Whak turned his attention back to his daughter, abjectly. It was hard for him not to be swallowed by the patterns and magic of events that were for him just an insight away from having meaning. He tried to be considerate.

"Get a job," he suggested.

"Thanks a lot," Lino sneered. "There are no jobs. Unless you want me to go and work for Jelli."

"No, no, no, don't go and work for Jelli." Frightful thought that two of his family should be in public relations. Besides the fact that Lino was completely unsuited to the work. "You'd go into a coma in a minute flat. Someone else." Lino was prone to periods of catatonic withdrawal that the best medical and psychiatric advice had failed to find a reason for, and no treatment, either, except frequent and large doses of anti-schizophrenic drugs. We can cure her by turning her into a vegetable, in other words. Whak had made it clear that a painful, antagonistic daughter was for him a better choice than a stick of broccoli, and since she had reached her early adulthood, Whak and Jelli had stopped trying to find the reason for her differences. He looked carefully at Lino's face. She was a perfect illustration of beauty that failed to come from within, her flawless skin and golden eyes utterly unillumed. She took after Jelli in looks, he considered, but after all his darkest moments in temperament and introspection.

"No, you're right, there are no jobs. If there were, I think I might have one."

"You?" Lino was surprised at the very idea. She clearly thought Whak was in some way not suited to work, which rang much the same bell in Whak's head as the discovery that he was under surveillance by Blue Suit: it's nice to be special, in a useless kind of way.

"Go join a social club or something. Go on a Wasteland tour," Whak tossed his hand skywards. "I'll pay."

"Jelli pays."

"Haven't you ever heard of the marriage partnership? We'll pay."

"Wasteland tours are for tourists."

"I have to go to the doctor. My eye is killing me."

"What about me?"

"I'm sorry, Lino, but you have to find your own entertainment." He wished it were not so, but over the years he had learned that helping his erratically autistic daughter was not helping her. "If I could make you happy, I would, believe me, but..."

"What?"

"I've got to go."

In fact, it was too early, but Whak had to escape from Lino. Everyone had to escape from Lino. Much as he loved her, she had a capacity for dragging him down into her darkness that he could only resist by not being there. He dressed, found the car keys, and took the front door way out so that he could check the street situation, which was not much improved. The neighbour's car had been pushed partway to the curb, but a dozen other abandoned vehicles were still lined up. A tow-truck operator was standing with cap in hand trying to decide where to begin.

"Hey," Whak called.

"Hey," the truckie called back.

"How about clearing these two?" Whak pointed at the cars which were blocking his driveway.

"Yeah, why not? Got to start somewhere."

"Terrific." Whak waved, turned back to his garage door, and stopped. The garage door, already a patchwork of riveted metal plates, was punctured in several places by circular holes. Like scorpion holes, but bigger, and rougher-edged. Whak groaned, then unlocked and lifted up the door. Jelli's car was gone, of course, but her car was a government-supplied SRM-resistant troop transporter, and his was a Mazda, and his car, if the pool of hydraulic fluid which was under it spake true, was crocodile food. But not entirely. Although he was practically useless with mechanical things, from necessity Whak had learned how to change hydraulic leads and to bleed brakes, because for some reason his car always seemed to be considered a morsel without peer by any SRM within cooee. He had spare leads - doesn't everyone? - locked in a wooden drawer where they were less likely to attract the metal-hungry little monsters. He set to work.

By the time Whak had brakes once more, he was in serious danger of being late for his late appointment. He hurtled down the street, onto the on-ramp, and exited at the shopping mall. He pulled into the car park, which was nearly empty. All these suburban super-complexes with their hectares of parking were anachronisms from the days of cheap fuel, disposable income, and reliable technology. They were vastly over-equipped for the world of forced, unpaid leisure and SRM snack attacks. In a corner of the car park given over to the carcasses of broken machinery and damaged goods, some pocket calculators were dismantling a teddy bear. Whak parked at a discreet distance, and took a moment to watch the law of the jungle in action. The teddy bear was a bipedal SRM with a spherical head that in no way resembled a bear of any sort. It was thrashing it's limbs against the tarmac while the pocket calculators used their extensive range of manipulators (no two pocket calculators shared the same combination, so folklore said) to dismantle it. All the useful parts equalled all the parts. The pocket calculators were shortly engaged in assembling something from the pile of bits they had accumulated - something that looked like another pocket calculator, except that it sported an abdomen made from a shiny metal ball. Whak raised a cheer as it came to life and clumped off with the others, a tribe of stiff-legged golems breeding, feeding, and fighting within the world of this car park. Whak thought it was wonderful. The rest of the world hated it.

The doctor's waiting room was packed, as they always seem to be. What did people who felt unwell do before doctors were invented? The caves must have been full of people in need of a kind word and an assurance that they were going to be all right, and when they got only a sour look and a sprig of herbs from the local witch, bitter seeds must have been planted. Whak thought that most human misery was due to no kind words when they were needed. He presented himself to the receptionist, who gave him no kind words either, and then put his backside onto a still-warm, (unpleasantly so, as if from the arse of someone fat and feverish) vinyl seat. It made his bottom itch.

Opposite sat a woman in her late twenties with eyes ringed by blackness, with a child who looked the same, on her lap. Faces grey with age were everywhere, grey with age and staring into their crystalline pasts. Whak looked carefully around, drinking in the hopelessness, but then his eyes fell on a man slightly older than himself, wearing tidy casual clothes, his face turned down into a neatly folded newspaper. It was rude, of course, but the search for the experience of truth often requires one to stare, so Whak stared. A little test of the eyes-upon-us theory. Eventually, the man looked up.

"I know you," Whak said instantly. "You're Dr Assok."

Whak couldn't claim to never forget a face, but he would always remember this one. Three years ago, during a period of untypical self-doubt, he had decided to Find a Job. Things were no better then than today, and interesting jobs were as now a hobby reserved for the governing classes, and Whak had no useful qualifications. He was forced to apply for positions that were sufficiently weird that no one else wanted them, or in some cases even knew what they were. Whak usually didn't know what they were, either, but in the frame of reference he operated in, that was a good thing. Or so he believed, until he found himself in a rather plain ugly looking building, several floors underground in it, in fact, naked under a cotton robe in a room full of computers and oscilloscopes and machines which he barely recognised, with a health questionnaire and rights waiver in front of him, talking to an excited-looking man in a white coat. Dr Assok. George, if Whak remembered aright.

All faces swivelled towards the man, who widened his eyes and narrowed his mouth.

After a moment, he said, "And you are?"

"Whak Puihare."

George Assok showed no recognition at all.

"You must remember," Whak told him. "You interviewed me for a job when you were working in some kind of secret laboratory. I didn't even get to know where it was, I was taken there by some real goony birds with shades so black they couldn't see their own wristwatches, and you were wearing the whole mad scientist outfit. Do you remember? You wanted subjects for some sort of viral exposure program or something, I never did understand whether it was the virus or me that you wanted exposed, and when you told me that you'd be taking brain biopsies before and after I ran around the room in one of those horrible hospital gowns that show your backside while the goony birds shouted at me. Is this ringing any bells?" Whak asked anxiously, because George Assok's face was becoming more and more agitated as he shook his newspaper at Whak and whispered, 'Shut up! Shut up!", but Whak in verbal train was not be derailed, and he continued.

"I hate needles. That's what biopsies are taken with, isn't it, BIG needles. What were you trying to find out? Germ warfare research, I guessed later. Was it germ warfare research?"

"I don't know what you're talking about!" Assok exploded. He turned a serious, concerned-looking face to all the people now looking back at him. "I don't know what he's talking about! This man is quite insane! You must be here to see the psychiatrist, is that right?"

"No, actually I have something in my eye."

"Well, get your eye seen to and leave me alone!" George Assok unfolded his newspaper to twice it's previous area and stuck it purposefully in front of his face. Funny how people think a symbolic barrier like that will stop anyone from talking to them. It certainly would not have stopped Whak, but there was a chime and a voice, which Whak didn't hear properly or understand at all, but George Assok clearly did, because he jumped up and marched quickly down the corridor to one of the examination rooms. A lot of people turned to watch him go.

"Strange bod," said the old man on the other side of Whak. "You trying to be sociable and all, and him saying you're a nutcase. Is that nice?"

"He's probably a bit sensitive, working in germ warfare," said Whak, placatingly.

"Terrible business. I didn't know we still did that sort of stuff."

"More than ever, my wife says."

"Terrible."

Whak agreed, and spent the next fifteen minutes trying to shut the old geezer up in a manner which didn't break his own strict rule of politeness: listen carefully, because there might be a poem in it, then ignore it. He was rescued when it came to be his turn to be examined. Puihare, Room 3.

With one vacuumed and polished eye patched, and the loud thudding echo of pain reverberating in his head, Whak drove slowly home. If experience is a rushing river in which we swim, and perception is a bowl of that river water, clearest when still, then what is a blinding headache? Whak did not feel still, so he did not try to compose a poem about his eye experience, at least not in the car. His remaining sight swam with photophobic sensitivity, so that he drove straight through most traffic lights without even seeing whether or not they were working. If they had been red, he normally would at least have slowed down, a conditioned reflex he supposed from the days when they had generally worked, and there had been enough cars on the road for them to be needed. It was still illegal to crash a light, though. The Consortium had to shore up the receipts somehow, now that income tax was so unreliable.

His street still looked like a used car lot. The tow truckie must have been called to some really serious snarl-up, or perhaps his winches and gear had a spot of SRM-itis, whichever, half the cars left in the morning madness were still blocking the way. As Whak drove up over the footpath, up the driveway, and into his garage, he noticed that there were two people walking up the long path from the gates. By the time he reached the front door, Lino had already answered it and was being talked at by the male component of the twosome. The other was a teenage girl, who was standing quietly while her companion spoke.

"Hi, Lino," Whak greeted her.

"Hi," she said.

"Who's this?" He nodded at the visitors. The man was wearing a brown plastic suit, yellow shoes, a crooked bow tie, none of which matched his age and condition. He was in his fifties, maybe sixties, and had a genuine pot belly which Whak could only refrain from staring at with great difficulty.

"Revital Church Elder Kutters," said the man, importantly. "An acolyte," he waved a hand at the girl. "Have you ever considered your place in the Universe, Mr...?"

"I'm not in the mood for this," Whak replied. "My eye hurts, my head hurts, and I'm an atheist."

"You do realise that the time of reckoning may soon be at hand? That the Hand of the Lord is visible in the world? Join us, my friend, and celebrate the creation of Life!" Kutters was clearly working himself into one of the sing-song celebrations which proselytising religions have always been prone to. "The Sign is the coming forth, from the very ground, of new life. Not like His first creatures, the new life is different so that we may recognise His Work. Rejoice! Prepare yourself to look upon the face of the Lord!"

"The new life might be here just to piss us off," Whak pointed out. "Get attention by aggravation. Plague of locust stuff."

Kutters put the brakes on his speech and cast a powerful and critical eye on Whak and Lino. He had been in this business long enough to recognise a tough assignment when he saw it.

"You should come to our Temple in the City," he said after a moment. "Come and meet with us. Discussion and revelation are our methods. You would be welcome." He took his leave, then, walking in a sideways fashion down the footpath to the gate, never actually turning away, still spouting phrases straight out of the Revital Handbook (which Whak happened to have read). It was interesting to observe. Especially when he put his hand on the hip of his acolyte as they made their way onwards, seeking more malleable minds to permeate with crap.

"Well," Whak shook his head sadly, "them is seriously deluded folks."

Lino, however, was no longer at the door. She had returned to the darkness and solitude of her bedroom, so Whak went to his study and worked there, unproductively, until hunger made him come out that afternoon. He saw then that Lino's door was open and couldn't resist looking in - he hadn't seen the inside of Lino's room for some time. The room was stark. Bare, neat, featureless, except for a picture above Lino's bed. A large photograph, black and white of course, of a man dancing with his cap in his hand. Whak had given her that picture when she was twelve, which was eight years ago now, and he wondered briefly if the monochrome girl was his own creation. He did not revisit his guilt today. What's done is done, he had decided long ago. Wonder where she's gone?

CHAPTER 8

The same morning, Jelli had peeled back her bedcovers and waited for the bite of the morning air to move her. Then she rose up and examined her naked self in the wardrobe mirror. Still clinging to the acceptable picture of the attractive 40ish woman, she thought. Being naturally small helped. The touch of the tarbrush too, perhaps. Her husband was rolled over facing the other way, a lump in the blankets, breathing loudly, with one arm sticking up in the air, drowning in the mattress. Jelli looked over at him once or twice as she dressed, not entirely sure of why.

She had a healthy breakfast. She always did. All PushRight executives did. It was like a badge of office: to become a figure of power at PushRight Creative Media, you had to toe a well-defined line for the years that it took to get the attention of, and the patronage of, the people at the top, and that meant that you had to become like them. Now that she finally was at the top herself, Jelli could define new corporate mores, if she liked, but the ones she had lived with for so long had become comfortable for the most part, so she went on living them. She had Whak, if she wanted to remind anyone that she was still an individual, which had both bright and cloudy sides, but still some of her staff probably thought of her as the living incarnation of policy. With lipstick and power nails.

She saw the holes in the garage door, but it was late, so she didn't leave Whak a note. Let the man stand on his own two feet. He'll notice all the brake fluid on the floor, and if he doesn't, he'll figure it out soon enough when he tries to stop at the intersection at the end of the street. That amused Jelli, because she was always telling Whak not to be so damned courteous on the road. Jelli clicked her car into growling life. The remote control that operated the doors had been eaten long ago, so she closed the garage door by hand.

Her car was actually an armoured personnel vehicle, which was supposed to withstand SRM forays by a combination of redundant parts and protective plates, but the best thing about it was the fact that Jelli never had to give way to anything but another humvee, and they were not a common sight off military bases. Not like the more conventional machine in the middle of the street, clearly a victim of a night-time feast. From it's position it appeared to have rolled down the hill, and from it's disembowelled condition it had been left in the open overnight. Because the machine Jelli was in, was so heavy, she hardly noticed as she clipped a corner and rotated the other car so that it blocked the street almost completely. What did it matter, anyway? It was SRM-bait.

She drove fast, hardly taking her foot off the accelerator pedal, so the trip to her work was a short one.

PushRight Creative Media was located in one of the still-habitable skyscrapers that lined up either side of what used to be the main shopping boulevard. Years ago, Jelli used to work on advertising accounts for half of the fashion stores that were now empty, or converted to food storehouses in expectation of the eventual collapse of the transport infrastructure, or, in many cases, report posts for the security forces of Blue Suit. She remembered those days as irresponsible and fun, and she knew that these now were hard, doom-laden times, but she had always accepted that the price to pay for climbing the ladder would be placing her work ahead of everything else, and she had done that, so if the world had not crumbled into shit at the same time as she was rising through it, she doubted that she would have noticed any difference.

There was a private lift which Jelli rode from the executive car park to the fifteenth floor, where her office was the largest, best situated, had the most windows, and generally reeked of privilege. Floors above this were deemed unsafe for human habitation. As Jelli passed by her PA's desk, Allynn rose up and followed her into the office.

"Tell me all," Jelli instructed as she opened her briefcase - it gave a faint popping sound as she released the catches, and the topmost file slid straight out into her lap - and turned on her computer. The computer beeped four times and died. "Shit. Don't tell me we've had an SRM in here. I thought we were safe enough this high up."

"An SRM? I don't think so," Allynn replied. "I think it's just you. You really do go through the equipment. This'll be your third workstation this year. What do you do to them?"

"I just turn the thing on in the morning and off at night," Jelli murmured. "But I used to be able to stop photocopiers at five paces, once." It was true. When she was near, recently serviced Xerox machines would chew paper, distort images, and cook toner cartridges just as she walked by. Whak said that this was a manifestation of one of his pet theories, personal entropy levels.

He claimed that Jelli and he had been attracted to each other, all that disappearing time ago, because they both generated disorder, he by emanating it, and she by absorbing it's opposite. He had written a piece about it on the side of the deserted Technology Museum, a long one, but all that Jelli could remember was

You carry a cloud of breakdown round
And wear things out by your presence
Every time you build a thought
Somewhere a star explodes

"Crap," Jelli said.

"I'm sorry?"

"Crap. My husband thinks that my life-force sucks all the order out of objects around me."

"Sounds like crap to me," Allynn agreed.

"Do you feel as if I'm sucking order out of you?" Jelli demanded. There was a brief hesitation in the other's face, which she noticed. "Oh, never mind. What's on the schedule?"

"A creative direction meeting with the Law and Order team at nine. Another Blue Suit meeting, at ten. And you're going over the plans for the next series of 'Who Needs Money?' at three."

"Blue Suit again, hey?" Jelli pushed her lower lip down with her finger, wetting it slightly in the process. "Has it been a week already?"

"Why do you have to have a meeting with him every week? They give me the willies, all those big men with guns he brings around with him."

"Hmm." She decided to give the ostensible reason, which might even have been the substantive: "It's because the Consortium Directors of Information and Justice want us to communicate with each other. Otherwise we might do, oh, an ad campaign about the virtues of reporting suspicious activities at the same time as Blue Suit is beginning a major program of surreptitious house searches, and the police would be bombarded with calls. Then the police would have to tell people that they haven't got the manpower to handle calls and our ad campaign which was intended to set the population on each other so they won't form activist groups would be wasted, and Blue Suit would get a lot of operatives identified in their neighbourhoods, and the public confidence in the police would go down, and generally we'd be running even faster towards the total collapse of civilisation as we know it." Jelli paused for breath and looked up into her PA's face, the expression on which was aghast. Allynn was so white at times. "Metaphorically speaking," she added quickly. No point in stampeding the natives. "Get me a coffee."

While Allynn got the coffee, she reflected on the progress of her personal agenda with Blue Suit. In the inter-outsourcer meetings, he had done his icy observing thing, making little comment, obviously itching to get away to more important business. Then there was the distraction of the thick carpet of her office floor under her knees, or the taste of him in her mouth, and then there was the usual prevarication about sharing information, or plans, or anything at all apart from spit. At this stage, she felt a little perplexed: what was Blue Suit getting out of this, apart from the best blow job on the planet? Or was that enough for him? Men could be such a puzzle, sometimes. All the men in her life certainly were.

Allynn brought the coffee, and also a huge folder almost bursting with Law and Order Project minutes. The trend to digital storage had never made it to really important stuff, and now that SRMs had turned the Internet into a billion kilometres of empty insulation, patchy voice lines, and defunct satellite stations, it never would. This reminder of what might have been made Jelli glum with the magnitude of her task and the quality of the tools she had to work with. She read over what had happened in the last meeting. Lots of good ideas, not much to support them. Proposals for gross psychological intervention through GOV1 entertainment, without any clear idea of the probable effects. Pleas for street polls to be funded and manned, without any agreement on what they would be polling about. Jelli shuddered.

Collapsing civilisations have their own dynamics. PushRight had an opportunity here to shape not just a few buying patterns and ephemeral styles, but the social context of the next generation. It was typical of Jelli that she had no doubts that PushRight, and more precisely, she, were the right people for the job, but a few team members were sadly less tuned in to social re-engineering. Some people had qualms about free will, self-determinism, human dignity. Jelli thought it all quite academic, since the Law & Order Project had not progressed past yelling at each other in meetings, but the fact was, she had to report some sort of progress soon. She began to prepare a series of re-appointments. Moving a few people around, rounding out their skills. All that bullshit. Really, signalling their dispensability. The threat of unemployment concentrates the mind wonderfully, as the saying goes, especially since unemployment meant loss of income, status, home, car, education facilities, and electronic consumer goods that worked, and cast the unfortunate out into the vicious rotten world that Jelli was trying to find ways to re-engineer. Life at the top meant a life that was almost as good as it once might have been, huge mansions and so forth, although Italian sports cars were just a memory. Life at the bottom meant, well, Jelli hoped she would never find out, but it was bad.

The Law and Order project was such an opinion polariser that even the most innocuous action point was usually debated bitterly before being allowed onto the minutes. This time there was an argument between Dukker's protégé Harrison and the news director over the virtue of spinning the news slant even further than they did already, to the point of outright fiction, even. The discussion raised real points of principle, which was likely why everyone ended up yelling at once. Jelli waited patiently until tension and exhaustion broke and the room fell silent as all present simultaneously released their pent breath, and then she changed the subject, brutally as only she could.

"If we could obtain Blue Suit's records of public surveillance for the past three years, what could we do with it?" she said clearly.

The silence of a deep breath turned into the silence of stupefaction.

"What couldn't we do with it?" asked an evangelistic young theorist at the back of the room.

"We could probably just turn the whole fucking world into a bunch of robots!" someone from the other camp shouted out. Instantly the crossfire started again as the opposing philosophies each tried to submerge the other with all manner of facts and figures and references and attributions and imputations. They probably thought Jelli had posed the question for no reason but to provoke this reaction. It was true that it had forced a few closet humanists into the open. And some from the social engineering side who she would rather see hanging by their necks than having any power over their fellow men. She took note of a few faces as she rose from her seat. She had to go, it was time for the inter-outsourcer meeting.

As she passed his seat, Dukker looked at her carefully. He knew her well.

"What's this data actually got in it?" he asked her.

"I don't know, yet."

"Yet?"

"That's what I said."

"You sure know where the money is," he said admiringly.

"And you sure know how to suck ass, Dukker," Jelli replied.

"True. But it's not my favourite piece of anatomy."

Jelli briskly strolled back to her office, rather pleased, and full of surpassing confidence. She passed the lift just as Blue Suit and his entourage emerged from it.

"Jelli, how are you?" Blue Suit smiled a cool smile. He touched her on the forearm. Jelli rose slightly into the pressure of his fingers, then drew away. Like all good sexual affairs, this one thrived on secrecy.

"This way," she called back. "Conference room six. Allynn! Catering for..." she turned back, flicked her eyes over the crowd, and did some mental arithmetic, "fourteen. Good God, you have more people around you every day." Creatures, Whak called them. It's not as hard as you might think to find people who will die for a charismatic master.

"A necessary precaution," Blue Suit said. "But these are not all bodyguards."

"I didn't say what kind of creatures they were."

"Five protectors, technical adviser, and recorder," Blue Suit said as he walked around the table in conference room six and sat himself at the top of the table. Jelli tried not to consider it a provocation. If she knew him any less well, she would have kicked his pleasantly muscular ass out of her seat. She wasn't sure yet whether he did these things knowing their effects on others, or whether he was so lacking in empathy that he didn't notice. His people quickly lined up down either side of him, four protectors standing, one sitting facing the door, and on his left side his recorder and the technical adviser, who was clearly discernible by the comparison of his complexion with the glowing healthy skin of the bodyguards. Jelli spoke polite nothing stuff while her team entered and arrayed themselves opposite.

"Agenda?" said Jelli. Pieces of paper were flicked across the glass table top. "Okay. Last meeting's minutes. Allynn?"

Allynn droned out the various decisions and actions of the last meeting, none of which were particularly interesting except the agreement that PushRight would notify Blue Suit, and vice versa, in the event of confidential information known to be leaked. Jelli didn't believe for a second that Blue Suit would tell her anything that he thought he could avoid, and Blue Suit surely thought the same of her. It was a feature of the inter-outsourcer meetings that each group attending did it's best to obfuscate and lie, whilst at the same time probing with their finest instruments for any iota of truth in what the other attendees let known.

Jelli was surprised, then, when Blue Suit made a statement.

"For some time, the Blue Suit Social Management Research Division has been investigating the statistical correlation between SRM teardown, as I believe it is called, and the incidence of crime, antisocial activity, and so on," he said. "I can tell you little about the theories being tested, but briefly, we are curious as to whether the connection is not so much the teardown factor as the physical presence of SRMs and their effects upon human psychology. To prove the point one way or the other, we wish to obtain a very large number of SRMs for purposes of experimentation."

This was a surprise. It sounded as if Blue Suit was intruding into PushRight's area of behavioural studies. Jelli wondered why he had brought it up.

"I recall a time when PushRight popularised a glass bottle collection, I was never quite clear on the reason for it, but this seems to be a similar kind of exercise. Can PushRight arrange an appropriate method of SRM collection?"

One of Jelli's creative directors pulled his face out of his chest and sat up. "Budget?" he asked.

"To be advised."

The creative director slumped back again. "To be advised," he muttered. "To be advised."

"Let's you and I discuss that in another meeting," Jelli put in quickly. She wanted to quiz Blue Suit about this in private. But, unable to leave the topic alone, she asked "But before we move on, why exactly do you require 'large numbers' of SRMs?"

The second creature to the left of Blue Suit leaned forward and began to speak excitedly and very quickly, looking straight ahead at Jelli with a fixed gaze, as if he seldom spoke to more than one person at a time.

"Well, theories of SRM origin are not at all settled, you know, and if we consider the Zone theory, which suggests a non-homogeneity of thermodynamic entropy at a macro level, we can by observing the rate of reproduction and other factors, especially the rate of reduction of structured materials in a controlled volume of space." He illustrated a controlled volume of space by shaping it out of air with his hands. "I prefer the ratio of Planck's constant to the n-dimensional root of the normal entropy coefficient of the observable Universe, I think that's definitely the best approximation, well..." Then he had to stop for air. He took a deep breath.

Jelli blinked at the mention of entropy, coincidental though it was, but before she could ask what it had to do with collecting SRMs, Blue Suit cut in.

"Any other new business?" he said coolly.

The second left hand creature froze while opening his mouth and cast a surprised glance around the table. There was a chorus of nos from that side, parrot-like, while Jelli's side looked at her for a sign. Initiative is such a hard thing to come by. Jelli decided to ask her questions of the second left hand creature later. She took a note of his appearance so that she could describe him when finding out who he was. He was about forty, thin, wearing a coarse weave cloth suit. He needed a haircut. His face was lined deeply in the cheeks, as if he sucked the inside of his mouth in too frequently or he had lost a great deal of weight. His lifeless blue eyes kept finding their way into his lap. Jelli surmised that he was frightened to a degree unusual even for an employee of Blue Suit. She wondered why.

"No further business," she agreed. Everyone began the ritual closing of untouched document folders and other stationery, and the air filled with the murmur of idle chat, but Jelli just sat, waiting for the room to empty. When only she, Allynn, and the Blue Suit entourage were left, she beckoned Allynn over.

"We'll carry on in my office," she said. Her office was the only room on the floor that was not monitored. As far as she knew.

"No doubt," Allynn replied.

Blue Suit's protectors refused, as usual, to leave him alone with anyone, anywhere, without first securing the area. When satisfied that Jelli's office was still as harmless as it had been this time last week, three of them took up stations outside her door, in front of Allynn's desk, by the water cooler, and between the entrances to the men's and women's toilets down the corridor. The other two goons, and the peculiar second left hand creature all departed. Jelli told Allynn to hold calls for the next hour.

"What's this SRM collection about?" Jelli asked as soon as the office door had clicked behind her. She unclipped the top of her suit. He did the same. Blue Suit stepped out of his trousers and hung them, folded neatly down the leg line, over the back of a chair.

"It is exactly as I said. We have an SRM research program. Technology breakdown is the single largest factor in social disintegration. If we can define the relationship between SRM populations and aberrant human behaviour, our objectives will be more easily accomplished. For that, we need samples."

"Strictly speaking, that sort of thing is PushRight's responsibility."

"Jelli, Jelli. We are all after the same thing. Let's not become bureaucrats." He put his hands around Jelli's breasts. She licked his chest.

"You were nervous about something," Jelli told him. "When your second left hand creature started talking about SRM origin theories. Why?"

They lay on the top of Jelli's desk. The polished wood was cool against her back.

"You misread me," Blue Suit said. "I am incapable of nervousness."

The vacant, intense expression he always wore during sex was on his face now, as their movement inched them slowly across the desktop. It was just sex, Jelli tried to remember, as the analytical part of her mind rapidly submerged. It was just sex, and orgasms are just positive feedback, and love is just bullshit. Remember that.

CHAPTER 9

The Wasteland was a source of varied emotions to the inhabitants of the city and beyond. It was there that the first sighting of an SRM occurred. It was like a hole chewed in the skirting board, out of which had recently appeared a large, rabid rat - compelling and at the same time fearsome. This was where the doom of civilisation had emerged. It was the door that should not have been opened. This was to some people the point where God's finger actually touched the ground. That was what the Revital Church believed, at any rate, and it was what Revital Church Elder Kutters was in the middle of proclaiming from the pulpit as Lino skulked into the church and sat as near as possible to the back of the room. She watched carefully as he boomed and gesticulated, and she watched the other people who had come to listen. She herself had come, not so much to listen to a sermon, as to feel the air, filled with belief and intense with hope, that belonged to people who thought that their insignificant lives were soon going to find a millisecond of meaning as they stood before their God and were judged. Lino was able to suspend a lifetime of Whak's atheistic influence and to hope that they were right, but her mind had been ploughed with too many rational arguments for her to have any more than wishes. Already she could tell that she was sitting though another failed attempt to find the meaning of her existence, but it was too soon to leave.

"Tomorrow, my friends, a selected group of worshippers, yes, of you, my friends, a select group and I will personally visit the Wasteland, the holiest of Earth's places, and mayhap a sign will be given to us! For it was there, in the cast-offs of our obscene worldly wealth, that God placed a reminder that it is not we who are all-powerful. Those who wish to take this pilgrimage, please remain with us after the service, and we will collect your entrance fee. For is it not so, that the ungodly of this world ask for payment for even the tasks set by our simple faith?"

Lino pouted and frowned. The Revital Church was going on a Wasteland tour. How gauche. There was a lot of shaking of heads going on in the crowded pews ahead of her, for such tours were expensive, and Lino could tell by the couture of the Revital congregation that lack of disposable income was practically a prerequisite for following the Elder Kutters. In fact, she was glaringly overdressed for the occasion, in her leather jacket, black shift dress and jackboots.

"Following the sign comes the flood, my friends. Do you want to be swept away with the ungodly? Do you want to see the fires of eternal damnation? Will God have nothingness in store for you? You can live after death, if you believe!"

Lino remembered that According To Whak, it didn't matter whether there was any way to live after death, because if you couldn't communicate, then to all intents and purposes you were dead, and to date, dead people had been very poor letter writers. There was an emaciated panhandler in church uniform creeping down the aisle rattling a brass canister, collecting a few coins. Lino searched her purse for small change and dropped a handful in when he stopped by her. The coins rattled exceedingly loud, it seemed to her, and for exceedingly long, until surely everyone in the church knew that someone down the back had more money than sense. But it's not my money, Lino told them all telepathically, it's not my money, it's Jelli's money, it's Consortium money, it's good behaviour money, I would rather be poor. But her message must have lacked conviction, because no one heard anything except the rattle of the coins.

Even Elder Kutters, way up in the pulpit, heard, looked up from his detailed notes, and peered down the room. Lino shifted her position sideways into the relative shadow by the wall, but she had been noticed. The sermon wrapped up quickly - Kutters seemed to have something else on his mind - and the congregation trailed out, Lino first. She could not escape from Elder Kutters, however. Somehow he had transported his corporeal form from the pulpit to outside the main doors even before Lino, moving as fast as she decently could without breaking into a run. She stepped out into the cold sunlight and instantly a hand clasped her forearm.

"Miss! How delightful to see you again. Did you find my sermon satisfying?" Elder Kutters pulled her around to face him. Lino, off-balance, tripped and fell forward. He pulled her upright and saved her from a fall, but she was now standing far too close to him for comfort.

"Let go of my arm," Lino snapped.

"Of course," Kutters dropped her arm, politely. "Your... father, is it? Is not here?"

"Yes, no," Lino answered concisely.

"Ah. He disapproves, no doubt."

"Yes, he disapproves." Actually, Lino thought, he would blow five fuses if he thought that his daughter was involved with the Revital Church. He'd take it more seriously than drug addiction or sexual promiscuity, not that there was any chance of either of those. Lino was not intending to lose her carefully nurtured inadequacies in the forgiveness of either drugs or sex. Pleasure must be taken to be given and she was not ready to do either. "Yes, he disapproves," she repeated. It sounded good. "He disapproves."

"So, he disapproves."

"I said that."

"Three times. He must disapprove a lot."

"What do you want?"

"I was hoping that you'd be interested in coming to the Wasteland with us tomorrow. It is a very holy place for Revitalists. I sense that a sign may be coming. I would like you to be there to witness it."

"A sign? A sign of what?"

"I don't know." At that moment, Kutters looked genuinely mystic. "But surely you want to find something to believe in."

Lino squinted at him. She did. But she was not going to say so, not even to her own parents, and definitely not to Elder Kutters.

"Come with us tomorrow," Kutters repeated. "I'll pay."

"Everybody wants to pay," Lino said. "All right. You pay." Instantly she hated herself for her inability to escape the flow. Hating herself for one thing or the other was something she did, and she hated herself for that, also. To prevent any sign of her self-loathing escaping, she walked with precisely even steps to the churchyard gate.

Elder Kutters called out after her "It will be a fulfilling experience for us all, my dear child."

By the time she had arrived home, Lino had turned her peculiar susceptibility to Kutter's suggestion into a cunning plan to rook Whak out of the money he had in his turn obtained from Jelli. She made her way directly to Whak's study and with an outflung arm threw the door open so that it dented the wall with the impact.

"Hi, Lino." Whak was sitting with his chin in the cup of his right hand, staring at his computer screen. "What do you like best? External eyeshots, or, pictures from the outside?" He tapped his screen with the end of a pencil.

"I'm going on a Wasteland tour tomorrow," Lino said, ignoring his question. "You said you'd pay."

"I did say that. You scoffed, I recall. How much is it?"

"I'll tell you when I get back. All right?"

Whak clearly had less important things on his mind. "Okay," he said. "Now, what about these words?"

"I don't care."

Whak nodded. "I guess you have to know the context," he said.

Lino avoided the implicit invitation to hear declaimed whatever he was working on now by saying "Okay then. You'll pay. It's expensive, you know." She felt nauseous as she gave him the opportunity to renege on their deal. She'd done the deal, got the commitment, now she should leave, but that was where she always failed to be true.

"Money, thank God, is not one of our current problems." Whak's gaze drifted back to his screen again. Lino slipped as quietly as she could back into the hall and closed the study door, BANG. As usual, her conscious desire to be silent and lay low was denied by her body, which took unilateral action without consulting her as to the consequences.

"Don't slam the door!" shouted Whak. Surely Lino's earliest remembered words.

The morning sky was grey as usual and the air filled with drizzle, and Lino's legs were cold and wet, and she regretted everything she had ever done, but particularly coming to the Wasteland. The Wasteland was square klicks in size, as big as the five dozen city blocks that it had once been, demolished for a shining new city centre that had never happened. For many years it had been the urban junkyard, full of the accumulated non-degradable material of the city, regularly topped up by one government subcontractor or the other settling upon it as a good home for dangerous waste or the wreckage of city blocks destroyed by improvements (read 'torn down before they fell down'). It was also a shrine. A shrine to the bony digit of Jehovah, if you were a Revitalist. A shrine to the visitation of an advanced alien civilisation, if you were an adherent of the Advance Force theory and took a certain view of it. Either way, a fine business proposition. Lino had met up with the Revitalist pilgrims at the gates and now she was seated in a small auditorium watching a multimedia extravaganza of SRM theology, which they all had to sit through before they would be escorted through a small section of the Wasteland by a qualified guide. Lino wondered what sort of qualifications you had to have.

Passed top of class in not stepping into biologically active slime. In front of her sat an assortment of Revitalist chaff, and on one side of her sat Elder Kutters, whom she noticed was more interested in her cleavage than the presentation. Lino tried to distract herself by focusing on the video, which was now showing a series of stills of different SRM types. There were a lot more types than she had realised. It appeared that the common varieties outside the Wasteland were fairly simple and unspecialised, whereas in here, in the primal soup, there were weirdies without end, some of them dangerous. Some of them ugly. Lino watched.

All these varieties of SRM have been observed in the area known as the Wasteland. SRMs, first observed within metres of this building, are now distributed worldwide and have seriously affected technological civilisation wherever they have appeared. It is still in the Wasteland, however, that conditions seem most favourable for whatever process brings SRMs into being. There are five main theories of SRM origin, but the question remains one of the great unanswered. The five theories are:

The Advance Force of Alien Invasion, suggesting that SRMs are a subtle weapon of an alien race which is seeking to weaken our technology to the point where we become an easy target for invasion.

The Zone of Anti-Entropy theory, suggesting that the Earth has drifted into a region of space with different physical laws which allow SRMs to spontaneously come into being.

The Government Experiment Gone Wrong theory, claiming that the whole worldwide situation is the result of a conspiracy of governments and scientists.

The Nature's Revenge on Man theory, which supposes that SRMs, along with this awful weather, may be Nature's reaction to the animal which destroys Nature, humans.

The Hand of God theory, in which SRMs are Precursors to the Second Coming of Christ, or other messianic figures.

"Huh," grunted Kutters.

Even today, ten years after they were first sighted, there is no agreement as to whether these things are in fact alive, or machines, or something else, but for the sake of simplicity, we at Wasteland Tours refer to them as 'life forms'. We apologise if this form of words offends the religious or other precepts of anyone present.

The screen showed old science fiction movie special effect sequences. It was obvious which theory the Wasteland Tours management believed.

SRMs may still be forming out of the waste and by-products of human civilisation, or they may all be reproductions, some better and some worse, from the original or originals. Although research is going on constantly into the origin and ultimately the control of SRMs, there are no answers. Today, you will venture into their world, like African explorers of the past, and see the most puzzling, dangerous, and destructive life forms on the planet in their natural habitat: amongst the remains of our own lives.

The screen froze and the voiceover stopped. From a side door on the small stage stepped a Guide, wearing a garish jacket with the word, guide, printed on it across the back, front, arms, all at different angles and in bright colours. The Guide was a slim young man with a fixed, calculating smile. He strolled to the centre of the stage and clapped his hands right next to his jacket mike, shaking the room and raising a shout of ear drummed anguish in return.

"Everybody awake, then?" he said cheerfully as the hubbub died away. "Good, good, good. I can't sit through that myself without falling asleep, but I suppose for anyone who's been dead for the last ten years it's a good recap of the world of the living. If you can call this living, eh?"

'My God, he's a cut-price talk show host', Lino thought.

"My name is Jim," the Guide said, "and I am your guide today. Please listen very carefully to what I tell you, and please do exactly what I ask when we are in the Wasteland, because although you may think that it is just a glorified junkyard, it can be a dangerous place." He pointed at the screen, which began to move again. "Watch this," he said.

On the screen, a Guide was shown, walking with his back to the camera, which followed him jerkily forward. Up one pile of car chassis. Along the ridge of huge, rusty pipes. At the end of the pipes, down and turn to face the mouth of one of them, an ugly looking hole with a trickle of brown water running out of it and in the shadows of the throat unknown things large and small making their own darkness. The Guide turned to the camera. It was Jim.

"Hello again," he said on the screen. "I'm going to show you what we mean about danger." He bent out of the picture for a moment. When he straightened up, he was holding a section of some metal extrusion, aluminium probably. The camera became glued to this bit of junk as he flicked it around like a ringmaster's cane. "See this interesting looking tunnel, here? There might be any number of arcane things in there. The famous Chang Hood would have been in and out of tunnels like this a dozen times a day as he searched for some discard that he could sell to supplement his SHA."

The image froze. It's fundamental fuzziness was revealed. Jim in person had some kind of remote control at hand. He attracted the attention of the audience by stepping out in front of his greater image.

"For those of you who didn't know, Chang Hood, a gentleman on the SHA, is the person who discovered and brought into the public eye the very first SRMs seen. He was a scavenger who lived in a block of apartments not far from here," he waved an arm westwards, "which sadly no longer exists, because the Consortium tore it down and sent the old people who lived there to Centres of Dignity." He took another visual circuit of the room and settled his stare on Lino, tilted his head slightly left and right as if drawing a bead, and smiled. "Sorry, everyone, I do apologise for my interruption, please let's continue."

Jim onscreen took his aluminium extrusion and poked it into the mouth of the pipe.

"Don't ever enter any location in the Wasteland where two objects at similar height are spaced less than five metres apart, and that means pipes, tubes, tunnels, corridors, or between two upright projections. Because this might happen to you." He flicked the extrusion sharply up and down. Halfway along it's length, it separated into two. The free piece separated into two again about a third further along, and splashed into the brown stream at the bottom of the pipe.

"Spiders," he said. "Unless any of you are return visitors - are any of you return visitors?" The audience sat dumbly staring at the screen, so he went on. "As I was saying, none of you will have heard of the variety of SRM known as spiders. They have never yet been seen outside the Wasteland, for reasons, which the technical types suspect to be related to their sensitivity to light. Or maybe there's a supply here of a specific material or food. Anyway, spiders are the biggest single danger out there. Spiders are SRMs which weave invisible monomolecular threads which will cut through anything. Lots of interest in spiders by industry, the military, and so on, but they can't keep the little monsters

under control yet. How do you avoid being cut to bits by spiders?
Simple: stay with your Guide."

"And your Guide will use this," in the auditorium, he picked a
spray can up from a table in the corner and turned the air neon
yellow with a quick burst, "to find any webs. Thank you."

"Thank you," said Jim. The screen went blank. "There are
other SRM types which can also be dangerous, and because none
of these more advanced types are common outside the Wasteland,
you will not recognise them. For example, there is some risk of
injury from scuttlebugs and drillheads. Either of those will cut
your shoes off your feet for the metal in the rivets. Which is why
we have to ask all of you now to proceed to the lockers and
remove jewellery, zippered coats, belts with buckles, and so on.
You will receive a receipt for your belongings. I'll meet you at the
security gate in five minutes." He walked off the side of the stage.

"Cut your shoe off?" Lino said. "I didn't know they could cut
your shoes off."

"There is no danger if God is with you," Elder Kutters assured
her, guiding her down the steps to the exit with a firm grip. "This
is all part of His plan."

Lino pulled away. "I'm not an old woman! I can walk down
stairs by myself, thank you very much." She marched ahead of
Kutters out of the auditorium and into the locker area, stripped off
her bracelet and handed it over to a short woman with ash-blonde
hair who never raised her eyes from the hands which held out this
or that trinket or item of clothing for her to lock away. Lino
studied the rest of her outfit and deemed it metal-free. Nearby,
Kutters was taking off his shoes. Good time to escape. Lino took
her receipt, stuffed it into her inside pocket, and followed the
signs to the security gate.

Jim the Guide was standing there with his hands in his coat
pockets and a cigarette of poor quality stuck in the corner of his
mouth. He was younger than he had appeared on stage, Lino now
saw. Maybe twenty-one or twenty-two. He was looking out
through the glass into the Wasteland.

"Can they get through this?" Lino asked, tapping the glass.

"Nope," said Jim.

"Why not? If they can cut your shoes off?"

"All right, yep," Jim smiled. In fact there was no serious
danger of any such thing. The Wasteland Tours spiel was
designed to maximise the client's feelings of excitement.

"What is it?" Lino asked angrily, stepping back from the glass in fear. "Yes or no?"

"You're a straight-answers sort of person, aren't you?" Jim turned away from the glass and looked at Lino with obvious appreciation, although whether for her looks or her attitude it was difficult to say.

"Yes or no? And if not why not? Shit, I sound like my mother."

"You sound like my mother."

"Don't insult my mother!"

"What?"

Lino fell silent and Jim put his Guide voice on, because the rest of the tour party was appearing from the locker room. Elder Kutters rallied his flock with a few exhortations and they all fell into line with the kind of efficiency that is achieved by either superb discipline or a high degree of suggestibility. At the end of the world there will be a mass outcrying of despair at the futility of accomplishment. Elder Kutters, however, having demonstrated his authority and by his expression well pleased with the range and power of his influence, spoke to Jim.

"We may proceed."

"I'm so glad." Jim pushed a button on the nearest wall. The glass wall slid to the left with a gentle rumbling and Jim led the way down a short ramp into the Wasteland.

CHAPTER 10

Lino In the Wasteland.

Jim began a running commentary on everything that they passed as they walked in double file into the irregular landscape of the Wasteland. He held a spray can in his hand, and it was clear from the shape of his jacket that there were several other items of equipment beneath it.

"First," he was saying, "we'll go to a spot where Wasteland Specials can be found. That's our term for SRMs that don't yet occur outside. Everyone stay close together and don't lag behind. You're not allowed to bring cameras or videocams in here, but we have a souvenir shop where you can get stills and movies of everything you're going to see today."

They walked through the corridors of a field of crushed car hulks, laid out in neat lines on an underbrush of broken concrete and bent reinforcing. Emerging into an open area of oil barrels, tyres, and rows of fallen power pylons, Jim pointed at a raised area to his left.

"Okay, see this pile of junk? We call that the Bump, and there are often hosenoses here. Keep your eyes peeled."

Lino hardly heard what he was saying. She was deep inside an unanswerable question loop that she had unwillingly triggered by her short altercation with Jim. She defended Jelli against no attack, but she hated Jelli. She couldn't find that emotion anywhere in her heart, so she must not hate her but love her. But she couldn't find that emotion anywhere in her heart, either, so she tried to find the answer by replaying all her most painful and all her most pleasant memories of her life, which inevitably began to involve Whak, her father. He didn't care, either, except there were times she could recall when he was the voice that reached into her nightmares and brought her back to her room in the night, but the memories were churning quickly and soon the unanswered question was, what was the question? Her heartbeat found an echo chamber behind her ear and began to thud.

Her mind cringing under the hammering of her pulse, she mechanically followed the tour, with Elder Kutters beside her and a short distance in front, Jim, the Guide.

"There's a hosenose hole right there," Jim announced suddenly. "Hosenoses are real interesting, they seem - wait, one's coming out." He motioned for silence, not that he needed to,

because all the eyes of the acolytes were glued to the shape
emerging from a neatly engineered trapdoor built into the side of
an 05 Honda Civic GTO with no roof. The hosenose was half a
metre long, and the apt possessor of a nose like a hose, a long,
bendy tube, clearly made of sections of aluminium cut from soft
drink cans, if the fragments of the world-famous logos were
anything to go by. The nose appeared first, waving around,
sniffing the air, if it was a nose, or looking carefully around, if it
was some other sort of sensory apparatus, or acting as a decoy, if
it was a front-mounted lizard tail, and no-one in the world knew
which. No-one knew how SRMs could see, or smell, or hear at
all, because, even now, no-one could tell how the meaningless bits
that made up an SRM's insides performed any sort of coherent
function. Jim was explaining all this in a lowered voice, when he
stopped and raised his hand again.

"Well, people, we have a predator."

"A what?" asked a woman in the party. "A what? Where?
That hoseynosey thing?"

"A predator," Jim repeated. "In other words, the hosenose is
about to be eaten."

"Oh."

Jim pointed a little uphill from the hosenose, which had now
emerged in full. It had two legs and two front appendages. Three
metres further up the slope, a shape was becoming exposed from
under the pile of bottletops, polystyrene hamburger cartons, and
deconstructed in-trays that made up the ground level hereabouts.

"A drillhead!" Jim was delighted. "Fairly new variety.
Cannibal type."

"You mean these things eat each other?" Elder Kutters, who
had paid little attention to date, heard an opening for a moral tale.
Jim looked at him and shook his head shortly.

"Not exactly. It depends what you mean by eat."

"I - "

"Shh! Watch!"

The drillhead was uncovered now. It was constructed far
more solidly than the hosenose. It gleamed with mechanical
perfection. It neither whirred nor clicked. Silently, it rose up
thirty centimetres on telescopic legs to obtain a better sighting of
the hosenose, and twin receptors of some kind spun left and right
on it's head, if that was a head, before recessing invisibly below
the surface. It lowered itself back to the ground. Everybody
relaxed, and one or two people looked critically at Jim, and then it

pounced. It shot straight up in the air on those same legs, left the ground, and from a height that could not be judged easily due to the greyness of the sky, fell directly onto the back of the hosenose. The drillhead was only half the size of it's victim, but heavy. It squashed the hosenose's back section as it landed. The hosenose struggled away on it's front limbs, but the drillhead's whole head began to spin at high speed and before the hosenose could move very far, it was impaled through the body, as the drillhead's neck shot out in the same way as it's feet and drove the cutting face through it's prey.

"Good kill," said Jim, nodding approvingly. The drillhead systematically removed from the body of the hosenose a series of small mechanical parts, which it either stashed on it's body or swallowed, but not knowing mouth from eyeball it was impossible to tell which. Jim the Guide took a few swift glances around which triangulated his position against the visible landmarks and then waved the party on, but shortly stopped again and brought up his spray can.

"Be careful here. This is spider country." He puffed a few clouds of shining yellow into the air to his left, and a sparse web appeared between a pylon and a water tank. "Those are new," Jim told everyone. "Spun last night. Spiders usually spin at night, we don't see them during the day."

"Have you ever seen one?" asked a young man who wore his hair in an imitation of Kutters' high-piled style. Jim shook his head.

"Not me," he said. "They're thought to be only active at night. But I do know some Guides who have seen them. And somewhere in the Wasteland there's supposed to be a secret Consortium research laboratory, so I suppose the people in there know more about them than we do."

The young man was not the sneering type, but he clearly doubted. "How do you know these aren't just ordinary spider webs?"

"You like to try them out?" Jim gestured the young man forward. "You want to run through there and tell me if they're SRM webs or not?" The young man declined. "Here, throw a can through them." Jim threw one himself. It left his hand with a small upwards acceleration, turned over with a lazy twist, and descended. It sliced in half as it crossed the thin yellow lines. There was a startling glitter of new metal. This demonstration fired an unexpected enthusiasm for destruction amongst the

Revitalists. Everyone in the tour, except Kutters, who was too dignified, if dignity is to be had in a brown plastic suit, and Lino, who was still busy in her sudden fugue, threw things through the SRM webs. They all scrabbled around for objects to throw, chucked them elbows-out in a cloud of projectile debris, and quickly grabbed another bit of junk and threw again. It was instant mania. It took Jim several minutes of shouting to calm then down from this great sport, and when he finally had them all back in line, wild-eyed and laughing, he said sternly, "You people should get out more often. Or something. Next time I tell you to do something, do it, and when I tell you to stop doing it, stop doing it, or I'll cut the tour short." Revitalist freakheads, he inserted between the lines. "We'll move on to Can Valley, next, where we'll find several more harmless SRM varieties. Follow me."

He lead them on, with Kutters and Lino now at the rear. As they entered a zone of relative flatness he recited the names of the landmarks they were passing.

"Can Hill, over there on your right, is composed almost entirely out of soft-drink cans. Straight ahead is the famous Leaning Carriage. Only the contractors who filled this area would be able to say why they stuck it end up like that." An inter-city train carriage was nose-first in the ground as if it had been fired at the wasteland from outer space, sticking into the surface and rising fifteen metres into the air at the nearly vertical.

"What do you think of this place?" Kutters asked Lino as they followed the others.

The part of Lino's mind not consumed by her fugue spoke automatically, like an answering machine woken by an unexpected call. "It's a dump. Full of little robots."

"Little robots that make more little robots. I think that makes them kin to ourselves. Do you not wonder about their ability to reproduce? It is written that only God can give life."

"Scorpions!" Jim called out in front. "Right, everyone, see this, look, I'll catch one. Scorpions have really sharp cutting blades, here, but they are harmless as long as you know how to hold them. One guide lost half his thumb to a scorpion last year, but not if you hold them like this, there, anyone want to have a close look? You'll never see one closer up than this!" Everyone pressed up close to see.

The First SRM Event.

Taking advantage of the distraction, Kutters guided Lino away, towards the railway carriage. Kutters was sensitive to the needs of others. He could tell immediately when a person was desperate for answers, looking for their personal God, or drowning in their introspections, as with Lino. But the reaction is what matters. A Rottweiler can tell when a person is scared, but is not likely to offer emotional support. Kutters, as part of his profession, had a special awareness of the weakness of Man. Sometimes he used this knowledge to feed some weaknesses of his own.

"You seem in need of comfort, my dear," he was saying as he steered Lino to the shadow of the railway carriage. "Let me offer you the hands of the Church."

Lino was not paying any attention to him, or to anything else. She walked, and her skin moved slightly under her dress, and her heartbeat sounded in her ear. Then the shadow of the carriage cut the air and she shivered, but darkness was her medium and the shade and the shiver woke her a little. She felt something bump her waist and looked down. It was an old, hairy, spotty hand, with a wedding ring, and it was sliding up her body towards her breasts.

"Aaaaaaaah!" she shrieked. Kutters hand jumped backwards into his coat pocket, and he turned immediately away from Lino towards the tour, his expression surprised and innocent and denials ready to emerge into the air like little fantasy balloons at the least pretext. All his disciples, and Jim, looked up from the scorpion lesson to see what the screaming was about, and they saw Lino, screaming, and Elder Kutters, who stood motionless like a snapshot, in the shadow of the railway carriage.

At that moment, from the windows of the railway carriage a dozen SRMs appeared, hand-sized many-legged things, which jumped into the air and seemed to float down until they touched the ground somewhere between the tour party and Lino and Kutters.

"What are those?" asked the young man with the doubtful expression.

"I don't know," Jim said slowly. "I've never seen... they might be, oh Jesus fucking Christ Almighty!"

Lino was stumbling over the ground, away from Kutters. Jim pushed his way through the Revitalist gaggle, shouting "Don't move! Don't move! Don't take another step!" but Lino's ears were turned off and she moved faster, breaking into a hopping jog as she jumped over this bit of rubbish and that, trying to get away from Kutters. Jim pulled out two spray cans and with a swift elbow to the neck of a bloke who didn't move out of his way fast enough for his liking, sprinted across the intervening ground with the practised legwork of a man who walked the Wasteland daily, spray cans in the air in front of him, spraying clouds of yellow paint left, right and ahead, still shouting at Lino to go back, go back.

Jim stopped dead some metres from Lino, reached out his arms at full length and held down the aerosol buttons. The paint drifted through the air in a rapidly dissipating cloud, and fell on Lino's arms and dress, so that she was gilded with the colour. She slowed. Jim went on shouting at her. She took a smaller step forward, looking at her arms, and because she was being sprayed with paint she began to get angry and looked up at Jim, standing in front of her, through a thin curtain of yellow mist and, set in the mist, bright yellow lines. She stopped when her face was almost touching the first of the lines and her eyes widened.

"DON'T MOVE!" Jim shouted in her face. "Those are SRM webs, so DON'T MOVE or you'll be cut to pieces!"

Lino took a step back. She looked at the filaments of yellow that hung in the air in front of her and she screamed again.

Her scream ended, and as if on a signal, the spiders which had jumped from the carriage began to move again. Their many legs were a blur as they raced in different directions, stopping momentarily here, then there, digging into the ground or crawling into the open ends of tins and the vents of old air conditioning units. Jim let his eyes move off Lino and saw them running exactly like crabs on the beach, little dashes and stops, each collecting, by the look of it, a pile of material which was stacked neatly and with perfect balance on their backs. But they were no longer the only SRMs in sight. The scorpion that Jim had dropped was as excited as the spiders, if that word could apply to SRMs, but instead of digging in the ground, it was tearing the trouser leg off the doubtful young man, who was dancing backwards and shouting "Let go! Leave me alone!", until the scorpion ripped off a section of cloth with side zip, and with movements too quick to appreciate, folded it small enough to tuck into a gap in it's carapace. At the same time, a host of other SRMs were appearing. Common ones, like the scorpion, pocket calculators, wheel jacks. Wasteland Specials like the drillhead, two drillheads, three, Jim began to feel apprehensive. A chorus of wails and terrified moans rose up. The tour party was being attacked by dozens of SRMs of different kinds, some Jim had never even heard described before. A woman was being systematically stripped naked by a kind of walking scissor which after slicing her outer clothes from her body, cutting her skin deeply so that blood ran down her arms and back, snipped the clips out of her brassiere and diced the metal parts into filings before apparently eating them. The tour party scattered in all directions, some even running towards Jim and Lino and Kutters, forcing Jim to spray them in the face with yellow paint before they bifurcated themselves on the webs. Three buzzing objects the size of tennis balls were rolling up and down the arms and chest of a man who had already lost his belt and shoes. They were shaving his jacket into dust.

Everywhere, SRMs were tearing up the surface, chopping junk pieces out of junk wholes, and removing from the human population everything possible, including, if the shocked recital "It cut my finger off! It cut my finger off!" was accurate, bodily parts.

Lino had shuddered into immobility. No SRM came near her at all. Kutters, who had not moved since Lino screamed, Jim, and the three who were now on the ground rubbing their eyes and shouting curses most inappropriate for Church members were also unassailed.

"What the fuck is going on?" Jim's eyes were wide and his mouth open. But already, whatever the fuck was going on was coming to an end. Over the next few seconds, the ground stopped crawling as the SRMs buried themselves back in the landscape, or stalked over the nearest hill, or lifted some hidden trapdoor and disappeared beneath it. The members of the tour party slid one by one to the ground, holding cuts, dismembered hands, the remains of clothes around their bodies. A section of the railway carriage slowly slid apart from the rest like the corner cut from a block of cheese and with a spectacular noise fell to the ground to Kutters' right.

Jim went over to the naked woman, sprawled with her big breasts pointing into the sky, pulled her up, and put his jacket over her.

"Tour's over," he said unnecessarily. From under his jacket he pulled out a radio, wondering why such a juicy bit of electronica had not been a target, and had the following conversation with the Tours Supervisor:

"Jim to Super."

After a crackling moment or two, there came an answer. "Yes Jim?"

"Need medical assistance out here urgently. We're by the leaning carriage."

"Help's on it's way. What's happened? Heart attack?"

"No."

"What then? You all right? Web problems?"

"No. It was a... an SRM attack."

"A what?"

"SRMs attacked the party. We have some severe injuries and shock victims."

"SRMs don't attack humans."   The super's voice was incredulous. Jim looked about him before he replied.

"Tell me about it," he said.

Eventually, there came from the Wasteland Tours building several other Guides who assisted in transporting the shocked and the wounded. Lino was slowly returning to the world, Jim noticed by the way she responded to a touch or a sound. Kutters was alert enough, but seemed unconcerned with his congregation, and kept looking at Lino in a curious manner. While all the paying customers were being tended and the ambulances were on their way, Jim was tapped on the shoulder. It was the Tour Supervisor, and he did not look particularly happy.

As Jim was being led off, Lino was starting to return to normal. She passed the boundary between the internal and the external, started, and looked herself over from shoulders to toes for any sign of damage, but there was none. Except for a coat of fluorescent yellow, she was unscathed by her experience. She remembered nothing but a fear of physical abuse. Her receptors were in perfect working order, but her responders were obviously not. She felt a chill of fear. She felt a rush of pleasure. She didn't like either one.

Kutters came up to her quietly. "Are you all right, Ms Puihare?" he asked, almost respectfully.

"Fuck off, you odious toad," Lino spat, and was surprised to find that Kutters did just that. He went quickly to the other side of the room, as far from Lino as he could, and sat there looking worried. 'Because he thinks I'm going to sue him. Or report him. All this is his fault', Lino thought, aware of how illogical that was, aware of the smell of blood and the sounds of pain.

The ambulances and police arrived at last. Everyone who wasn't too dysfunctional to speak was asked if they had any idea what had occurred. No-one did, so they were asked to contact the police if they thought of anything, and one by staggering one they went back out onto the wide empty street beside the Wasteland and took their various ways. Lino accepted a ride in a police carrier back to her home.

Meanwhile, Jim was seated in the supervisor's office, seated with foreboding by his side.

"What the hell happened out there?" asked the supervisor, standing with his hand on the edge of his desk, unlit cigarette as pointing finger.

"I haven't got the faintest idea," Jim answered, "except that every SRM within fifty metres went totally ape. Types came to the surface I've never even heard of, let alone seen."

"Well, listen up, boy, because there's a bunch of media creeps outside who are going to make hay out of this, and they're not going to make hay at the expense of Wasteland Tours Limited. I have just had the word from on high about this."

"News travels fast."

"News travelling fast is fine as long as it's the news that the boss wants to travel. And the news that the boss wants to travel is this: Incompetent Wasteland Guide leads tour party into known dangerous area, tour party attacked."

"That's crap. There are no dangerous areas. And I'm the best Guide you've got."

"Let me finish." In his best-guide-we-what? voice. "Wasteland Tours Limited regrets the incident and assures the public that the Guide responsible has been removed from his duties."

"You mean sacked." Jim would have liked to get angry at that point, but he was still on the downside of the days events, and he couldn't find the emotional strength needed for any sort of reaction at all.

"Uh-huh."

"But it was nothing to do with me! We take tour parties to that spot every day!"

"Not any more, we don't. And I know it wasn't your fault. Nobody could have predicted something like this." The supervisor looked worried. "But anyway, this is damage control time, Jimmy. If the public knew that this was a totally random thing, they'd stay away, but if they think it was human error and that human has been removed, they'll keep coming."

"Do you think it's a good idea for them to keep coming?"

"Shit, if they don't I'm back on the SHA, and that's not enough."

"You don't care if someone gets killed, then."

"I care, but one thing like this doesn't mean shit." The supervisor had let self-interest take over from reason, Jim saw, and he could hardly blame him for that. It was the way people survived. If he wasn't taking a fall, Jim would likely have used the same rationalisation. But since he was taking a fall:

"What's in it for me?"

"Keep your mouth shut and we'll go on paying you half wages under the counter."

"In writing?"

"Don't be stupid."

"If you don't pay, I'll talk."

"If you don't talk, we'll pay."

Jim trusted him. Jim believed in deals. Jim was naive like that. People are suggestible immediately after shocking events.

CHAPTER 11

Whak Discovers Pitfights.

Since the wholesale demolition of transmitters and studio equipment throughout the land, the role of television as entertainment had almost ceased to be. Television was now restricted to the PushRight channel, GOV1, consisting entirely of attitudinally-slanted role model showcases and advertisements for products which might not even exist, the ads for which associated genuinely good values with things that the Consortium currently wanted the public to think were good. Like young women with handsome boyfriends shown swimming in tropical waters, saying how good life could be on the SHA if a common-sense budget was followed. Message, whatever's wrong with your life, it's your fault. Like students in sports cars (sports cars? Nobody made sports cars anymore) extolling the virtues of education, as if having an education was going to help when technology finally collapsed altogether and the population began to plummet to naturally sustainable levels. And right now, Whak was watching a GOV1 soap. God knows why, he certainly didn't, except perhaps out of professional interest in the simplistic plots and obvious structural techniques. He didn't know the names of any of the characters and he hated them all intensely, because, good guy or bad guy, they were all mouthpieces for PushRight Creative Media, and seeing them and hearing them always reminded him that his wife was the intellectual whore of the invisibles who were trying to hold the status quo against powers greater than they. Whak did not admire foredoomed stands against all odds.

"No more," he decided. He went over and turned the off the TV. "What happened to entertainment? Do I care? Do I have time for entertainment? There's work to be done." But today the house was cold, and he was alone, and it was that dark time outside. Jelli was at a meeting. Lino was still slowly surfacing from her last encounter with reality - Whak always wondered whether she would be the same if she had a different father, different genetic makeup, different upbringing by parents with solid, unimaginative values, but the question was who would I be if I wasn't me, and there's no answer to that, is there? At any rate, Lino had not emerged from her room in the two days since the SRM event which despite Wasteland Tours Limited's best efforts had spent a busy day on the front pages of the spittlerags and gained two seconds of flat denial on the GOV1 newscast. Whak guessed that Wasteland Tours stock was not a good buy at present.

Of course, she must have come out of her room, Whak knew. She could only hold her water so long. She had to eat. But she must be waiting until no-one was about. He remembered that she used to do just that when she was about eight years old: her small, dark, serious face (always serious, even then) would peer around the corner of her door, and if she saw anyone (usually Whak) she would retract her neck back into her room and quietly close the door. Withdrawn to the point of autism, the child psychiatrist had said. How could two people so immersed in the art of communication, a poet, damn it, and a bloody advertising executive, how could two such hotshot talkers and writers instil this insularity in their only child?

Whak had no answer to that, either, no matter how many times he asked it.

He went to his desk and tried to pour what he felt into words, but he was distracted by the irregular rising and falling noise coming from outside.

"What is that?" Whak asked his screen. He went to the window. Across the street was another row of houses, but there was an open space, and beyond that, Coolio Park. There had been a time when the park glowed until late with flood lamps and people played football and other sports there at night, but them flood lamps got ate, and now the playing fields and the cycle paths and the other leisure edifices were unused outside daylight.

Except Whak could plainly see the nimbus in the sky that could only be caused by an intense source of light, over there in the park.

Whak often walked at night, in fact he did most of his public work in the peace of three in the morning. He took his old leather satchel, heavy with spray cans, from it's hook and went out to investigate the new thing in the park. He crossed the road and proceeded up the street alongside the expensive homes. He noted, as he passed the gates and post boxes for the hundredth time, that he knew none of the families associated with the displayed names. Perhaps Jelli did. He didn't think it necessary to be acquainted with every family in the street, in fact, he preferred to hypothesise about the human condition from the solitude of his study, rather than experience it in person. The hotshot talker and writer shuns humanity, it seems.

He turned into the park entrance, which occupied the gap between the three-story home of the Enrights, or so the plaque said, and the high wall surrounding the Yangs, whose house was not even visible. Dogs growled as he walked by. Then he entered the park, and the source of the illumination became apparent. In the section of the park allocated to sporting venues, there was a skateboard rink, a huge one, with spectator seats raised up high around it, curving and overlapping walls so that it was hard to guess whether the construction was supposed to be functional or otherwise. Whak had a vague idea that it had won some design award. He thought he recalled saying at the time that there would be prizes for street lamp design next, and that the significant thing about great art was that when you looked at it, you didn't think, I could do that. Well, he was wrong. Now, at this distance, in the darkness, with the complex shape lit from within by overpowering halogen brightness, Whak admitted that the skateboard rink was impressive. Light was beaming vertically out of the arena, and it could have been mistaken for a crashed spaceship, or an outlandish attempt by star-crazed architects to communicate with the sky. But more, there were the shadows of people moving on the walls, and dimly discernible were many people standing around it, half-lit, and more appearing from the south side of the park.

Whak walked closer, until he could see the entrance at the side of the rink. There, the people arriving were one by one being stopped by a couple of large men who by the looks of it were taking money or checking tickets before letting anybody in. There was a big board of some sort set up to the left of the entrance, and another person was writing on it. Whak was within earshot now.

"Odds, odds, odds! Place your bets! Favourite's on a slide! Put your money on the new shiner, come on, come on, put your money down! Thank you, sir, here's your chit, now who's going to even the odds here? Come on, come on, it's five to three, five to three. More booths inside, go on through, ladies and gents."

Whak gave the situation a quick risk analysis and decided that it looked undangerous enough for him to emerge from behind the bushes, and so he did. The two big men were still selling door tickets, or so he assumed, but the numbers were dropping, and then there was the roar that can only be made by a crowd of hundreds of people who have just been shown whatever they are waiting for. As Whak approached the rink to see what the fuss was about, he was immediately impeded by the ticket men.

"Ten bucks a seat," said the largest man.

"Do you take eftpos?" This was a joke. Eftpos had died the day SRMs annihilated the central banking systems. That had been one of the bright spots of the fall of technological darkness. Ownership of property had shifted mightily to the proletariat on Mortgage Free Day.

"What? Do we look as if we take eftpos?"

"No, I guess not."

Whak could only see the entrance to the rink past the shoulders of the two bouncers cum doormen, not what lay beyond. He peered and the smaller bouncer, still twice his size, pushed him downwards with a hand the size of a tennis racquet on his shoulder.

"No peeking," he said in a surprisingly polite tone. "You the law?"

"He's not the law," the other was positive.

"No, you're right. Then you're a nosy parker. You want to go in, you pay."

"All right. I'll just go get some money."

"You do that."

"What am I paying for, anyway?"

"He doesn't know what he's paying for!" The bigger man guffawed, and the two of them exchanged snickers. "If you don't know, then you shouldn't be here. Get lost, go on, before we lose our sense of humour." He waved Whak away, and Whak after one or two backward steps changed direction and orientation and went over to the bookie, who was rather glumly rubbing the last line of figures off his whiteboard and mumbling to himself. He was a much more humanly sized individual, slightly shorter than Whak, and he was wearing another one of those plastic suits which seemed to be fashionable, or cheap, and which made the wearer look like a computer animation, for those who remembered such things.

"Excuse me," Whak said as he approached, loudly to be heard over the crowd sounds that came from the rink.

"Closed," the bookie said instantly. "The event's started. Not taking any more bets."

"I don't want to place a bet."

"Lucky for you, then, because I'm closed. And I wouldn't take your bet, anyway. You look like a blue suit to me."

"Oh, come off it!" Whak couldn't believe his ears. "Me a blue suit! There are blue suits watching me! There's probably some underpaid young jerkoff crouching under the picnic tables right now with an infrared scope, wondering what I'm doing out here, if he's got the brains to wonder, which he probably hasn't or he wouldn't spend his time spying on people! Me a blue suit! I'm the antithesis of Blue Suit!" Whak was insulted. He would rather be called a failed poet and a parasite on his family than be accused of working for the Consortium's security agency, Jelli-propaganda-minister or no.

The bookie quailed at this outburst of passion. "Under what picnic tables?" he asked, looking around.

"Oh Christ, man, will you just answer one question?" But just then a familiar tennis-racket hand took Whak by the collar and lifted him slightly into the air so that he had to stand on tip-toe to avoid neck injury. The bouncers must have become concerned at Whak's motives. Without a word, they turned him around on his toes so that he faced the darkness from which he had come, and flicked him away, stumbling and spinning and finally tripping up on his own left foot and crashing down in a heap.

Bastards, Whak thought without much heat. He got up and studied the rink, the light and the sound. The crowd noises were settled now. Whatever was going on in there, it was periodic. He walked away a short distance and looked back again when there was another increase in volume. Got to see what's going on, he decided.

He made sure that there were enough trees and darkness between him and the rink so that the bouncers couldn't see him, then chose the biggest tree nearby - an oak, ideally enough, with solid horizontal branches stretching wide and high enough for his purpose. He climbed up onto one of those branches and craned to see the rink. Not high enough, wrong side. He eased around the trunk, nearly fell, then his foot found another branch and he balanced there for a second, then pushed off and clutched desperately. His position was still insecure. He slipped again and was now hanging on like a possum underneath the branch. His soft hands were scratched raw by the bark. He was certainly going to fall, and he cast a worried look at the ground, invisible blackness, probably covered with large and knobbly surface roots for cracking spines on, and began to release his legs from the branch so that he would at least fall feet first, when a voice spoke above him.

Whak/Assok Up Tree

"For God's sake, grab hold of this."

The voice was impatient. A yellow rope fell down in front of Whak's face and he snatched it with one hand. It was sufficient for him to regain control. He got his other hand involved and pulled himself back up onto the topside of the branch.

"Thanks," he said to the foliage above him.

"Just get down and go away."

"I'm not going yet," Whak replied. He reached up and took a grip on the next branch, planted his feet against the trunk and rather successfully walked himself up, swung his legs over and sat down. He was high enough to see the rink, now, but first he looked for the owner of the voice, who was still above him, so, since the climbing was easier up here, he quickly gained another level. In the shadows he could now see another person sitting, much as himself, astride the branch, and as his eyes adjusted there came recognition.

"George Assok!" he said, very surprised. "What are you doing here?"

"Oh, it's you." George Assok was also surprised, and obviously displeased. "I might ask you the same question."

"Yes, you might, but since you're here with a videocam, a tripod, and a portable computer, I think you have more to explain than I." Whak looked around at the panoply of equipment that Assok had set up on the branch. The tripod was a monopod, in fact, screwed into the branch and supporting the sophisticated video camera, the lens of which whirred every few seconds as it autofocussed on whatever it was pointed at. Currently, straight at Whak's stomach.

"Please move out of the line of sight," Assok snapped, ignoring Whak's question. "I didn't save you so that you could get in the way."

"Oh." Whak could think of no response to this. He didn't consider a helping hand up the tree as a great service, for he had fallen out of higher trees than this in his time. It hurt, but physical pain was easier to bear than an unwarranted sense of obligation. He dropped the subject, shuffled out of the way, and swivelled his head to find where the camera was pointing. Into the rink, of course. While Whak strained his eyes to see what was happening in there, George Assok reached up and retrieved from above his head a pair of binoculars and began to observe.

"What's happening in there?" Whak asked after a minute.

"Pitfight," Assok said shortly.

"What?"

"Pitfight. SRM pitfight." Assok put down the binoculars and made a sardonic smile appear on his face. "Entertainment," he added. "Gambling."

"Really?" Whak was delighted to have encountered such a thing. "You mean, those people are betting on a fight between SRMs? Where do they get them from? What kind of SRMs? How do they get them to fight?" Delight faded as he reflected on the way that mistakes of the past reappear as interesting new mistakes with false moustaches. "Is this wise?"

George Assok flicked a maybug away from his face and gave Whak a new look that held a degree of approval. "No, it is not."

Whak had no idea whether they were talking about the same thing or not. "I think our thoughts may have failed to collide," he said, but Assok was taking a look through his viewfinder and not listening.

"There's two unusual varieties being set up now," he said.

Whak took advantage of the other man's spare eye being shut to borrow the binoculars and take a look for himself. He was not very good at seeing through binoculars. He fiddled with the focus and his left eye started to water, but he saw that the in the centre of the skateboard rink was a raised platform like a circular boxing ring, except that instead of ropes it was surrounded by a low wooden wall. All around it were people with shouting mouths, their arms in the air, and behind them more people on seats built higher on the rink's acceleration curves. Too many people. If the police bothered to enforce safety regulations anymore, this would be the place to start. Where were the police? This pitfight shit looked like fun, and fun was largely illegal. He put his gaze back into the central ring. He could see that there were two large SRMs in there, one at each side, but he couldn't see the detail that George Assok obviously could through his 120 times digital zoom. Where did he obtain such equipment? The crowd noise intensified, and he saw that someone was playing ringmaster, winding up the audience, gesticulating and shouting. Coincident with the peak of audience agitation, the two SRMs advanced on each other. One extended some sort of periscope. The other leaped forward and simultaneously produced what must have been a spinning blade, because the protrusion fell and the de-periscoped SRM moved with unbelievable rapidity to the side. There was a flicker of something between the two machines that was too fast to interpret, and the blade-spinner fell neatly into two halves. Crowd hysteria became general amidst a great waving of what at this distance appeared to be small pieces of paper, probably betting slips.

"That was entertainment?" Whak asked rhetorically.

"For them it was entertainment. For me, it was research."

"Research?"

But Assok had said more than too much. He unscrewed his monopod, put his video into a hard plastic case, and put his hand out.

"My binoculars, please."

"Just tell me, what are you spying on all this for?"

"I am not spying on this, I am observing it."

"Yes, yes, why?"

"I'm not at liberty to say."

"I suppose you're still involved in all that germ warfare stuff."

"I am not involved in any biological warfare research, and I never have been. As a matter of fact, I'm not even employed by the government. This is strictly personal."

Whak looked dubious.

"Jelli says that anyone who has a working VCR is employed by the government."

George Assok was reaching out to take hold of the binoculars which hung from Whak's neck, but at these words he paused and took another one of those careful looks which were apparently the return of his attention from wherever he usually foraged.

"What's your name again?" he asked.

"Whak Puihare."

"Unusual name." Whak did not respond by relating the history of his family the way he might have done in more social situations. "I've only ever heard of one other Puihare. Chief executive at Pushright. Jelli Puihare. Your wife?"

"My wife."

"Might I ask what the husband of the person in charge of the Consortium's propaganda arm is doing up a tree in Coolio Park at midnight?"

"No, you may not." Whak smiled cheerfully. Since he never planned anything, and had no ulterior motive for being anywhere, least of all here, he felt himself utterly absolved of having to give explanations for anything. "But you could tell me what you're doing here," he added.

Assok thought about that for a moment.

"Come with me," he said.

CHAPTER 12

Jelli's Late Night Meeting

Since the last PushRight/Blue Suit gabbleday, Jelli had been thinking seriously, for she was a serious woman, about this SRM Collection that Blue Suit wanted organised. For purposes of experimentation, no less, which made it another of the half dozen or so research projects into SRMs that was going on at any moment. That was certainly a good nipple to attach to, if funding was your criterion, because no-one expected such projects to ever produce any results. Jelli was certain, however, that funding was not Blue Suit's motivation. She saw all subcontractor budgets and expenditure reports in the course of reporting the mental state of the nation to the Consortium: mass psychology and market research were inseparable parts of governing a disintegrating world. PushRight was the power it was because it knew everything. Jelli wished that it was true. One of the things she didn't know was how Blue Suit managed to obtain huge grants, often with laughably thin justifications. Either security had a special place in the Consortium's budgetary picture, or he had somebody in his pocket. She suspected both.

"What is this Blue Suit Research Division?" Jelli asked. "What does it do? Why is Blue Suit doing SRM research? Only the military is still seriously researching SRMs. Why is Blue Suit suddenly interested? And how dare they butt into our area of expertise? Behavioural psychology is our charter, not his."

Allynn coughed.

"Perhaps," she suggested, "they think that they might be able to get rid of them. If there are no SRMs it will bring back the days of wealth and happiness."

"Days of wealth and happiness. Good God, Allynn, listen to yourself. You sound like a PushRight soap. You sound like the characters in Friendly Fellowes Family Fun Time. Wealth and Happiness. Might be a good episode title. But no, that's not it. It's perfectly true, and it sounds reasonable, but in fact if SRMs were wiped out, Blue Suit would actually suffer. They'd have no role in a world of steadily improving lifestyle. One of their main functions, apart from punishing the innocent and the guilty each according to their needs, is to give the people a purpose, to spy on their neighbours. There's no justification for that except in times

92

of war and disaster. I'm perfectly sure that Blue Suit's objectives have little to do with eliminating SRMs."

Allynn wore the same wounded expression that she always did when Jelli let the full glare of the sun onto her.

"Well," she eventually replied, "then why are they collecting them?"

"I wish I knew," Jelli said unhappily. "Not to work out the ratio of SRM population to assault and murder, though."

She would have to find a way of obtaining more from her dalliance with Blue Suit. He was as uncommunicative as Whak was not. Apart from skin friction, Jelli was getting nothing out of him at all. Men usually became protective, tractable, and slightly stupid when Jelli had fucked them - except for Whak, who became more entirely Whak. Blue Suit was not following that pattern at all. The manipulative pig, she thought. She consoled herself for the moment with the knowledge that he was getting nothing from her, either: she had done nothing so far to get this Collection of his happening, and wasn't sure that she was going to. She could always find reasons for indefinite delay.

"The weekly meeting's tonight," said Allynn.

"So I see." Jelli had an agenda in her hand. "Why so late?"

"It was the only free space on everyone's schedules, and the Consortium says that we have to meet every week."

"Yes, that's true." Jelli thought about her alternatives. "Have we managed to place anyone in Blue Suit's staff yet?" Allynn was very good at placing infiltrators, oddly enough. Jelli thought her methods came straight from twentieth-century spy novels, but so what? They were her private spell books, and they worked.

"No. They recruit from their own. Nobody gets to work in the administration without two years of reliable street work. It'll take us another year to get anyone close."

"In a year we'll be eating each other's children."

"Ugh. You say the most terrible things."

"My husband said that one." Jelli scratched her earlobe. Such verbal snapshots did not bother her. "So we have no sources inside. We'll have to rely on sex and tactics, then." She reached for the phone, hoping that it was working. "I better tell Whak."

"Tell Whak what?" Allynn looked alert. She obviously thought that Jelli's life was run on television drama principles. Jelli gave her a condescending look.

"That I'm going to be late. What did you think I was going to tell him?"

The phone was functioning well, as phones go. While she was listening to the sound of whales through a drainpipe for the inevitable three minutes that it took Whak to just finish this one line, frown at it, declaim it, reject it, and come to the phone, she sent Allynn away.

"Go get me something on Second Left hand Creature," she instructed.

"Who?"

"The techo that was at the last meeting. Sedric someone. Check the minutes."

"But the meeting's at nine tonight."

"That gives you eight hours to find out something useful. Get to it," Jelli ordered. Allynn hurried off to do her bidding. Whak picked up the receiver.

"Hello?"

"Whak, it's Jelli."

"So it is."

"I'm going to be late home."

"Ah hah." Whak was not surprised. "How late?"

"Very late. I've got a meeting that starts at nine."

"I thought that if a person couldn't manage to do their job between eight and six then they were either inefficient, or stupid, or both." Whak never missed a chance to recite back Jelli's own generalisations, at times when they were least true. The best belief is a short-lived one. Jelli assured him that this time she was held ransom by someone else's inefficiencies, not her own.

"Well, I'll be waiting for you," he said.

"How's Lino?" Jelli asked.

"No idea. Incommunicado. Sucks food out of the fridge by direct mental contact."

"She'll snap out of it eventually."

"Maybe. She's isn't well equipped for witnessing violence."

"And you are?"

"I'm not sure," Whak said slowly, after a pause. "Why? Are you expecting some?"

"No, of course not! I've got to go, I'll see you tonight."

"Bye."

There had been dozens of attempts to clear areas of SRMs, from simply scouring a city block and melting down every SRM encountered, to a series of designs for SRM capture that brought new meaning to the better mousetrap, but none of this had succeeded. If cleared from an area, they returned to it. If captured by some harebrained device, they soon after ceased to approach such devices except to dismantle them for parts. Their interior workings were still not understood. Two SRMs that appeared to be close relatives on the outside could have completely different interiors, to such an extent that SRMa might be crammed with intricately inter-linked pieces of metal, plastic and silicon, and SRMb might be to all intents and purposes an empty shell, lined with obtuse patterns. They clearly contained within their genesis a seed from another set of laws. Otherwise rational men and women had been caught proposing that when an SRM wished to move it's leg, it sent a signal from within it's information processor (wherever that was) and generated a response in some universal energy field which made the leg move. This was the way Aquinas thought that the soul of man asked God to move the mundane flesh, before the purpose of the nervous system was discovered, and was just as likely to be true.

The documents that Allynn had collected made interesting reading, Jelli thought as she sat behind her monster of a desk. None of them, however, suggested any link between antisocial behaviour and SRM teardown. That idea appeared to have come straight from the Blue Suit disinformation service. So far as capturing the beasts was concerned, though, Blue Suit was right on the money. The best way to restrain an SRM continued to be to grip it tightly in a human hand.

Allyn, who been given no option, and Dukker, who as senior account manager could not always escape his routine responsibilities, were looking out the window at the nightscape of the city. Shadows and darkness, glimmering light. Dukker had brought along his young thing Harrison, from the Law and Order Project. Perhaps for a cuddle in the car on the way home.

Jelli excused most of her people from these late night meetings. She thought that that the chances of survival for advertising executives on the streets after dark were poor. She closed one folder and opened another. She now knew as much as she had ever wished to about SRMs. She knew a little about the Second Left hand Creature, too. He was a mathematician with many publications in the field of self-regulating systems and cosmology. She also knew, with the instinct that had helped her to shape the flesh of her less successful colleagues into stairs, that the Blue Suit Research Division was more than it appeared. If she could only figure out what it was.

95

"Arriving," Allynn said over her shoulder. That meant that down on the street, she had spied a cavalcade approaching through the dark. Allynn fetched Harrison, and then Jelli got up, stretched, and went to conference room three, drawing the others behind her as if she exuded impossible amounts of gravity. She adjusted her face while she waited for the meeting to begin.

Then the room began to fill up with protectors, and as soon as there was a bright-eyed warrior, who would die for honour, positioned in every corner in their sharp woollen suits, in strode Blue Suit, followed by Second Left hand Creature and some baggage. Blue Suit looked, as usual, like a dictator from a seceded American state, immaculately dressed and lightly tanned. He nodded at Jelli and took her hand from the table, inclined his head briefly and said "Charmed to see you again, Jelli."

"Thank you." She savoured his good looks. She felt again the uncontrolled sensation in her solar plexus. "Shall we begin?"

The words were echoed by the sound of half a dozen folders opening, pens were poised, and they began.

The meeting progressed like all it's predecessors, boringly. They had read the previous minutes and debated over various words that might or might not have been said at the time, but which in hindsight should have been different or not said at all, and they had notified each other of mundane plans and uninteresting actions of interest. Jelli could see that Allynn was drawing spiderwebs in the margins of her notebook, some orb and some funnel. At last, Blue Suit tilted back his head and said "SRM Collection Program."

"Ah," said Jelli. The start of the news.

"We have not yet heard from you regarding a plan for this."

"I've been wanting to talk to you about it. In fact, we're very interested in your project," Jelli assured him. "To help you, we have to understand the objectives. Can you explain the purpose of the collection to us again?"

Second Left hand Creature leaned forward, but was silenced by a stare. Blue Suit took it upon himself to answer.

"I will go back to the basic principles of things," he began. "As you know, Blue Suit is subcontracted to the Consortium to provide security services and control of undesirable social trends. We are a service-oriented organisation and we take our role very seriously. Now, the sort of trends that we have to deal with include a wide range of antisocial behaviour patterns. Organised crime, gang activities, violence, destruction of public property, rioting, and so forth. And it's getting worse as the depredations of SRMs continue."

"You're saying that society is falling apart, basically," Jelli put in. "We know that."

"The task of Blue Suit becomes more difficult with each passing day, so, interpreting our contract creatively, we believe that we should take steps to understand the effect SRMs have on human behaviour. With understanding comes power. We may be able to return society to the status quo ante. By experimenting with large numbers of SRMs, with the data we at Blue Suit already have on aberrant behaviour, we expect to find counteractive procedures."

Jelli had to strongly resist shaking her head at every word Blue Suit uttered. It sounded too much like rote. It was too thick and too thin at the same time.

"There have been a lot of people who tried to understand SRMs, all of whom have so far failed to get anywhere," she pointed out.

"The previous efforts have been directed towards understanding the principles behind SRM construction, and that has meant, on the whole, studying SRMs in isolation. Nothing exists in isolation. What is the point of excising the tumour if the disease is metastatic? Our paradigm will be quite different. We are following some very interesting lines of research that we expect to be successful."

"So the collection is for what?" Jelli didn't like Blue Suit's metaphor very much. She had always felt an unreasonable fear of cancer, despite it's steadily reducing incidence.

When the Knife Fell
When the knife fell on my metastatic breast
the instant before it parted my lumpy skin
I thought, in my next life
I'll not smoke I'll not do drugs I'll not party party
because all those things are wrong
and the penalty for fun
is death.

"High-density test populations, of course."

Jelli made a note on the block of paper in front of her, adding to it, 'testing what?'

"As a matter of fact, if it would make it any easier," Second Left hand Creature put in, clearly continuing a thought he had prepared earlier, "we don't need an example of every single variety. A broad cross-section would be sufficient."

"I disagree," Blue Suit said severely, causing Second Left hand Creature to cringe back against his chair. "We need as many samples of all types as possible. That is the commission."

Jelli made another note. 'How many types are there? Does anybody know?'

"What kind of techniques are you going to be testing?" she asked.

"That is classified."

"Where is the testing to take place?"

"That is also classified."

"It has a sort of genocidal ring to it, doesn't it? Round them up, experiment on them. Then when you're through with them, what? Destroy them, no doubt."

He stood up, leaned across the conference table and said, very carefully so that everybody could understand him "SRMs are destroying civilisation. They are killing us. There is no point in talking about them in human terms. They are not even alive. They have to be destroyed. Every piece of knowledge we gain is a weapon against them."

"Yes, all right, all right," Jelli said placatingly. So, he was trying to destroy them. An amusing thought crossed her mind, to which she could not resist seeing the reaction from Blue Suit. "It would be interesting if they turned out to be intelligent, don't you think?"

Second Left hand Creature perked up at this and without reference to anyone, began to chatter.

"That's a possibility, although intelligence, that's a very emotive word, don't you know, very imprecise, because people consider intelligence in biological terms, and mechanical intelligence, that could be quite different, very hard to quantify, and where do you say, well, this is sentient and this isn't, when there's no equivalent comparison that you can make? We do it all instinctively with our fellow animals, but it's a different matter with something non-biological. There are only human-subjective self-awareness tests, and whether self-awareness is a critical aspect of intelligence is a semantic issue which may never be proven." He looked owlish. "Mathematically, I mean."

He was quite guileless, Jelli now realised, and said whatever came into his head, not thinking of consequences until afterwards, which he now did. He suddenly became frightened, looked at Blue Suit, and fell silent.

"I thought that the scientific viewpoint is that if you can't communicate to it, it isn't intelligent," Jelli smiled, "or at least, it might as well not be." She noted, 'SRM intelligence? Are they investigating SRM intelligence?'

Blue Suit stared at her. "Could you please wait outside?" he said, and Jelli thought he was talking to her, so that he could disembowel Second Left hand Creature in private, perhaps, but he was talking to everyone else. The meeting was over, anyhow. With obvious displeasure, Blue Suit's bodyguards left the room, followed closely by Second Left hand Creature, who was positively eager to depart, and with a loose wave of Jelli's fingers, Dukker and Harrison. The door closed. The corridor became empty.

"I often wish that I could achieve my aims without the help of technicians," said Blue Suit. Jelli knew what he meant.

"I'm sure you keep him with you for good reasons," she consoled him, "even if he is a walking information leakage."

"Indeed. He was not my first choice for the job, I'm afraid."

"Why do you need a mathematician? And a cosmologist, to boot." Jelli decided it was time to put some knowledge on the table and see what rats came running.

There was a rather long silence. Jelli could feel some sort of tension building. She continued to look steadily at Blue Suit, who did the same to her, and as is common with extended eye contact with the opposite sex, Jelli began to feel aroused, and as her face and muscle tone softened fractionally and her expression developed a predatory slant, so did Blue Suit.

"I wanted to talk to you alone, about the things Colville was just saying." Blue Suit possessed the ability to ignore so totally what had just been said that even the person who said it wondered whether it had been spoken or not.

"Who?" Jelli answered dreamily.

"Colville."

"Oh, him."

"What he says is perfectly possible, in theory, SRMs might be intelligent in some arbitrary sense. But I have the public safety and wellbeing to consider. It's perfectly obvious that SRMs are draining the lifeblood of civilisation away like an army of bloodsucking insects." He looked at his arms and hands as if he expected to see them covered with the insects in question. "You know the statistics as well as I do. Crime rates are incredible. Suicide is ten times more prevalent than the decade before SRMs. The economy has shrunk by sixty-two percent in the last three years alone."

"Well, at least it stopped us from destroying the planet. Some people think that growth is not an unmitigated good, you know."

"Some people think that dead people live on clouds and have wings," Blue Suit said dismissively. "Imagine if it became generally believed that SRMs are intelligent. Soon enough, there'd be a committee set up somewhere in the 'elected administration' to investigate their lower socio-economic status, and they'd be made eligible for the SHA. That's just the kind of idiocy that we have to deal with!"

"All right, I see your point." Jelli did indeed see his point, idiocy wise.

"And then there's the Advance Force Theory."

"That SRMs are the precursor of an invasion by creatures from another planet? That's absurd."

"Perhaps. All I know is that we can't take the chance."

"You're not serious, surely." But Blue Suit was very much serious. He walked around the table and stood over her, leaning down face to face, and when he spoke his voice was lower and for the first time since Jelli had known him, held an urgent note. She wondered if it was real.

"Don't dismiss the unlikely because you don't want to believe it. Is it worth risking the future of all humanity for the dubious virtue of being polite? Do you want to tiptoe around these monsters in fear of violating their inalienable rights until we're debating morality in caves when their mother ship arrives? What is more important, the current ethical stance, or the continuation of the species?" He was so intense now, that Jelli could not resist. She touched his groin with the tips of her fingers, and when he didn't move, pulled on him with her other hand until he was standing between her legs. He pulled her up to her feet and they kissed, violently, one of Jelli's legs now coiled around his thighs. His body felt good, he smelt good. The zipper of Jelli's jumpsuit slid slowly down, exposing the tops of her breasts.

"Shall I minute this?" asked Allynn loudly.

Blue Suit's eyes widened in a gratifyingly shocked fashion, and he stepped back. Jelli slid down into her chair, breathing heavily.

It took a couple of breaths before Blue Suit spoke, but when he did, his voice was once again an unperturbed drone. "We can continue this discussion later," he said.

"Yes, we must do that." She began to zip up and tidy up. "In the meantime, I'll set up a team to prepare ideas on the SRM collection, a bonanza holiday prize for the most collected, or whatever."

"Good. I will be looking forward to seeing your proposals." He gave Allynn's back a puzzled glance as he followed her to the door, and then he was gone and his minions. Allynn returned to find Jelli in her own office, looking through the liquor cabinet.

"Nicely timed, Allynn."

"Huh. You were enjoying it." She sounded slightly upset.

"You have to enjoy it. They can tell if you're not enjoying it. The difference is whether you care when they stop," Jelli replied defensively. For reasons she couldn't articulate, she didn't want Allynn to think that she was screwing Blue Suit because she liked it, although damn it she did. In spite of what she had just said, she was aroused. "I swear I don't know how you manage to be so inconspicuous." She attempted to change the subject.

"I just take the seat in the corner and keep my eyes on the table."

"It wouldn't work for me."

"No," Allynn agreed, "it wouldn't."

Jelli poured a glass of something strong and transparent and offered it to Allynn, who refused politely, so Jelli drank it. "I still don't understand what he's up to. One of every SRM variety. But there's more going on than just behaviour studies, if Second Left hand Creature's reaction was anything to go by."

"What was all that alien invasion stuff? Does he really believe that?"

"No, I don't think so. He gives a lot of very plausible reasons for wanting to collect SRMs, but they're all lies. I want to know two things: why does he want one of every kind, and what is he really going to do with them? Answer me those, Allynn."

"Why don't you ask him?"

Jelli had been asking herself that very question for some time. There was no simple explanation she could give, but she did find something to say.

"We don't have that kind of relationship. Maybe it's time we did."

CHAPTER 13

Whak visits Assok's Lab

Walking through the park at midnight was a fine thing, Whak was thinking, made even more fine by the prospect of mystery. George Assok, his hands full of carrycases, was walking in front, leading the way to wherever he might be going. Whak had no idea of what was in store, and he liked it. They left the park by one of the rusty iron gates at the west side, entering into streets that Whak had only ever driven through before, and he was surprised to notice for the first time that the houses on this side of Coolio park were smaller, older, and definitely less expensive than the north. Instead of large well-fenced properties enclosing the wealthy, here was a mixture of ticktacky and tenements. On the park side of the street, and running in both directions until it disappeared in the night, was a grey, bare stone wall. Not even graffitied. Whak's hands itched to spray words on it, but there were no words ready.

"You like West Coolio?" Assok saw Whak's face under the first and only working streetlamp they passed and drew comment.

"It's all, ah, poor," was all Whak could say. It was not that he didn't know what it was like to be poor, or that he thought poorness offensive. It was that it was the truth. Assok took it badly, however.

"Well, not everybody can afford to live on North Coolio, you know, Puihare. Most people are poor. I'm poor. See these houses? Poor people live in them. Those that can be lived in. You have the privileged life of a government employee." He sounded distinctly envious.

"I know that," Whak said humbly. "I didn't know that it was either that or this."

"Pretty much," Assok muttered.

They crossed the street and took a side road, on which the housing gradually became even more decrepit than on the main drive. Here the tenements were completely unlit by any sign of life. Outside one of the ugliest, Assok stopped.

"Welcome to my home," he said. "Come in."

Cracked security glass in the double entrance, concrete bare on the hall floor, and elevator doors standing open to the shaft. Whak looked up the stairs, a receding passageway of twisted boards and bent banisters, but he was not required to use them. George Assok took him to a heavy metal door at the back of the hall and down a short flight of concrete steps. The metal door slammed with a death row boom, and Assok switched on the lights.

"This is interesting," Whak said, looking around. It was not so much a home as a laboratory. Although Whak had never studied the sciences, it reminded him of a university chemistry lab, with benches scattered over a wide area of basement, bad lights swinging on chains over them, electronic equipment of arcane sorts flashing and beeping, and a faint smell of methylated spirits. George Assok placed his stuff carefully on a table.

"How did a person like you," he said with unconscious condescension, "come to be married to the PushRight CEO?"

"Do you want the non-stop raving loony answer or the dry and serious explanation?" Whak asked right back in the same tone of voice. Assok was taken aback.

"Never mind," he said. "Puihare, I think you can help me with something important."

"Well, I like helping people. Your lab isn't as nice as that last one. Funding cut? Everybody's funding has been cut." Whak walked around the room. It was a big room, and their voices echoed. He stopped by a bench and looked over the paraphernalia. There was a glass cylinder with large insectoid legs in it. "What the hell is this?"

"For God's sake, Puihare. Be serious for a moment. That is an experiment I'm conducting on SRM type VIII - wagglers, as you probably know them. I want to know if they can regenerate from partial body parts."

"Jesus." Whak stared into the cylinder.

"Doesn't anybody ever think about these things? SRMs can repair themselves. SRMs can adapt to their environment."

"Skills worth having, I suppose. And what's this?" Whak was looking at a computer screen on which a series of small circles were tracing a pattern back and forth.

"It's an intelligence test. A test of an intelligence test."

"Intelligence? You mean, you're testing them to see if they're intelligent, and at the same time you're cutting their legs off to see if they build new ones?"

"Oh, they definitely build new ones. It's whether the legs can build a new body that I'm interested in."

The small windows which peered out below street level were suddenly bright with the single headlight of a passing vehicle. Shadows danced around the room. Whak was not sure what to say.

"But if they're intelligent," he stopped, at a loss for words.

"I doubt that they feel pain. They have nothing even analogous to a nervous system. Any intelligence they might have is going to be so different from ours that you can forget about ever communicating with them."

"I'd call cutting their legs off a form of communication." Whak kept walking around the room. He had a destructive curiosity when it came to the blind philosophies of humankind. He saw a spiky SRM head mounted on a panel, with dozens of electrical probes attached to every visible projection. "Or their heads."

"I didn't ask you here to discuss the right to life of SRMs." George Assok waved him towards some large construction that occupied one wall. It was a series of fish tanks, six metres long in all, connected together by clear plastic pipes, and looking to Whak like a still for fermentation of scientist's brains, except that it did not hold liquids bubbling colourfully and frothing violently, but SRMs. Of course. Everything to do with George Assok spelled SRM.

"So what is this?" asked Whak.

Assok coughed. "It's like this. When you and I met the first time, five years ago, I was working in the field of nanotechnology. Not," he shook a finger at Whak before he could interrupt, "not germ warfare. Nanotech is the most powerful application of quantum physics imaginable, even more than electronics. It has the capacity to completely change the way we manipulate our environment. It's not just extreme miniaturisation - machines at the scale I'm talking about are working with completely different classes of objects to what we are used to. Individual molecules. Isn't it amazing that an incomplete theory like quantum mechanics has provided us with nearly all the major advances in practical physics since early last century?"

"Oh yes," Whak replied. "So what is this?"

"I'm getting to that. I used to dream of a world where all the basics of life - including food - were created directly from available raw materials by nanomachines, or at least by systems based upon the same principles as nanomachines. It was never going to be easy, of course. There are all sorts of difficult areas, programming, control, activation, deactivation, efficiency, power source, to name a few, but the one that stopped us dead was replication fidelity. Did you know that the first nanomachines were literally made by hand using multiscalar manipulators? Those early machines were microscopic, it's true, but they were just miniatures of basic machines that we use in everyday life, levels, pumps and so forth. It's only in the last few years that we've come up with a device that automates the build process." An inanely proud expression crossed his face. "An advance that I had a great part in. But then the replication fidelity issue arose. The other problem with nanomachines is that they don't endure. To accomplish anything useful, you need nanomachines that able to both do the requisite task and construct more nanomachines of the required design. Nanoviruses, we call them. But it doesn't work. Within a few generations, the descendent nanoviruses degrade to the point where the replication cycle breaks down."

"Wrong answer, then?" Whak felt very much as if he was being lectured in Russian on sub-nuclear physics.

"Not if the replication fidelity problem can be solved."

"So, how does this little story lead us to this room full of SRMs?"

"For reasons I don't think I need to go into now, I have had to pursue some alternative lines of inquiry into this problem. It's often useful to look for inspiration in naturally occurring systems."

"I like trees, myself."

"Yes, so do I, but in this case I mean SRMs. SRMs must also have a replication fidelity issue. So do biological creatures, of course, but the principles are different. I have been studying the evolution of SRMs. Not how they exist, or what their power source is, or any of the other unanswered questions, but only how they maintain a reasonably consistent instruction set from one generation to the next."

Whak found that he was also interested in the answer to that question. "Have you found out anything?"

"I'll explain by showing you the results, if you don't mind." He turned to the wall of fish tanks. "I built this series of tanks two years ago."

"Bravo. Nice work."

"I placed a simple SRM variety, the amphibian of SRMs if you like, in tank number 1. Then I supplied it with high quality raw materials. And as you might expect, it reproduced. I've got records of the number of times it reproduced, and what variations occurred, and the time lag between each, and the relationship between an arbitrarily assigned quotient of organisation for the raw materials and the rate of reproduction. Everything. Each time a clear differentiation appeared, I separated it into the next tank. The connectors can be closed off, you see."

Whak and Assok were walking slowly along the wall, looking into tank after tank, as Assok spoke. Whak stopped and stared at a SRM type he had never before even heard of, a centipedal thing as big as a bicycle inner tube, with very obvious cutting jaws.

"I soon found that I had to reinforce the tanks. The first few tanks are just armoured glass. Not all SRMs have cutting capabilities, and the early varieties were reasonably easy to contain. Later, I started using fused quartz, and these last two are made out of a material that I, er, obtained from my previous employment, and I can't tell you what it's made of, because structural polymers are not my field of expertise."

"Nor mine," Whak agreed. "What exactly was your previous employment?" He observed that George Assok took a few seconds, then, to struggle with himself before answering.

"I used to be scientific director at a company called Smalltech. I had to leave under difficult circumstances."

"So now you've set out on your own, funded by secret sympathisers, to prove that you're right and the establishment is wrong, and have reached the point where you have to find powerful friends through whom you can reveal the truth? Good plot."

"I don't have secret sympathisers," George Assok said in exasperated tones. "I funded all this myself. I stole what I couldn't buy. There is no private research into SRMs anymore. The scientific community has lost it's will to live. With these pitiful resources, I am learning things about SRMs that nobody else knows. There's new physics waiting to be discovered. Look at that!" He pointed a rigid finger at the last tank in the series.

Meet the octopede

It held a large SRM which was obviously derived from the centipede, but it had lost a great many limbs since then, now possessing no more than eight. It had a large head out of which came several different antennae, and it had eyes, big globular ones that resembled the eyes of no animal or insect, but did remind

Whak of the coated lenses of an optical film camera, of the sort that Japan no longer produced. It was watching the two men.

"It's watching us," Whak said, alarmed. "Is it intelligent?"

"How do I know?   It's difficult enough to measure the intelligence of a human being. At the moment I'd say that it wouldn't be in that tank if it was intelligent. But it might become intelligent. Do you see what has happened here? The first tank holds an amphibian. The last tank holds a reptile, you might say, or better. SRMs are refining the design, Puihare. They don't just fortuitously construct a better version of themselves by lucking onto the right materials for the job or by coding errors in whatever passes for assembly instructions in whatever passes for their brains.   They are driven by something. Their evolution is purposeful.   Purposeful evolution eliminates the need for replication fidelity."

"I thought they mutated. That's how we evolve, isn't it? Mutation?"

"Mutation is always going on. It doesn't cause evolution in itself. Evolution is caused by changes in a creature's environment, causing one of those mutations to become favourable over what has, until then, been the norm. But look at these tanks! Identical environments. No stress. Unlimited food supply. There is no advantage to be had by improved teeth or more intelligence. But there it is, generational change, at a speed no biological system could contemplate."

Whak could see that. Getting slightly irate, he said "What does all this prove? Why are you so excited about it? Do you mind getting to the point? Or is it a secret? I don't like secrets. Secrets are lies." He tapped the nearest tank sharply with his finger in time with the last three words, and the watchful octopede swivelled it's sensory equipment to focus on him, causing him to take a couple of rapid steps back. "That one's strange," he added.

"They're all strange," Assok said. He went over to the other side of the room, with Whak right behind. Whak saw that here was a bed, low metal-framed and uncomfortable-looking. Assok sat down on it.

"You sleep in this room, with all these SRMs around?"

"SRMs only approach human beings if they are carrying metal fabrications or electronic parts, copper connectors or silicon wafers, for example. Do you want to hear the whole story or not?"

Whak burst out "Shit, George, you need a television in here.
Didn't you hear about Wasteland Tours? The tour party was
attacked right out of the blue, for no reason whatever! They don't
let any metal or electronic stuff like that on tours."

"I didn't hear about that," Assok said, a doubtful expression
forming.

"Well," Whak had to admit, "it only got about five seconds on
the news. It was suppressed, Jelli tells me. I don't approve,
secrets are lies, you know."

"Yes, yes, so you said. Did you found out about this through
Pushright?"

"No, through Lino. My daughter. She was there." Whak
shook his head. "It was pretty awful, apparently. She still won't
come out of her room."

George Assok was not interested in the location of Whak's
daughter. "This could be very important. Very important," he
said. "Purposeful evolution, and entirely new behaviour. They
attacked the tour party, you say?"

"Attacked it. Stole their shoe leather," Whak exaggerated.
"Tore all their clothes off."

"That's interesting. Very unusual. I should go there." He
gave a short laugh. "Thirty years ago a famous physicist was
saying that we now had the basic laws of the Universe all worked
out. A hundred years before that, a famous physicist was saying
the same thing. I don't think anyone would say it now."

"Perhaps the Universe doesn't have any basic laws," Whak
suggested.

"Everything has basic laws. Anyway, I have formulated a
hypothesis, which I haven't finished telling you, which is this:
instead of maintaining a relatively fixed specification, like
biological forms, which only attain new instruction sets by a
combination of random mutation and evolutionary pressure,
SRMs are purposefully modifying and improving their own
design. The SRM instruction set is much larger than the physical
implementations we observe on the streets. I propose that the
scorpions and wagglers and so forth are only a projection of these
meta-instructions into the physical world. The complete
instruction set exists as an amalgam of all the subsets, that is, all
the SRMs that currently exist. The meta-instructions provide the
purpose behind purposeful evolution."

"That sounds all upside down to me," Whak said scornfully.
This didn't agree with his view of things at all. "You're saying

that a collection of individuals are really just expressions of the sum of all their attributes. That's meaningless."

George was surprised to find that Whak had a logical bone in him. He nodded. "It does if you say it like that. But I'm not suggesting that there are information patterns in the Universe which exist independently of any physical reality. I'm suggesting that SRMs possess a collective instruction set that is communicated piecemeal as required. If the potential of purposeful evolution is revealed at all by my experiment here, SRMs may have the capacity to surpass humans, so far as ability to manipulate their environment goes. At which point," he ended dramatically, "the end of our species becomes a real possibility."

Whak raised his eyebrows.

"Isn't that obvious?" he said lightly, for while aware that Assok was serious, in his heart he could not believe in the extinction of humanity. Humans are such a perfectly exploitative animal, and there are so damned many of them. The streets, deserted except for shining metal bugs with bulging braincases, taking their seemingly random routes to and from city blocks collapsed from neglected age into a morass of stone, wire, and human bones - it was hard to contemplate.

"Is it? Purposeful SRM evolution could be interpreted as evidence that the Zone theory is correct, and that the Earth has entered a space region of different physical laws, including spontaneous organisation of matter, or equally it could be evidence of the Advance Force theory, that SRMs are sophisticated pre-programmed robots designed to weaken our technology and make us a pushover for an interstellar invasion." Assok paused for breath.

"It could also support the Hand of God theory," Whak added.

"You don't believe that, do you?"

"My opinion doesn't affect reality, as far as I know. Whatever the truth is, we'll find out eventually, one way or the other." A sudden thought. "So do you think this SRM event in the Wasteland is something to do with this?"

"It could be. The point is, we are facing an even bigger threat than is currently realised, but at the same time, I have the foundations in place for a leap forward in nanotechnology. I can use this meta-instruction approach to control nanomachine reproduction, by introducing inter-nano communication into the clade. Nanotech could give us the power to compete with SRMs.

I need to communicate this to someone with influence." He looked nervous. "Someone who can protect me."

That sounded like paranoia to Whak. It was late now, and he was tired. "This is great stuff, George, but I think I'll go home now."

"But I need you to speak to your wife!"

"Well, I can't speak to my wife by telepathy, George."

"No, no! You don't know what I want you to say, yet!"

"I could say, Jelli darling, I met the most fascinating man today, and he'd like you to use your power and influence to cause a world-wide panic."

"That's exactly what I don't want you to say."

"Well, what do you want? I want to go home and sleep."

"I need her to confirm something, before I say any more. Can you ask her to find something out for me?"

"Something confidential, illegal, or dirty?" Whak considered. He was a stranger to consideration, but it was useful at times. "No, I don't think so, " he decided after a few seconds. "I don't actually know you from Adam, George, and you might not be what you appear to be, and the days of freedom are long over. If you'll excuse me now, I'll be going." Whak looked around for the stairs, located them, and put his words into action, but he was not able to break away so easily. Assok followed him up the stairs, back through the dingy foyer, and out onto the street, still trying in a circumlocutory way to tell Whak what exactly it was he wanted.

Whak took a breath of cool night air and looked up and down the street. "Which way is home?"

"That way is back to the park. But tell me you'll at least ask your wife to find out what Blue Suit is doing!"

"Blue Suit?" Whak stopped short. "Well, if you want to know what Blue Suit is doing, we could just ask him." He pointed down the road to a collection of angular shadows.

"Who?" Assok cast a frightened stare in the same direction.

"My personal representative of the observing classes. My very own blue suit." He waved, not knowing whether anyone was there or not. The effect on George Assok was immediate.

"Oh my God."

With those words, George Assok leaped backwards into the equivalent shadows on this side of the street, hunched down into a shape and size similar to a rubbish sack, and ceased to move. Whak looked at him and would have asked, what the hell are you doing, but the rubbish bag shape made rapid little waving movements and whispered desperately "Away! Go Away!", so he took a few steps, looked back, and caught a final glimpse of his strange acquaintance, still crouching, creeping slowly off in the darkness, and then Whak was alone on the broken pavement.

"Mad," he murmured. "Everyone I meet is mad."

On the way home, he stopped at the Coolio Park wall. A late night conversation with a lunatic had to be worth a swift line of words.

two men walking towards an idea
one with no answers and one with no fear
the idea is a foetus that fell from it's nest
they stood over it's last breath
last words strangled by death
the unspoken word dies in your sleep.

He liked it. He went back through the gate, got lost in the park, and didn't get home until dawn. His sense of direction had never been good.

That day, Lino came out of her room.

CHAPTER 14

Lino goes to town

Lino came out of her room early. Jelli was still in the house, drinking black coffee and reading a document about the relationship between low income and hostility to authority, a tautological state that she thought it might be interesting to invert. What would the key elements have to be? Government as protector of the weak, the Consortium as the expression of the voice of the poor. There must be a version of the truth that worked for that.

"Where's breakfast?" asked Lino.

Jelli was surprised. "Wherever it usually is, Lino darling."

"Whak usually gets my breakfast."

"I'm not Whak, Lino, and he's not awake. Nice to see you out and about again." She went back to reading. She suspected the reason that rebellion grew so well on poverty was because it was beneficial, up to a point. It gave the underprivileged something to direct their anger. Jelli's job was to prevent that anger from igniting. Something else to direct their anger. She scratched her forehead. It would be so much easier if it was the rich, well-educated component of the population that boiled over with resentment. Trouble was, they had little to be resentful about, except BMW deprivation. And there weren't that many of them any more, either. SRMs had been a powerful force for redistribution of wealth. Of course, they were still rich. Jelli herself had more wealth than she could ever spend, especially now that there was almost nothing to spend it on. There were even mega-rich, but they seemed to be in hiding, living on isolated estates, waiting for these dangerous times to pass. As a result, their existence had taken on mythical status amongst the much more numerous poor. They were thought (correctly) to be the secret force behind the Consortium, for example.

"Can you give me a lift into town?" Lino asked, through a mouthful of bran flakes.

"Yes." Jelli did not look up. "Of course."

Perhaps if PushRight began to say that there was a falling out between the Consortium and the wealthy and privileged, some kind of tax punishment perhaps, the effect would be to identify the Consortium with the lower economic classes, and peace and law-abiding conformity would reign upon earth. Jelli wondered what her psych team would think.

"I said, let's go then!" Lino said loudly, startling Jelli back to the breakfast bar.

"All right, when I've finished my coffee! Don't shout at me!"

"You shout at me."

"I can't remember the last time I shouted at you!" Jelli said, truthfully, and wished she had said nothing, because the true reply, "I can't remember the last time you said anything to me," was right on Lino's lips. She pretended that it didn't hurt.

"Lino, please, I've got to finish reading this paper before we go. Don't you have to brush your teeth or something? And put a bra on."

"I'll wait in the car." Lino gulped half a cup of black coffee and went to the door. "And I'm fine, thanks."

Just at that moment, Whak appeared, clad in a kimono and clearly still half asleep.

"Strange night," he began, but Lino interrupted him.

"We're just going, Whak. Tell us later."

"Oh, Lino," Whak noticed her. "How are you? How's the mental interior?"

"I'm perfectly all right. I'm going into town. I've got to see someone."

"You're not going to that godawful Revital Church again, are you?" Whak asked immediately. "I mean, first day out of your room, don't let them shovel shit all over you again."

It was the wrong thing to say. Lino became intensely calm.

"I was in my room because I wanted to be in my room. Don't make it sound like I have to be locked up until I'm well enough to face the world, because I can face the world any time. Come on Jelli, let's go."

Whak was sorry he had spoken. He showed a big lower lip. He and Jelli nodded courteously at each other as Jelli shoved her still-unfinished read into her briefcase and squashed it down closed. They kissed cheeks as Jelli walked past him to follow Lino out the door.

"Is she all right?" Whak asked.

"Who knows?" Jelli replied. "She's an adult."

"I'm not sure that I'm an adult, Jelli."

"Neither am I. I'll see you tonight, unless you decide to go out again." There was a faint rebuke in her words. Whak started to object.

"Last night? I was only out last night because I met a very unusual - " Jelli's car horn made a sound like the sudden scream of a thousand cats, and he winced and stopped.

"Tell me later," Jelli said, and went out the door.

She climbed into her great beast of a car, and slid her briefcase over the seat so that it occupied the space between her and Lino, who was drumming her fingers on the dashboard impatiently. Jelli said to her "Where to?"

"Oh, anywhere."

"I thought you had to see someone!"

"Well, I do. Drop me, oh, outside your work."

Jelli was unreasonably irritated by Lino's sudden indifference. She started driving, determined to ignore her for the rest of the trip. Although usually she had the patience of a blind snake, this time she couldn't contain her increasingly vile mood for long enough. After ten minutes of driving in silence, during which she gradually became more irritated and Lino's face remained apparently glued to the window, Jelli snapped.

"So are you going to see somebody or not?"

"I said I was," Lino answered. "What I do is my business!"

"And who I give a lift to is my business," Jelli snapped. She had not meant to threaten immediate expulsion from the car, but that was what Lino decided that she meant.

"Fine," she said in that dramatic and serious tone that she had used earlier on Whak. She turned from the glass. Like a young child, she had the ability to fill her eyes with the utmost loathing and hate. Jelli wished that she could also fill them with love, but that emotion seemed to be missing from her, or at least, Jelli had never seen it. You see in others what you wish for in yourself. "Then let me out."

The next intersection possessed working traffic lights, and whether Jelli wished to or not, she was obliged to stop there. Numbers of other vehicles, lashtogethers mostly, pulled up beside and behind. Lino opened her door, stepped out, and walked off without a further word.

"Well, shut the damned door! Bitch!" Jelli screamed at her. She reached across - the humvee was a big car, and she had to stretch - and pulled the door shut, and as she straightened up she screamed again. A scorpion suddenly appeared in the dead centre of her windscreen, smiled a toothy smile, and began to cut a hole in the bonnet.

"Get off!" Jelli shouted.

Jelli's car is eaten

Kunk.

She looked up to where that noise had emanated. Above her head, a section of roof was beginning to melt. Melt? Jelli took no more than two seconds removing herself from the car. Standing by the bonnet, she saw another SRM poised on the roof with a bright light in its mouth. A welder. That was a Wasteland type that she had only heard tell of before. Something touched her leg. She jumped backwards and narrowly avoided another metal insect, a crocodile this time, emerging from underneath her indestructible car with a section of metal in its clutches. Jelli wasn't sure what the section of metal was, but she knew, with unhappy certainty, that it was something vital. It always was, where crocs were concerned. A small SRM, of tubular appearance, emerged from the exhaust pipe. Then another. The scorpion had by now opened up the bonnet like a can of soup and was pulling out a pair of thick black cables. Jelli took a step backwards, and was subjected to the howling horns of the vehicles in that lane, but she kept backing away from her own car. It was practically crawling with SRMs, now. They appeared as if from out of the ground, perhaps she had stopped over a manhole, but Jelli was not about to try and find out. She continued to walk backwards until she reached the opposite pavement, where she found a crowd of pedestrians (suddenly they were fellow pedestrians) watching with interest the consumption of her vehicle. She stood with them while the mighty humvee was reduced, with startling rapidity, to the bare husk of an automobile.

"Well shit," said an old brown man beside her. "I never seen that happen before."

Lino saw none of this. She had walked away from Jelli's car swiftly and not looked back, and now she was fifty metres down the street and around a corner. Before the fight with Jelli, the inevitable fight, the never-ending fight, she had been intending to go to the Revital Church, as Whak suspected, but not to listen while Kutters declaimed his non-existent insights. She was hoping, rather, to kick him repeatedly in the groin. She was capable of it. Lino, when angry, had absolutely no empathy for any other person whatsoever, and she was angry with Kutters, for trying to touch her breasts and for being an opportunist door-to-door salesman of rehashed biblical rhetoric. His hunger for her flesh had exposed all that resonant sermonising as calculated, emotional fish-hooks. She despised insincerity. He had no kind of message that Lino could use to understand her life. She was severely disappointed.

She was not going to go there anymore, however. It was now too far to walk, for one thing, and she suddenly felt tired and drained of emotion. Instead, she walked down the street that she had randomly chosen. She walked for several minutes and came to one of the streets dotted with bars and slums that ran away from the city centre. She was lost, by this time, and there were people watching her go by in her expensive clothes. It was the leather jacket in particular that got the attention of a young man, unshaven except for his head, who was thin enough of build to fit into that fine piece of black cowhide. He lifted himself off a concrete step and began to follow her, as she took her bearings from the horizon of lifeless skyscrapers and turned right.

Jelli took a taxi to the PushRight building. She hated taxis. They were always dirty, they stank of the urine of many drunks, and they were driven by sullen men who thought their customers stupid. When she arrived at work, she was in that state which people reach when all their hates have piled upon them. Allynn saw her coming out of the lift and, making a perfect reading from the length of the office, went to her desk and pretended to be searching for something. Jelli stopped right there beside her, her eyes slitted, and said "What have we done about the SRM Collection?"

"Nothing," Allynn said promptly. "As per your instructions."

"Well, do something about it NOW!" Jelli shouted. She pulled at her collar, which was grimed with the dirt of a un-airconditioned cab, and went on in a more controlled tone. "Do you know what has happened to me today? Have you any idea? My daughter came out of her room, that's what happened. And my car was eaten. I have just paid fifteen dollars taxi fare to an obese, half-naked Spaniard with infected pustules all over the back of his neck, who took me three blocks the wrong way while I screamed at him to turn around. So suddenly I think, life could be pleasant, if it wasn't for SRMs. Apart from not driving my daughter insane or ripping my car to pieces, we could have clean taxis and drivers who don't drool. I no longer care what Blue Suit is doing about SRMs, as long as it's something! Bring me the SRM Collection folder."

Suddenly Jelli was seeing things from a very Blue Suit perspective. SRMs were ruining her life! They were bringing down civilisation! It was time to do something about it!

She went into her office. Had a coffee. Washed. Allynn brought her the folder, she opened it, and began to conjure out of the constant rain of interplanetary bullshit that falls around us at all times, the scheme that would provide Blue Suit with all the SRMs he desired. For much as it pained her to give Blue Suit anything more than orgasms without a visible payback, right this second she didn't give a shit.

Jim saves Lino

Since the SRM event at the Wasteland and his dismissal and obloquy as the guide responsible for leading innocent tourists into danger, Jim had been forced to look for a new profession. General unemployment in the open economy was horrendous, but in the real world, nearly everyone had their tasks, their skills, their special patch on which they grew their incomes. Workforce statistics for migratory hunters look pretty bad, but they're all fully employed staying alive. Jim was pretty pissed off by the fact that Wasteland Tours had almost instantly folded before the verbal ink was dry on his agreement to leave quietly, but shit, it added up the same way however it happened. He wasn't going to be getting any half pay for keeping his mouth shut. That was over before it began, and he had to find another job.

He very quickly realised that his time as a Guide had given him two invaluable assets. He knew a hell of a lot about SRMs, and he knew how to get around the Wasteland without losing either his freedom or parts of his body. Useless skills, some people might have thought, but they would have been unaware of the latest and greatest entertainment available on the street, SRM pitfighting. Jim had known a little about this phenomenon, but it had not caught his imagination until a couple of days ago when he was down at the bar spending a little of his remaining money on a beer and a number. The number man told him how bad business was these days.

"You know, when TV stopped working properly and everybody joined the slums, heh, that was good, you know. They used to say that one day everybody was going to be rich, but everybody got poor instead. Heh heh. That was good for the numbers. A little hope, a little profit, a lot of numbers, that was good times."

"So what's wrong?" Jim asked. "You don't look like this story has a happy ending."

"It's the pitfights, Jim man, they're ripping our guts out."

"Oh, the pitfights."

"Yeah, the pitfights. It's thanks to Cousin Sinfine, not my cousin, he's a Cousin. Of the big man." The number man rolled his eyes skywards. Jim guessed that he meant one of the Uncles, as they called themselves. Uncles, Cousins, and Nephews, normal-sounding family members, except that these were the old men who had survived the crime wars, their smart young lieutenants, and the grunts that they used to kill people. To Jim, the violent Nephews were as much a part of life as the police, or the number man, or the street chimps.

"He's a smart shark," the number man went on. "He's started these pitfights. I come around and have to point my boys at twice the usual punters to shake out dollars. Everyone has spent their money at the pitfights. SRMs, shit, if they want fighting they should have fucking men fighting. Who wants to see crocodile machines fight? Where's the blood in that?"

"There's no blood in horse-racing, either," said Jim, "but people still watch it."

"Give me your dollars, boy, and shut up."

It was then Jim realised that he might be in the right place at the right time. If there were SRM pitfights, there must be winners and losers, and the losers would have to be replaced. Jim had seen many SRM altercations in the Wasteland, and they were inevitably fatal for one participant. This Sinfine bod, or his street men, would be on the lookout for new talent. Jim could see a class of SRM suppliers arising, who would scour the city for the biggest, meanest, fastest, deadliest SRMs, and earn a share of the gate for their labour. He knew the Wasteland backwards, and there was no better place to find obscure and hopefully crowd-pleasing varieties. He thought about showing up at a pitfight with a brace of drillheads. They would dismantle any crocodile in less than ten seconds. He went back to his shoebox, nodding enthusiastically to the tune of his new future.

Later that day, he took the hours-long walk to the Wasteland, where he stood staring in the glass fences at the spots he knew so well, where the drillheads and the spiders lived (although he didn't think he'd try to take any spiders anywhere. He valued his limbs too much for that).

He looked at the security cameras mounted at the top of the fence pillars and chuckled. They didn't work, they never had worked for as long as he'd been a Guide. Their insides had been eaten the very first night they had been put up. The cables running along the top of the barrier were ostentatiously supported by large ceramic insulators, but that was no problem, either. They weren't live. Five thousand volts was one of the few things that had been found to discourage SRMs, but Wasteland Tours had never been able to afford the cost of keeping the wire hot, and now that they had closed down, it didn't matter. Jim had no doubt he could get in there, collect a couple of money-spinners, and get out again, as often as he liked.

Now, the other end of the equation. Who was the buyer? Somehow, he would have to get himself introduced to someone at the pitfights.

He was still waiting for that introduction. While waiting, he was planning his first acquisition trip into the Wasteland. In the spirit of illegal entry, he had armed himself with a sack, bolt-cutters, and his balaclava, but he still needed gloves. He had a need for a morning cup of sood, too, and he was out. He left his small third-floor room and as he stepped out onto the street. He observed the tail end of a beautiful young woman ahead of him, which would have been a pleasant sight if there hadn't been also been one of the street's chimpanzees walking quickly to catch her up. Jim hurried and was right behind the other two when he heard the chimp accost her.

"Hey, nice jacket," said the man.

The young woman said nothing. She did the common thing. She ignored him and hoped that the he'd leave her alone. If this had been a real chimpanzee there might have been a chance, but humans are much more able to modify their behavioural programming than most animals. Lying on her back and letting him sniff her belly might have been more successful. The chimp grabbed the collar of the jacket as she tried to walk away and hauled her back, which made her lose her balance. She fell onto the cracked pavement and the young man with the wish for her jacket began to roughly peel it from her shoulders.

"Hi," Jim said, a smile on his lips. He smiled even wider as the chimp looked up and snarled "She's mine, so fuck off."

"Never make demands from a crouching position," Jim advised him. The chimp's face changed as he suddenly became aware of his vulnerability, just as Jim kicked him under the jaw.

As the foot connected, his neck seemed to stretch to half as long again and his whole body lifted slightly into the air, then he fell stunned across the young woman. Jim stepped over the two bodies and roughly pushed the chimp off the pile.

"Are you all right?" he asked as the young woman picked herself up. "Hey, I know you."

Lino's face was frozen, but since that was the way Jim had seen her most often, he thought this to be normal. He asked her again.

"Are you all right?"

"Yes," Lino said flatly.

"I guess I saved you again," Jim said cheerfully.

Lino did not answer. She straightened her clothes and began to walk away.

"Hey!" Jim wasn't going to put up with this. "Hey! It's Lino, isn't it?"

"Yes," said Lino. Her face remained glazed.

"You look all shook up, Lino. You need to sit down for a bit. Would you like me to buy you a drink?" Jim pulled out a cigarette and lit it while he waited for Lino to make some response, but she just stood and watched him. "You knew how to speak English last time we met, I think."

"I know how to speak English," Lino echoed.

"Are you all right?"

"What do you mean?"

Jim suddenly dropped down onto his knees and clasped his hands together in front of his chin. "Thank you for saving me," he said dramatically. Lino stared at him, then her face changed a little. "Ah, you can smile."

"I'm sorry. I'm feeling very tired." Lino took a deep breath. "Thank you."

"No problem. How about a drink?"

"All right."

There was a metallic noise from behind them. Lino, who could see that way, gasped, and Jim spun on his heels to see the chimpanzee getting to his feet. The clicking sound was not from the switchblade he had pulled from his pocket. Jim pointed. "Look out," he warned the chimp. "There's an SRM behind you."

The youth looked. There was a cat-sized scorpion, way out of the normal size range, right there on the footpath. He squinted at it, then poked at it's sensory apparatus with his blade. The scorpion extended it's cutting tool and whirred in a strange way, both blankly mechanical and threatening at the same time.

"Jesus," said the chimp, backing away. He looked at Jim and Lino, who were already walking off, and put a hand to his painful jaw. "Ah, to hell with it."

CHAPTER 15

Jim and Lino have Coffee

Jim took Lino to a nearby Sood Shop and ordered two soods and two beers. The shop was down an alley so narrow that from their window table, he and Lino could count the bricks on the opposite wall, except where they were obscured by a large pile of rubbish. Neither of them said anything until the drinks arrived. Lino counted bricks, it seemed, and Jim studied the side of her face. While stirring two sugars into his weak and phoney espresso, Jim pointed out that bad things seemed to happen to her.

"Not usually," Lino replied.

"I've only met you twice, and the first time SRMs attacked a whole bunch of innocent bystanders, and the second time you're being turned over. You're a hundred percent in trouble."

"Fine. Then don't meet me again." Lino spoke carelessly. It wasn't that she wanted to push Jim away, but a statement of her self-worth. She had no reason to think that Jim wanted to meet her again. Jim was a little annoyed, as people are when their judgement of another is assumed to be wanting.

"You don't have many friends, I'll bet." He was trying to sting her, but she answered as smoothly as if he had remarked on the weather.

"I don't have any friends. I never meet anybody," she said, pouring her beer.

"What about work, school? You must have met some people there."

"I don't work. I was educated at home. I did my degree by correspondence. " Jim was impressed. Only wealthy people bothered to get degrees. He wondered what her degree was in. Ancient Greek seemed the most likely. "I don't go out much," she finished up.

"Why not?"

"I get upset." She gave up this information painfully.

"I'll bet, if every time you go out something bad happens."

At that moment, Jim's chair was clipped by the shop door as someone hurried in. The shop was busy, because it was cheap, and in this part of town, almost nobody had a job. There was no morning migration to the city offices. There were a lot of people on the street during the day, instead. So the place was crowded, and there was a lot of smoke and noise, but Jim naturally tuned in to the old guy who had just bumped his chair.

" - pulled the whole car to bits. Real quick, too. It was shit funny to watch. The woman, she got out and just walked backwards till she hit the kerb, scared shitless, she was."

Jim put up a 'stay-here' hand to Lino and pushed his way up to the bar.

"Another sood, with some more coffee flavour in it this time, eh?" he said. He turned to the man with the story. "What's pulling cars to bits?"

The old guy shrunk his eyes into his shiny brown skull and glittered at him suspiciously. Eavesdroppers can be dangerous. "Who wants to know?" he said in a voice little more than a whisper.

"I'm Jim. I'm just a neighbour. Live over there on Combine Street." He turned to the counter hand. "Tell him I'm all right, will you?"

"Pay for your sood."

"Jesus. Here. Am I all right or aren't I?"

"He's all right. No blue suit."

The old guy nodded a couple of times. "Okay," he said. "It's nothing. Out on the arterial there was this rich bitch in some kind of flash armoured car. Stopped at the lights, got torn up by SRMs. That's all."

"They tore up a car at the lights, just like that?" Jim was amazed. SRMs didn't usually go for moving objects, and the definition of a stationary object was one that hadn't moved lately. Cars at the lights hardly qualified.

"That's what I said."

"Sure. You did. Thanks. Interesting."

The other grunted and turned to face the other way.

Jim went back to his table. Lino was watching his face, but she asked no questions. He quickly finished his second sood and suggested that he take her to her home.

"You don't need to," Lino said. Some people say such things only to give their benefactors an out. Or it can be an independence unto death thing, I'll help you, but no, you needn't bother, I couldn't ask you, no. I don't want to owe you. I don't want you that close. That's where Lino's voice came from.

"You think you're going to get home safe from here?" said Jim. "Where do you live?"

"North Coolio."

"North Coolio?" Jim knew that Coolio Park was where the pitfights were. "Don't all you North Coolio types have cars?"

"I can't drive," Lino admitted, slightly shamefaced. "I got a lift with my mother."

"So where's she?"

"Why are you always interrogating me? She's at work, I suppose. I got out at some lights." She saw that Jim was waiting for some more. "We had an argument."

"So you got out and went for a walk down Combine Street. Bad choice. The guy at the bar said a car got ripped up by SRMs out on the highway just now. You see it?"

"No." Lino shuddered. "I don't want to see another SRM, ever."

"No, I guess you wouldn't." Jim looked thoughtful. "Got any money? It's a long walk to North Coolio, we'd be better in a taxi."

"I've got enough for a taxi." She went blank, again, which Jim took to mean that she had more than taxi fare, but stealing her money wasn't his plan. She was a sweet looking female, and he thought it might be nice to make love to her some day, but he also thought that she was the focal point of a lot of strangeness. That interested him.

"Let's find a cab, then," he said.

the white plastic sky reminds me of the side of my fridge

Whak read the line over for the fiftieth time today. He flicked the venetians open and looked up into that plastic sky, perpetually overcast white or grey, which did indeed remind him of the side of a fridge. Perhaps it was the literal reporting of what he felt that was wrong. Perhaps he should pull some cheap tricks. *The side of my fridge reminds me of the sky,* for example. Or start something new. There was a time when he could find inspiration and material in the way that human complacency had been shaken to pieces by SRMs. He thanked the mechanical beasts for that, but the stream had run dry for him. The warnings of the artists had been translated into the attitude of the masses so damn quickly that the artists hadn't even finished saying what they had to say before they were redundant.

He was rescued from what was quickly becoming a serious moment of angst by the sight of Lino entering the property at the gate. There was a young man with her. Whak watched them both walk up the path. They didn't touch, he noticed. His little leap of the heart died.

"Better put in an appearance," he said to himself. In the hall he found Lino, trying to close the door on Jim.

She was saying "Goodbye! Thank you, and goodbye!"

"Can't I come in for a minute?" said Jim, once more finding this infernal woman the rudest person he had ever encountered, and he had encountered a lot of assholes in his time. "You can't just say, thank you and goodbye. It's not a very big thank you, then, is that it?"

"What's happening?" Whak broke in.

Lino let go of the door. Jim stumbled in as the pressure on his pushing arm abated, and Lino tried to get around Whak in the direction of her room, but he put out an arm and blocked her way.

"Who's this?" he asked her.

"His name is Jim."

"And who is he?"

"I'm a friend of Lino's," Jim volunteered.

"I don't have any friends," Lino said coldly.

"Maybe some friends have you," said Whak, giving her a serious look, then transferring it to Jim. "Come in," he said. Jim looked around. He was in. Whak waved a directing hand down the hall and they all ended up in the kitchen. "Coffee?" Whak asked.

"Yes," Lino replied. Jim nodded. Everyone wanted coffee. Jim was watching Whak.

"I'm Lino's father, by the way. My name's Whak."

"I'm Jim."

"So, what brings you and Lino to this place and time?"

"I saved her from a chimp on Combine."

"A chimp on Combine. Good work." Whak seemed to be congratulating him on his choiceness of expression rather than his rescue work. Jim noticed that he sub-vocalised the phrase a couple of times more before he went on. "So, Lino, you didn't quite get to town. What happened? You and Jelli had a fight, I suppose." He seemed to find this uncommonly amusing. After he had finished chuckling to himself, he went on. "What do you do, Jim?"

"He's a Guide," Lino answered for him.

"I was a Guide. I got the boot when the SRMs attacked my tour party. But it wasn't my fault," he added hastily as Whak's eyes spiralled in on him. "Wasteland Tours made a deal with me. They said they'd pay me off if I kept quiet about what happened.

But they haven't paid, and they're not going to, because they've gone out of business anyway."

"Lucky for you." Jim looked puzzled, so Whak explained what he meant. "You're saved the embarrassment of a wrong decision by reaching the same result regardless. So, you were the tour guide that day. What did happen?"

"Does he always talk like this?" Jim asked Lino, who scowled and nodded. "What did happen to what?"

"When the SRMs attacked. Lino hasn't told me."

"Well, she must have told you something." He looked at her. She seemed to have withdrawn to about three galaxies away since the appearance of her father.

"Not much. I heard more on the news, and there wasn't very much of that. Why did they attack?"

"I've got no idea. It was like they'd had a signal or something. They just went insane. Attacked everything that moved. Except me, and the old guy, and Lino. We were all by the leaning carriage - that's a landmark - and the rest of the party were out in the open. But the spiders came from the carriage in the first place. They came leaping out."

"So you and Lino and this old guy were left alone?"

"Yes. We were."

"Maybe there's something funny about that carriage."

"Naah. I've been there hundreds of times. Nothing weird has ever happened before."

"Interesting job, touring the Wasteland every day?"

Jim thought for a bit. "Not after the first few months. Watching SRMs evolve can be a bit dull after a while."

"Watching SRMs evolve? I'm wondering if this attack is something to do with that. Are they getting more aggressive? I met a man last night who thinks that they have a plan, well, he doesn't quite say it like that, but that's the way I'd say it if I thought what he does. They've got a plan. They're probably building a giant robotic brain in the centre of the earth."

"Don't say things like that! They're creepy enough as it is!" Lino finally had something to say. She pushed her empty cup away so violently that it toppled off the opposite side of the table and Jim only just caught it before it hit the floor. "I'm going to my room. Goodbye." She left the kitchen.

"I'd better go, then." Jim stood up. "Thanks for the coffee. Good. Real stuff?"

"Real stuff," Whak agreed. "You're consorting with the rich and powerful now, Jim." He laughed again, but not as easily as before.

As he walked back down the path to the street, Jim wondered if that was true. He also wondered how it was he had left the house without arranging for a further meeting with Lino. No doubt he could turn up at the tall door and knock, and Lino (or possibly Whak, or the mysterious unseen Jelli) might answer, and he could play it by ear from there. He intended to. He had a feeling that she was going to help him in his quest to become rich.

Now, however, he was going to take advantage of the fact that he had somehow ended up near Coolio Park. Tonight, he was going to the pitfights.

The SRM Collection Ad

Tonight, Jelli was early. As soon as she was in the door, the house reverberated to the sound of Lino's bedroom door being ostentatiously and loudly slammed. Jelli cast one negative gaze down the hall, then threw herself into an armchair, stretched her legs over the side of it and asked Whak to get her a drink. As he returned to the room with a couple of tumblers of alcohol, she looked at her watch and asked him to turn on the TV.

"It's a bit soon for mindless blobbage, isn't it?" Whak asked as he flicked the switch.

"Sshh. There's a Pushright ad on."

"Aren't they all Pushright ads?"

"Well, yes, they are, but there's one in particular I want to see. Thanks," Jelli added as he gave her the drink. "Damn programmers have stuffed up the schedule again, I see. This show was supposed to be over three minutes ago."

"Maybe a flying cockroach ate their clock. Or maybe they're all under arrest, and this show is going to continue without pause or ad break forever."

"That would not be according to schedule," Jelli said without humour. "Ah, credits. Ssh."

The credits indeed rolled, and the familiar GOV1 logo and theme music came next. Whak sighed but endured, and at last the ad appeared.

Big graphical letters: SRM BOUNTY

Voiceover (dramatic): It had to come. The battle has begun.

Several short segments of SRMs dismantling new-looking televisions, computers, and household appliances, shot with lurid jerky close-ups and big pixel size

Voiceover: Your government needs your help. In the ongoing struggle to ensure a better life for all citizens, in the fight against the common enemy, in the quest for knowledge.

Slow-motion, calmly lit shot of a gleaming white laboratory where handsome, serious men and beautiful, smiling women study large-screen displays of what might be SRM schematics

Voiceover: To aid our research and achieve the technology we need to bring employment, freedom, and happiness to all people, we ask you to capture as many SRMs as possible and deliver them to this address.

Street address of Blue Suit Offices appears, superimposed over a picture of the Guggenheim Museum.

Sexy female voice: For every SRM delivered, a bounty will be payable, according to a sliding scale, published at a Post Office near you.

An advertisement for Sood followed. The drink with more kick than flavour.

"Well," said Whak, "that was interesting. Kind of heavy-handed on the 'your government loves you' angle, of course."

Jelli frowned at him. "They didn't quite put it across the way I instructed them, no," she said, "but it's not bad. We should see some results from this."

"We should see what results?"

"People will start delivering SRMs for research. I expect that at least zero point six percent of the population will be motivated enough by the bounty to go out and catch as many SRMs as they can. The morons we're aiming this at will be happy, busy, and have purpose and objectives in their lives. What could be better?"

"Delivering them where? To Blue Suit? What's he doing?"

Jelli kept a perfectly straight face. "I don't actually know," she replied. "He's got some high-powered people working on something, he claims it's mass behaviour analysis, but I don't think that's the true story. I'm sure he's leading another attempt to wipe them out. Anything that might help get rid of SRMs has to be good. Did I tell you my car was completely wrecked today by another one of these SRM attacks? It was just torn to pieces! Nobody had ever seen anything like it. I had to catch a taxi home! It really brought home to me how much better off we would be without SRMs. All the consumer electronics, high tech manufacturing, home appliances that worked, that we used to have ten years ago, back again."

Whak ignored the wish list. "Another SRM attack? And you were there?"

"I was the target. Or my car was."

"Your car? I thought - "

"That it was supposed to be SRM-proof, yes. Well it wasn't. SRM resistant, they said."

"And you don't know 'exactly' what Blue Suit is doing."

"No! And I don't care!"

Whak thought that everybody should care what megalomaniacal autocrats who ran security services in an age of increasing fascism did. That suddenly reminded him of George Assok. "I met a man last night," he told Jelli, "who wanted me to find out what Blue Suit is doing. He didn't make it very clear what he thought it might be, though."

Jelli, who was sipping her drink as Whak said this, obtained a slightly fearful expression. She put her drink down carefully on the coffee table.

"Who was this person?" she asked. "Whak, you're already under observation. If you weren't my husband, you'd be in a secure area by now."

"Why? For writing poetry?"

"For writing poetry, yes. For all the things that you do that disturb Blue Suit."

"Blue Suit is too easily disturbed."

"All right, but that doesn't change the facts, Whak!"

Whak knew that. He knew he was under Jelli's protection. It wasn't that he didn't think before he spoke, it was just that he didn't usually think of anything that made him not want to speak. Honesty is the best thing anyone can achieve with their life.

Jelli took her drink back from the table, having reduced Whak to nonverbal dejection, and repeated her question.

"Who was this man last night?"

"He's a strange chap. Does research into SRMs, by the sound of it. I went to his place with him, after the pitfight - "

"Pitfight?" Jelli looked wildly around for the connection any of this had with pitfights. "What pitfight?"

"They hold them in Coolio Park. SRM fights. People gamble on them."

Jelli nodded fiercely. "I know what a pitfight is."

"Let me tell you about George. He had all sorts of experiments on SRMs going in his where he lives. Intelligence tests. Do you think SRMs might be intelligent?"

Jelli did not feel happy at the way this question seemed to recur so often. Blue Suit was right, SRM intelligence was a dangerous prospect, best left unanswered. But equally, it was an obvious question in the face of SRM behaviour how they could perform tasks of complexity that baffled the best technology that still survived, such as building more of their own kind. "They might be. An insect is intelligent, isn't it?"

"I mean intelligent like reasoning intelligence." Whak saw Jelli dismiss the question and rather than argue the point, went on talking. "This guy says that SRM evolution is according to a plan. Purposeful, he called it. And he asked me to find out what Blue Suit was up to."

"What plan? How did he expect you to find anything out?" Jelli began to get agitated, now. She took short steps back and forth in front of Whak, paused in his face, and then more steps. "What does he think Blue Suit is up to?"

"I don't know. He knew who you were, though," Whak nodded at her. "He used to work for some place called Smalltech, he said. Nanotechnology outfit, apparently."

"Nanotechnology. That's..."

"That's a big word," Whak said, po-faced.

Jelli stopped her pacing. Now she had a slit-eyed, concentrating expression, and she stood still while she ran some scenarios, but she still didn't know enough to decide whether there was any advantage for her in all this. She had to find out more.

"Whak," she said in honeyed tones, "why don't you ask this person to tell you what he knows about Blue Suit."

"He asked me to ask you to tell me what you know about Blue Suit."

"Whose side are you on?" Jelli raged. "Mine, or a complete stranger who you met in Coolio Park?"

"That's not what I meant. But if he wants to know what you know, why should you think he knows anything that you might want to know? Shit, this is bad for my metre. A minute ago, you were telling me to behave myself and not get into trouble, and now you're telling me to collect information for you."

"There's a difference between being locked up for being stupid and being locked up for doing something important. Just ask him, Whak!"

Whak gave a silly grin. "Well, I would," he said, "but I've forgotten where he lives."

CHAPTER 16

Jim Goes to the Pitfights

Now it was dark, and Jim had no trouble at all locating the illuminated skateboard rink in which the SRM fights were held. Unlike Whak, he had no trouble gaining admittance, even with no money. He hung back a while until he observed a group approaching the rink with an extra-large suitcase, one of those black plastic ones that usually hold massive camera lenses (of the sort George Assok was focussing on the pitfight floor right this very second) but this case, Jim was sure, held one or more SRMs wrapped up in newspaper. He promptly joined the group at the rear. He gained entrance by looking seriously around at the critical moment, just as they passed the two monsters at the gate, and asking the man in front of him a question guaranteed to evoke a response, like, "Hey, how do two cockroaches dismantle a drillhead?"

"What?" said the man in front, shaking his head. He was about the same size as Jim, a few years older, and wore a moustache and a gun, if Jim guessed aright. Now that they were through the gate, Jim moved up next to him.

"I said, how do two cockroaches dismantle a drillhead?" Jim was not dismayed by the gun angle. Many people on Combine Street wore guns and the rest wished they could afford one.

"Is this a fucking riddle or something?"

"No way. This is a demonstration of my incredible depth of knowledge about SRMs," said Jim. He was in, it seemed, but he always pushed his luck until it broke. "I'm an expert."

"Ah-huh," the other said. "Get lost, smart boy."

"Okay. See you on the losers list." Jim started to walk away into the seat-seeking flow that went left when the competitors, like this group he had joined, went right.

"What is a drillhead, anyway?" the man suddenly asked.

Jim looked back. "Wasteland variety. Cuts most things to bits, but two cockroaches can take it down. I've seen it happen. They creep into it's lateral sensor holes and next thing you see is lots of baby cockroaches. Sex takes two, I guess."

The man with the moustache smiled briefly. "So I've heard," he agreed. "Now, what do you actually want?"

"I'm an SRM whizz. I used to work the Wasteland for the tour company. I figure I've got contacts and facts. I could be a very good technical adviser." Jim was making most of this up as he went along. But hey, why should he do the chimp work, climbing electric fences and letting scissor-mouthed tin bugs have three goes and you're out with his fingers as bait, when he might be able to do the brain job? "Anyway, who are you?" he asked politely.

"Nobody. But I know some people who are somebody. All right, technical adviser, let's see if the boss wants to hear you."

"Right." Jim looked ahead into what he imagined must be the competitors holding area. Although the rink was dazzlingly bright, half a dozen suns cooking the tops of everyone's heads with sheer photon power, he was looking down a short flight of concrete stairs into darkness. "Down there?"

"Down there."

There is a simple relationship between outcome and acceptable risk that people consider every day, and Jim considered it now. The holding area was unknown territory, away from the crowd, amongst strangers, and poorly lit. The possible gain was a new career for Jim Truly. He hesitated no more than two seconds. "Fine," he said, and went down the stairs, in front of his moustached acquaintance.

"Pass," said a voice.

"He's with me."

"OK, Sergi." Being with Sergi apparently qualified as a pass. They went a few steps further into the darkness, by which time Jim's eyes were starting to adjust and he could see that the holding area was a locker room. Standing in groups around the benches and coat hooks were exactly the sort of people Jim imagined would be involved in this business, hard-lookers, small-timers, smooth-looking guys who must be the money men, and of course the guns, any one of whom looked to be more financial than any of the participants. There must be a link between a smart personal appearance and the willingness to kill. The people, though, took little of Jim's attention. He followed Sergi, whoever Sergi was, and he scanned the cages and boxes and cases of SRMs that had been brought for the fights.

"Crocs. Huh," he muttered as he saw a distinctive tail section waving through the gaps of a wooden box. "Everybody's favourite." Then the side of the box exploded into a cloud of splinters, and the croc was briefly in view, running across the floor, across Jim's path. Not one to miss an opportunity, Jim quickly reached down and grabbed the croc by the nose. It thrashed it's tail once and then, as he knew crocs do when impeded by a vertical force, played dead. Jim held it down for a few seconds to make sure, then let the owner (who tried to pretend that he had it all under control, and if he didn't, it was Jim's fault) have his creature back. Sergi looked impressed.

"So, you might be more than a big mouth," he said.

"I think so."

"Who's this?" Another man approached. This was a fashionable gun type. Jim estimated his rank as one Sergi and a bit. As Sergi explained who and what Jim claimed to be, the gun looked him up and down in the estimating way that men of violence do. Jim did his best not to appear intimidated. When Sergi had finished, the gun man nodded at him and then at Jim.

"You're a handler," he said. "We've got a handler."

Jim didn't try to push the technical adviser line with this one. Instead, he asked, "Do you win?"

"Often enough."

"Well, then you don't need me."

Two minutes later, Jim was wondering at the monotony of things as he was being explained to yet another member of the chain. However, this final person was the money man, executive power was his, and like most money men, he was astute at identifying possibilities. His name was Eric.

"Handler hotshot, you say. We've got a handler."

"That's what I told him."

"On the other hand, if we had two handlers, we could put twice as many crocs in the ring, win twice as often."

"More than twice as often," Jim said. "And I can get better varieties than crocs."

"What's better than a croc?" Eric asked immediately.

"Am I in?"

Eric's face twisted around as thoughts apparently crowded into first the left corner of his brain, then the right. "Trial," he suggested at last. "If we don't win all your fights, you're out."

"What do I get out of this?" Jim demanded.

"Handler pay."

"And a cut of the winnings. Ten percent."

"Hah! Win the next five fights and we'll talk about it." Eric was amused. He took out a thin dark rollup and put a match to his face, exhaled odoriferous smoke over Jim's head. "But it won't be ten percent, no matter how good you are."

That was enough for Jim. Winning the next five fights, he thought, will be a piece of golden piss. His thoughts went back to climbing the dead electric fence into the Wasteland, prime reservoir of SRM species, and he cast his gaze around the holding room and over the boxes and cases and traps full of SRMs. All of you, he thought, are old news. All of you.

Albert Shefykas

GOV1 reached ten percent of homes. It was unlikely that anyone in those homes, richer than the average, would see Jelli's advertisement and then leap out their door with sack in hand and coal miners' lantern perched on their brow to hunt SRMs.

Jelli did not expect it. But she did expect that the word would creep. So it was that after some few days, the news was common in Combine Street, for example, or the slums by the motorway, and in the basements of the crumbling skyscrapers on the south of the city. SRMs were worth money.

This was not news to Jim, of course, or anyone else involved in the pitfight game, but it sure as hell was news to people like Albert Shefykas, who lived in the boiler room of the National Mutual Building on the corner of deserted Queen and Eleven Streets, near the Wasteland. He heard it from the Sweep, a fat lummox of a man who was always stained with sweat and food, who heard it from a kid who stole a TV from somewhere in the suburbs. The Sweep was Albert's only real contact with the outside of his boiler room, into which he had retreated years ago and from which he emerged only when he was pressed by hunger, or more often, when his animals were. He looked after a dozen stray cats and dogs in there, giving them food bits picked from other people's rubbish and talking to them under his breath. He dreamed of buying packets of cat biscuits and tins of dog food as he slept in the cold and unused boiler. One morning, he woke to the sound of the thin metal door at the top of the stairs clanging as the Sweep came in to empty his dustcart into the big hole, where during one of the riots, probably, someone with a jackhammer or a stick of dynamite had broken open a piece of floor three metres wide that disappeared through a tangle of subterranean pipes and cavities into hell, for all anyone knew. Whether the Sweep was paid to do his work or he did it out of some inner need was not something Albert had ever asked him.

"Hey Albert. You hear about SRMs?" The Sweep's voice
was always hoarse, so he sounded like a talking frog, a likeness
not dispelled by his large belly and wide, lipless mouth.
"No," Albert shook his head.
"They're paying for them. You catch them, take them in, they
pay you for them. Easy money!"
"How much money?" was the first thing Albert asked, but
like most people, the Sweep only knew what he'd been told. All
else that Albert found out from him was that the captured SRMs
were to be collected at the Blue Suit building. Now that put
hesitation in Albert's mind, but the thought of negotiable currency
- unpeople like Albert could not even get the SHA - was so
compelling that he eventually decided that he could brave the
headquarters of oppression with a sackful of mechanical bugs, if it
meant being able to buy dog food. He went to the nearest public
noticeboard, along with about a hundred other people who had an
interest, and read the scale of payments there. Around him, too
many voices merged into a litany of estimation.
"Teddy Bears, five bucks. That's easy money. Those stupid
things all freeze up soon as you look at them. Scorpions three
bucks. Hey, those things bite. Pocket calculators five bucks, yeah.
Crocs, ten dollars, shit, I've seen them in the fights, no way am I
going anywhere near a croc. They can hurt you. Not for ten
bucks. Others. What are others? Oh, others. Spot prices. Well
how much is that? What other sorts are there?"
Albert listened and shrugged. He didn't need to know. He
was going to stick to known varieties, thank you, and get the
stated bounty, if he could catch any. He was a percentage man. It
hadn't got him very far in life, but he still thought that low risk
and low return was the safe bet. When you've got more than
enough, if you lose then you've still got enough. When you
haven't got enough to begin with, the edge of the razor is a lot
closer to your dilated eyeball and looks a lot sharper. And there
were the animals to think about. What would they do without
Albert? In fact, the dogs would return to running in a pack around
the decaying remnant of the financial district, to be shot, run over,
or caught and eaten. The cats would slip back into the air-
conditioning ducts from whence he had enticed them, return to
living on rodents, and no trace of Albert would remain in their flat
skulls. Albert felt sad when those thoughts went through him,
which was how it seemed to him. Thoughts were outside events
that passed like through his head like freight trains, unloading

nothing. It was better like that, because, moments later, he had forgotten that the animals didn't need him and was reasonably happy again. He walked slowly back to his boiler and once the door had rattled closed behind him, he started looking for a sack. In the cupboards, in the air ducts. He had to have a sack.

"No damn sack," he said to himself. He sat on a pipe with his elbows on a valve wheel and made squeaking noises at a grey tomcat, which ignored him. Most of the dogs were asleep. He reached over and scratched an eczema-ridden hound gently behind the ear, and it snarled without opening it's eyes. While he was leaning over, Albert found himself looking down the Hole where the Sweep tipped his dust. There was a single beam of light, coming from another hole in the wall, that at this time of day shone down into the darkness. Albert saw something shiny move down there.

"Walking money!" he started, leaning forward further. SRMs right here, under his boiler room. He was ecstatic. He wondered if there were any old sacks or bags down there, too. That would be too much luck, but he had to find out. He went to the broken edge of the hole, and carefully began to climb into it. Albert was not a fit man, and even when young he had not been nimble. Where the concrete had been smashed open were rusty bits of reinforcing rods, bent spiderlegs that his tentative grip found painfully rough. He found a foothold on some unseen object and looked at the blood leaking from one of his palms, and even as he decided that the trip down to hell was beyond him, whatever he was standing on capsized him into the air. He dangled by one arm - shouting with pain - his body twisting slowly around like a corpse on a rope, for a few seconds, and then he fell.

His thigh broke as he hit the pile of concrete and rubbish at the bottom, but it didn't matter, because his velocity was still high enough to throw him face backwards down the slope, and when his head struck, he stopped caring about his leg, because he was dead.

His dogs would have eaten him, but not being members of the tree-climbing family, they couldn't figure out how to get down to the slowly intensifying smell of meat. Days later, the Sweep came and, without looking, he dumped another dustcart full of rubbish down the Hole, and then later, another. Albert was slowly buried in beer bottles and cereal boxes and, ironically, empty tins of dog food. No one wondered where he had gone.

Jim visits Lino at Home

"How's your SRM collection going?" Whak asked Jelli.

"It's not my SRM collection, it's Blue Suit's. Can't you tell the difference?"

"Sure! Sure I can tell the difference," Whak nodded emphatically. "You're shorter, and he's got no tits. Oh, and I think you have a heart."

"Whak," Jelli put on her warning voice.

"Sorry. So how's it going, anyway?"

"It's going very well. Thousands of SRMs are being handed in. It's really given the target population segment something to keep their minds occupied. It's pushing the hunter-gatherer button dead centre, and that's such a fundamental aspect of the human psyche that activating it gives a sense of worth and pride even to something as mundane as collecting those crazy machines for money."

"Hmm," Whak said doubtfully. "I can't see this leading to anything good, to be honest."

"Oh, and those pitfights you told me about."

"Yes?"

"They're illegal, you know."

Whak put on a horrified face. "No!" he groaned, putting a clawed hand to his chest. "Oh, no! Not illegal!"

"All right, have your joke. But if they're illegal, they'll be cracked down on soon enough. The current Consortium policy is to enforce the law, in case you haven't noticed."

"There wasn't much sign of law enforcement the other night. They're probably paying off the police."

Jelli in turn looked horrified. "Paying off the police? We don't live in a Mediterranean state, you know!"

"Oh come on. Everybody knows the police are paid off for everything from street gambling to drug pushing. Pit fighting wouldn't be anything special."

"Well, they can't pay off Blue Suit."

"What is this admiration for Blue Suit? And what is this 'illegal-is-wrong' attitude? Since when did what the law says have anything to do with what is acceptable and right?"

"That is a bohemian attitude, Whak. The law is the codification of civilised standards and should be observed. Just because it changes from time to time doesn't make it any less valid." Jelli was quoting straight from Law and Order Project papers, but he wasn't to know that. He thought it was her opinion, arrived at like his after careful thought.

"It changes," Whak said carefully, "because people like me and, I thought, people like you, act according to their consciences, not the conscience of some eighteenth-century Lord of England or some self-serving politician who gets a law passed to push up the price of land he happens to own!"

Jelli enjoyed an argument, most of the time, but she cut this one short. "Just don't go to the pitfights, Whak. If you get dragged in during some bust, it will be very difficult for me to protect you."

Whak drew himself up in a way that Jelli recognised as preceding the sudden vocal birth of a poem, but before a single word of it escaped his lips, the doorbell rang.

"Get that, will you Whak?"

"I - "

Ding dong. Whak shut his mouth. He walked heavily down the hall and threw the front door open and thrust his glaring face forward into the daylight, thinking damn that woman, if she's losing her integrity then what the hell does she have left?

"What?" he snarled.

"Hello, Mr Puihare," said Jim. "Is Lino in?"

CHAPTER 17

They all go out

Whak stared at Jim in confusion, not quite recognising him. Last time they had met, Jim had been wearing canvas trousers and a tee-shirt, but now he wore a thick leather jacket, black, similar to Lino's, and shoes better than those Whak was wearing. He waited for a moment, and when Whak did not reply, he asked again.

"Is Lino in?"

"Yes!" Whak reconnected. "Ah, Jim."

"Is there any chance of seeing her?"

"You can try."

"Then can I come in?"

"Yes, yes. Of course. Sorry. I've just been talking with Jelli, and I was thinking about something else. Come in. Nice jacket."

"Thanks. I just bought it. I got a new job."

"Oh, congratulations. I had a job, once. Didn't really like it. Interfered with my sex life. What are you doing?" Whak guided Jim down the hall towards Lino's door. Jelli stepped out of the kitchen and because Jim was holding half a conversation with Whak on his right, he walked straight into her.

"Oh, sorry," he said, looking down. Jelli was smaller than Lino, but she was very obviously the same stock, and seeing her dressed as she was, had the effect of seeing Lino in twenty years after two divorces. It was good.

"And you are?" Jelli said coldly.

"This is Jim," Whak explained. "He was the tour guide on Lino's trip to the Wasteland."

"Oh, yes." 'And what exactly is he doing here?' was left unsaid.

"He wants to see Lino," Whak continued. "So if you could slide to the left, my dear, the route would be clear." He made little waving motions with his hand, directing her out of the way, and took Jim past her. With Jelli watching him with shaking head from five steps behind and Jim watching him with ill-concealed anticipation from the side, he knocked on Lino's door.

"What?" Lino called.

Whak made a prompting motion at Jim and looked back at the door. He wondered whether Jim would discover the opening mantra that had always eluded him and Jelli.

"It's Jim," Jim said.

Lino's door opened. Jim went in. The door closed. For a moment, both Whak and Jelli stared at it, as if expecting Jim to be vomited back, but no sound or sign came from within. Whak turned back to Jelli. "And just what the hell do you want? To sing a song of praise of Blue Suit? I might buy a blue suit, myself. I can tell supermarket checkout operators that my spies are everywhere and that I know their every thought. Do you think I'm as good looking as him?"

"No," Jelli replied flatly. "I don't."

Whak sat at the kitchen table with Jelli facing him and wondered vaguely whether anything sexual was going on in Lino's bedroom. It had always seemed a question that he would never have to ask. Lino's puberty, adolescence, and now young adulthood all seemed to merge into a continuous process of rejection of others, others' minds, others' bodies. Whak thought sex was a great communicator, whereas Jelli thought sex was a fine weapon, but dangerous in the wrong hands like any other, so it was Jelli who finally asked.

"What do you suppose they're doing in there?"

"Jim's been in there half an hour. Anything they might be doing could have been done twice over by now." Whak scratched his stubble. "That's longer than I've been in her room for years. Good, isn't it?"

"I don't remember what colour her wallpaper is," Jelli admitted.

"Blue." That reminded him. "Jelli, what is Blue Suit doing with all those SRMs?"

"I told you, I don't know. Why don't you find that mad scientist you told me about and ask him?"

"I should try, I suppose."

"Damn right." Jelli looked at her watch. "I've got to go to the office." She always said it like that. Got to go, not I'm going or I want to go or I need to go.

"But it's late." Whak looked out the window at the darkness.

"Got a meeting." Jelli went to get her briefcase. Almost as soon as she was gone, Lino and Jim came into the kitchen together.

"I'm going out," Lino told Whak.

"Well, that makes everybody. You're going out, Jelli's going out, and," he rose to his feet, "I'm going out. Let's all go out."

Jelli has sex with Blue Suit
They all went out.

Jelli went in her new car, a dark grey, low-slung coupe with pseudobiological styling, made predominantly out of plastic. She missed sitting high over the rest of the traffic like a queen in her litter, an expression that always reminded Whak of cats, but the fact was, she could no longer trust the brute invulnerability approach. The new theory was, with all those other cars on the road, constructed out of metal and full of hydraulics and circuitry, the utterly dumb plastic car would be the last thing to be eaten. OK, Jelli thought as she drove through the darkness, but what about at night? There are no other cars on the road. A chewy plastic snack might be better than no snack at all.

She drove faster. She was going to meet Blue Suit and she didn't want to be late. So far this relationship had been a dismal flop, so far as advantages for Jelli went, although the sex was quite enjoyable. She had arranged tonight's meeting, therefore, with results in mind, and what she was most interested in, now more than ever, was what Blue Suit was really up to with his SRM Collection. Why did he have Second Left hand Creature with him so often? Did he really believe in the Advance Force Theory? Jelli's judgement was that he believed in nothing that he hadn't personally tortured to death. Perhaps tonight, with just the two of them alone, she would find out some truth.

The PushRight offices were a twenty-four-hour operation. The GOV1 studio was always busy with programmers, editors, live teams, and so forth, and security and SRM sweepers came out at night to prowl the fire stairs and creep the passageways. The executive floor at this time was near deserted, however, and that was how Jelli wanted it for tonight.

She poured herself a glass of wine and waited. No Allynn tonight. No bodyguards or Second Left hand Creature. She ran her hands over her face and tilted back her head and sighed in a way that was not happy, or sad, or content. The drug of sexual anticipation was more powerful than any of that forebrain stuff.

The elevator gonged, and a few moments later Blue Suit stepped into her office, alone, his protectors left behind in the foyer. Jelli quickly ended up naked, but this time Blue Suit retained most of his clothes. That probably meant something,

something male security related, but Jelli liked it, and said nothing. She put her head back so that her neck extended past the edge of her desk, put her feet on either side of Blue Suit's trousered thighs, and concentrated on enjoying the moment.

She got there first, which meant she had to keep on going, and she got there again, which was great, but she could no longer control the gasping and snarling sounds that were her natural reaction to pleasure. At last, Blue Suit silently expressed himself and, after the correct interval of somnolence, she reached over her shoulder, opened a drawer, pulled out a box of tissues, and cleaned herself. Then she sat up on her desk cross-legged, cool wood against her hot groin. Now it was business. She decided to be blunt.

"We said that we'd start sharing some information."

Blue Suit was straightening his shirt, and while he made the tuck immaculate he did not answer. Once he was happy with his appearance, he pulled one of the visitor chairs over to the desk and sat. As if conducting business with a naked woman sitting on a desk was a daily occurrence, he spoke.

"What did you have in mind?"

"Well," Jelli squinted and tossed her head from side to side as if she had only just thought of this. "We have the Law and Order project that is something of a shambles." Blue Suit looked serious and said nothing, so she went on. "It would help a lot if we had some information on public response to law enforcement. Such as your organisation has. And as you say, you have a huge amount of information on behaviour and crime. What do you do with all that data?"

"We study it," Blue Suit said vaguely. "As I told you, it's classified."

Jelli thought it likely that they used it to threaten and blackmail, but sharing trust doesn't necessarily follow sharing flesh. "We'd like to study it, too."

"Perhaps we can let you have some edited extracts." Blue Suit suddenly switched subjects. "How is the SRM Collection progressing? I saw your advertisements on GOV1."

"It's hitting the right demographic," Jelli said. "There's a poster campaign to follow. What is it really all about?"

Blue Suit sat up and looked at her closely, but he did not reply.

"I don't see what advantage you get from it," she continued, "unless you plan to be a figure in the history books. The man who saved the world - somehow - from the SRM menace."

"I will be a figure in the history books regardless," he said, "but that is part of it."

"So how are you going to do it?"

"I have already told you. We are going to construct test areas with unusually high SRM populations and measure the deviation of aberrant behaviour from our established baseline," Blue Suit recited blandly.

"That's crap. You're up to something."

"Why not assume that I have a genuine desire to save the world?"

"Because the payback for that is too immaterial. You go for instant gratification," Jelli said.

He shook his head. "Not true," he said. "I plan for the future. A future where there is a proven antidote for SRMs."

That was a strange way of putting it, Jelli thought. A proven antidote for SRMs, what did that imply? She sighed.

"So you won't tell me any more about it. What else can we co-operate on?" she asked.

"The SRM Collection is important, Jelli. It is going to make a difference to the world that you cannot possibly imagine."

Jelli hated that expression. "I can imagine most things," she said tartly.

"Can you imagine a world without SRMs?"

"I used to live in one. I can remember it."

"You would like it back. Everyone would like the return of that world. The wealth! The opportunities! The dreams! All that can be restored."

"How?"

Blue Suit leaned back in his chair. "I have, ah, cornered the market, I think is the best choice of words, in a certain field of technology."

Jelli became interested. He was giving her information. That was what this relationship was all about, as far as she was concerned. Bearing in mind the connection with the man Whak had told her about, he had to be referring to nanotechnology. That was what Whak had said. She tried to remember what exactly nanotechnology was.

"So this isn't about behaviour control? I thought not. Then what is it?"

"That information is not for disclosure." He looked her over carefully, his eyes dwelling no longer on her breasts and her groin than any other part of her body. "Now, put some clothes on, Jelli. I have to leave."

She wriggled into her suit and walked to the lift with him. Holding down the door open button, he said "An excellent meeting. We must do this again."

"Yes," Jelli said thoughtfully, "we must."

He left. Jelli waited until the lift indicator showed L2, then went back to her office and sat at her desk.

"I think it's time I learned more about this nanotechnology stuff," she said, unconsciously squeezing one breast.

Whak seeks Assok

At about the time that Jelli was reaching into Blue Suit's trousers, Whak was looking up a certain tree in Coolio Park. Stupid, he was thinking, because the pitfight stadium was dark this night, and there could be no reason for George Assok to be here. He wondered how the people who came in lines like ants to watch the fights, knew not to tonight. Perhaps the power of word of mouth. Jelli would be interested. He fell into one of those trance-like moments, looking up into leaves with cool night air moving gently and the smell of night honeysuckle faintly around him.

"Hmmm," he grunted after a few seconds. "So let's see. We came down out of the tree and went, ah, right." He turned that way and walked across the park towards the dark horizon. Nothing looked any more familiar than anything else did, but that was a state Whak knew and understood. At length, he came to the western boundary of the park, and by walking alongside the high wall he found the gates, unmistakable, big, ornate ironwork that needed paint.

"Entering purgatory now," he said as he gripped one gate and felt it's weight. When he took his hand away, it was brown with rust. Always prone to flight of fancy, he began to imagine that he had died and that these gates were the physical embodiment of his transmigration from the land of the living to the nothingness of death. He had a soft spot for Greek mythology and their implacably physical Gods. Of course, death could never happen to him, or anyone else, because the universe is bounded by your birth at one end and by your ceasing to be conscious at the other, so you can never die. His imagination had him firmly in its grip, however, and he could not escape the sensation that his hand was covered with blood.

He stepped from the world of the living. There was no moon tonight, so the only light was the intermittent street lamp across the road. Whak tried to remember which way Assok had gone from here, at the same time wishing that some form of life would appear to rid him of this feeling of detachment from the earth, and his wish was immediately answered by a resounding thump to his right. Whak was by now in a mental state equivalent to the first man on Mars in the deserted City of Time, and he screamed and threw his hands up in front of his face as if hiding behind his hands was going to save him from the emergence of the Insect King. Luckily for Whak, the sound was caused not by any of the gargantuan arthropods, which he saw in his infrequent nightmares, but by the body of a man hitting the ground after falling off the park wall. The new arrival picked himself up and dusted off his overcoat - a singularly ridiculous garment for climbing walls, Whak observed. Then he turned to Whak and spoke severely.

"If you hadn't hung around this gate for so long, I wouldn't have lost my balance."

Whak wrinkled his eyebrows. "I'm sorry," he said, "but I fail to understand any connection between me, and you falling off walls."

"Never mind," said the other, still dusting his overcoat. Then Whak realised who he was, not by his face or any other feature, but by the way he turned and began trying to climb back up the wall. He leaped and grabbed and scuffled furiously with his feet, like a cat trying to run up sheer glass. He had observed the same technique on the slippery elm. It was Whak's blue suit. Intense curiosity boiled up in him.

"Hey, I know who you are. You're my blue suit. Tell me, how do you feel about spying on people all the time? Isn't it hard to find an ethical justification for what you do? What would you do if you had information that would cause harm to a person?" He had more questions, but his blue suit managed to hoist himself onto the wall. "Give me an answer!"

A puddle of face looked down. This man inhabited the dim-lit distance even when he was in arm's reach. "Well?"

His blue suit whispered fiercely.

"Listen, you pompous wealthy bastard, I don't care if you're taken by Blue Suit and put through the pet food factory. I don't care if you can't sleep at night for fear of me. All I care about is keeping my job. You lazy parasites don't have to worry about that, you don't have to work, you can let your days and years slide by one perfect fucking day after another. And you know what? Your life is a boring life, Puihare. You lead a boring life."

Then he dropped off the other side of the wall, Whak assumed by accident if the curses were anything to go by.

"A boring life," Whak said, slightly upset. "Shit."

He abandoned his search for George Assok, at least for tonight. He went home.

CHAPTER 18

The Alley Party

The taxi took Jim and Lino to one of those social gatherings that had replaced televised entertainment and expensive night-clubs as the scene to be seen. The entertainment was known as alley parties. Alley parties were loud and druggy and crowded and fun. They were held in alleys or streets, either abandoned, or where the residents could be made to go away. The entrance of the chosen street was barricaded with cars and a truckload of amplifiers, speakers and instruments was parked in the middle of the road. Twenty percent of the door took care of the police. An alley party was a good place to dance, to fight, to buy drugs, to flare violently as all around you the world disappeared through it's own arsehole. Whak, who had an interest in stellar physics, had written a poem about this very thing, in large blue writing on the unused observatory building.

> burn your insides to a cinder
> let your balance start to falter
> feel your body start to render
> gravity is getting weaker
> shine a little brightly now.

If Jim of Combine Street, had heard this, he would have neither understood, nor cared about his lack of comprehension. Jim hadn't yet obtained enough of his personal needs to begin worrying about his contribution to the culture. He was rather pleased to be a meaningless component of a decaying machine. It was a vast improvement over being either a Guide, or a SHAman. He was earning big money. He could afford to take Lino out. He fingered his leather jacket proudly, pulled out his new wallet and paid their way into the alley.

When he passed through the gate, Jim looked for faces that he might recognise. He had friends, he thought, among the ex-Guides of ex-Wasteland Tours, but it seemed that none of them could afford to go out, and besides, the alley party was a uniquely criminal occasion. You had to be a part of the ungoverned to be here, or in other words, you had to have enough confidence in the power of the police bribes to accept the risk of being raided, arrested and sent to one of the Centres for Self-Examination out in the dysfunctional countryside. In fact, Jim didn't really consider handling SRMs for the pitfights to be criminal. Or leading groups of uglies into the deserted Wasteland for replacement fighters. Or setting up a favourite for a fall by introducing another, unheard of specimen into the arena. Jim was now working on an 'if-not-me-then-someone-else' basis.

"Let's get a drink," Jim said to Lino. She was observing the crowd and didn't answer. A small stage had been erected at the back of the music truck, and near it about a hundred people were dancing to the sounds made by a dozen musicians. They played shiny brass and polished wood instruments, heavily amplified, and the music had a strong beat and percussion in robot time that sent the cavorters this way and that according to the steps of their dance. Lino was watching them and frowning.

"Whak says that once, everyone danced different dances. All at the same time, " Lino said, pointing. "Now everyone does the same dance." She seemed sad about it.

"Let's get a drink," Jim repeated. He had an idea that Lino could become as hard to understand as her father was unless he kept her attention on simple things. On the plus side, she was beautiful and she had a mind, and Jim felt more of a man when he was with such a woman. As soon as he had enough money from the pitfights to rent a nice place, this courting game could end and they could try their bodies out. The thought of it made him shiver. He decided right then that he would have to risk some bets at the pitfights, on his own team of course, if he was to avoid this constant feeling of readiness in his balls. 'This must be what love is', he thought. 'Testicle pressure'. That didn't diminish it any in Jim's eyes. The bar was set up in the dining room of a restaurant. The window had been smashed out and the broken glass crunched under their feet as they pushed through the mixture of going and coming people around it.

"Beer?" Jim asked loudly.

Lino shook her head. "Whisky," she answered.

"Whisky? It won't be real whisky, you know."

"That's OK." She was watching people again. Jim got the drinks. The infallibly grey sky was long since obliterated by the night. Somewhere near the bandstand a smoke generator was puffing, and a series of projections started floating in the air over the alley. Some were music video and some were advertising

microclips of extreme violence or passion. Jim stared up at them.
"Hey, look at those! Wonder how they got the gear for that?"

"Funds for Government Advertising, probably." Lino glanced up, then away. "They'll be full of subliminal stuff."

"Government? In an alley party? There's no government here, girl." Jim studied the sky, anyway. "What kind of subliminal stuff?"

"You know, pictures of things that they want us to think are good, like, I don't know, people all wearing the same clothes and obeying orders, and then a picture of something we really like, like..." She tapered off. Jim tried to see pictures of naked tits in the sky, but all he saw was a man jumping through a window full of stars and a flythrough of one of the great cities of the past, probably Paris.

"And don't call me 'girl'. The government might not be here, but I'll bet PushRight Creative Media is. She's everywhere." She took another bitter look upwards, and Jim saw that her mood had suddenly moved right to the edge of doom. This changed Jim's attitude very swiftly. He predicted a rapid downhill spiral for his evening's entertainment unless he started to make this lady think about the sound of quakeful music and maybe got her pissed.

"Knock this back," he suggested. He turned back to the bar and ordered again, thanking the pitfights for filling his wallet. When their second drinks were in their hands, he suggested that they go and join the dance, and they were pushing towards it when the smell of drugs filled the air even more solidly than the lights, the music, or the clouds of bad tobacco. Jim put his arm around Lino's waist and diverted her towards a group of laughing men and women who were sitting at the street tables of a pizza place which had been subjugated to the needs of the party. These people were rolling up dope on the red tablecloths and laying out red and white capsules and tiny pink tablets. Jim ignored the pharmaceuticals. Since the economy collapsed, drugs that could be brewed up in the bath had replaced the more expensive tropical imports like cocaine and heroin, but purity and safety were not in the guarantee, and he knew one or two who had popped more brain cells than they had wished. Instead, he went to a table that seemed to be stacked high with joints and began to ask how much they were.

Lino was dragging along behind. She hadn't rejected his hand, but neither had she let herself be pulled any closer to Jim than absolutely necessary. Circumstances of full body contact are important. Because she was an arm's reach behind Jim, when she passed the pink pill table the woman sitting there caught her eye.

"Had a fight, Red?" the Lucy asked. Jim had stopped at the next table, so Lino, who was wearing a red shift, could stay most distant from him, without actually losing contact, by staying at this table.

"No," she replied. She took a sip of her whisky. While Jim haggled over the price of a joint, she watched this woman idly shift a few pills from one side of the table to the other. "What are those?" she asked.

"Hallugics." The Lucy held one out on the upturned tip of her index finger. "Want to try one?" She smiled persuasively. "You'll forget everything but the moment with this."

Lino had never taken anything stronger than alcohol, but then, she had never been to an alley party, and she never had been towed by the arm through a crowd of strangely dressed men and half-naked women either. She was excited by all this newness. She was excited by the fact of Jim and by the touch of his hand on her side, but that also frightened her a little, because she might have to trust him, and she had never trusted anyone before. Except, maybe, Whak. More than anything, though, she heard the words forget everything but the moment. She licked her finger, picked the pink pill off the other woman's as neatly as any practised pill-popper, and tossed it into her mouth.

"You've got to pay for that," the Lucy said sharply, seeing her merchandise disappear. "And now would be good, because in five minutes you might not be able to."

Meanwhile, Jim had finished buying two good-smelling rollups. He turned around and saw Lino handing the Lucy some cash. "Lino! What are you doing? Don't buy that shit!"

"Too late," said the Lucy. "She's swallowed it."

Jim's eyes rolled. "Oh, fuck," he said.

"What's the matter?" Lino demanded. "Can't I do what I want? You want me to come here and go there, and when I want to do something, you say, oh, fuck. Why shouldn't I take something? You're buying dope, aren't you?"

"Yes, but," Jim got no further.

"So you can buy dope, then I can buy dope. What's wrong with that? What's in those cigarettes?"

"Hash and tobacco."

"Well, I don't like tobacco."

"Do you like hash?"

"I don't know."

"But you like hallugics. You like hallugics, and you don't know whether you like hash or not. You've never taken anything like this before in your life, have you?"

For a moment, Jim wondered if he had pushed one of Lino's innumerable psycho buttons. He couldn't get through an hour with her, it seemed, without her turning on a severe sulk or a fit of aggression about something. She didn't answer him straight away. She stared at him. Her face began to change into tears or a smile - there is an instant when it can be either. It turned out to be a smile.

"No," she agreed. "I never have. But I'm glad I did."

Jim shook his head. "You might not be so glad tomorrow when you're still coming down," he said, but Lino wasn't listening anymore. She was eye-scanning, slowly, the whole alley, from the barricade of old cars and rubbish skips across the entrance, to the dead end of the street, where the wobbly brickwork of the apartment buildings towered up until they merged with the sky.

"Isn't everything colourful," she said.

"Shit. It's starting," was Jim's answer. He was almost tempted to turn back to the Lucy and get one for himself, but he resisted. He would have to be straight to keep Lino under control for the rest of the night. She was still looking around. An expression of flicker-eyed glee was gradually taking over her face, a physical disruption that seemed to change her into a different person. She pointed to the dancing swarm.

"Dance!" she said as if it had just been invented, and clearly forgetting her earlier comments. "Yes!" She lifted her arms and waved them back and forth in arrhythmic mimicry of the hundred limbs moving more or less as one, then took off at a fast walk. Jim caught up with her as she pushed her way into the dance. He wished she would press up against him the way she was to the complete stranger that she was trying to pass. The complete stranger enjoyed it. He reached for a handful of buttock, but Jim slapped his arm away.

"Hands off," he snapped. The stranger shrugged. Jim pushed on. In what must have been the geometric centre of the crowd, Lino stopped pushing and danced. It was not at all the dance that everybody else was doing. The top of her body writhed left and right, her arms above her head, and her legs stepped mechanically in a circle around Jim, who, truth be told, was not a confident dancer. He tried to do the same as the people around them.

Hands forward, half turn, hands side, dip, but Lino collided with him, so that was the end of that idea. She was so bright now that it hurt to look. She giggled and rotated three hundred and sixty degrees, half a centimetre away from his chest, then resumed her dance. Jim liked the experience of Lino on drugs, but he was acutely aware that he was no more able to communicate with her than before. As over their heads the projectors enacted a symbolic planetary collision, he began to realise that whatever state she was in, psychopath or snake goddess, he could get no closer to her than her need for distance dictated.

Rainbows of flame flickered stroboscopically. Lino became many different coloured Linos. People around them were starting to notice that somewhere the designated dance steps were not being followed. A gap began to open up, an unpopulated circle that divorced Lino and Jim from the joys of synchronisation. There were disapproving eyes on them. Jim was nervous at this. He knew that the type of people that he had seen as they came in could decide to make violence over another's refusal to keep to the beat. When society was strong and law was powerful, these same people would have danced their feelings of the moment, but now that order was in short supply, they invented the necessary limits to behaviour. Of course, the first rule of survival is never be seen to be different.

The projectors went out. The sky went dark.

The music lost the lead saxophone, violin, and keyboard, leaving only bass, drums, and trombone.

All over the alley party, people froze where they stood in the darkness and wondered what was happening.

Lino kept dancing.

Jim, like everyone else, stopped moving and listened - for sirens - and looked - for police, but there were no such signs. As the lack of police became apparent, fear left and instead angry murmurs arose from all directions. Jim heard shouts from the music truck. The affected musicians shook their instruments in the air and showed by their elaborate gestures that their amplifiers were dead.

"SRMs," Jim said quietly. He turned to Lino, who would spend the rest of the night on another planet. "Every time I go anywhere with you, we have problems with SRMs. Lino?"

She danced.

"Lino!" He was going to pull her arm, but there was something underfoot as he moved and he tripped and fell down on his side on the ground. A pocket calculator activated-deactivated its LCD sensor panel in his face. It was like being blinked at. Jim blinked back. "Oh, great. You're the one who wrecked the music, I'll bet."

He would have lost. He got back to his feet to many screams and shouts and even gunshots, all happening because the blinking pocket calculator was not alone. The alley party was being gate-crashed. From out of the gutters and the gratings and the walls, SRMs were appearing. Jim, remembering the Event and how soft is flesh and how sharp is metal, looked frantically for a safe place, but there were none. He thought he could see nothing as deadly as a spider amongst the varieties that were scattering around the area, but the light was low. All he could really see was people jumping out of the way of small dark shapes with many legs. But this time they were not attacking anything biological. He saw a buzzsaw - now that was rare, and a good potential for his team - coming straight towards them. Fast, rolling on one ball-shaped foot in the heedless, undeviating way that SRMs moved, Buzzsaws usually sliced sections off their prey and dragged the captured limb, tail, or whatever away for disassembly and use. Jim had seen them at work once or twice, and he knew that what their cutting blades were made of was mysteriously sharp and tough. It's blades were out and spinning. Jim could see toes and feet going missing unless he acted quickly.

"Lino!" he shouted in her ear. "Lino! Come with me!" But she was far gone on her trip, now, and her eyes weren't seeing him and her ears weren't hearing him, and when he tried to pull her with him, she unwound from his arm like an eel and threw back her head and rotated her shoulders and spun around again. Someone running crashed into Jim's back and knocked him down again. A lot of people were running, either from the brawl that was in progress by the music truck, or from the SRMs. SRMs frightened people. It was a big part of the appeal of pitfights. They were beginning to frighten Jim, but when he lifted his head off the footpath and saw in front of his nose the buzzsaw, waving its front limbs in the air, twisting and spinning on the spot, keeping a beat, dancing, for an instant the fear he felt was not only of SRMs.

It was of Lino. Her face was turned upwards and the perspective turned her into mostly legs and hips, but when she spun left, the SRM spun left, and when she moved back, so did it. She was dancing with the buzzsaw. It with she.

It was only a moment before his instant of fear was overtaken by a thought. Jim got upright again and in the dark, the shouting and the violence, he knew what he had to do. He had to see Cousin Sinfine, and soon.

CHAPTER 19

Introducing Sinfine

Sinfine was a hard man to see, under normal circumstances. He was, by his own estimation, an important man, on the fast track to the top of his profession, and therefore powerful. He had personally invented (in fact, stolen from a big mouth, bright boy who was now dead) the lucrative pitfight concept, and was in charge of the whole region's gambling business. Sinfine was into retailing. He moved more drugs through his alley parties than most of the more conventional Cousins could by doing wholesale deals with the little bag pushers, and he had the police departments of half the country in his pocket. There was a cloud in his life, however, and the name of that cloud was Blue Suit. Police could be bribed. Blue Suit could not. Police would obey Sinfine, except when Blue Suit told them otherwise.

Sinfine disliked the uncertainty that this always introduced into what should have been a simple and reliable process of making money hand over fist, but the fact was that Blue Suit didn't care for money, or appearances, or any of the other things that usually enabled Sinfine to get a hold over his enemies. He only cared about power, and sad to say he had a lot more of that than Sinfine, or Sinfine's boss, or Sinfine's boss's boss. Sinfine would have liked to have had him killed, but he had weighed the risk of not succeeding on the first try and decided that he was wiser to endure the bastard.

But he wasn't a fool, as he often reminded people, and he knew that good ideas have to be cultivated and stolen when the hard work is done and the moment is right, so he was approachable.

The entertainment business demanded a peripatetic commander, but today he was in residence at his very expensive home in North Coolio, three blocks from where the Puihares lived. It was one of those places where, in the days of finer weather, people lived in and around the vast swimming pool. Now, the grey skies reflected in the water gave the pool area a depressing appearance, but Sinfine was not sensitive to such nuances and gave not a shit for the beaten way his women watched for a glimpse of sunlight as they adjusted their swimsuits around their unnoticeable tan lines. He sat at a table under the veranda and drank iced soda water with lemon while one of his lieutenants flicked through a pile of papers and remarked briefly on each. Then the man stopped turning pages over and reread the paper in his hand, frowning.

"Alley party at Dern and Widmarck got zapped by SRMs," he said after a minute.

"And?"

"And people got pissed off. Demanded their money back, that kind of thing." The lieutenant looked at the piece of paper again. "Gave them free entrance to the next one. Party got cut short, drug and alcohol sales were poor."

Sinfine banged his glass on the table. "I fucking hate those machines! They're like great big fucking insects, and I hate insects. Crawling around. I stay well clear of them. Never know what they're going to do. You hear about the Wasteland Tour thing? They went berserk, that's what they fucking did. I've never been into that fucking place and I never will. Even if the pitfights do make us a packet. How's the gambling take this week?"

"Pitfights are up. Offsite betting is, anyway. At the arenas it's down a bit."

"Down? Why the fuck is it down?"

"I don't know, Sinfine, it's just down. Not much. Just down."

It was not unusual for the pitfight take to be up and down from time to time but Sinfine was perpetually nervous about it. He beat up on all the other Cousins about how great he was to have thought of it and how important he was therefore, and if it ever failed to deliver then he would be the boasting failure, a laughing stock. It was a prospect that Sinfine found particularly awful. Loss of prestige and respect was a dangerous thing in the present age, especially for one as irritatingly arrogant as he, because the chances were that he would then be killed by another Cousin and, worse, the Uncles would just slap the offender gently on the wrist. Naughty Cousin. Don't kill Sinfine again.

So, it was at a vulnerable moment for Sinfine that Jim checked the piece of paper in his hand, looked at the enormous brass numbers bolted to the high wall around Sinfine's home, and began to walk up the driveway. This place was even more impressive than the Puihare's. The house was three stories tall and built of white stone, with a red tile roof that had a couple of circular damaged areas that Jim could see quite plainly. There was a flight of stairs leading up to the door - which was three times taller and wider than strictly necessary - and a dozen tall palms were potted one to a step.

Obviously, like the Puihare's place, the electronic surveillance gear that all these kinds of places used to have was not working, but there were older ways of protecting a property. Jim heard barking.

"Oh oh," he said. He began to run up the stairs. He had just reached the top step when three large, black dogs raced around the side of the house. Jim was never very comfortable with dogs. He pounded on the door while the dogs drew nearer and louder. He saw a doorbell switch and held it down. He tried not to smell afraid.

The door opened just as the dogs were arraying themselves in a growling triangle behind him.

"Yes?" It was a woman in a maid's uniform.

"Ah, I'm here to see Mr Sinfine." The dogs continued to make the sound of an overpowered lawnmower.

"He is expecting you?"

"No. I just came."

"Hmph." The woman looked down at him from her slightly elevated position. What Jim had said might once have cut no ice, but since telephones were not very reliable anymore, and communication technology generally was on the slide, it was now practically acceptable to arrive unannounced at the doors of the rich and famous. The woman snapped her fingers and the dogs stopped growling. "All right," she said. "Come in."

This female, whom he decided must be some kind of personal security guard, took Jim to the poolside. She certainly was no ordinary maid. She made him stand in plain view behind a set of bifold glass doors while she went out to the gaggle of people arranged by the pool. Jim could see that she spoke to someone about him without taking her eyes away from the doors where he stood. He felt a little nervous. He had decided to come direct to Sinfine, rather than try to pass a message up the chain, to his team owner, to the team owner's cut-taker, and so on up the line, for no other reason that he was an impatient son of a bitch. There was just no way that he could sit around waiting for that sort of bounce-around. What was more, he didn't trust anyone else not to cut him out of the deal in some way. If he dealt directly with the top - well, the man at the top couldn't spend his whole time screwing everybody. He had to give credit where due. Or he'd have no organisation left. Wasn't that so? By reciting this argument to himself, Jim mollified his fears. He put on his most confident face as the non-maid came back.

"What do you want?" she asked. Jim realised that she had not asked him previously what he was here for. Maybe knowing things was not safe. Or maybe asking questions was not safe. Jim would have liked to have known which.

"I've got something that'll make pitfight heaven," he said, "and I want to sell it."

Jelli thinks about Blue Suit

Jelli was forced to admit that she had had not a sniff of Blue Suit's surveillance data, and that rankled. Not as much, though, as the increasing mystery of the SRM Collection, or more precisely, the project behind it that needed however many hundreds of thousands of SRMs. Blue Suit had told her enough to make her think that it was probably dangerous and certainly important. Cornered technologies. Saving the world. From her close observation, she felt uncomfortably certain that whatever was going on, the aim would be more to dominate the world than save it. The man who controlled the SRM plague would be a hero, of course, but heroes have a short span in the public eye, and no power whatsoever. Blue Suit's ambitions ran higher than that.

High-tech projects were extremely expensive these days, and no matter who it was that approved Blue Suit's excessive budgets, there was just so much Consortium funding to go around. The word was that next financial year it would be even less. It was a time for centralisation and take-overs. PushRight was on the inner circle of strategy and budgets. If Blue Suit made a spectacular cock-up, then Jelli might even be able to convince the Consortium to put Blue Suit Security Services under her wing. Then the Law and Order project would have all the population and surveillance data she could wish for. So, she hoped that he would fail, but at the same time, she realised that she was going to miss him if he did. He was an arrogant, insular, scheming commissar who shared nothing, but all those epithets applied equally well to her. It distressed her just a little to think that they had such a lot in common.

One thing that she was certain about was that Blue Suit wasn't going to tell her much more. She needed new sources. She needed that George character that Whak had bumped into. She also needed to do some work, she realised with a start, looking at the clock. She picked up the phone.

"Allynn, arrange a contact session with our reaction report squad. For tomorrow. And get me the minutes of the last Law and Order meeting, damn it, I have to find out what they're up to this week. Did you know that young idiot Harrison put forward a proposal that we incite some kinds of petty crime as a safety valve for uncorrectables? My God. I don't care how much sense it makes, it's political suicide." Dukker had probably promoted him in order to look good by comparison. Jelli knew how it worked. She had led a few sacrificial goats to the altar in her time. "Oh, and the last Blue Suit minutes. And this week's management performance reports. And get me everything you can find out about nanotechnology."

Allynn was not fazed. "Is your workstation working, or do you want physical copies?" she asked.

"Physical copies. I can't read anything on my screen, it's lost contrast, or brightness, or something. Get me a new one."

Allynn made a face. "They'll take a while to print," she said.

Jelli took advantage of the while to take a cruise around the office. In the PushRight offices every small team had it's own partitioned work area, some of which were further partitioned into smaller offices. On this floor, the executive floor, there were always meetings going on, some louder than others, and it was when Jelli passed doors that bulged with passion that she liked to step in and cast embers on the flames. If she could find any doors that bulged with passion. Today it all stank of routine. Jelli hated routine. At length she decided to go down to the TV studio and see if anything needed a shake-up down there. She came out of the lift on the TV floor and went straight past the receptionist, who put on a wide but unfeeling smile for her, and pushed open the doors to the production chamber.

In theory, PushRight didn't have any monopoly on television broadcast, but the equipment was serious SRM bait, so keeping the transmitters going required a constant flow of hard-to-get components and cash. Also, Jelli considered that having control of television was so important to PushRight's task of moulding the public psyche, that she had bribed an official to block licence applications. Program production was done in various other locations around the country under constant advisement, but from this building came the news. It might have been because Jelli understood the symbolic importance of a free press that PushRight, rather than Blue Suit or some other intelligence service, was entrusted with it.

In the production chamber were the usual flashing lights and monitors, and the usual line-up of hypertensive videomedia people, sitting and standing, looking over their equipment at a dim window which was as wide as the wall. She saw the head producer look sharply in her direction and away, and she smiled to herself. The cost of keeping GOV1 running was so high that interruptions to a shooting schedule were sackable offences.

She went over to the glass and watched the news reader, a beautiful young blonde woman, they were all beautiful young blonde women, for a minute, making imperceptible nods as the girl rolled off a near-perfect series of subtle emphases that changed the tenor of what she was saying from neutral to slyly judgmental. Neatly done. So Jelli was all the more surprised when the blonde woman said, in the few seconds she had between items "How can I be speaking this bullshit?"

"You do it well," the producer said soothingly into his microphone. "Keep up the good work."

"Who is that?" Jelli turned to the producer and asked.

"That's Elizabeth Furth. Anchor evening news."

"Does she have an attitude problem?"

"She's a Revitalist," shrugged the producer. "If that means she has an attitude problem, then she does."

"She doesn't sound like a Revitalist," Jelli said, looking at her. "And she doesn't look much like a Revitalist, either."

"What does a Revitalist look like?" The producer was one of those who think that all generalisations are inherently wrong, which is one generalisation that is inherently wrong. By their nature, generalisations are usually right.

Jelli played it straight. "A Revitalist looks like a someone who believes in what she has been told, and by what she just said, she doesn't."

"She does a good job," the producer said defensively. It was his responsibility. "She does all the semantics beautifully."

"Granted." The woman was now reading a feel-good piece about a family who had made a new life for themselves in one of the agricultural districts. The more families that could be convinced to leave the crumbling infrastructure of the cities and take up the hoe, the less strain there would be on the distribution chain. Jelli doubted that the public had ever realised how dependent on reliable bulk transportation their sophisticated lives had been, before SRMs.

At length, Jelli decided that she had better things to do than watch the news. She went back up to her office. On the corner of her desk was the pile of papers she had asked Allynn to prepare. She took the thick folder of reports off the top and spent the next hour reading the awful preparations of the PushRight managerial level. It made her worry for the future even more than the latest production statistics, which were included in the employment trends analysis attached to one paper. Surely, when she was a middle manager she had not relied solely on buzzspeak and drivel? It seemed so long ago now that she couldn't remember.

Jelli says Find Assok, Whak!

The next paper was a one-page note authored by Allynn. It said 'Nanotechnology is the applied science of molecular mechanics, involving machines on the order of one billionth of a metre in size. The potential uses for nanotechnology include biomechanics, complex component fabrication, and self-adaptive systems. Nanotechnology research and development has been abandoned for several years. There are no projects extant. The records show that three out of the only four qualified professionals in the field died, of natural causes and accidents, over a four month period in 2018-2019. The whereabouts of the surviving academic, Doctor George Assok, is unknown.'

Clutching the note, and pushing the rest of the pile to the side of her desk, Jelli grabbed her phone and dialled Whak's study line. It rang and rang and rang, as it always did when she phoned Whak. At length, he answered. Jelli always thought that his voice sounded weak and far away when she spoke to him through the telephone, as if he was speaking to it from across the room, which he probably was.

"Hello?" he said.

"Whak, it's Jelli."

"Hello," he said cheerfully. "I've just had a great theme come to me."

"Have you tracked down your mental patient friend yet?"

There was the sound of Whak scratching his head. How he could be across the room when he spoke yet inside the telephone when he scratched his head was just one of those paradoxes involving Whak and machinery. "If you mean George Assok, he's not a mental patient. As far as I know, and he's not my friend, either. The first time I met him he wanted to take biopsies of my cerebellum."

"I'm sure he had very sound reasons for wanting bits of your brain, Whak. But have you found him?"

"No, I got tired of walking around Coolio Park in the middle of the night with only my blue suit for company. Why?"

"I need you to find him." Jelli was surprised by the way her tone gave away her urgency. It was a voice she would never have used with anyone but Whak.

"Oh." He understood. His voice became gentler. "What for?"

"I need to know what he knows. It's very important."

"It's war, is it?"

"Yes." She realised abruptly that it was. A contained little conflict with only two players, but none the less significant for that. The blitzkrieg and the bedroom.

"War is a wonderful antidote for good manners, isn't it?"

"Find George Assok, Whak."

"All right, all right. I'll look for him tonight."

There stands a statue in Coolio Park
Clutching a kipper or a lark
You can't tell which because it's too dark
I thought this was a car park.

CHAPTER 20

Lino exists!

When Whak put the phone down, the first thing he did was go and see if Lino was in. She had been a lot less predictable lately. It used to be Lino in, Lino out, Lino in room, periodic sightings of Lino reported in the hallway, but since she had met Jim, it had become more difficult to tell where she was and what she was feeling. Whak had half a lifetime of controlled drug abuse and all-night parties behind him - much of which he regretted, now, as a simple waste of time - so he had been interested some days ago to see Lino staggering out of her room about three in the afternoon with all the symptoms of being wired out of her skull. Anyone else, he would have asked what they had been on the night before, but because it was Lino he pretended not to notice her bloodshot eyes or when she drank four blacks in succession and claimed that she had seen a cat in the refrigerator.

Today, he knocked loudly on her door. He couldn't resist a good knock. Then he opened it, just a bit, and stuck his face in. Lino's room was in half-light because she always had the curtains drawn, but it was light enough for him to see that Lino still meticulously organised every item and every corner. It was a heartless sort of place, Whak thought, but he knew that lack of heart and too much heart can look very much the same from the outside.

"Lino?" he called.

"What?" she snapped.

He noticed that the bump on the bed was his daughter.

"Just seeing if you were in."

"It's none of your business whether I'm in or not, is it?"

"No, but I have some interest in what you're doing and where you're going."

"Oh yes. Do you have an interest in where Jelli is and where she's going? Do you really think she works late every night?"

"Not every night. Sometimes she's home early." Whak didn't want to discuss reasons if he could avoid it. He knew that Jelli always came home. "She'll probably be home early tonight."

"Huh."

"I might be going out later."

"So?"

"So nothing. Are you going out?"

"Yes. I'm going out with Jim."

"Good!" Whak was still feeling positive about Lino's sudden relationship with a male. But he thought of something. "Oh, Lino. Are you using contraceptives?"

Lino jumped off her bed and rushed over to the door where Whak was standing. He knew that she would find that question offensive, ether because she was and didn't want her parents to know it, or she didn't need to and didn't want her parents to know it. Either way, it was strange for a woman of twenty years of age. So he expected her to shout in his face, or use her fiercest eyes on him, but he wasn't prepared for this. She hit him solidly in the chest with both arms so that he stumbled backwards out the door, which she slammed nearly on his face. Physical action! Lino existed in the world! He was practically delighted.

"Does that mean yes?" he asked the door, but it didn't answer.

Jim takes Lino to Sinfine

Jelli did come home early, so it was unexpectedly appropriate that by eleven o'clock she was the only person left in the house. It was her own doing. First Lino was collected by Jim. Jelli was finishing her dinner when there was a thunderous knocking at the front door.

"Don't we have a doorbell?" she asked.

"Not since the SRMs made a little baby SRM out of the bell housing, no," Whak said, pouring himself a beer. "That'll probably be Lino's young man."

"I don't like him."

"You've only met him for five seconds. Try again. He might improve. I think he's better than nobody at all, in fact he's a lot better than nobody at all. He seems to have a bit of ambition, which is more than most kids, and he actually has a job."

"What kind of job?"

"Ah. Well, I don't know. He used to be Guide, and now I don't know. But he looks like he has a job. He was wearing a new jacket last time I saw him."

"Okay," Jelli said, getting up. "Let's go let him in, then." She walked quickly to the door - the house was large enough that people would be fairly patient, standing there on the top step, but there were limits - and pulled the door open. It was Jim.

"Yes," she said to him. He smiled confidently in reply, at her and at Whak, who was standing behind her so that his head was visible behind her shoulder.

"Is Lino in?"

"Yes," Jelli replied, but she didn't let him in. "What do you do for a living, Jim?"

He was quick on his verbal feet, Whak was pleased to see. He hardly hesitated before he said "Surely you don't classify human beings on the basis of what they are forced by circumstances to do in order to make a living."

"Cut the crap, kid!" Jelli snarled. "That kind of liberal bullshit went out before you were born! Yes, I do classify people by what they do. If you work bars, you're a barman. If you rob houses, you're a thief. What do you do?"

"At the moment," Jim said carefully, "I am an SRM handler."

"A what?"

"An SRM handler. For the pitfights."

"Oh great. A criminal."

"It's not criminal, it's just underground."

In the background, Whak's face was thoughtful. He pushed forward a step. "Let him in, Jelli."

Jelli looked at both of them suspiciously. "Come in," she said ungraciously.

"Thanks."

Jelli stepped back inside. As Jim crossed the threshold, Whak spoke to him earnestly.

"Is it right," he said, "to set SRMs against each other for our entertainment? I have heard it said that they're intelligent, or potentially so."

"Mr Puihare - "

'Whak, please. Nobody calls me Mr." It didn't suit him, that was true. Rather than the gravity and seriousness of a Mr, there were times like now when he had some of the worry and vulnerability of a child.

"I don't know whether it's right or not, but if I didn't do this, I'd be on the SHA, and somebody else would be doing it instead."

"Don't go on, Whak," Jelli cut Whak off before he could start another sentence, because although she was all in favour of interrogating this young punk, it was not his views on interspecies morality that she wanted to hear. She was not sure what it was that she did want, however. While she looked for another question, Lino's voice came bouncing down the hall.

"Is that Jim?"

"Yes, it's Jim," Whak called back.

"Coming!"   She also bounced down the hall.   She was exposing as much of her skin as the temperature allowed around the edges of a loose, scoop neck dress. Her coat was over one arm and her bag over the other. "Let's go," she said to Jim as soon as she came close enough to speak.

"Ah, goodnight, Mr and Mrs Puihare." Jim tried to be polite, but Lino made it difficult. She grabbed his arm.

"Come on."

"What time will you be back?" Whak asked. He always did the clock watching.

"Later. Maybe never," Lino said to him, but she also smiled at him, and he was so enchanted that he just smiled and giggled as she swept Jim down the path.

"You are such a sap," Jelli said from behind him.

"Thanks." Whak was embarrassed.

"I suppose she's got to go out with somebody."

"If she's ever going to build a relationship with anybody but us, she has to."

"I hope she gets along better with him than she does with me." Jelli spoke wryly, but Whak thought there was a wish to be contradicted there, so he did.

"You get along better than you think."

"How can two people get along better than they think? You get along by thinking that you get along."

"Leave the human insights to me, Jelli."

"If you leave the judgement calls to me. And by the way, when are you going to find George Assok for me?"

"Oh shit, Jelli, why can't you hire somebody to find him?"

"I have hired someone to find him, or at least, I've had Allynn trying to trace him, and you know what? He can't be found. He doesn't get the SHA, he doesn't seem to pay any tax, either, not that many people do, and his last known address is, get this, three years old. So you're the only person who's seen him lately." She tapped him on the chest in her intimate way, putting a little lingering extra pressure on each tap and each word. "So find him. I want to know what he knows."

"I saw in him the park."

"Go back to the park."

Whak looked out the open door. The larger stars were just popping shakily into existence in the slightly thinner haze that covered the sky at night. "Too early," he said. "I'll go out later."

"Later?"

"So where are we going?" asked Lino. "And how are we getting there?"

Jim shook his head. She amazed him.

"You'll go anywhere, wouldn't you?" he asked, taking her hand and feeling some surprise that she didn't remove it from his grasp almost immediately. "I thought you'd be knocked down a peg or two by the last time we went out. Taking hallugics, you crazy bitch."

"I enjoyed it. It was much better than what the doctors used to give me. What happened at the end?"

"You don't remember? You were completely off your face, I guess." Jim stopped walking and turned to face her. Lino stopped walking, too. "Lino, have you noticed that every time you get upset or anything like that, then SRMs seem to turn up and act crazy?"

It was obviously the wrong thing to say. Her face grew slightly blank and the air between them chilled instantly. "N-no," she stuttered slightly. "That's not true."

"Well, it is true. Every time I've seen you, something out of the ordinary happens and it's always got SRMs involved in it. You were at the Wasteland when the attack happened. When you were mugged by that chimp, an SRM attacked him right there on the street. SRMs ate your mother's car after you had a fight with her. And at the alley party, while you were too blitzed to know what was happening, another SRM event happened, all the sound gear was wrecked. Why?"

"I don't know." Lino was completely frozen-faced now. She drew her hand sharply out of Jim's palm. "I don't know. It's not me. How do you know it isn't you? You were at all those places."

"I wasn't in your mother's car."

"Neither was I."

"That's true." Jim saw that any further discussion was going to be bad for his plans. He took half a step on his way, half a step back, and hoped she would go with him. "Let's go."

"Where?"

"I promised I'd visit my boss. He lives around here." Jim didn't like telling Lino such an isolated truth, but he was nervous that she might leave him cold if he told her what he had in mind. "Coming?"

She said nothing and she looked daggers, but she followed him across the street and up the hill. She was either on or she was off, and now she was definitely off. When they were approaching Sinfine's abode, Jim thought he had better try to oil her up a bit. He didn't want her walking out of the deal.

"This guy's not really my boss," he started.

"Then who the hell is he and why did you lie to me?" Lino never held her tongue on politeness where her wellbeing was concerned, a trait she probably got from Jelli. "Well?"

"He's the boss of the whole pitfight scene. He's very, very important and if I want to make it big in this business, I've got to get close to him."

"He's a crook, isn't he?"

"I guess so. But people like me don't live the way people like you live. I don't live in a big house and my old man doesn't own two cars. If I want to survive, I've got to do whatever I have to do, and if I have to do deals with the pitfight boss, then I do deals with the pitfight boss. Understand? I want to be a success. How long do you think you'll be seeing me if I go on being a nothing SRM handler?" Jim was unusually forceful, in the way Lino had seen only once before, at the Wasteland, when he spoke about the Centres of Dignity. She felt his anger, so different from her own, as if through a layer of water.

She only said "My mother owns the cars, not my father. My father's just a poet."

"Oh, well, right."

By now they were on Sinfine's driveway. Jim looked left and right and didn't see the dogs, but when they reached the big stairs, there they were again, growling. Jim had not been issued with any special instructions with regard to the dogs. He stepped in front of Lino and said, rather weakly "Shoo!"

The dogs stopped growling and padded quietly away.

"Obedient dogs," Jim said with a trace of his usual bravado.

"Yes," Lino replied. She pointed to a window in which a face was looking through the gauzy curtains. "Obeying that person there, I bet. Let's get this over with. I want to go out tonight."

"Yeah." Jim banged on the door. As before, the woman dressed as a maid answered.

"Here to see Sinfine," Jim said. He glared at the woman. "Again," he added.

"Step inside," the woman waved them in. She closed the door behind them and checked Jim down for weapons. Then she ran her hands over Lino's clothes in the same way. Lino twitched and blinked and looked at Jim, who tried to indicate with his hands that it was all fine and nothing to be concerned about, but he missed the point, of course. Lino wasn't worried about entering a house where a weapons check was part of the way in, but she hated to be touched. Even letting Jim touch her was only possible when she was in her extrovert phase, and although she had been happy enough when they left her home, she could feel herself plunging down the steep side of the rollercoaster. The number of blows to her fragile balance was starting to tell.

"Relax, Lino," Jim whispered to her as they were marched along the corridor.

"Relax," she echoed.

They were led to that selfsame poolside table where Jim had been presented to Sinfine a few days before. The nightfall was well progressed, and Sinfine was sitting there in the bright and shadow cast by the wall lights, dressed in a dark suit despite the dull humidity. He nodded briefly to Jim and looked hard at Lino.

"So this is her," he said. He stood up. He was short. He looked Lino over from hips to hair while she let her vacant eyes slide around him. Jim was about to protest when Sinfine turned back to him and said "Quite a looker."

"I have ears," Lino said. Her voice was flat. "You're quite short."

Sinfine was still facing Jim. He saw Sinfine's eyes became very hard for a moment, then he laughed, a groaning sort of chuckle that did not make Jim feel any more relaxed than before.

"Sit down," he said, and to the maid, "Get some drinks." The maid disappeared into the building and Jim and Lino found themselves seated facing the pool. A big goon who kept patting his jacket as if he was afraid he had forgotten his gun was watching them from under a palm tree, and Sinfine began to get chatty.

"So she drives SRMs crazy, huh?"

Lino said nothing.

"I've seen her do it," Jim nodded.

"I'm going to have to see it, too." Sinfine waved at the goon, who reached behind the palm, brought out a box, and brought it to the table. Jim knew that it was an SRM case like the ones he used at the pitfights, and started to protest.

"Hey, don't do anything with that!" But Sinfine told him to shut the fuck up and the goon put a painful squeeze on his shoulder. Jim tried to warn Lino, but before he could say more than take it easy, the goon knuckle-clipped him lightly on the mouth, which silenced him with surprising suddenness.

"A little test," Sinfine said. He picked up the case and with one quick movement, opened it and threw the contents onto the table. It was a scorpion.

Of course, since the Wasteland, Lino had hated SRMs. Non-receptive though she had been at the time, the sounds of people screaming and the sight of bits of human hands lying in the dirt had left her terrified of ever being near one again. Jim had deliberately refrained from telling her about her little dance at the alley party because he knew that she would sooner distrust him than believe it. Right now, she was encased in glass, but through that glass she saw the scorpion waving it's segmented sensor unit in front of her eyes and with an almost inaudibly high-pitched shriek she fell backwards off her chair.

At the same moment, the scorpion made a dash for freedom. Like a streak of grey ribbon it disappeared off the table and hit the ground between the pool and the floor-to-ceiling windows on that side of the house. The goon ran after it, but by the time he reached the house the scorpion was nowhere to be seen, and he turned back towards Sinfine for instructions. What he saw when he looked back was Jim kneeling beside Lino, who was sprawled on her back with her arms sticking up, and Sinfine, now standing, looking alarmed, and pointing towards the house.

"Look!" Sinfine shouted. The goon turned back. Jim looked up. On the glass before him, a metal butterfly about half a metre across had appeared. The image of a beetle's wings unfolding from under it's shell struck his mind. The butterfly pushed off into the air, failed to achieve flight, and fell down on the head of the goon, who shouted, ran around in tight little circles striking at the butterfly with his hands, and finally dislodged it, whereupon it fell onto the paving. Before Jim could say or do anything to prevent it, the goon jumped up and down on it, pounding it into a pile of metal fragments.

Lino was still paralysed on the ground. Jim left her while he went to look at the butterfly.

"Scorpions don't have wings," he said, half to himself. The goon, breathing heavily, gave the wreckage one last stamp of his boot.

"That was no scorpion," he said, breathing hard. It is interesting how some people, even professional killers, react to the feel of insectoid claws near their faces.

"It's difficult to tell, now," Jim pointed out.

"Well, that was great," Sinfine was taking a sip of his lime water over by the table. "We may have something here."

Jim went back and managed, with the help of the goon, to get Lino back in her chair. She was twitching slightly, now. Jim hoped that that was a good sign rather than a bad one.

"She wasn't supposed to get hurt," he said to Sinfine.

"She's not hurt. She's just freaked out. She'll come out of it by and by." Sinfine studied her with a decidedly sexual intent for a few seconds. "Quite a looker," he repeated.

"It gets worse the more she's upset," Jim was upset, himself, and words were falling out of his mouth without his being fully conscious of them. "Every time, she's been out of her mind or off her face."

"Is that so?" Sinfine smiled rapaciously. "That's interesting."

CHAPTER 21

Jim, Lino, Sinfine @ Pitfight

Lino did come around, after about twenty minutes. During those minutes, Sinfine, sipping his lime water, conjectured about the impact she might have on a pitfight, and Jim wished he had never suggested it. When Lino all of a sudden jerked out a hand, grabbed the edge of the table, and took a deep, noisy breath, Jim jumped to her side.

"Shit, I'm sorry, Lino. I didn't expect this. Lino?"

She didn't go through any confused state this time. She passed immediately from autistic to aggressive. "You cunt," she snarled at him. She saw Sinfine grinning at her like a plastic lips advertisement and pulled herself upright in her chair. "We're still here," she said. Instantly, she became passive again.

"Not for long." Sinfine looked at his wrist. "It's time to go down to the pitfight." He pointed at Jim. "Move."

They were loaded into a smart looking tank of a car. How Sinfine kept the thing on the road was anyone's guess. It was plenty dark, now, and as Jim looked out of the car window there were parts of the world that had sunk completely beyond view into the unifying blackness. Light pollution was a thing of the past. The few astronomers that were left would have been delighted if they could have placed their hands on the great optical instruments of the past, but naturally, pointless exploration of the unreachable universe was, if not forbidden, unfunded. Only radio astronomy was kept alive, just in case the Advance Force Theory had any teeth. Somewhere there were hordes of well-qualified astrophysicists playing rorschach with static. Jim did the same with the shadows.

Lino stared out the other window into the equally impenetrable darkness that existed wherever she looked and wondered why she could not affect her surroundings. Why she couldn't stop bad things from happening. Why she couldn't think, light, and see light. She tried it. She thought, light. The car turned at the gates of Coolio Park, the light of the pitfight rink spilled out like a gaudy fountain and the beam of light that always emitted from the centre shot into the sky. The contrast with the night was sudden and alarming. Lino knew very well that the light was already there before her thought, but she gasped, nonetheless, and fell back.

Sinfine looked back from the front passenger seat and laughed his painful laugh at the sight of Lino cowering away from the window.

"That's where we're going," he said. "Biggest arena in the city. Pretty, isn't it? Looks fucking terrible in the daylight. Take us right up to the gates, Emery."

The goon cum driver, who had now acquired the name Emery, swung the car off the road and began to drive up the wide park walkway. It was not clear of pedestrians, but he let the engine roar a little bit and the group of people ahead leaped out of the way like frightened rabbits.

The big car stopped.

"Out, out, out," Sinfine said impatiently. "The fights are ready to start."

"I should be with my team," Jim said. As soon as he had spoken he felt Lino's cold stare upon him. "Lino, why don't you come have a look at the team rooms?"

"Don't be the fucking clever boy, Jim. She's not here for the tourist trip," Sinfine waved them ahead. Behind them was Emery, and the two door goons were only the advance guard. Jim knew that there were another half dozen large and heavy individuals, with no empathy for the pain of others, patrolling the aisles and the perimeter. He shrugged and followed Sinfine's pointing hand. He had begun to lose faith in his idea, that Lino would spice up the pitfights just by being there, and Sinfine would be so grateful that he would share a portion of the take with him. It sounded stupid even as he reiterated it to himself.

As he entered the arena he observed automatically that it was a good crowd. The seating was full, the aisles were busy, and the odds boards, that were prominently displayed on every available flat surface, were surrounded by punters waving their money. Jim found himself looking for the odds on his team, but he was pushed forward by Emery and into the stairway that led to the private boxes. He had never been up to the private boxes before. He looked back at Lino. Since she had woken after the scorpion episode at Sinfine's, she had fallen back into the lifeless, pointless state that she suffered at the Wasteland. She stopped walking up these stairs every few steps and when pushed impersonally by Emery, started again. Her entire appearance had shifted. Her eyes were dull, her perfect body was now just flesh, and her hair

seemed to have grown heavy. Strangely enough, Jim felt the
reverse happening to him. He was vitally alert. He felt Sinfine's
casual willingness to inflict pain emanating from the back of the
line. He reached the corridor behind the private boxes.

"That one," Sinfine called. "The first one. Go in there."

Sinfine had not actually threatened Jim, or Lino, with any
harm, and except for dumping an SRM in front of them, Sinfine
had not done them any harm. Even the SRM would have caused
no more than a fright for anyone but Lino. It wasn't his fault that
Lino was autistic, schizophrenic, or whatever the hell she was.
But despite all that, Jim had not been able to refuse when he was
pushed into the car, ordered up the stairs, and now he opened the
door to the private box and meekly stepped inside.

'What am I doing?' he wondered. 'Am I going to stand here
while he does God knows what to us?' In the streets where Jim
lived and was brought up, there had been no shortage of violent
crime. There was one in particular that he remembered. The
owner of a tiny tobacco shop, and his entire family, had been
surprised one afternoon, marched upstairs to their equally tiny
home and there one by one murdered in retribution for not having
sufficient funds in the till for the murderer's expectation. Jim had
always wondered why they had all stood there and let themselves
be killed. But of course, he was not in any danger like that. He
was going to be robbed of his idea and just as bad, Lino was going
to have the living shit frightened out of her, if she hadn't already
and if any sort of sensation was going to reach her now.

Emery closed the door. Sinfine went to the window.

"Good view. Need a telescope to see the action, but I don't
give a shit for the action. All I care about is how big the crowd is.
Tonight, it's big. Sit down." He looked out the window again and
when he looked back and saw Jim and Lino still standing, he said
in the same voice, "Sit down, assholes."

Jim sat. He pulled Lino down beside him. The seats in the
box were arranged as if the window was a giant TV, like they
used to make in Japan before it became Mushi-no-esa, SRM-food.
The seats were separate pieces of furniture. Jim and Lino were
sitting on a long sofa. Emery and Sinfine continued to stand.

"I invented this," Sinfine told Jim, lying. He didn't look at
Lino. "It took me right up the ranks. I was a little bit like you,
once, a bigmouth straight off Combine Street. But big difference?
I was smart. You are not so smart, Jim."

Jim wisely made no reply.

"So anyway," Sinfine might have been disappointed that Jim didn't bite, but he didn't show it. "Anyway, I feel, protective. That's the word. I want to protect the pitfights, because that way I protect me. Simple. And you know they say that if you stand still then you're really going backwards."

"So that's where I come in." Jim said.

"That's where your sexy friend here comes in, although she doesn't look so sexy right now. What's wrong with her, anyway?"

"I don't know. She's a bit crazy."

"That's fine. I'm a bit crazy, too." Sinfine smiled. "So, you've told me that she excites SRMs, and we've tried her out, and it looks like you might be right. And then you told me that it happens when she's 'upset'. So we're going to upset her, right here, and see what happens."

"What do you mean, upset her?"

Sinfine ignored the question. "If she sends the SRMs down there into a screaming fit, that's good. The punters love it when the fucking bugs get worked up. Sometimes, don't know why they do it, might be just that day's catch, they are wild, vicious. Yeah, vicious. Never been able to make them do it to order, though. Let's see if your girlfriend does the business."

"What do you mean, upset her?"

"Well, she likes you, doesn't she?"

Jim was horrified to see Emery drawing out his gun. He jumped to his feet. Emery grabbed him by the upper arm and pulled him over to the window. Sinfine pulled Lino up and dragged her over to Jim. She was still in her dangling puppet state. She looked at Jim with no particular interest, as if he was no more or less to her than the sofa she had just left. Sinfine pushed her to the window and made her look out.

"SRMs down there, little girl. Lots of big, ugly, sharp, metal bugs. Crawling all over you. Make them go crazy." He rattled her head back and forth. "Make them hate each other! Make them want to kill each other!"

Jim wanted to say, it doesn't work like that, but he was focussed completely on Emery's gun and couldn't break away. Lino gave no reaction at all. She went on looking out the window. There didn't seem to be any machine reaction in the pitfight ring.

"Okay," Sinfine decided. "Look here." He turned Lino around so she was facing Jim and Emery. "See Jim? You like him. He's going to die."

Emery began to raise his gun.

"No!" Jim shouted. He jerked his arm out of Emery's grip. He didn't know if Sinfine was pushing for a reaction or whether this was for real, but he knew that he wasn't going to stand there and let them kill him just because he couldn't believe it was going to happen. He knocked Emery's gun hand downwards and backfisted him squarely on the nose, which cracked loudly. Emery fell back against the wall with a grunt. Jim took a millionth of a second out to evaluate the situation and decided that for better or worse, he had to abandon Lino to Sinfine. He ran to the door and was out of the box and on his way down the stairs before he heard Emery's voice.

"Stop, you fool," he heard. The next thing he expected to hear was a gunshot, but as he turned down the second flight there was a great roar from the arena, and he heard Sinfine's shout "Shitting Jesus! Look at that!"

Jim didn't have Sinfine's vantage point any longer, but as he exited the door at the bottom of the stairs, he understood just what the shitting Jesus Sinfine had been shouting about. He ran straight into a riot. There was a tide of people roaring out of the arena with all the noise and chaos of a beach-crashing wave. Jim found that he could do nothing but to try and match his speed and direction to that of the crowd. He saw a man lose his feet and become a footpath for a hundred others. He tried to pull the man to his feet as he was swept past, but it quickly turned into Jim's life or his. Before he too was pulled down, he dropped the hand he had grabbed. 'That guy is a goner', he thought. And then, 'what has happened to Lino?'

From the outside, the gates of the arena appeared to vomit out a tumbling mass of bodies, shadows in the darkness, indistinguishable from each other as they expanded like a boiling gas from the opening. Following simple thermodynamic behaviour, they slowed and grouped as their distance from the arena increased, until there were clots of humans drifting randomly about the park, dissipating more or less rapidly towards the perimeter. A few people stopped near the arena, perhaps drawn back because there was someone missing. Jim was amongst them.

Sinfine looked down on the empty arena. Empty except for an occasional SRM, buzzing madly from under a seat, or leaping unexpectedly from a hanging light. Empty except for a few bodies, maybe alive and maybe not, that were either crushed by the stampede or killed by the precise dismantling methods of the SRMs. Sinfine had not been so busy with his threats to kill Jim that he had not kept an eye on the ring. At the start of an SRM match, the two teams of handlers, cheerleaders, and so forth would line up at the opposite ends of the arena with their boxes of bugs piled beside them in the order that they had stated. It was actually a team event, full of strategy, like the incomprehensible English game, cricket. The type of SRM and the size, strength, and speed of the contestants was offset by the cunning of the handlers, who would pit a scorpion or two against one of the new drillhead variety (still Jim's favourite) in order to wear it down before letting a crocodile or a buzzsaw finish it off, or not. That was where the odds came in. It had been the start of a round. The boxes were stacked. The announcer was winding up the crowd and the two handlers were shouting and gesticulating aggressively at each other. Then all the SRMs on the platform simultaneously broke out of their cages. They drilled or cut or sliced through the sides. They snipped their chains. The cages were reasonably effective against SRMs in their normal purposeless state, but they did little to stop them now. The handlers stopped midway through their obscene gestures and the announcer began to stutter. The SRMs did not mill about as animals might have done if released into a strange environment. They moved at top speed in straight lines into the crowd. From the passageway to the handling pens came dozens more. The biggest, best equipped SRMs that people motivated by profit could collect took the most exact direction between themselves and the nearest source of raw materials. Shoes. Bracelets. Watches. Sinfine took binoculars from the table by the couch and through them saw a body with both eyes missing. That's what you get for wearing sunglasses at night, he told himself. Behind him, he could hear Emery breathing loudly through his mouth.

"Get this place cleaned up," he told him. "Get rid of the bodies. Pay the police. Jesus. What a mess. What a fucking disaster." He looked away from the window. Lino was sitting on the couch. "You were advertised as a bomb, woman. Not a fucking nuke."

He slapped her face, hard. Lino's face remained calm.

"You awake? Hey! Jesus. She's catatonic again." Sinfine peered down the front of her dress. "Nice tits," he said. Emery agreed. "Well, I'm not into fucking zombies, myself. Maybe when she wakes up." He had second thoughts. "Or maybe not,

not if she's going to make a swarm of cyberbugs tear my fucking dick off. Jesus. She's got to be good for something."

"Think that this'll screw the fights, Sinfine?"

Sinfine looked angry.

"Of course it'll screw the fights, moron!" He looked thoughtful. "Maybe for a couple of days. I'll turn it around. Real danger. Real excitement. All that shit. But I don't think I'll use her again."

"Not for this, anyway," Emery nodded.

Whak And Assok Up Tree

There were other witnesses that night.

Whak left his home when the bright lights over Coolio Park told him that it was a pitfight night.

"You're mad, Whak," Jelli told him sharply. "You can't wander around Coolio Park in the middle of the night at the best of times, and if you say that one of these illegal gatherings is happening, the park will be full of undesirables. You'll be robbed. Knocked on the head. Killed."

"You want me to find George Assok, don't you?"

"Yes, but in daylight."

"He's not to be found in daylight. Anyway, I go out at this time quite frequently and the worst thing that's happened to me lately is that I've been called boring. After that, being knocked on the head and killed will be light relief."

"Very funny."

"He'll only be out there if there's a pitfight on. He watches them."

"I thought he was a scientist, not a sports commentator."

"He's cataloguing SRMs, I think. Has anybody catalogued all the different kinds of SRM?"

"The SRM Collection, probably. Why?"

"Interesting that Blue Suit and George Assok are both doing the same thing."

"Totally unrelated events, probably."

"And George Assok says that Blue Suit is up to something."

"Christ! I think Blue Suit is up to something! You think Blue Suit is up to something! Of course he's up to something! What I want to know is, what?"

"Calm down. Your hair is starting to thin." Whak opened the front door and sniffed the air while Jelli unconsciously scratched her head. "It's getting cooler," he said. "Well, see you later."

"And when you find him, don't let go until you have answers. Right?"

"Right."

Whak pulled his jacket closed and went. He remembered walks in the night many years ago that had been conducted in the psychedelic wash of the city lights, but as usual only the two streetlamps, at opposite ends of the street, were alive. In contrast, when Whak arrived at the base of George Assok's oak tree, as he thought of it, the pitfight arena was alive with sound and light. People still streamed into the rink. Odds men were shouting and changing their boards.

Whak looked into the tree.

"You up there?" he called. After a few seconds, he thought he saw some branches moving. "Coming up," he said, and climbed. It was an easy tree to climb, if you started on the right side of it, but Whak still managed to bash his head squarely on the underside of the oak's second tier of horizontal arms. "God damn it," he grunted. "Assok! Are you up there?"

"Yes, I'm up here." George Assok's voice suggested that he would have preferred it if Whak now fell to his doom rather than intruded.

"Oh good," Whak said. "Next floor, oak leaves, views of the arena, and mad scientists. Going up!" He struggled his way onto the next level and found Assok perched like a giant owl looking through his videocam out of a hole in the canopy of leaves.

"What do you want?" Assok snapped, taking his eye from the viewfinder.

Whak was momentarily stuck for what he did want. Was he here to help George Assok, or Jelli Puihare? Was to help one to help the other, or not?

"I thought you wanted me to talk to Jelli for you," he said at last.

"That was before I knew that you were being watched by Blue Suit. Are you being watched now?" He looked nervously around the branch.

"Why are you so worried about Blue Suit?"

"Isn't everybody?"

That was what Jelli had said, nearly enough.

"Yes, I suppose so. But Jelli seems to think that you must know something specific. She'd like to take Blue Suit down a peg. Why don't we go and see her?"

"In secret?"

"In our underpants, if you like."

George Assok pretended to play with his monitoring equipment while he thought about it. Before he could make any reply, there came a sudden silence from the direction of the arena. Both he and Whak stared over at it.

"What's happening?" Whak asked.

"I don't know - " Assok peered through the viewfinder and fiddled with the zoom. "Good God. Look!"

"How can I look? My eyes aren't on stalks. You've got the video. What's happening?"

The silence disappeared. A panicky noise, the sound of five hundred people fleeing, scared, from the arena, replaced it. George and Whak watched with puzzlement and a little fear as the pitfight audience exploded. The crowd flowed smoothly but screams and other sounds made it clear that the exodus was not an orderly one. Behind the mass of people, a few buglike creatures were removing the nails from one of the betting stalls as it fell into pieces.

"They went mad," George said a few minutes later, when there were only a few staggering bodies left below them. "They attacked the crowd. They took apart everything even vaguely related to their usual diet."

"I told you. SRMs do attack people. Like that time in the Wasteland."

"And now."

Whak looked grim. "Start of a trend," he said.

"So it seems."

CHAPTER 22

Blue Suit knows Assok

Blue Suit was pleased with the way he had Jelli panting after him like a pedigree spaniel. She was a unique female, obviously hungry for power, obviously caring little for what it took to claim that power. With a streak of humanity, as shown by her attachment to her peculiar husband, but one that didn't surface often enough to be a problem. He felt a surge of pleasure as he thought about her. Powerful women were as powerfully attractive to him as power itself. Having the pleasure of her body satisfied him at a level that a mere tactical outmanoeuvring could never have achieved, and distracted her attention from his real objectives, allowing him to use PushRight resources for the SRM Collection with only the thinnest of explanations. But in spite of that, she was now at least partly aware of the significance of the Collection to his plans. She had excellent strategic skills, and as he didn't trust her yet, he would have to begin making precautionary plans. He thought that later, he might make Jelli a more permanent part of his life. Strange sensations writhed in his chest, but he didn't recognise them. He wasn't on a first-name basis with his heart.

Today he intended to make an inspection visit to the pseudonymous SRM Collection Program, which was the vehicle for his plans to join the ranks of history. He had not been to the project station since shortly after it was commissioned. First, though, he had reports to review. He let his office administrator know that he wanted the daily update.

A few minutes later, the Chief of Observation knocked politely on the office door. No-one ever walked in on Blue Suit without knocking, for the simple reason that it was impossible to guess what he might be doing. Even if the arrival had just been sent for, Blue Suit might have taken the intervening moments to place a call to one of the invisible Consortium politicos over whom he had the power of ruination, or one of the spies he had watching his spies might have been ushered in ahead. Not today. Blue Suit pressed the buzzer. It was a device he had always admired when he had been a pupil in a corrective boarding school and always getting into trouble. He would be sent to wait outside the principal's office, the door of which was always shut. He would stand there for what felt like hours, wondering whether this time he was going to escape with just a verbal or whether he was to be beaten. Then there would be a buzz and a light on the wall by the door would glow, and he would have to go in and meet whatever his fate was to be that day.

He considered now that all that terror had done him good.

"Observation report, sir," said the man on his carpet. He looked eager. He had some news.

"Today, spare me all the statistics on nationwide absenteeism, drug dealing, and anarchist guerrillas. We know all that. You look constipated. What is it?"

"George Assok, sir. He's been seen."

Blue Suit looked slightly constipated, himself, at the name. "Where?" he asked.

"In this city, as a matter of fact. The Coolio Park area, sir."

"Who saw him? What duty were they assigned?"

The Chief of Observation looked at his documents. "He was seen by the observer assigned to... eh,"

"Who?"

"Whak Puihare, sir." The Chief of Observation pronounced it 'whack'.

Blue Suit sat motionless for long enough that the Chief of Observation wondered if he wanted the next report. "Sir?"

"Be quiet."

So, Jelli had found George Assok, the missing scientist. How she knew about his importance was baffling, and would have to be discovered. And, she was using her own husband as an operative. How charmingly ruthless, he thought. She had depths. This could be the start of what might be a long and interesting conversation. He felt a pang, however, that, in spite of their time together, Jelli had chosen to be his enemy.

"Collect him," he said. "I want him."

"What about Whak Puihare, sir?"

Strictly speaking, being in the company of known criminals, even arbitrary ones like George Assok, was reason for detention. Blue Suit decided that arresting Whak now might allow him to appease Jelli, later, by releasing him, and was therefore worth doing.

"Collect him as well."

"Isn't he the husband of the PushRight CEO?"

"That is not your problem," Blue Suit told him coldly. "Collect him."

"Yes, sir."

The Project Station

As soon as the Chief of Observation left, Blue Suit made ready to inspect the Collection Project. First, he rang Sedric Colville at the project station. The phone line crackled violently as if it was being chewed by a hoard of electronic termites, which might well have been the case.

"Everything is going very well," Colville said, excitedly. He always sounded excited when he was surrounded with millions of dollars worth of hard-to-get technology. "We're conducting an isolation test today. My designs look very promising. They should do everything you've asked for. Replication fidelity is still a problem at the moment," he added as an afterthought, "but I expect to solve that in the next few months."

"I'm doing a site visit," Blue Suit told him.

"Today?"

"Yes."

"Oh. Yes. Very good." His voice became overly agreeable. "Should I postpone the isolation test?"

"Is it dangerous?"

"Oh, no, not really," Colville hastened to assure him.

Blue Suit disliked Colville intensely, not least because he was so easy to frighten. "Postpone it," he said arbitrarily. "I want your attention while I'm there. I don't want to be standing around while you scream at your computer."

"Oh. All right, then."

"And I want to inspect the holding pens. There have been some unusual SRM events lately, and I want you to be able to prove that the pens are escape-proof."

"They're escape-proof. I designed them!" Colville said, peevishly. "The electrostatic containment field is over twenty kilovolts when fully charged, and it has multiple redundant power supplies."

"Be ready. I'll be there in an hour." He put the buzzing, whistling handset down and straightened his jacket. He never took his jacket off, even though it meant sitting bolt upright so as to avoid wrinkles in the back. What was a Blue Suit without a jacket? He took the elevator to the underground car park and was met there by the usual bevy of protectors. No-one had ever tried to kill him that he was aware of, but he preferred to take no chances, and he had found it useful on several occasions to have a small private army around him. He and his army rode out of Blue Suit Headquarters in their huge black cars, the image and the purpose at one with each other.

The project station was a secret, if not a very well-kept one. There had been rumours for years that there was a government research laboratory hidden in the Wasteland somewhere, and for the first few years it had been only that, a rumour. When Blue Suit had first conceived the ideas that he was now sure would solve the SRM pestilence and make him instantly one of the most powerful men in the world, he had moved quickly and silently to construct a facility exactly where common knowledge said it was already. Because no-one had ever found it there, when it was not there, he deemed it unlikely that anyone would bother to look again. He had overlooked the existence of Wasteland Tours and their Guides, who made it their profession to prowl the Wasteland in search of good spots for tourist thrills. Even so, no Guide had ever found Blue Suit's facility, but fleets of big black cars arriving in the dead of night and sitting under guard for hours on the opposite side of the street were a dead giveaway. It had been Jim, in fact, who had started a sweepstake on who would locate the mysterious place first, but the matter had never been settled.

The cars drew up, as usual, on the other side of the wide road from the Wasteland.

"Way is clear for you, sir." Blue Suit's situation controller, his senior protector, opened the door on the pavement side. Blue Suit got out, walked quickly to the utterly decayed pile of bricks that still resembled a tenement or some other kind of building and entered it through a hole shaped like a door. There were what all senses suggested to be seriously unsafe stairs leading to the basement. Blue Suit tramped heavily down. The stairs were probably the strongest part of the entire building, having been replaced and then camouflaged at great expense to look as uninviting as possible. At the bottom of them was a shambles of fallen masonry and other assorted crap that made progress impossible unless you knew where to walk in the darkness, but Blue Suit and his cronies did know and were not dismayed, and finally, there was a very impressive door, three metres high and two wide, knobbled with ship rivets. They all passed through after a brief password exchange through a grille, and a degree of pushing and shoving when the hydraulics failed to operate. Now they were in a smooth-walled tunnel under the road between the blocks of disused slums and the Wasteland itself.

One day, the Wasteland might reach out and encompass these gangrenous parts of the city. Blue Suit did not consider it likely only because he could imagine no mechanism by which it could happen, as junkyards grow by accretion, and the Wasteland was no longer a permitted dumping ground, but he had forebodings, none the less.

He came up out of the ground into the project station. The Lab, as Colville always called it, but it was far more than a laboratory, even more than a multi-million-dollar one appointed with enough computer power and technical manufacturing capability to provide a complete experimental environment for dozens of technicians. It was Blue Suit's alternate headquarters. It had office space and communication gear for all his essential personnel. It was buried under the surface of the Wasteland, and even Blue Suit could not have said exactly where. As he entered the station, Sedric Colville broke away from an animated conversation with an arm-waving woman in the compulsory boring white lab coat and hurried over.

"Welcome," he said unnecessarily, as if all this was his and Blue Suit was a visiting venture capitalist. "What would you like to look at?"

"Everything," Blue Suit answered. "But first," he continued while the other's face grew alarmed, "I want your personal report on progress." He snapped his fingers and pointed. "Into my office." He had an office here, reserved for his use. Colville babbled about how he had not had enough notice of today's visit and how his report wasn't ready or complete and how there were many technicalities, which he would have to explain to the ultimate boredom and non-instruction of all, and that the latest designs were still being refined and the modelling computer had been upgraded and all his files had been lost. By the time Blue Suit, his protectors, and Colville were in the office, he seemed to have run dry and stood blinking and scratching his arm until Blue Suit brought him back to attention by drumming his fingers slowly on the desk, twice.

"I prefer your reports to be a little more structured, if you don't mind," he said with no trace of politeness. "Begin again."

Colville took a deep breath, saw Blue Suit frowning at him, and managed with an obvious effort to restrain himself from another episode of babblemania.

"Yes," he said instead. "Very well. Ah, this will be somewhat summarised."

"Good."

"We have completed the tests of the prototype design 8 version 211."

"And?"

"It is extremely effective at SRM neutralisation. It exhibits excellent self-reprogramming capabilities, identifying the difference in composition between any given SRM variant and adapting it's deconstructive radicals accordingly," Colville said in a voice that should have been smug, but Blue Suit knew from his tone that there was a bad news part to this story.

"But?"

"Ah. Well, like the others, it has an unacceptably high mutation rate. It is proving to be a very difficult to strike the balance between adaptability to multiple compositions, and uncontrollable and eventually fatal mutation of the nanovirus."

"So you are doing what?"

"Well, according to Elbe's theorem, there is a self-cancelling but infinitely recursive construct similar, in fact, to some of the well-known chaos sets, but unrelated, which... " He noticed the fingers beginning their drum roll again. "We're trying a governing mechanism which will cause the mutations to cycle through a limited number of variations."

"Good, " Blue Suit nodded. "The problem is solvable, I take it?"

For once, Second Left hand Creature managed to assume an air of dignity. "All problems are solvable, given the right approach," he said clearly. "Of course, access to the work of others would speed the process."

"The work of others is not available to you."

Colville returned to his impersonation of a scared rabbit in the spotlight of Blue Suit's eyes. "Of course not. We can manage perfectly well without him. He probably has nothing of value to contribute, anyway."

"Perhaps. Now, I would like a look at the design workshop and the testing procedures."

"Why? I mean, of course. Is there anything in particular that you want explained?"

"I'll think of some questions," Blue Suit smiled. "You think of some answers."

While Blue Suit was getting the guided tour of the design workshop, which bore no resemblance to a workshop of any sort, but was rather a large room full of desks on which workstations were surrounded by piles of paper and disposable cups, he made a point of providing motivation. In his terms, this meant threatening dismissal, disciplinary action, and unpersonhood on Sedric Colville at every opportunity. When he stepped into the workshop, the sound level diminished steadily from the moment he was recognised until within a few seconds of nudging and whispering the entire room was silent.

"Ah, the workshop," said Colville. "Everyone, we have a surprise visit from the director of Blue Suit today. We'll be just moving around the room for a few minutes. Please go on with whatever you were doing."

They obviously didn't. The silence continued as Colville and Blue Suit went from workstation to workstation. At the first screen, a blond young man with a terrible squint was using his mouse to cut squares out of what appeared to be a circuit diagram and drop them onto another window.

"What is he doing?" Blue Suit asked.

Colville moved his jaw around as if winding up for speech. "Well, he's pulling small sections of the nanovirus design out of the entire plan. The other window is a runtime simulator. He can run logic checks and regressions on the piece of the full design that he's working on, amend it, and put it back."

"Is this the isolation test you were talking about?"

"No, no. An isolation test is an actual physical deployment test. In the isolation chamber. We can go there next."

Blue Suit watched the squares of nanovirus being moved around. "Is it safe to work on parts of the design like this? The whole is always an unpredictable assemblage of parts. What happens if the behaviour when tested alone differs from the behaviour when complete?"

"Very good point." Colville was surprised at Blue Suit's acumen, and showed it. "And in fact that's exactly what happens. Exactly. Computerised simulation testing doesn't actually correspond to the behaviour of the physical nanovirus, there are discrepancies. It's a case of if we knew everything that could go wrong, we wouldn't need to do physical isolation tests. Do you want to see one?"

"No. I haven't time. But show me the procedures."

"Of course. Ah, this way. Okay, everyone. Thank you."

Colville took Blue Suit and the two protectors, who were never more than a step behind, back past the entrance and through a pair of wooden doors. The doors were at least half a metre thick. Blue Suit glanced at them significantly, but Colville was insensible to any visual prompts. Blue Suit had to ask him outright. He slapped him on the shoulder with the back of his hand.

"Why are the doors so thick?" he asked.

"Organic material. Wood." Colville always fell into an uninformative staccato pattern of speech when faced with unexpected questions, no matter how harmless.

"I can see that."

"I, I mean it, the nanovirus is nonorganically biased. Which means," he added quickly, "which means that it will only affect nonorganic materials. Metal, silicon, and so forth. It's made of those materials. It won't reproduce without access to those same materials. It's targeted for SRMs."

"So the doors?"

"Well, in the unlikely event that the nanovirus escapes the isolation chamber before we think it's ready, this whole area is lined with wood. Organic material, you see."

Blue Suit looked at the ceiling and the walls. They could have been any material. They were painted grey. "So we're already in the isolation chamber," he said.

"No, no. This is the safe area. The isolation chamber is at the end of this corridor." Colville went on walking. Blue Suit asked him one more question.

"And if the nanovirus does escape into this area, what then?"

Colville stopped walking.

"It is extremely unlikely," he replied with a faint hint of determination. "If it did happen, we have a deactivation agent. We expose this area to the agent, the nanovirus shuts down."

Blue Suit was satisfied. "Good," he said.

They moved on. At the end of the wooden corridor there was another pair of doors, and then a large room, in the centre of which was a tubular object which nearly reached the ceiling. The left wall was a lattice of SRM enclosures resembling a post office delivery box system, for those who remembered such things, except the boxes were bigger.

"SRM enclosures," Colville said, pointing at them. "Only one of each type is kept here at one time, because of space requirements more than anything. Duplicate specimens are kept on the next floor down, in similar cages. We have over forty thousand SRMs at this station now. PushRight's scheme is supplying several thousand more a week. Really, we have an oversupply."

"Then destroy the excess common types," Blue Suit told him.

"But there are thousands coming in per week! Couldn't we tell PushRight to call off the collection?"

Blue Suit sighed. Technical people could be so short-sighted, even in their own areas of expertise. "No. The objective is to collect one of every type. New types arise frequently. How are we going to be sure that the nanovirus is effective against all types if we stop the collection? By the time we release the nanovirus, there could be any number of new varieties which are immune to it or which have unpredictable reactions to it, and the objective is not to slow them down. The objective is to wipe them out."

"Of course, of course."

There was another reason why Blue Suit wanted a large number of SRMs under lock and key, but Second Left hand Creature had no need to know of it. When he had cleared the planet of SRMs and was feted everywhere as the saviour of technological society, when he had been elevated by the collective gratitude of the mankind to the sort of power he deserved, then a secret supply of SRMs would be a wonderful way of maintaining his position. When a few inexplicable SRM outbreaks occurred across the country, who would be able to dispute that in order to protect civilisation against reinfection, he required total executive power? No-one would know that it was he who had caused the outbreaks in the first place.

Of course, to maintain the secret, a number of untrustworthy and irritating people would have to be dead, but that was the price of order.

CHAPTER 23

Whak and Assok are Chased

"Let's get out of here," George Assok said abruptly. He swiftly packed up his observation equipment. "Come on," he said to Whak.

"Where?"

"We'll go back to my place. We need to talk."

The night was silent, now, except for occasional engine music from the road surrounding the park. The brilliant lights of the arena accentuated the depopulation by illuminating the emptiness.

"We're not even going to be able to get out of this tree in secret," Whak said. "We'll be the only moving things in sight."

"Just follow me. I've had years of practice at this."

"I meant to ask you about that. Why are you so paranoid about Blue Suit?"

"I'll tell you," George Assok hissed, "when we're safe."

Whak thought they were pretty safe at the top of the oak, but he signalled his okay. Assok slipped silently down the back of the tree, the side facing away from the arena and it's pitiless brightness. Whak followed him into the shadows. They crawled into a garden that ran alongside the path. Only old men with nothing else to do tended these gardens now. Often enough, Whak had seen liver-spotted, trembling gardeners walking in their ancient bliss around Coolio Park, stopping here and there to pull a weed or snip a branch with the secateurs that they all seemed to have in their trouser pockets. He wished they got right in and cut tunnels, because all the dead sticking-out wood was scratching his face and risking his eyes. After Whak's knees had become sore and dirty, George Assok decided that they were far enough away from the arena to emerge.

"That was less fun that I expected," Whak said as they stood up.

"This is not a game, Puihare."

"What is it, then?"

"It's life and death. My death. I don't want Blue Suit to find me."

They walked, not on the path, but from garden edge to garden edge.

"Why not?" Whak asked. He received no answer. "Aren't you ever going to tell me anything?" he demanded. He heard a sound from the emptiness behind them, telling him that it was not as empty as it appeared. "Did you hear that? Someone's nearby." As he finished speaking, three beams of light suddenly sliced the night into pieces of blinding candlepower and glistening colours. It switched off Whak's night vision completely. When the lights swung away from them he was left standing in a field of pulsating purple. The lights swung back, sought them out and pinned them to the night. Someone shouted.

"You two! Stop where you are!"

"Run!" Assok pushed Whak in the direction of the park walls. "Run!" He took his own advice. He dropped his equipment and sprinted with surprising speed away from the voice. Almost immediately, Whak heard several strange popping noises, which, he decided after a second, were gunshots. "Run," he said to himself, and he did. He took off in the same direction George Assok had taken. He heard some more popping noises and the python of fear rose up in his throat to choke him. He gasped for air and his body went on running while his mind observed with interest that animal reflexes still seemed to have all the necessary strategies for survival. He ducked and weaved and kept low as he ran twice as fast as he thought he was capable after the dim shadow of Assok.

The gunshots became fainter.

After a minute, Whak caught up with Assok at the wall of the park. He could hear feet pounding the ground somewhere behind, mixed up with his own heartbeat which pounded louder in his chest.

"Over the wall!" Assok whispered. He motioned for Whak to make his hands a hoist. He climbed up on Whak's clasped hands and counted aloud "One, two, three." At the count of three, Whak propelled him skywards. He looked up at the top of the wall. Assok sat across it, outlined in orange by the faint street light glow.

"Come on!" Assok reached down. Whak jumped, grabbed, and Assok hauled.

"Stop!" shouted their pursuer, or pursuers. Whak was less interested in the numbers than the fact that he was being shot at. He had no intention of stopping. He threw his body across the top of the wall, across the broken glass imbedded in the concrete, flipped his legs up and kept going.

Jim follows Sinfine

At about the same time, Sinfine was leaving the pitfight arena. He stood by his car as Emery carried Lino out of the arena as if she was a shopfront dummy, under his arm. He manoeuvred her head and shoulders through the rear driver's side door and pushed her into a roughly sitting position.

"I can't believe this fucking woman is so much trouble," said Sinfine as he climbed into the front. "And I can't believe you let that little twerp get away." Jim was bigger than Sinfine, in fact, but Sinfine referred to anybody less powerful than himself as little. "Let's get this bitch back to my place and send somebody out here to bury the bodies."

"Yes, sir," Emery answered snappily. He did not think this a good time to act even slightly equal with the boss. He turned the start key. There was no responding burble of petrol power. He tried again. Nothing. The car wouldn't start.

Rubbing his nose where Jim had dented the cartilage, Emery opened the bonnet, got out of the car and went around the front to see what was the problem. He shone a small torch into the engine compartment. It was unusually full of empty air. SRMs had removed the fuel injection system, all the electrics and the aircon.

"Uh, Mr Sinfine," Emery said hesitantly.

Sinfine's shout of anguish echoed distantly around the acoustically designed arena. It attracted the attention of what was probably the only other person left in the park. Jim peered out from behind one of the abandoned odds boards that were leaning on the side of the arena and watched Sinfine striding away in obvious anger, with Emery and his mannequin burden struggling to keep up. He withdrew back into the darkness and took several deep breaths, trying to draw up as much of the illusion of safety that existed in this hiding place as possible. When he left here, he was going to be in serious danger. How could he have been stupid enough to believe that a man like Sinfine would share anything with a nobody like himself? From what Jim had just seen, Sinfine would far prefer killing to sharing. So to actually think of following him was inviting a high risk of death. Jim was stricken thoughtful by the fact that he was going to follow Sinfine anyway. Because of Lino. God damn her. He waited until the sound of Sinfine cursing Lino, SRMs and Emery was distant, then came out of hiding and, taking infinite care to remain silent, he pursued the beacon of Sinfine's voice, across Coolio Park, out onto the north side, and through the dark and silent streets to the gate of Sinfine's mansion.

There, he decided that to venture any further would be foolhardy in the extreme. Instead, he crossed the road, located a suitably bushy tree, and climbed into it. From there, he could observe Sinfine's house and all that came and went. Jim figured two things. That if Sinfine was going to kill Lino, he would have done it at the arena, and that if he was going to keep her alive, he would sooner or later want to move her from his house. Jim settled down in as comfortable a position as he could and prepared for a long wait.

George Assok's Story

When Whak hit the ground he was momentarily stunned, and when George Assok jumped down almost on top of him, pulled him to his feet, and shouted in his ear, he felt no particular sense of urgency.

"Run! Run!" George shouted at him, pulling him along and waving his pointing finger across the street. "Come on! Run! This way!"

"I need practice at this," he told Assok.

"You need to RUN!"

From behind them came the grunting and scrabbling sounds of large, heavy men climbing the wall. Whak blinked and all the adrenaline that had evaporated with the relief of finding himself still alive, if dazed, on the concrete footpath rejoined his blood and accelerated his brain. He ran. He and George Assok crossed the street, took the first available exit and ran on, further, until they were sure that there was no pursuit. They had come to a section of South Coolio that was utterly uninhabited except by SHAmen and rats, a mini-Wasteland piled high with the wreckage of a lifestyle passed into oblivion. Whak stared into the darkness. If it hadn't been for a moon somewhere, the exact position in the sky was impossible to tell, the clouds diffused the lunar glow, he would have been blind.

"Where are we?" he whispered.

"I know where we are," Assok replied at the same volume. "I often come here. There are SRMs here."

"There are SRMs everywhere," Whak scratched his cheeks. His unshaven skin rasped so loudly that he cringed. Assok's eyes flashed rather whiter than Whak expected. George was so easily upset.

"Actually, SRMs are not everywhere. They congregate in areas of high material availability and low exposure. Like the Wasteland, and here, and in underground pipelines and the like. And always near, but not too near to high density human populations. Follow me. We'll go back to my place."

"Who were those people chasing us?"

"Blue Suit, almost certainly."

"Why would Blue Suit chase us?"

"I doubt that they were chasing you," Assok said sharply. "They were chasing me."

"Oh, well, congratulations. You must be honoured," Whak snapped back. The experience of being shot at for the first time in his life had given him an uncontrollable excess of tension, which he converted smoothly into sarcasm. "So why are they chasing you?"

Assok began to walk, Whak had no choice but to follow before he vanished completely into the night. "Well?"

"Well what?"

"Why is Blue Suit chasing you?"

"I really don't know," George said evasively.

Now that was too much for Whak. "Bullshit!" he said loudly. A strange thing about uninhabited buildings is that they echo much more than the same buildings would if alive with families and businesses. The open faces of broken glass seem to suck sound into a complex wave tunnel and spew it back with doubled force. Whak's voice resounded up and down the street.

"Quiet!" Assok hissed. He kept walking. After a moment, he spoke again. "I told you I used to work on an nanotech research project."

"And?"

George Assok was just as likely to use mathematics as physical engineering to prove and disprove his suppositions, since the world of physical things became a little blurred at the scale of nanomachines, and both quantum mechanics and cosmological theory began to play a part in understanding what could and could not be. Nanotech could do to the physical world, what electronics had done to information processing technology, which had moved from books filled with symbolic characters to silent cubes of aligned molecules. Nanotech would take the manufacturing industry from brute casting and shaping of metal and plastic, to a degree of control over the physical universe previously unimagined except by the undisciplined dreams of fiction.

Assuming that a number of difficult questions could be answered. Energy supply was a problem. A clade of nanomachines designed to draw power from ambient kinetics had been a failure, although they might be a good basis for a refrigeration system. George was now trying visible radiation as an alternative, stealing a few quanta from the low and high ends of the spectrum. He could have produced a cloud of darkness, if he'd wanted to, by widening the frequencies to be tapped. Programming new nanomachine behaviour was, in effect, designing new types of machines, and the more complex the objective, somehow, the more beautiful and strange the machines became.

George was well known throughout the nanoresearch community. He was thought by most of his peers to be brilliant, probably without equal. Most of this lustre was the reflection from his greatest contribution to the field, the nanoconstructor. George had developed a system which allowed nanodesigns to be directly translated into reality, via a simple computer interface to a fantastically unsimple device the shape of a shoebox and about half the size. George had spent over a year hand-building the thousands of stable, non-motile protonanos inside the shoebox. Under the electron microscope, they looked like a colony of sponges, bulbous clusters of metallic ions at their heads, single strands of gold atoms connecting their roots. They were attached to a wafer of silicon which had, etched into it's surface, a powerful set of parallel processors. All that computing power did, was turn whatever instructions came in the port on the side of the shoebox into environment modifiers for the nanos, points of electromagnetism, angstroms across, at which scale their behaviour became almost monopolar. George had to have help in building the program on Smalltech's modelling system. In fact he'd had lots of help. Simulation programmers, VLSI designers, electronic gurus, all kinds of skills had been needed. But in the end, it was George Assok's creation. The nanoconstructor was able to produce a physical implementation of practically any design you might wish to download, as long as you followed the Assok API. It had changed the game from one of time and painstaking manual effort to one of conception and imagination.

Right now, the nanoconstructor sat idly in the controlled room where physical tests were carried out, while George used the simulation interface to guide the development of features he wanted the next generation of nanomachines to possess for their paltry twenty or thirty iterations before they broke down and became an undifferentiated cloud of complex molecules. George was as happy as he had ever been in his life, even if all this was so confidential that he wasn't allowed to visit his own dentist for fear that under the influence of nitrous oxide he might let something slip. Now he could forget about the painful task of building nanothings and concentrate on the exciting part, making them work.

In spite of the secrecy surrounding the nanoconstructor, he was allowed limited liaison with senior people at other companies working in the field, even the military, although the military budget was meagre. Most of their money was spent attempting to SRM-proof their installations, planes, ships, missiles, and the like. A few carriers floating aimlessly around the Atlantic without navigation or engine control showed that they had their hands full.

SRMs were wearing down the civilian industrial complex, as well. When some of his esteemed colleagues began to drop out of sight, he assumed at first that their projects were being closed down. The man he knew at the giant software company, for example, well, software needs computers to run it on. The SRMs had cut the number of personal computers in the world by ninety-nine percent. George wasn't surprised when that company went belly-up.

But George wondered enough, and felt enough of a gloat that he was not they, to call up one of his more respected friends for the gossip on the failed projects. He sat on his tall lab stool and after two or three noisy disconnections - what was happening to the phones these days? - he made contact with the reception.

"I'm sorry, but John Firely no longer works here," he was told.

Surprised, George asked where he had gone.

"I'm not able to give out that information over the phone," the reception told him, but there was a human inside the regulations as it turned out, because he added "but he isn't working for anybody. He died."

"Why?" George asked.

"Why does anyone die? He dropped dead. Heart attack, they said. Thank you for calling." Click.

John Firely dead of a heart attack. That spelled the end of that company's nanoresearch, for without John they were rudderless, just as Smalltech would be, even more so, he told himself, rudderless without George Assok. John had been a brilliant theorist. He had made some fascinating hypotheses about the statistics of order in noncommunicating groups. Wrong, but fascinating.

Not a man to waste time on sentiment, George turned back to his workstation and focussed his mind on replication fidelity. It had to be overcome if there were ever to be mass production nanomachines. But it nagged him, the death of Firely. And he had not had any answer to the closure of the other projects, staffed as they were by idiots, but nanotech projects nonetheless. If there was a reason that nanotech projects were being abandoned, he should find out about it. This one might be next on the list. Forewarned is forearmed, and so on and so forth. He shrank the simprog he was training, looked up a number on his contact manager, and picked up the phone again.

A few minutes later, he put it down. His acquaintance at WestLibVar was also dead of a heart attack. That was an improbable coincidence. He thought about it in a disbelieving way for a few seconds, then went back to teaching his simprog to differentiate between broken and working p-junctions. People die of heart attacks all the time. Academia and edge research make for stressful lives. Poor colleague at WestLibVar. What was his name again?

Another day, he had this difficult problem in transtensor math, which was a discipline in which the young Senior Academician Ortlovoksky in Boston, was unexcelled. That was a long-distance call, but when information is needed, it is needed, so George, all email attempts failing, faxed the man. He got a message back by e-mail that Ortlovoksky was dead of a fatal fall from a window.

George scratched his chin and worried about the life expectancy of nanotech researchers, although it worried him rather more that he would now have to spend a week getting up to speed on this difficult area of transtensors before he could transform his latest idea on directed replication into the network of molecules that would effect it. Maybe more than a week, since his time was not entirely his own. There were management meetings, staff meetings, lab meetings, technical meetings, budgetary meetings, planning meetings, progress meetings. He cast an eye over his appointments. Then, just as he was nodding with satisfaction at his clear afternoon, an alarm went off. The alarm went off. The SRM siren.

The corridors outside George's rooms immediately filled with people running to their stations. An SRM ingress was one of the worst things that could happen to an institute as reliant on computer technology and fine engineering as Smalltech. All staff had trained long for the day when even one of the technology-eating machines was reported on-site. There were procedures to be followed that would render this building SRM-free in minutes, theoretical procedures admittedly, but George was confident they would work.

He turned off his workstation, took the CD-W out, put it in a cardboard sleeve, put it his pocket, threw a paper bag over the rest, and went into the corridor. Quickly, all the time quickly. Nonetheless, he was one of the last out, so the corridor was filled with people's backs all apparently walking away from him, as if he had suddenly joined in a ballet of galaxies. He started for the main entrance, which was his mustering point. Coming towards him he suddenly saw people's fronts. A man in a dark suit, no, three men in dark suits. One was a youngish man and the other two were both older and bigger.

"Are you George Assok?" the younger man asked him sharply.

"No. That's his office, there."

George's answer surprised him, but then it was his job to derive certainties from unrelated facts. The three men swept past him and went on in the direction of his office. George walked as quickly as he could, without breaking into a run, towards the main entrance. There were only a couple of other people in the corridor, now. Checking on stragglers. There was Colville, the mathematician, he had been very useful in the development of the nanoconstructor, useless at transtensors, unfortunately, his interest was in finite number theorem. George thought that line of work to be distracting rather than edifying. Colville saw him and came right over, chatting cheerily as if this was just a drill and not a very real danger to all their work. Perhaps it was a drill. George asked him as much.

"Ah, I really don't know," Colville said, surprised. "I supposed it was. Do you think it's a real emergency, then?"

George tried to push past him, but he stood stupidly in the way like a ruminating animal. George, feeling an unspecific fear, the worst kind, shoved him violently.

"Out of the way!" he shouted at him. Colville fell back with great alarm, George looked over his shoulder, and there were the three men running up the corridor. The certainty that George had derived from the quickly successive deaths of several of his colleagues, a hypothesis he did not wish to put to experimental test, was that these three men were here to kill him. The trouble with an assumption like that is that you can't take the chance that you might be wrong. George sprinted for the exit.

He heard Colville wailing something in a high-pitched voice, and took another look behind him. The smaller man was holding Colville by the arm while the other two were galloping at impressive speed across the linoleum. Clearly, he was not going to escape them if he continued in a linear fashion. George ducked into the next doorway on his right that he came to.

The room he had just entered was one of the chemical laboratories. There were the usual tall benches lined up down either side and the middle the room, like a student lab, or like an exhibition of the versatility of pyrex. A few bunsens were pushing their blue fingers into the air. At the window end there was a rack of glass-stoppered bottles. Tall, wooden-framed windows in the far wall cast diffuse shadows over it all. George ran down an aisle and leaped onto a table, and behind him he heard the crash of the flap doors slamming. The two men stopped, one at the end of each bench, looked meaningfully at each other, and started to advance on him at a casual walking pace.

George grabbed a pair of bottles and shook the stoppers out. Acrid fumes immediately rose from the openings. He had not had time to select by label, and these were nitric acid by the smell of it, a poor choice, since it had little immediate effect on skin. Luckily his predatory assailants did not know that. Or unluckily, since they both stopped and slowly drew short and ugly-looking automatic weapons from under their jackets.

George had never believed in negotiating with a man with a gun. He hurled the two bottles at them with all his strength and threw himself, with no clear idea of what lay beyond the shining glass, through the window.

Extreme happiness, tempered with terror. Grass existed beyond the window, at a reasonably high elevation. George was not injured. Neither were the two men who jumped out right behind him with their guns seeking silently and smoothly behind their darting eyes. But the first man had leaped too far. He landed almost on top of George, who almost by accident toppled him by entangling legs. His weapon gave forth a rude sound, and George found blood spattered on his shirt. The other assassin was swinging the hole end of his gun to bear. George, frozen on the ground with his legs wrapped around a dead man's knees, waited to hear the fart of death. Instead, the gun was pounced upon and wrenched from the hands of the assassin by the energetic leap of a teddy bear which, on landing, proceeded to remove various bits of the weapon at near-invisible speeds. The little homunculus' robotic delight was short-lived. The assassin crushed it underfoot, snatched back the gun, and made a fast assessment of it's fitness for killing people. By the time he looked up a second or two later, George was running across the car park into the crowd at Muster Point Two.

Hidden amongst all the other white coats, George struggled to control his gasping breath. As soon as the all-clear sounded, he slipped away, past his own car, out the side gate of the complex, and into a taxi. He wasn't going back. Someone was trying to kill him. The same someone may have already succeeded in killing John Firely, Ortlovoksky, and that WestLibVar fellow. That spoke of an unnerving thoroughness. He pressed the CD-W in his breast pocket against his heart.

He didn't go home, either. Once he had his breath and his powerful analytical mind back, he realised that once an attempt like this has been made, there is never again any chance of a normal life. It was time to disappear.

"I have found I have a surprising facility for living on the run," George finished. "Some time ago, I reached the limit of what I can do without equipment and funding, and that's when I turned to studying SRMs for clues as to how they maintained the integrity of their instruction sets." He saw Whak's face, sighed deeply and got to the point. "And, I think it was Blue Suit who killed my colleagues. He wants nanotechnology to himself."

Whak tripped as he kicked a brick and with that excuse, did not attempt to argue the point.

"Where are we going?" he asked after he regained his balance.

"My place."

"Don't you think they'll be waiting for you there?"

"I'm hoping that they don't know where it is."

"That's a good hope," Whak said.

CHAPTER 24

Sinfine sees the Advert

I find out with great distress
That my creative output is limited
And that instead of pouring out on demand
Sometimes it must be grown, carefully like a crystal
Only to find that when almost perfect
It grows heads like a medusa
And that is I suppose what happens
If you get too close to reality.

Sinfine was too close to reality. A simple thing had turned without warning into a large ugly hairy circumstance which made him both unhappy and nervous. The physical appearance of this disaster was lying like a stringless puppet on his chaise-longue, her tits half fallen out of her dress and one shoe nowhere in sight. Sinfine watched Lino moodily as a line of saliva began to roll down the side of her chin. It made Sinfine feel ill.

"Fucking wipe her face," he told Emery. Emery did so. "Prop her up. Shake her tits down. Jesus, she looks like a drug death. Have you called the clean-up boys?" Emery nodded. "Good. Any cops down there yet?"

"Not so far, Mr Sinfine sir," Emery said. He had just come from a long telephone call to one of the specialists that the Cousins occasionally employed, and a damage control team would soon be arriving at the Coolio pitfight arena in authentic ambulances, accompanied by phoney detectives and enough cash to close the eyes of any police who might come by. Not that there was much chance of that. Undermanned and underfunded police were not highly motivated to explore known dens of crime in the dead of night, especially when their own bosses were already paid to ignore the pitfights wherever they might be held. And it was the dead of night. It was coming around to two ay-em. Emery yawned.

"Am I keeping you up?" Sinfine snapped at him. "Jesus Christ. I've got a major fucking disaster on my hands and you're falling asleep. Total shit. Dead punters. We've got some serious advertising to do. Experience the thrill of the fucking pitfights, if you dare. That sort of stuff. What's on TV?" He looked around for the remote control.

Emery found it cut into pieces on the floor. "Looks like an SRM got it, Mr Sinfine."

"We never used to get SRMs in here." Sinfine stared at Lino. "And my beautiful car. Go see the old geezer next door about another one." He pulled out a cigarette. "That Jim bastard was right. She's a monster." Emery turned on the TV by hand and a cheerful GOV1 ad announcer appeared to tell the audience about the ads that they were going to see in just a few minutes. Then,

Big graphical letters, SRM BOUNTY

Voiceover (dramatic): It had to come. The battle has begun.

"What the fuck is this?" Sinfine asked plaintively. He groped for the remote and when he remembered that it was no more, he gestured for Emery to turn it up. He watched it intently until the street address of Blue Suit Offices appeared, then he snapped his fingers several times, as if he was attracting the attention of the TV. "Get that address written down." He went on snapping his fingers while Emery quickly found a pen and paper. "Beautiful," he said, "just beautiful. Show it to me." He looked hard at Emery's handwriting. "This is Blue Suit's address," he announced eventually. "Blue Suit is collecting SRMs. Now isn't that interesting."

Jim and the Old Man

Morning dew settled clammily upon Jim's upturned face. He awoke, rolled off his branch, bounced off another, and only his arboreal descent saved him from a more precipitous kind.

"Ow," he muttered, pulling himself back onto his night perch. He guessed from the brightness of the sky that he had slept for a couple of hours. Not good. Lino could have been taken from the house in those two hours. He peered across the street. Sinfine's house was curtained and silent, or he assumed it was silent. The tree above his head was cacophonous with birdsong and made any judgement of sound levels impossible. Jim had not previously noticed that the decrease in human industry was balanced by an equal increase in the bird population. Once the racket had penetrated his attention, he could not rid himself of it and with a curse he shinnied down the trunk, waited for a few cars to pass and under their cover crossed the street.

By positioning himself near the gates of Sinfine's property he lost his view, but gained faint audio. After half an hour he heard a car start up.

"Oh shit, oh fuck," he said under his breath. If Lino was in the car then he would lose her for sure. He looked quickly up and down the street. Further down the street, there were a few cars on the side of the road, probably broken down, but they were too far away. He ignored them. He put his head fractionally around the gate. The car that he had heard was moving down the driveway. He couldn't see who was in it. It rolled past him onto the street and he stole a complete inventory of its contents before he turned quickly and pretended that he had been walking in that direction the whole time. Lino was not in the car. He breathed relief. Instead, two men, with the unmistakable goony style, sent out on some mission of mayhem perhaps. The car did him the favour of turning in the other direction and roaring away.

His relief was short-lived, however, because he quickly returned to the question of whether Lino was still in the building. He went over to one of the abandoned cars, sat inside it, and tried to think.

After a time, he wondered whether there were other entrances to the property than the front gates. Not every abode in North Coolio was a barricaded fortress. From the back seat of the old Chevrolet he could see part of the grounds of the house next door. A tall wall divided the two properties, but it deserved inspection. Jim slipped into the adjoining estate and under the cover of several more discarded Chevrolets and Mercedes, which he was surprised to discover littered around the lawn, he reached the dividing wall. There he climbed up onto the roof of an old wagon and saw that there was a point further up the property where he might be able to jump across onto a garage or similar low building. He climbed back down the wagon and as his feet touched the earth a man spoke.

"Nice view?"

It was an old man. He was wrinkled, white-haired, and rheumy-eyed, and his hand, which he was using to point at the top of the wall, was trembling. Jim thought that all the old people had been moved to Centres of Dignity, and before he could override his mouth, he said so.

"No, only poor old people," the old man told him. "I'm a rich old person. Now, young man, what are you doing on my Mercedes? Looking over walls? Spying on my next door neighbour, are you?"

"Yes," Jim answered.

"Good, that's what I thought you were doing. Come inside."

"I can't come inside. My girlfriend's in there."

"Really?" Unless you have seen an old person at least once before, an old man's face is impossible to read, and Jim had no idea what he was thinking, but his tone of voice was amused. "We have a love triangle?"

"No, nothing like that. She's been kidnapped. And she's sick."

"I remember a kidnapping once where the victim was a diabetic child," the old man was triggered into a memory that was probably at least as real to him as Jim was. "The parents paid and the child died. There was a lot of that in the old days. I didn't think kidnapping happened much anymore. Nobody cares enough to pay the ransom, you see. What's wrong with her?"

"I don't know, exactly. She's like in a trance. She doesn't react to anything."

"Oh, catatonic withdrawal. Had a shock, has she?"

"You might say that. Sinfine tried to kill me in front of her."

"Mr Sinfine is a Cousin, you know," said the old man as if that excused him of any responsibility for his actions. "Come inside. You can see better from there."

"How do you know I'm not going to rob you or kill you?" Jim asked as they walked up to the old man's house.

"You could have killed me already. Anyway, I don't care. All I care about now is my cars. I'm hoping to restore another one of them before I die. I did a car for Sinfine, you know. A 1996 Buick 420 sedan. Beautiful."

"I think it got eaten by SRMs last night."

The old man sighed deeply. "They'll get them all one day. There won't be any cars left at all. Don't go in there, that's the workshop." Jim had no intention or method of going in there. There had huge, wooden doors, chained shut. "Up the stairs."

Jim remembered the last time he had been directed up stairs. He felt a bursting anxiety for Lino.

"Come on," said the old man. "You can see right into his living room from up here." He started climbing the steps at a geriatric pace. Jim took one step, and waited, and then another, and waited, while his heart ached with anticipation. He had never felt this physical pain in his chest before. He wondered if it was a strained rib.

"There," the old man said as he finally reached the top of the stairs. "Go on through."

Jim rushed ahead and found a large lounge, almost entirely filled with furniture so that it was a maze of narrow gaps between this armchair and that cabinet or a garishly papered wall and a line of vase stands. But there was a window that looked straight out and down onto Sinfine's house.

"She's in there," Jim clenched his fists and shook them back and forth. He could see Lino sitting on a couch not fifteen metres away. Emery was talking on the telephone. The maid came into the room and said something to Emery, who left. Sinfine appeared from another door and stood looking at Lino.

"What are they saying?" Jim demanded of the air.

The old man now arrived at the window. He stared out of it.

"Sinfine just said, 'I'm putting you somewhere safe'," the old man told Jim.

"How do you know that?"

"I'm half deaf. I have to read lips at least part of the time. Now he's saying to that woman that she should take her to the something house."

"That what house?"

"I didn't get that bit," apologised the old man. "I have to blink sometimes." In fact he blinked with parkinsonian frequency. "The something house. She says right now, and he's looking the other way now so I don't know."

Jim stepped back from the window. "Well, thanks," he said. "You've really helped me. I don't know what I can ever do for you, but thank you."

"Its okay. I think helping people should be encouraged these days." He was still looking out the window. "Your girlfriend is moving," he told Jim. "She's standing up. That other woman's taking her to the door. She's doing what she's told."

"She does that. When she's like this, you can push her and she walks."

"Maybe not catatonia, then. Is she schizophrenic?"

"I don't know. Yes. She's either really happy or she's really miserable. Is that schizophrenia?"

"Sounds something like it."

"I need to follow her."

"Need a car?"

"Yes!"

Whak and Assok discuss SRMs

George Assok was right, thank God, that Blue Suit still didn't know where he lived. He led Whak down highway and byway, between buildings, until they reached the street on which he lived. There they both waited for a further long and boring time, standing behind a bus shelter, until Assok considered the street to be both empty and unobserved.

"All right," he said at last. "Let's go." He scuttled across the road under the protection of an intense band of shadow. Whak did the same. He climbed in his own basement window. Whak did the same. He looked around his laboratory, while Whak collapsed onto a pipeframe chair that stood against the wall.

"No-one's been here," George announced.

"If they had been, we'd be dead now, wouldn't we?"

George was now looking on the brighter side of things. "They may not have been trying to kill us," he said. "Blue Suit may want to know what I know."

"And what do you know?"

George Assok sat down on an identical chair. "I understand," he began, "that Blue Suit is financing an SRM collection project."

"I heard that. Jelli told me. It was on GOV1." Whak looked around the room. There was no television in sight.

"So it's true." George's long face stretched even further. "This is bad, Puihare. Very bad. It confirms what I already believed. Blue Suit killed John Firely, Ortlovoksky, and that other fellow."

"How does it prove that?"

George looked surprised that his word should be questioned. He snapped "Well, it doesn't. Not directly. But one additional piece of information will prove it. I want you to find out exactly what they plan to do with the SRMs they collect."

"Everybody wants me to find things out, lately," Whak sighed. "Why does that matter?"

"It matters because if they are going to test nanoviruses - "

"Nanoviruses?"

"Yes, nanoviruses," Assok said impatiently. "I've already told you what they are. Self-adaptive, reproductive nanomachines designed to attack specific molecular structures and reconstruct them into descendent nanoviruses. Dismantlers. I was working on the principles of nanoviruses at Smalltech. We had already manufactured some very simplistic nanoviruses that could, for example, reverse crystal growth."

"Dismantle a crystal? What sort of crystal?" Whak had visions of diamonds dissolving into the air, elegant and expensive women screaming as their tiaras evaporated, champagne spilling out of vaporising flutes.

"Silica, as it happens, although it doesn't matter what sort. The target for the nanovirus is programmed in at design time. It could be anything."

Whak's imagining turned to beaches empty of sand and he grew more serious. He liked beaches. He liked having glass in his windows. He preferred fine crystal wineglasses to plastic tumblers.

"What happens if these nanoviruses get out?" he asked. "They sound worse than SRMs. What if they dismantle everything?"

"Ah, well, that would be a problem, wouldn't it?" To Whak's great mystification, George looked pleased. "That's getting back to the replication fidelity issue, isn't it? Yes, it could cause serious problems. But since the second law of thermodynamics has yet to be repealed, the tendency is for nanomachines of all types to degrade into disorganised matter, rather faster than desired."

"I'm glad of that."

"As I'm sure you know, however, whenever self-replication occurs in an environment of natural selection, incremental advantageous mutations accumulate."

"Which means?" Whak asked, exasperated.

"Which means that if nanomachines are designed to reproduce themselves in an adaptive mode, that is if the nanoviral design is used, as I would to affect a wide-ranging population of SRMs, then they could mutate out of control."

"Fucking Christ, George."

"If Blue Suit's project is working with nanoviruses, it has the potential to destroy a lot more than SRMs. My research into SRMs and purposeful evolution has suggested some techniques that might reduce the risk considerably."

"You're not doing stuff with these nanoviruses here, are you?" Whak demanded.

"No, I can't. I haven't got the equipment. I wish I could. It's very hard to develop new concepts without testing."

"Jesus, George! You're talking about things that could eat the planet and you're planning to make them in your garage! What if you let these germs out and they develop a taste for oxygen, for

God's sake? Or water? The whole world could end up a floating ball of microscopic machines!"

"You can't dismantle an oxygen molecule, you fool. The risks are infinitesimal, almost nil, and besides, we have to take risks to obtain knowledge. The world is in a crisis. Nanotechnology is a perfectly valid way to solve it. We must have knowledge to survive."

"We must have oxygen to survive," Whak said loudly.

"Sshh! They could be looking for us out on the street right now."

"Who can blame them?" Whak glanced up at the dirty windows that opened into the world below footpath level. "They probably think you're as crazy as I do. Although," he added, "that doesn't make me want to kill you."

"You're wasting your time and mine by complaining about what I'm not even doing, when out there in the Wasteland, Blue Suit almost certainly has an army of semi-competent technicians working on the same thing, and without my knowledge to guide them, either. We have to act. We have to get somebody with some influence on our side. Your wife."

Whak was suddenly struck by the circularity of the problem and the solution, and he groaned and rubbed his eyes, which were feeling the strain of twenty hours open. "SRMs, nanoviruses. Nanoviruses, SRMs. The cure is worse than the disease. You said that SRM's might develop intelligence, didn't you? Why not wait until the SRMs get smart enough that we can talk to them? Then we can just ask them politely to stop eating our brake leads."

"That's ridiculous and you know it. There's no point in saying things like that. Listen, I'm not trying to help Blue Suit, I'm trying to help the human race. I want Blue Suit's SRM project stopped before it does something irreversible. And one other thing. We can probably discount the nanoviruses-run-amok scenario, but what if Blue Suit releases his nanoviruses and they fail to exterminate SRMs? What will the SRM meta-instructions make of that? If SRMs evolve towards intelligence when they're left alone, what might happen if they are threatened with extinction? What will that do to their rate of development? It's a disaster whichever way you look at it."

He shook Whak roughly by the shoulder as if he was a disobedient child, which in George Assok's eyes he probably was. "I have to talk to Jelli."

CHAPTER 25

Jelli - Lino is missing!

Jelli looked around the house for her family. She was unused to awaking in a bed without the undefinable presence, the smell perhaps, of a male body nearby. It was sufficiently unusual for Whak to be out of bed before her that she did not even make herself a coffee before looking into his study. Which was empty.

"Where are you, Whak?" she said to herself. "Didn't you come home last night?" That would be uniquely unusual. She checked the living room and the conservatory, although Whak never used the conservatory, because as he said, it was a sweltering glasshouse by day and a freezing glasshouse by night and it had nowhere to sit that wasn't too exposed to the light or too much in the shade. All of which Jelli understood to mean that Whak disliked the conservatory for some other reason, which he could not translate into a mutually intelligible form. She thought it might be because he had lost his portable computer to an SRM there, long ago, and Whak made absurd attachment to the tools of his trade, but that was just a guess.

She went down the hall and hesitated outside Lino's bedroom. As she had remarked to Whak just the previous day, it was a long time since she had entered Lino's room. There was a tension between her and her daughter that had existed since the moment of birth, Jelli seemed to remember, which had survived and outlasted the bond of motherhood. Come to that, whatever part of Jelli was supposed to produce the all-encompassing loving stuff that reportedly poured out of other women more regularly then menstrual blood, she could not identify it. Words that might have been said she had never found time to say. Jelli's words were not an extension of her heart the way that Whak's words were an extension of his mind.

It seemed to her that in her ideal world, she would be happier than this.

She knocked loudly on Lino's door.

"Lino!" she called. She hammered even more loudly. If she was going to have another confrontation between her urgent life and Lino's indifference, she might as well be the aggressor. "Lino! Have you seen Whak?"

No reply. Well, in the words of some comedian of the last century, she wasn't going to take no reply for an answer. She turned the handle and pushed the door open. Whak was right. The room was tidy and blue. Tidy, blue, and unoccupied. Unbelievable! Lino was out and Whak was out. Was this a wife-and-mother desertion? Jelli looked at her watch, which she seldom took off even to sleep.

"I have to go to work," she told Lino's empty room. "All you missing family members had better be here when I get back." Whenever that was going to be. She went back to the bedroom and finished her dress by wrapping herself in a few metres of coloured fabric. Thus bandaged up, she stopped in the kitchen for her caffeine jolt, took another, disturbed glance around the empty house, and went to work. But as she went through the garage access door, the phone rang.

Incoming telephone calls at the Puihare home were something of a rarity, since there were not many private telephones that worked or public telephone lines that were reliable. The telephone was not an answerphone, either. The RAM that all the answerfaxes of the previous decade needed to function was choice SRM fodder. The normal household phone now was no phone, but if you were important enough to possess one it was a low-tech affair. The door had closed behind Jelli before she realised that she was not in the office and that answering the phone was up to her. All this meant that she had to unlock the garage door and rush back through the house to the kitchen where the phone lay by her unwashed breakfast cup.

"Jelli Puihare," she said into the mouthpiece.

"Hi, it's Whak."

"Whak! Where the hell are you?"

"I-can't-tell-you," Whak chanted with faintly Gregorian intonations.

"What do you mean by that?"

"I'm with George."

"George?"

"Yes. You know George."

While Jelli was reviewing her person list, she heard Whak saying at a distance, "All right, George, you already said that." Then, "Jelli? You'd know the answer to this. Is our phone bugged?"

"Well, yes, probably."

"Shit." In the background, "The phone's bugged." To Jelli, "Why didn't you ever tell me this before? Where can I call you?"

"At work. Whak, where's Lino?"

"I don't know, where is Lino?"

"She's not here. She didn't come home last night."

"What?" Whak became agitated. That had never happened before. It should have done, but it hadn't. "That's not like Lino. Something must have happened to her. That miserable bastard Jim."

"You said he was better than nobody, remember," Jelli told him with some malice. "And that he had some ambition."

"Do you want to score points or find Lino? She could be hurt. Or cataleptic. Or anything. You know how she reacts to things."

Jelli did indeed know how she reacted to things, and the edge of Whak's panic began to cut into what until now had been her feeling of only mild concern. Blood started to well up around the edges. Lino was missing. Lino was missing. Jelli dealt with the unfamiliar emotion this fact engendered by snapping into executive mode.

"I can't find her, I have to go to work. You'll have to find her. When are you going to be here?"

"I'm coming straight home," Whak replied.

"I'll call you from work." Jelli hung up.

Assok's fear of Blue Suit

Whak also hung up. He turned to George Assok.

"I've got to go," he said. "My daughter is missing."

"You didn't arrange a meeting!" George wailed. "You didn't tell her that I need to see her! You didn't tell her anything!"

"There are more important things going on," Whak replied. He looked around. "Where's the stairs?" he asked. George paid no attention to his question.

"What can be more important than the survival of the species?" he demanded.

"The survival of my daughter," said Whak. "However paradoxical that might be to you. The survival of the species is the survival of individuals." He remembered the layout of Assok's rambling basement and went to the stairs, with George behind him, issuing a steady stream of complaint.

"I have to go and find my daughter," he told him again. "She's not well. She's got a psychological condition. She freezes up. She could be in danger."

"It will only take a moment for you to arrange a meeting with your wife!" said George.

"I will, I will arrange a meeting with Jelli, but first I have to find my daughter. Look, she might be home by the time I get there." Whak reached the top step and found an assortment of mortises and clasps all over the inside of the large metal door. "You going to let me out?" he asked.

Assok unlocked and unclipped the door.

"Thanks," Whak said. He went through the foyer, past the gaping liftshaft, and pushed open the street level doors. George Assok was still right behind him, still pleading.

"Which way is north, again?" Whak asked him. When George indicated a direction, he nodded. "Hey, I'm starting to develop a sense of direction," he said, but not cheerfully. "Well, thanks for the pyjama party, George, and for the midnight race from death. I'll call you as soon as I've made arrangements with Jelli. What's your telephone number?"

"You can't call in on that line. It's piggybacked on a house line in North Coolio. I have to repair the cable every two weeks because of caterpillar damage. And it's illegal. I don't even know the number. Every time I use it I'm afraid that telecom technicians will kick my door down. We'll have to meet somewhere. In the Park."

Now the two men were walking along the street towards Coolio Park. Whak wished that George would leave him alone. Whak had only Lino on his mind, and he found that there was no room in him at present for the end of mankind, or even the destruction of the planet. Some things are too big and undefined to deal with, even for a poet. He reached the end of the street and made ready to cross.

"The sooner I speak to your wife, the earlier we can begin to put pressure on the Consortium to stop Blue Suit," Assok was mumbling. "His technical people might blunder at any time. The risks are mounting. Who knows what stage they're at, but I suspect advanced testing, if the SRM Collection is what I think it is."

Whak reached the park side of the street. 'Where is Lino?' he was thinking. To find Lino, he thought, he first had to find Jim. So where was Jim?

"So what do you think it is?" he asked disinterestedly.

"They must need so many samples because they are testing nanoviruses against the entire spectrum of SRM types. Although even so, it's strange that they want such vast numbers."

A large car suddenly appeared from around the bend ahead of them. George Assok stopped dead. Whak felt oddly compelled to do the same. Both men shrank against the wall. The car passed them without any variation in speed and George sighed in relief. As they stepped away from the wall, a second car appeared, driven with either little experience or great haste, or both, for it screeched as it swung around the curve, stopped momentarily to realign itself with the road, and then screamed again as it accelerated. It swept past.

"What was all that about?" Whak said. "Do we keep following the wall?"

"Yes, yes."

They continued as they had before. Whak trying to find Lino or Jim within the small-scale universe residing in his head, and George Assok endlessly repeating his demand to be put in contact with Jelli. Then the second car suddenly reappeared, coming back down the other side of the street. It pulled over to the kerb slightly ahead of them.

"Hey!" called the driver. "Hey, Mr Puihare! I mean, Whak!"

"Jim," Whak said thoughtfully. "So. The penis of God is erect today, it seems."

Blue Suit to meet Sinfine

Blue Suit was reading PushRight Creative Media's annual budget disclosure and wondering what he would be able to accomplish with it, if it was his, when a communication appeared at his desk in the form of the Chief of Observation. He buzzed, knocked, came in, and stood at attention. Blue Suit liked the military precision aspect of his business.

"What is it?" Blue Suit asked him.

"The observers assigned to collecting Whak Puihare and George Assok have lost them, sir."

Blue Suit put his elbows on the desk and leaned his forehead on one hand in a gesture of expiring patience. "Why didn't you use control officers? They are trained in person collection. Observers are trained in observing. Use the right resources for the right job next time. Put control officers onto it. No, wait, put protectors onto it. They, at least, succeed or die. Anything else?"

"Yes sir. We have a message from a Cousin."

"Cousin who?"

"Cousin Sinfine, sir."

"Pitfights, I believe."

"That's right, sir. You keep up with the data, sir."

"Just keep to the facts. What does he want?"

"He asked for a meeting, sir," the Chief said nervously, "with yourself, personally."

"Dangerous for both of us, I think. Do we have any information about his activities?"

"Some, sir. Last night, there was an SRM event of some magnitude at the Coolio Park pitfight arena. At least ten deaths, we understand. The Cousins cleaned it all up before we could examine the scene."

"SRM event? Another one? That makes three, doesn't it?"

"Another one, yes sir. Three."

"And this one at a pitfight. Cousin Sinfine must be hurting in the pocket. Well, there's no harm in us having a word. It might be interesting. He might know something about these events. I'll meet with him at one of our open-air setups. Organise it."

"Yes sir. When?"

"When I have a free hour. Check with my PA. And catch George Assok. I might be needing him. Don't make any more mistakes."

"No, sir."

The Chief of Observation left. Blue Suit always found the few moments after a person left his office to be a vacant hole in his usually well-structured mind. He disliked being disturbed for that reason. Sometimes irregular thoughts intruded at such times. On this occasion, the thought that took up the empty space without invitation was particularly unpleasant. Had Jelli had George Assok hidden away for all this time? Was she, and now he felt an unfamiliar wave of doubt, more aware of his plans than he believed? If she was, then getting his hands on Assok and what Assok knew could become a very complicated thing indeed.

Whak, Assok, and Jim together

Whak ran across the road, reached in the car window and tried to drag Jim out of the car by his shirt.

"Where's Lino? Where's Lino? What have you done with Lino?" he shouted. Jim, now bent at an unusual angle with his shoulders caught in the window frame, tried to answer, but Whak's incessant jerking and pulling knocked the words away. George Assok began to tug urgently on Whak's arm.

"Don't make such a scene," he told Whak. "Keep it down! There'll still be Blue Suits looking for us! Quiet!" He looked rapidly in all directions, then without warning he opened a car door and slipped into the back. "Get in!" he told Whak. "Get out of sight!"

After a few more seconds of bouncing Jim off the door frame, Whak calmed down enough to hear this exhortation. Great tranquilliser, physically assaulting the incarnation of your fears. He pulled open the driver's door.

"Move over," he told Jim. "Your driving sucks." He pushed Jim across to the passenger seat and climbed in. He did not refrain from shaking Jim so violently that flecks of his spit struck the windscreen.

"Where's Lino?" he repeated.

"He can't answer you while you're rattling him like that," George Assok put in. Whak reluctantly let go of Jim's arm and asked him yet again, "Where's Lino?"

"I don't know," Jim answered after a few seconds of reorientation. He held up a defensive hand as Whak made to grab him again. "I don't know, exactly. But I know the general area." He saw Whak's eyes starting to focus in clearly different directions and took it to mean that he had better explain himself, and fast. Although Jim was very capable of looking after himself in normal circumstances, he was smaller than Whak, Whak was motivated in a way that Jim could never be, and Jim was, as he knew damn well, fully deserving of whatever Whak wanted to hand out.

"I took Lino to the pitfights," he started half-truthfully. "Lino made the SRMs go mad. They tore the place up. Killed people. I lost her in the crowd, and next thing I knew, Sinfine had her."

"Who is Sinfine?" Whak said. His voice was no longer that of the harmless poet.

"Sinfine," George Assok told him from the back seat, "is the criminal boss in charge of pitfight gambling."

"Yeah," Jim agreed. "That's Sinfine. He kidnapped Lino."

"Why would the pitfight boss want to kidnap Lino?" Whak asked.

"What do you mean, Lino made the SRMs go mad?" George asked at the same time. He and Whak looked at each other, then at Jim. Whak was becoming more distraught by the moment. He was panting with the effort of controlling his instinct to pound Jim to a bloody pulp.

"To get more people at the pitfights! She makes SRMs go crazy! Don't tell me you don't know about it!" Jim answered both questions at once. "She's done it at least three times. The Wasteland, at an alley party, and last night at the pitfight. She starts going all frozen, and suddenly all these SRMs come out of nowhere, really hungry." He saw Whak's face. "It really happened!"

"We know," Assok said. "We were watching. I've got it on tape." He frowned. "No, I haven't, because I lost my videocam. Damn."

"And Lino was in there," Whak stared out the windscreen. "And now she's kidnapped by this Sinfine character. So where is she? What is he going to do with her?"

"I don't know what he's going to do with her, but I heard he was sending her to a place near the Wasteland. I know that part of town. There aren't that many places she could be."

"Then let's go there," Whak said. He stuck the car into drive. It rolled smoothly forward. Whak starting winding in his paternal protection zones until he reached a state that allowed him to hear the engine over the sound of his own heartbeat, then he said "Why does Lino make SRMs go crazy?"

Neither of the passengers answered. Whak kicked down and the car, which happened to be a 1999 Ford Fairmont - no safety belts and the brake booster's faulty, the old man said, which is very appropriate for a man in your position - jumped forward, causing Jim and George Assok to be thrown back in their seats.

Righting himself, George offered an opinion on the fundamental improbability of any form of communication with SRMs. He got as far as the fundamental improbability part of his pronouncement when the Ford passed one of the gates into Coolio Park and all three men saw a crowd gathered there. Whak slowed down. The rubberneck impulse was a spinal short-circuit with Whak.

"Don't slow down!" George shouted. "Go faster!"

But Whak didn't go faster. He drove past the crowd of similarly dressed men that were standing in lines on the footpath. When George Assok threw himself on the floor of the car and began to moan with fear, Whak realised that he was rolling slowly past a concentration of blue suits. Through his open window, he heard an authoritative voice saying "- last seen in this area. These men must be collected. They have been officially decitizened. We have observation of the collectees both at this end of the park and in some adjacent streets. Move in groups of two. Use voice hail for backup and notification."

"Jargon-ridden clones," Whak said. "Decitizened. It's a hallmark of the fascists, this reinvention of language. They invoke unthinkable actions by giving them another name and the funny part is, no one notices that they're breaking taboo because the trigger words are never said. I should write a poem about it."

"It's us they're talking about," Assok told him from behind the seat.

Jim looked alarmed. "Let's drive faster, Whak," he suggested. Whak couldn't stop looking at the lines of blue suits. There must have been a hundred of them. But then the line stopped, and he was looking instead at the cracked plaster of the Coolio Park perimeter wall.

"I guess they didn't see us," he said as they accelerated away.

"Nonetheless," George Assok picked himself off the floor and brushed dust off his jacket, "nonetheless, I suggest that we stop driving around town as if we're on a holiday junket from the beach district and hide. You heard them. We're decitizens. Jim," he went on before Whak could confuse the issue, talent for which he had in abundance, "where can we hide?"

"Combine Street's safe," Jim said immediately.

"Then let's go there."

As he drove, Whak looked in the side view mirror at the wall of Coolio Park as it rolled past, and he thought about laying low while his daughter was in the hands of the man who ran the pitfights, and fear of the future grew very strong inside him.

CHAPTER 26

Sinfine meets Blue Suit

One of Sinfine's little joys was to enter into a negotiation with a strong set of cards. Regardless of what he had to sell or what he wanted to buy, he was on the push, ridiculously overconfident in his wares, unwavering in his assumption that their value was what he claimed, uncomprehending of the usually more measured approach of his customers. Like the man who got laid by asking every woman he met to sleep with him, he had achieved success with his life because he had been lucky enough to deal with a proportion of credulous suckers slightly higher than the statistical mean.

On the other hand, one of Sinfine's failings was that he seldom recognised when to suck ass. He had got into trouble in that score with the Uncles of the Cousins, stupid designations all of them, but they were traditional. Don't mess with tradition unless you want a fight that lasts more than one lifetime. Anyway, it was in this non-ass-sucking frame of mind that he was going to the meeting with Blue Suit. It was not unheard of for legally appointed, high-ranking officials and powerful outsourcers to have fireside chats with their equivalents from one dark side or another, but it was unusual, and there was vast potential for betrayal and mayhem.

Whak had often wondered what security arrangements were in place when Blue Suit had his monthly performance reviews with the Devil. He would never know the answer to that, but Sinfine would have been able to tell him, because they could not have been much different from the arrangements that he and Blue Suit had agreed to for this very day.

Firstly, the meeting place had been chosen to be both as public as possible and as difficult to observe as could be contrived, opposing attributes that had been reconciled by a favourite trick of the old CIA, an open air meeting, and where else than in the Wasteland. On the next point, which in the best example of the drop was come alone, both men chose instead to bring force. For every protector of Blue Suit arrayed against the background of rubbish there was a goon of Sinfine's. Blue Suit flunkey collides with Sinfine heavy, annihilating both with concomitant release of semi-free bosses. Or so it might have been. Instead, they all occupied locations well separated from each other and exchanged hard looks. From the air the pattern of humans would have allowed measurement of each side's self-confidence with mathematical exactitude. And the last point, that had been the most difficult to accomplish, was the simultaneous arrival of all parties so as to prevent priming the site, which entailed an ongoing telephone conversation between Emery and Blue Suit's situation controller, arranging the meeting place while the meetees were already en route to their as-yet-undefined rendezvous.

Mobile telephones were a dream of halcyon days. Sinfine's driver had to stop every time they passed a working telephone to find out what arrangements Emery and the other guy had reached so far. Cousins and their nephews muscling into bars and Sood Shops and grocery stores made for a lot of nervous tension in the district, but at last the runaround interval came to an end. Sinfine's driver came back to the car, a replacement, courtesy of the creepy old guy next door, and Sinfine snarled at him.

"Have they fucking settled the scene yet?"

"Yes, Mr Sinfine. It's to be in the Wasteland, Mr Sinfine."

"Oh Jesus Christ. Right there with all the fucking bugs all round us. What a dumbshit idea."

"It's going to be on the Tours side, sir, that's an open area."

"Damn good thing." Sinfine settled back from his position of outrage. The fact was he hated the bugs worse than anything else he could think of. He hated them, and his fortunes were built on them. There was nothing unprecedented about this. There were plenty of eighteenth-century millionaires whose wealth was built on the bodies of the classes and races they despised. Take any British shipping magnate of the period, ask him to pay a visit to Togoland, and observe the disgust and nausea. Sinfine preferred not to visit the source of his riches, but he preferred not to deal with Blue Suit, either, and he was doing it. The car rolled into the empty Wasteland Tours car park with Blue Suit's long black limousine just before it. Before either man got out of their cars, four more vehicles arrived and their respective punks lined up. The scene was established.

Blue Suit stepped into the open, not even glancing at his protectors. He stood by his car until Sinfine followed suit. The two men walked towards each other. Sinfine was in sell mode and swaggered right up to Blue Suit so that they were face in face.

"Kindly move back a step," Blue Suit told him, "or my protectors will be forced to kill you."

"Shit," Sinfine said, stepping back swiftly. "Take it fucking easy, will you?"

Blue Suit looked at him distastefully. "What do you want?" he asked.

"Right to the point, I like that," Sinfine told him. "It's not what I want, uh... " He was looking for an appellation, but there was none to be found. "...Blue Suit. Is that what they call you?"

"It's what you can call me."

"It's not what I want, anyway. It's what you want. I've got something you are going to want to have."

"What makes you think that?"

"You're interested in SRMs, aren't you?"

"I have as many SRMs as I could possibly require."

"This isn't an SRM."

"What is it?"

Sinfine made the groaning noise that he used for laughter. "It's a girl," he said.

"I have no need of girls," Blue Suit was perplexed. His estimation of this obnoxious Cousin was oscillating around zero. "Why should you want to sell a girl? Slavery is economically infeasible at present."

"This girl can make SRMs go crazy."

Blue Suit became much more interested. "How?" he demanded.

"I don't fucking know. Do I look like a fucking scientist?"

"No. You do not look like a scientist."

"She's in a trance, right? And when she comes out of the trance, you just upset her, like stick a gun in her face, and pow! SRMs go crazy. I've seen it. She made the fucking bugs rip up my pitfight the other night. Now, you're interested in SRMs, I bet you're interested in any way of talking to them. She talks to them."

"This is all hearsay." But he was interested. If there was a link between SRMs and the human brain, he had to know about it. It might be a useful tool in creating havoc. SRM events were much more visible and destructive than normal SRM activity. Or someone might come up with a way of controlling it and duplicating it and making, who knows, SRM repellers or remote controls. That would sweep his plans into oblivion.

"I'm here, and I say. I saw it."

"Nonetheless, I'll need some more information. And what exactly do you want from me?"

"I haven't decided yet. Money would be good, but protection might be better. You know, like you let me know when the other Cousins are up to something. And where the Uncles might be having a pow-wow. I know you know that sort of shit. You can tell the police to fuck off, too. I've got a big future in the Cousins, with a little help from Blue Suit. Might be to our mutual advantage to deal together, don't you think so?"

Blue Suit didn't think so, as a matter of fact. His plans precluded any power-sharing arrangements with the Uncles and Cousins. But he made no show of this.

"Who is this girl?" he asked.

"Who cares who she is? It's what she is that matters, not who. She's some girl. I got her from a pitfight handler. I've got her fucking wallet here. Let's see," Sinfine flicked open a small billfold. "She's Ly-no Poeyharry. And she's somewhere you are not going to find her without my help. So how about it?"

It took all of Blue Suit's self-control - and he had plenty - to refrain from reacting to the name. Lino Puihare. Jelli's daughter. Exhilarating possibilities burst from this fact and exploded with flashes of tantalising futures. Lino Puihare. The leverage available by having Jelli's daughter was effectively infinite, if he read Jelli aright. And on top of that, the girl supposedly had this talent. He didn't take that very seriously, but the fact that she might made her disposition a matter of national security, which made it the business of Blue Suit. He would be undeniably acting within his charter if he took her into custody.

"Who knows about this girl's alleged ability?" he asked.

"Just me and my man, you, and the boy wonder who brought her to me in the first place. It's tighter than a virgin's asshole."

"What have you done about this 'boy wonder'?"

"I've got my men looking out for him."

"You don't have him?"

"He kind of ran off. Don't worry about him. He's dead."

"Not yet, however." Blue Suit hated this kind of sloppy security. "I would prefer it if this was confidential for the time being. I leave the missing person up to you."

"No problem. Now what about you and me, deal-wise?"

"I will be in touch." Blue Suit took a step towards his car. Sinfine looked puzzled, then angry.

"You will be in touch? What kind of duckout is that? Do you want this fucking deal or not?"

"I will let you know. In the meantime, I will be asking for some proof of what you say."

"Proof? What fucking proof do you want? I'll set her off on the middle of the bridge and let the bugs tip the fucking traffic into the harbour, if you want."

"I'm sure we can find a less spectacular option, Mr Sinfine. I must leave now." Blue Suit turned his back on the Cousin and went to his car, disappeared therein, and a moment later the car quietly departed. The remaining bodies in the equation then separated from their opposites. Two minutes later, the car park was empty.

Sinfine's unstoppable deal had not been as irresistible as he had hoped, and the mood in which he had felt that with a suitcase and a bomb he could take over New York City was fast dissipating. Still, he thought, it could have gone worse. Blue Suit was interested, there was no mistaking that. All he had to do was keep this Lino bitch under wraps and then get the bastard Blue Suit, whoever he was, to support him in a variety of violent ways, and pretty soon after some bloody internecine warfare, Cousin Sinfine would be Uncle Sinfine. All because of a pitfight handler named Jim. Sinfine would have to shake his hand before he killed him.

With these thoughts, Sinfine told his driver to stop at the next Cousin-owned bar and make a call to Emery. Tell him, he told the driver, to meet me around the other side of the Wasteland. I'm going to have a look at this Lino bitch.

Emery had a lot further to come than Sinfine did. Sinfine got there first. He walked past a detached four-story that had an alley running down either side of it, turned down the alley and stopped in front of what appeared to be a boarded-over door.

"Get on with it, jerkoff," he told his driver. "Knock. Ta-da-di-da-daah."

The driver knocked, ta-da-di-da-daah, and the boarded-up door revealed itself as a fully operational door with a few boards nailed to the outside of it. The fact was that the current generation of crime had learned a lot of it's tricks of the trade by watching TV shows. Just like the Fortune 500, the Mafia and all the other big orgs of the past had taken a terrible beating when their technology stopped working. It didn't pay anymore to rely on complicated international money transfer programs and jet airliners full of cocaine. That way of doing business, and all the people who did it, had dropped out of the picture and into the vacuum had stepped the Uncles and Cousins, small time no longer, but sadly, thus far, cursed with a lack of infrastructure. When the Mafia had wanted to disappear someone for a few days, they had a Sheraton Hotel penthouse at their disposal. Those were the days. The Cousins had condemned housing estates.

Still, Sinfine had made this particular hideaway more comfortable than most, because he never knew when he might be the person needing to hide in it. Sinfine and his driver went in.

"Get me a drink," Sinfine told the door guard, whose name happened to be Horse. He looked more like a mule. "What room is she in?" He looked up the stairs. "Okay. I'm going to have a look at her." He went up and pushed open the door to the room the guard had indicated. It was a bedroom of inordinate size, perhaps ten metres wide and fifteen long, almost as large as Sinfine's swimming pool. The boundaries of the safe house paid no attention to the pre-existing buildings, rather it penetrated into the surrounding derelicts, giving the wrongful impression that it was the remnants of a larger construction, the floors and paint of which was being dissolved from the outside. At the opposite end of the room was a king-size bed with Lino there arrayed in a corpselike position, feet together and hands clasped. Sinfine went closer.

"She hasn't snapped out of it yet, then," he said.

"No, sir, she hasn't," the guard, who had followed him up the stairs, answered.

"Well, get the doctor to have a look at her! She's a valuable fucking asset, moron!"

Horse jumped to attention. Sinfine's goon squad all knew that the best reaction to his unpredictable eruptions of temper was instant action. "Yes, sir," he said and looked at the door. "Okay to leave you alone here, Mr Sinfine?"

"Does it look to you like she's going to overpower me and escape?"

"No sir." Horse hurried downstairs to get the doctor. The house had a semiresident doctor, because this was where any wounded Sinfine man went to be stitched up, or chopped up, depending on whether he was dead or not. If it wasn't a Sinfine man, the line between stitching and chopping had been known to move around a bit. When he was alone with Lino, Sinfine frowned, then reached down the front of her dress and squeezed one of her nipples, hard. No reaction.

"Just checking," he said. "Where's the doctor? I want to be sure you're going to wake up enough to put on another demonstration."

Emery arrived outside a little later. His life was becoming too busy. Already today, after no sleep the night of the pitfight and little last night, he had arranged with the old car guy to put all the SRM damage to the Buick to rights, organised a big tag and flyer campaign in the city to pull the punters back to the Coolio arena, played telephone hockey with Blue Suit's goddamned Senior Protector, put the capture and kill word out on Jim, and now he was back on the accompany Sinfine and do what he was told detail, which he loathed. In spite of his large size and general hired-killer appearance, he was also a brains man. One day, he hoped, there would be an opening for a new Cousin, and he was going to be it. Not by a recommendation from Sinfine, though. Sinfine never recommended anybody for anything except sudden death.

Because Emery was thinking uncool thoughts, he was less careful than usual, and so he did not notice that he was being observed.

From a crumbled brick frame window on the opposite side of the alley and a floor above ground, someone knelt, watching Emery step up to the boarded-up entranceway, drum rhythmically on it, and after waiting a moment for it to open, enter. The watcher took out a paper notebook and painstakingly recorded what had transpired, closed the notebook again, put it back into his jacket pocket, and returned to the position he had occupied before with head resting on heel of hand and elbow resting on window ledge. It must happen all the time that knowledge is collected, recorded, and then for a time lays unreceived in the in-tray of the universe. There must be a law of disconservation of facts, formulating the obvious truth that information does not exist unless it is communicated.

Another uncommunicated fact, there was still another person in the alley. On the same side of the alley as, and out of sight of, the first floor window a figure slipped out from behind the obligatory pile of bricks, bottles, doorframes and plastic bags of domestic refuse so long abandoned that they had lost even the capacity to stink. Silently, this third person edged along the wall to the dead end of the alley, and then disappeared through an unseen opening.

Emery meanwhile had met up with Sinfine in the bedroom.

"About time you got here," Sinfine told him. "Find out where the fucking doctor is."

"He's on his way." Emery had picked up this piece of news as he passed through the ground floor. "Should be here in a few minutes." He looked at the bed and Lino. "Still out cold?"

"She's not out cold, she's in a cocksucking coma. Maybe she burned out all her fuses when she stirred up the bugs like that. Anyway, I want her awake. She's no use to me like this."

"What did Blue Suit say?" Emery had to admit to a little bit of admiration for Sinfine. There was no way he would have dared a meeting with Blue Suit the way Sinfine had. Blue Suit could have squashed him like a disturbing moth at the candlelight of his upmarket restaurant repast. Of course the difference between Emery and Sinfine was that Sinfine ran those kinds of risks without even knowing that he was doing it. At Emery's question, he looked pleased with himself.

"He's ready to do a deal," he said importantly. "Soon as I decide what he's got that I want."

"What's he got that you don't want?" Emery asked. "Sir," he added quickly. Sinfine gave him a cold stare.

"You just make sure the doctor wakes this bitch up," he said. "I want her ready for action, and soon."

CHAPTER 27

Jelli has lost her family

The disappearance of Jelli's entire family was now two days past, and although she called home every time she remembered to, Whak had failed to return as he had promised, and of Lino there was not a sign. Jelli was sitting at her desk staring at the telephone when Allynn came into her office.

"Reports from GOV1 Advertising, Behavioural Sampling, and Law and Order," Allynn said, dropping the thin folders onto the corner of the desk.

"Hmmm."

"What do you think has happened?"

"I'm trying to work that out," Jelli said without shifting her eyes from the telephone.

"Have you heard anything from the police?" asked Allynn.

"The police don't care unless it's a murder, and even then they only want to know if it's somebody famous. Whak is only famous if you can read. I should have had Whak written into the Adventures of the Agee Family, then the police commissioner would have jumped to attention. He loves that show. Which shows the quality of people we have in the police force. Idiots." She decided to stare instead at the pile of folders Allynn had just dropped. "I told the police to pick up that Jim character, and they just looked in their records and said, he doesn't exist. Hardly anybody exists if you go by police records. I knew that he was up to something. Whak said oh, no, he's okay, but I knew. I can tell when somebody's got a scam going." She put a hand up to one eye. "Oh shit, I'm crying," she complained.

"Well, of course you're crying, you're upset," Allynn told her. "Your family's missing. You should be hysterical. You should be screaming. Even if you do treat them terribly most of the time. You still love them."

"What sort of love is that?" Jelli said sadly. "I cheat on Whak and I only speak to Lino when we're having a fight. They probably left me. I would leave me. Except they wouldn't have all gone separately like that. If they were leaving they would have waited until the morning and then both gone at the same time, and what about Jim? It's something else. And Lino wouldn't leave. Whak might leave. Whak might disappear for a week because he wanted to learn something about himself or so he could write an epic in a cave or so he could study my reaction, damn him. You know, I've got no control over him at all. I suppose that's why I keep him. It's like living with a wild animal."

"Sounds fun."

"Unpredictable. Not fun. Educational. I've got power over everybody else that I know, I've got some sort of control over them. I can sack you. I can embarrass Consortium officials. I can screw Blue Suit until his testicles hurt. And so on. But Whak I can't touch. He just doesn't care. He'd find it absolutely fascinating to be carted off to an agridistrict and made to tend maize. He'd write a poem about it."

Allynn thought that was unlikely, but she said nothing.

"And Lino doesn't care, either, but she wouldn't just leave. It's only when she's up that she can even leave her room, let alone her entire life."

"They'll be all right." Allynn spoke soothingly, as if to a child who could be convinced by words that things were not as they seemed. Fortunately, Jelli was too concerned about Lino and Whak to be insulted.

"Be sensible, Allynn. If anyone else disappeared for two days, we'd be saying, they're history." She had slow tears on her cheeks, now. "Fuck these emotions."

"Everybody has them."

"Give me those folders."

Allynn pushed them across the desk. Jelli picked up the Behavioural Sampling report and flicked through the small selection of charts and tables. Not finding anything there to comment on, she dropped it and took the next folder in the pile. And the next. And the next.

"Why don't you take some time off? You're not needed here," Allynn asked, realising almost as soon as she had said it that she had with one breath tried to take away Jelli's only distractant and suggested that what she did was unimportant. "At the moment, I mean," she quickly added.

"Sit at home wondering where everyone is instead of sitting here wondering where everyone is. Great idea, Allynn," Jelli said sarcastically. She looked at the Law and Order Project report. "So, they've finally admitted that they can't establish a correlation between criminal offence frequency and the acceptance of authority shown in TV drama. I could have told them that."

"You did, I think."

"But they had to prove it scientifically at great expense. Well, I could have been wrong." She wiped her face dry. "But I wasn't. I seldom am. Got that?"

"I know." But people who are seldom wrong seldom need to make such claims.

Jelli held the Law and Order folder up in front of her face and for a moment she was the indefatigable CEO of PushRight Creative Media Inc once again.

"There is someone else I can get to look for Whak and Lino," she muttered. "He'll be able to find them. Why didn't I think of it before?"

"Not Blue Suit." Allynn made a shocked face.

"Yes. Why not?"

Jelli didn't actually want to ask Blue Suit for help. She didn't really want to even think about Blue Suit at this moment, because she didn't want to see him while she felt so vulnerable. But he might be able to find out what had happened to Whak and Lino. He might be responsible for whatever had happened to Whak and Lino, which was all the more reason to see him.

"Arrange it," she told Allynn.

At Jim's Apartment

Jim's apartment on the third floor of a Combine Street ex-office block was neither large nor comfortable, but it had a good view. It was a single room affair, except for the toilet, which was panelled off. It worked. It was plumbed into the building system so that a bucketful of water thrown in after use flushed the excrements way down below, into the sewers Jim hoped, although he couldn't be certain. The kitchen was a gas-fired three-ring stove hooked up to a cylinder of propane gas. A guy came around every couple of weeks and for a few dollars swapped the empty for a full. The windows had, when new, been mirrored, and by some over-engineered miracle the coating had survived the intervening years of constant neglect. The third floor was just high enough to escape the shattered fate of windows closer to the street, too. Jim liked it up here, but he had admitted that it was not made up for three men to spend two long days in without ever leaving. George Assok was a toilet hog, for example, and Whak had started mumbling verses to himself, which meant that the chance of them surviving another two days without violence was slight.   There was no telephone, of course, so they were incommunicado and could not even have the release of letting important people in their lives, if any of them apart from Whak had lives with important people in them, know where they were.

On the bright side, it wasn't strictly true that there had been three men in here for two days.

"Where's Jim gone?" George Assok asked for the tenth time. "When is he coming back? Why did he go out? He'll lead our enemies to us!"

"Please stop," Whak told him. "The melodrama pains me."

"You'll be less concerned about your artistic sensibilities when a horde of Blue Suits burst in that door guns with blazing and kill us both."

"I'm sure," said Whak. He was being flippant, but whoever directed his mental picture show thought that the suggestion had great possibilities. In the vivid but unseeing way that visualisation always happened for him, as if he was remembering something recent, he saw the door fly open as George had said, guns waving at the ends of suit jacket arms, he and George falling bloody to the floor. "Ridiculous," he snorted. So he was caught utterly by surprise when the door did fly open, just as he had imagined, and revealed nothing more dangerous than Jim.

"Don't do that," he said when he recovered from the shock. "George was just saying..."

"Never mind that," George broke in. "Where have you been? We wake up, you're not here, you could have gone to Blue Suit for all we knew. If we'd had any sense we would have left here as soon as we saw you were missing." He looked at Whak angrily. It had been Whak who had insisted on staying.

"Not without my daughter," Whak said again, for the record.

"That's where I went," Jim told them. He closed the door behind him and rubbed his eyes tiredly. "I think I've found where they've got her."

Whak started forward. "Where?" he asked. "Where have they got her?"

"Like I said, down near the Wasteland. But I know what building. I saw Sinfine's offsider go there."

"What did you think you were doing?" George Assok was still angry. "We're trying to escape being killed by Blue Suit and you go out and walk around in broad daylight as bold a brass. If you'd been picked up then they'd have found out where we are."

"I don't care about you and Blue Suit," Whak told him. "I'm only interested in Lino."

"It wasn't broad daylight," Jim put in. "I left before dawn. It's still only ten o'clock. And no-one knows that you're with me. Blue Suit isn't after me, it's Sinfine who wants me out of the way."

Whak gave him a sharp look. "Why?" he asked.

"Why?"

"Why does Sinfine want you out of the way? Because you're a witness? What does he care?"

"Well, I don't know. But he does." Jim looked uncomfortable. "How are we going to get Lino out of there?" He was changing the subject, Whak saw, but at the moment there were admittedly more important things to worry about.

"Lead the way," he said. "And let's avail ourselves of a telephone, somewhere. Jelli must be out of her mind."

Whak had always thought, as he watched the two-dimensional heroes of the small screen, that there could be no adventure in a world where everyone acted in a careful and thoughtful manner. The good guy would not be in such terrible trouble if only he had been wise enough not to get out of bed that morning. Or if he had refused to do what the equally two-dimensional shady character had silkily suggested, or if he had not been staring blindly at the heroine's well-presented breasts when he should have been paying attention to what the scriptwriter had in store. That assumption had proved to be wanting. He had acted in his most reasonable manner and still, here he was in a Combine Street shoebox with a street chimp and a deranged scientist.

He had laughed along with everyone else at the common mistake of calling friends and family when on the run with the inevitable consequence that they all died as the protagonists tracked them with predictable efficiency until the penultimate scenes. But here in the real world he couldn't believe that every telephone in the city was bugged or that Blue Suit or anyone else had the ability any longer to trace a call. He glared at George Assok as he opened his mouth.

"I'm calling Jelli," he said. "Don't argue."

George Assok obviously wanted to argue, but he closed his mouth again. Jim pointed his finger at the door.

"Let's go then," he said.

"I'd rather stay here," Assok said.

"Alone? This Sinfine person might turn up anytime, George." Whak smiled happily. "I'm sure he'll think that you're a friend of Jim's. He'll ask you where he is. He'll ask and ask and ask. He'll ask your fingers and he'll ask your toes." Whak had no idea whether any of this was true, but he certainly hoped it was.

"He'll ask really hard," Jim agreed.

"God," Assok mumbled. "The fate of the world hangs in the balance and we're stumbling around the city after your daughter."

"One crisis at a time, George." Whak went out of the door.

Jelli asks Blue Suit for Help

Blue Suit was not surprised to hear from Jelli. Once he had become aware of her manoeuvring of George Assok via her husband, his admiration for her had increased, and now that neither Assok nor Whak Puihare were to be found, he imagined that she was responsible for their current whereabouts and safety and that she wanted to talk trade. He was open to it, especially since he had the hole card. He would soon have Lino. He wondered what Jelli would have to offer in return.

They met this time at the Blue Suit offices, which gave him the extra edge of being seated in his own empire. He looked at his watch and at the door of his office. She was late. To keep the king waiting in his castle. Edge nullification, deliberate without doubt.

Then she arrived, and Blue Suit let her seat herself before he spoke. She had that Allynn woman with her, unfortunately. Jelli crossed her legs in her casual way and looked into Blue Suit's eyes and instantly emanated sexual availability in a way that he had seen her do before. Blue Suit did not try to analyse how Jelli was able to produce the effect without any apparent motive cause or organ, but simply enjoyed it.

"Hello Jelli. Charming to see you," he said.

"Yes," Jelli replied politely. "Charming."

"You have something you wish to discuss?"

Jelli nodded.

"I have a problem," she said, looking at her hands. She glanced up and caught a glimpse of expression on Blue Suit's face, but she wasn't sure what expression it was. "I thought you might be able to help me with it." She went back to submissively studying her lap.

This was not what Blue Suit had expected. Her subdued manner was charming and he wondered if it was genuine. He thought that he would ask her next time they had sex.

"Go on," Blue Suit said.

Jelli looked up. "My husband and daughter are missing." She watched Blue Suit closely as she spoke, and saw that he was surprised. That was a relief. "I haven't seen either of them for two days."

"The police are in charge of locating missing persons," Blue Suit pointed out. If she didn't know where her husband was, then she didn't know where George Assok was, either. Or so she claimed.

"The police aren't interested unless there's a body. They give up on missing person cases before you finish telling them the details. I think you might have a better chance of finding them." Jelli leaned forward and put her hand on Blue Suit's desk, not far from his.

"What do you know?" Blue Suit asked, very seriously. His own hands pulsed. He wanted to take her and pull her across the desk.

"Nothing," Jelli lied. She wasn't about to mention the fact that Whak was last heard of in the company of an eccentric, paranoid nanotechnology researcher. She was not yet sure whether George Assok was a force for good or for ill in her life.

"Then what do you think has happened?"

"Lino went out two nights ago with a young man about whom I know almost nothing. His name was Jim. They went out, and they haven't come back." She forced herself to be fair. "Although to be honest I wouldn't have known if Lino came home and then went out again. She slips in and out as she pleases."

"I could have the local observation records for that night processed for women of her description," Blue Suit offered. "I'll need photographs."

"I would have thought you'd have photographs of everyone in the world by now," said Jelli. "But I brought some." She got them out of her bag and passed them over. There was one of Whak, looking dopey, and one of Lino, looking surly. She waited until he returned his gaze to her face and then went on talking.

"Whak went out the same night, the 17th. I think he went to the pitfight in Coolio Park. I told him that he was running a risk." She had actually told him to get his ass out there and make like a spy for her, which made anything that had happened to him her fault. "You should clean those pitfights up," she told Blue Suit pointedly, but he brushed it aside.

"It's a police matter, I'm afraid. No security implications. However, there was an SRM event at the Coolio Park pitfight on that date."

"SRM event?" Jelli said in a startled voice. "Another one?"

"There have been several," Blue Suit nodded. "As I have always maintained, SRMs are a danger to human beings at many levels and all efforts should be made to eliminate them."

"Your Collection Project should be well on the way to achieving that, shouldn't it?"

"We are making progress," he said guardedly.

"You're saying that Whak might have been caught up in the pitfight event?"

"Possibly. I don't want you to worry unduly until that is confirmed or denied."

"All right, I won't," said Jelli, well aware that Whak had spoken to her day after the pitfight and that whatever had happened to him now, it was nothing to do with SRMs, except in the sense that everything in the world was something to do with SRMs. "Another thing."

"Yes?"

"Until my family's whereabouts is known, I don't think we should hold any more private meetings." This was the stick and the carrot in one. She leaned forward and spoke under her breath. "I can't be with you when I don't know what's happened to them."

This was the second time in the past few days that Jelli had caused him feelings that he did not wish to have. As another wave of something, doubt, loss, or desire, crashed down, and his chest tightened, he said smoothly "I quite understand."

Jelli noted with some surprise that if he had felt disappointment or rejection, he didn't show it. She stood up and motioned for Allynn, who suddenly rematerialised from nothingness, to do the same. "When do you think you'll have some news?"

"Soon, I hope," said Blue Suit absently. He was trying to push all the unhappiness she was causing him down below the consciousness level, so that he could think. He was aware that he was angry. A wide-ranging anger, but largely directed at Jelli. "Soon."

CHAPTER 28

Emery goes to the House

"One thing I hate," said Sinfine as he accepted a glass of lime water from the maid, whom he trusted with both food and household security. "One thing I hate is doctors. Always saying they have to know this and they have to check that and they can't just stick a needle in. And another thing is no fucking telephones. Why can't we run a telephone line to the other house? I want to know if the doc has woken her up yet."

"A telephone line wouldn't last very long, Mr Sinfine." Emery was standing at attention beside the table. "Not that close to the Wasteland. SRM teardown is real bad there."

"What about a radio? What's wrong with that?"

"Be like a homing beacon, sir. Everybody would know where the place was."

"Shit." Sinfine looked at the telephone that he had sitting on an ornate little stand by the wall. "Let's use fucking smoke signals to run our business, then."

"Same problem, sir. Too easily traced."

"I was kidding, moron! Jesus Christ." Sinfine drummed his fingers. "Go down to the house and find out what the doctor's found out. Go!"

"What about the ticket run? You told me to get tonight's tickets out to the nephews."

"Fuck the ticket run. Get someone else to do it."

"Those tickets are worth a lot of money to us. The odds men can't start the bets until they have them."

Sinfine's eyes would have cut glass. "Get this straight, ticket-run-man. Those tickets aren't worth anything to you. They're worth something to me. Since when did we become us? You'll get your pay whether you do the ticket run or not. It doesn't take a genius to tell the nephews who's on tonight. Doesn't take a genius to go down to the house and find out what I want to know, either. Doesn't take a genius to know when to do what he's fucking told."

Emery went. Either way, he got to get away from Sinfine for an hour.

Whak, Assok, Jim go to House

Whak drove while Jim directed and George Assok took his customary position low down and out of sight on the back seat.

"You comfortable back there?" Whak asked him.

"Fine, thanks," Assok replied.

"As a scientist, don't you think that you're granting too much power to bad luck? The chance of anyone who's looking for you seeing your face go by at..." Whak inspected the speedo, "eighty k's, is low, I bet."

"I like it down here. You're advertising our presence quite widely enough without any help from me."

"They're not looking for me, you said."

"They might be now."

"Turn left," Jim said. He tried not to get involved in the ongoing argument between Whak and the other guy, George, about who was chasing whom. So far as he was concerned, Whak was here because he was Lino's father, and Assok was here because he was with Whak. The fact that they both seemed to be on the run from Blue Suit, or maybe only George was, didn't matter a shit. He was on the run from Sinfine. Being on the run was a fact of existence. He reflected that this always seemed to have been the case, ever since his father left and his mother died a few years later of what some smart-ass at the time deemed a broken heart, at a time in his adolescence that might have been programmed to render his life one of hustle to survive.

"Better park," he suggested. "We're getting close."

"The hero swung his battle-weary stallion into a convenient angle park," Whak said flatly. The other two said nothing. If Whak wanted to play a light song to cover his fears, that was fine with them. They were wishing that they had ways to deal with their own.

The street that they were now in ran between two rows of utterly gutted buildings that must once have been warehouses and depots of various kinds. Some of the buildings were collapsed, so that through glassless frames piles of fallen bricks and ceiling plaster could be seen.

"Where is she?" Whak said. He cast his eyes about the vista of abandonment impatiently.

"This way," said Jim. He set off in a cautious keep-near-the-wall manner in a southerly direction. The further south you went in this city, the more the world lost all flavour of man, the champion of order. As they skulked, Whak asked questions.

"What's this connection between Lino and SRMs?" He didn't indicate whom he was speaking to, so at first nobody answered him, and then both the others tried to speak at once.

"It's when she gets, you know, stressed. She goes all quiet and then, wham, the SRMs come," Jim said when they had all stopped talking. He went on, "and then she just loses it altogether. Goes completely mindzip."

"Completely mindzip," Whak muttered.

"Smalltech did some research into this very phenomenon once," George volunteered from behind. He seemed quite at home, creeping through desolate streets amongst rusty skips and burned-out vehicles, walking like a duck. "I believe that was the project that you volunteered for, Puihare."

"You wanted to take brain biopsies," Whak shuddered. "You must have been insane to think anyone would let you take brain biopsies. My brain is private property."

"In fact, we did get some samples of brain tissue," George said brightly. "But it turned out that the correlation between brain tissue abnormalities and hypothetical SRM to human relationships was insignificant."

"What were you trying to find out?"

"Down this alley. In that door," Jim directed.

"It was suggested once that SRMs tended to congregate in areas of human activity. Smalltech was trying to establish some kind of link."

"Well, of course they congregate in areas of human activity. Where else will they find the junk they need to make more SRMs?" Whak said scornfully. "I hate it when millions of dollars are spent proving that goddamned traffic deaths are related to the number of cars on the road, or airliner crashes are directly proportional to uncontrolled landings. Don't any of you have any common sense?"

"Science is the history of common sense being wrong."

"Up the stairs. We've got to go across to the other side. The place I think Lino's being held is across the next alley. We can look it over from this building." Jim was paying little attention to Whak and George Assok's conversation.

Whak got to the landing at the top of the stairs and looked across the shattered interior. Bits of rafter and joist hung crooked from the floor above, and half of this floor was protruding into the floor below that. Whak put out a testing foot. The floor felt distinctly spongy.

"Have you been in here before?" he asked as Jim stepped out across the maze of holes and other obstacles.

"Nope," Jim replied. He edged past a section of the floor that
he judged to be unsafe. "I think we should go one at a time. And
better keep quiet."

"Definitely."

"Why are we doing this?" Assok complained. "We can look
this place over from the ground, can't we? Why does everything
have to be so dangerous?"

Whak followed Jim. He was heavier. The floor creaked
everywhere he stood. He was tiptoeing, as if his weight could be
reduced by careful balance, over a line of nails that stuck up from
where a wall must have been untidily removed. Walls, he
thought, are usually built over floor joists. The gaps between the
nails were slightly smaller than his shoe size, and when he
accidentally lowered his heel a fraction he was rebuked by a sharp
pain. He took a longer step and found himself on a small section
of tiles that must once have been a bathroom. Ahead of him, Jim
was trying to find a way around a gap in the floor. He glanced
down.

"Hey, there's a body down there," he said, leaned forward a
little too much, and fell into the hole.

Jim disappeared in regulation silence. Whak was not so well-
disciplined.

"Jim!" he shouted, and as quickly as his continued survival
would allow, he moved over to look into the hole. Jim was
hanging onto a crossbeam a metre below him, with his arms and
kicking furiously. Below that, the next level down had practically
no floor at all, and below that it was a long drop to the basement,
where another hole picked up where this one left off. A fall from
the height Jim was dangling at would almost certainly break his
legs.

"You're not going to fly by kicking your legs," Whak told
him, relieved that he had not already fallen. He put out an arm,
but he couldn't reach. Behind him, George Assok said "Ouch,
damn."

"Walk on your toes, George," Whak called to him. "And
hurry up."

"Yeah, hurry up!" Jim looked considerably less self-assured
dangling in space. Below him, Whak saw a pair of seriously
mangy dogs appear and look up at Jim's legs with an expression
and saliva volume that suggested hunger.

"Dogs don't eat people," he said consolingly.

"Get me up!"

Assok arrived at Whak's elbow. "Hmm," he said, studying the situation. "We need a pole."

There were no poles. When Whak tried to remove a rafter from a nearby collapse, it collapsed further, filling the air with plaster dust that choked him and made his eyes sting.

Jim called "What about a rope?"

The dogs started to bark.

"Dogs don't eat people," Whak told everyone again. "They're just excited."

"They're rabid! Get me out of this!"

Trousers are always useful for covering and warmth, but Whak had never expected to use them for a rescue. Both he and George Assok stood braced with the stale air of the condemned building cooling their hairy thighs while Jim clutched at the makeshift rope and they pulled him slowly up until he could drag his body over the edge.

"Thanks," he gasped after a few moments.

"No problem," Whak replied. "Where now?"

"Can I put my trousers back on before we throw ourselves into the next disaster, if you don't mind?" Assok said. They both re-donned their pants.

"There's a body down there," Jim pointed. "See the arm sticking out?"

"It's probably a mannequin," Whak told him. "Otherwise the dogs would be eating it."

The three men made it to the windows on the opposite side of the building with only a nail in George's foot and a glass cut to his arm paid in toll, and looked down onto the boarded-up door that led to Sinfine's safe house. They spoke quietly together.

"That's the place," Jim said. He rubbed his shoulder and made a pained face. "She's in there. I think."

"Well, why don't we go in there and get her?" Whak asked. "There's no place for fear where love is involved, is there?" He frowned. "Although death does seem to be watching us closely. What do you think, George?"

"I think we should at least find another way in than through the front door," George said. He studied the door for a moment. "None of us are trained in hostage recapture, I take it?"

"You take it correctly," Whak nodded grimly. "No hidden talents."

"Someone's approaching," said George.

"That's Emery," Jim told them both. "He's Sinfine's number two, I think."

"Great!" Whak made fists. "Let's jump him and trade him for Lino!"

"He's got a gun," Jim said.

"Oh."

"Sinfine isn't the kind of guy you want to be doing deals with, either," Jim spoke from experience. Whak gave him another hard look, but did not pursue it.

Emery knocked on the door. After a minute, he knocked again.

"They're not letting him in," Whak murmured.

Emery knocked one more time, then he went back up the alley and returned with a crowbar. After a couple of efficient applications of this tool, the door swung open. The three men watching him looked briefly at each other - what the fuck is going on? - and fell silent.

Emery entered the building. Two minutes later, he came running out again. He looked along the alley in both directions, but fortunately not upwards, and then sprinted off to where he must have left his car. The boarded-up door hung open.

Whak grabbed Jim's arm. "What's happening?" he demanded.

"I don't know!" Jim was as puzzled as the others.

"Let's go and find out, then," Whak said. He put his head out the window, then his legs. "There's a big pile of stuff down there," he said. "Wish me luck." He jumped.

"You fucking crazy man!" Jim called after him. But the fall was really only half a floor. The big pile of stuff that Whak landed in was not soft, but at least it stopped his fall after only a couple of metres. Whak rolled down the junkpile with a series of grunts and pained yelps, met the pavement and got back to his feet.

"No problem," he winced. "Coming?" He ran across the street and in the door. Jim found himself with no option but to leap out the window after him. George Assok did not. He found other choices.

"I'll catch up," he called down to Jim when the young man had finished staggering about wiping what seemed to be copious quantities of dog shit off his feet. "I'll find another way down."

"It's only me that falls into dogshit," Jim assured him, "but okay. Don't attract any attention!"

George found it unbelievable that one of these lunatics who had dragged him out onto the streets at a time when all their lives were in danger should tell him not to attract any attention. He disappeared from the window. Jim would have liked to have smelt less of crap, but he also wanted to find out what was happening in the house, so he just grabbed a piece of cloth from the general heap of garbage and followed after Whak, trying to wipe his shoes as he ran.

As he entered the house, the grey decay outside was shockingly replaced by neatness and quality. If he had been able to draw comparisons with a four star hotel of a decade earlier, this room would have lost, but to Jim it was as luxurious as either the Puihare's or Sinfine's castles, and he stopped for a second just inside the door to make sure that his memories were complete and that he had not just awoken from an amnesiac dream. Behind him there came a footstep and he whirled around only to find George Assok.

"Where's Puihare?" George asked.

"In here somewhere." Jim went looking. He found a man lying face down on a rug that was efficiently blotting up his blood. There were several bullet holes in the man's shirt. Assok turned the dead face sideways and shook his head, while Jim looked in the next room, which was empty. As he came back to George, he saw him examining another body attached to a pair of legs, which stuck out from another doorway opposite.

"Is he..."

"He's dead," said Assok. "Have you found him?"

"No."

"I'm up here," Whak's voice came from above. There was a mezzanine balcony that Jim and George Assok only now noticed. "Lino isn't here," he said sadly.

"It looks like that's a good thing, Puihare," said George, almost gently. "Everybody who is here is dead."

"If Lino isn't here, than I think we should piss off away from this place, and fast," suggested Jim. "Bad things have happened here."

"Yeah. Obviously. Let's go." Whak came down the stairs wearing an intent expression, a grey shadow of mind trying to expand fast enough in every direction to capture a fleeing fact. But there were no facts. There were no clues. It was a dead end.

The smoke trail from a burning cigarette paper

Lino felt sensations. She didn't want to feel anything, but the windlike rushing, starting as a whisper in the distance and drawing closer to where she rotated in darkness, forced her to listen. There was now something other than herself. Then, still not wanting, she peeled open her inner eyes to discover more about this other something and saw curvaceous walls of indeterminate colour that spun with the imponderability and rightness of the stars, as slowly as, as forever as the dreamtime, changing and unchanging as a moment without memory.

The wind spoke.

But I'm happy, Lino thought uselessly, because she had been happy before she thought, and the return of thought brought with it the return of pain. The wind didn't care. It rushed louder. Time restarted. Lino and the wind travelled together.

The doctor pulled the needle out of her arm and thought briefly about hepatitis, AIDS, and other diseases that when he was younger he might have thought good reason to throw the shiny silver shaft away, then wiped it carefully with spirits and put it back into his bag. He jerked his head around at the sounds from downstairs. He went to the door.

"What's happening down there?" he called. There was a spattering sort of noise, and then the doctor didn't care, anymore, about anything. Stolen happiness can bring with it surprises.

"What now?" Whak saw a packet of cigarettes poking from the pocket of a dead man and jerked them out. "I gave these up once," he said, pulled one out and stuck it crookedly in the corner of his mouth.

"You want to light that?" Jim asked, lighting his own.

"Not right now," he said around the cigarette. "Later." He shook his head and shoulders like a large dog after a swim. "What now?" he repeated.

"We leave," George agreed with Jim.

"I mean, how do we find Lino?"

"I don't know," Jim admitted.

"We have to find Lino."

The three men went back out the boarded-up door and took the ground level route to their car, a half-block walk, but safer than trying to cross inside the ruins. They were almost back on the wider road that separated these wrecks of buildings from the Wasteland, when two men stepped out, one from each side of the alley's mouth. Like everyone else in the world, it seemed, except for Whak, George and Jim, they had guns.

"Don't move," the one on the left said. "You're under arrest."

CHAPTER 29

Whak and Assok arrested

The two men conversed animatedly, without once looking away from Whak, George Assok, and Jim, who while held at gunpoint tried to see a way past them that did not involve being shot dead.

"Are these the guys?"

"I don't know, do I? They're here, aren't they?"

"You got the pictures?"

"Yeah."

"Well let's see them."

The man with the images slowly reached into his coat. He drew out a few sheets of paper and did a focus flicker from Whak's face to the pictures that made Whak feel slightly, empathetically, dizzy.

"You George Assok?" he asked Whak.

"Wrong picture," Whak told him.

The man turned his eyes onto the real George Assok.

"You George Assok?" he asked in exactly the same tone as before.

"Herman Kithing," George said without hesitation. "Electronics engineer." He made to get out his wallet.

"Don't move," said the other man.

"Who are you people?" George asked, every nuance a man mistaken for someone else.

"Blue Suit," said the man on the right. He spent a bit more time shifting his gaze rapidly from the papers in his hand to the faces of his prisoners. Whak's eyes began to lose focus in sympathy and he leaned heavily to one side. He had always been susceptible to suggestion, even when he was not in such a charged state as he was at present.

"Hey, you, stand straight," the man told him, but it was out of Whak's hands. He keeled over.

"Christ," said the one without the pictures. Waving his gun in an alarming fashion, he edged up to Whak and slapped him roughly. As he stood up and faced the other man, he was turned away from Jim, who, seeing his opportunity, took a flying leaping dash for one of the broken square faces that looked out from the alley walls. One of the two blue suits took a desultory potshot at him, but when he disappeared headfirst into a window they immediately lost interest.

The one with the pictures said "Forget him. He's not on the list. Let's not be too efficient. Remember what happened when team ninety-four brought in the son of a Consortium director because he was with a subversive."

"Yeah," said the other. "De-employment all round."

"Big mistake. But these two," he waggled his pistol at George Assok and Whak, who was shakily climbing to his feet, "are them, all right. George Assok, right?"

"Herman Kithing," George Assok said firmly. "If you'll just let me get out my ID..."

"ID can be forged. Don't ask me when I last saw an ID that wasn't forged. No, you're him. And this fainting violet here is Whak Puihare, right?"

"Hum," said Whak.

"Just walk around this side of us, that's it. OK. Keep your arms out from your sides."

"We haven't got the car," the other one suddenly realised. "Mike went back to report to Observation. We'll have to take them back to the Station." There ensued a lively discussion as to whether it was acceptable or not to take suspects and prisoners to the Station, because apparently it was classified.

"Why are you arresting us?" Whak asked.

"Sorry, but your having that information is not necessary for successful execution of our mission. Start walking. Straight down this road."

Whak and George Assok walked in front of the two blue suits, responding like two farm animals to commands that steered them around the perimeter of the Wasteland. The wide road, full of potholes, separated them from the tall glass that in turn separated the mountain of discarded stuff from the outside world. Whak spoke to George Assok as they trudged in tones that echoed despair.

"Why are they arresting me? Whak Puihare? George Assok, yes, you're on the run as it is, but why arrest a burned-out dissident poet? I'm not likely to cause any harm." He clutched his fingers together in front of him as he walked, supplicating at the parade of his own fear.

"God, Puihare," George said disgustedly. "Why not just shoot me and save Blue Suit the trouble?"

"Told you he was Assok," said one of the two blue suits. The other nodded seriously.

"All I want is to get my daughter back," Whak continued.

"I'd worry about staying alive for the moment," said George.

They reached a building that was barely distinguishable from rubble and were guided through a hole in what was left of the facade, then down into darkness. One of their captors brought out a hand torch, and suddenly the great door hidden in the basement loomed up. Mounted on the wall was a small voice grille.

"Move back," said one of the blue suits behind them. He stepped in front of them, struck the door sharply with the heel of his hand and spoke into the grille. The door creaked open a little. He put his shoulder against it and pushed. "You two," said the other blue suit, "push."

"What happened to automatic doors?" Whak grunted as he heaved against the riveted surface.

"Broken down," the Suit next to him answered. "This door breaks down a lot. Replacement door parts are hard to get."

"That's what you get with the extinction of technological society," Assok told him.

"We no longer stand on the shoulders of Gods, but in their waste-baskets," Whak added.

"Cheerful bastards, aren't you?"

"You'd do better if your daughter was kidnapped and you were arrested and threatened for no reason at all?" Whak asked.

"Don't expect anything good and you won't be disappointed, I always say," the rearmost blue suit advised them. The door was finally open. Inside, another pair of blue suits returned, panting, to their posts by the voice grille. "Keep walking."

"At least oil the hinges next time," Whak muttered as he moved forward. He looked at the curved walls. "We're in a sewer," he announced.

"Keep going."

They came out in a room that was structurally similar to a car park. There were massive concrete pillars growing out of the concrete floor, holding up the concrete ceiling at an uncomfortably low altitude above their heads. Some pillars, clad with panels, formed the boundaries of large enclosed areas. Smaller offices were built-in along the walls. There were dozens of people in sight, moving around, carrying folders, stacks of paper, piles of optical disks. The faint smell of sood drifted from a vending machine.

"Lock them up in one of the offices."

Assok Meets Colville

But before they could be hustled out of sight, a man turned from the sood machine, looked across the room, and called out. "George Assok!" The man came rushing over, spilling sood down his lab coat in the process. He didn't seem to notice.

"Ex-Smalltech," George muttered to Whak. "Doesn't mind working for murderers, obviously."

"George Assok!" the man repeated. He tapped himself on the chest. "Sedric Linus Colville! Imagine you turning up here like this!"

"He's under arrest," one of the blue suits broke in. He shook his gun-holding hand to draw attention to it. "He's to be held for Blue Suit."

Sedric Linus Colville was a twitchy, Whak observed. He twitched now. And like many twitchy people that Whak knew, when he found himself thwarted, he became more dogged. He drew his skinny self up and put on authority.

"I'm in charge here," he said.

The blue suit with the handful of gun disagreed with that. "You're not in charge of Blue Suit operations," he said.

"I am in charge of this installation. This is my project."

"Yes, but these are political subversives. We're only holding them here for convenience."

"They're in my project building, so they're under my jurisdiction." Colville was looking confident.

"I'm afraid I'll have to call for instructions."

"Fine, do that. In the meantime, I want this man to accompany me." He pointed at George Assok. "I have some technical issues I wish to discuss with him."

One blue suit looked doubtful, but the other said "They're still in the building. They aren't going anywhere."

"All right," the first one decided. "You stick with them. Anything looks like a problem, you shoot to wound, right? I'll call in and report."

The other blue suit was younger than his partner, and found shooting to wound an enchanting proposition. "You bet," he said. He pulled out his gun, checked it, and put it away again. "Any trouble from you two and you'll be walking with a limp," he told

George and Whak in a matter-of-fact way. He nodded at Colville.
"OK," he said.

"Come with me," Colville grabbed George's arm and dragged
him off, immediately beginning a technical monologue that Whak
only heard enough to recognise as largely mathematical. Whak
trailed, and the young blue suit with the fascination for wounding
followed him. Whak noticed that George was being drawn into
an argument with the man who had introduced himself as Sedric
Colville.

"You'll never stabilise the cycle using that method," George
was saying. "Haven't you noticed the way physical tests deviate
from the model? There's an additional factor, I've..." He stopped
and pulled away.

"What additional factor?" Colville demanded, but George was
standing arms folded and unyielding.

He said "At Smalltech we were looking for ways to advance
civilisation, improve the human condition, with self-adaptive
nanomachines. But that's not the aim here, is it?"

"The first step to improving the human condition, yes, the
first step," Colville stuttered, "is to get rid of SRMs. Even now,
they tear down faster as we can build up. This is a fight for
survival, George."

"You listen to Blue Suit too much."

"He pays the bills," Sedric rebutted.

"That's not a good criterion to work with, Sedric. Even if
what you're doing here succeeds, which I doubt, what then?
You're giving the power of nanotechnology to Blue Suit! How
can you work for him? He kills people! What will a man like that
do with nanomachines?" George pointedly turned away from
Colville and made like a statue right in the middle of the
passageway between two rows of desks. Colville became, if
possible, even more agitated and dogged than before.

"Oh, so you doubt that we'll succeed, do you? Have you seen
enough to make that judgement? Operative, bring them with me.
This way. This way. I'll show you what we've accomplished
while you've been hiding and getting involved with God knows
what kinds of disreputable people," he stared briefly at Whak with
a curious expression of fear on his face. "Criminals and terrorists
I don't doubt. While you chose to run away with your knowledge,
we have developed nanomachines with that reproduce without
error up to fifty iterations! Yes! Of course, there are some, some
little wrinkles to be ironed out," he added dismissively.

"Like the fifty-first generation," George muttered.

"We'll find the answer to reproductive fidelity any day now!" Colville snapped back. "It's an incremental process!"

"No it isn't. It's a fundamental error in theory, Sedric. You never have been good at fundamentals."

Whak sighed. Now the two scientists were descending to ad hominem, a sure sign that things were not going well. His dim hope that the twitchy Colville might be some form of rescue was dying fast.

"And what have you achieved in your time in the wilderness?" Colville went on.

"Nothing. How could I? Of course, I already had achieved fifty nanogenerations before I was attacked and chased into hiding," George told him loftily.

Colville was taken aback. He quickly recovered his erratic poise, however, and beckoned to the blue suit. "Come along to the isolation chamber. There's a test scheduled." He made a shaking gesture with both hands as if he was sizing an escaped trout. "I'll show you where the leading edge is," he told George Assok. "Come."

Whak nudged George as they followed the excitable Sedric, and spoke low.

"Do you have to wind him up like that? Can't you get him to turn us loose? I've got to find Lino. And should you be telling him every damn thing about your crazy machines? Things are bad enough without you letting every other narrow-minded technobigot with the wisdom of a lab rat know all your secrets."

"I haven't told him any secrets, and I'm not going to."

"What's this isolation chamber?"

"I can guess. A facility for testing nanoviruses."

"Oh shit. Isn't that superenormously dangerous?"

"Depends. It takes time, even at exponential rates, for the process to reach macro scale. Scale is important."

"What sort of scale needs an isolation chamber?"

"Large scale." George's eyes whitened as he spoke. In the room they had just entered, the floor-to-ceiling tube that comprised the isolation chamber was illuminated by a blue light. It possessed all the attributes of early science-fiction cinema, including a disturbing hum that faintly tickled the back of Whak's ears. Several technicians were working around the chamber and at a pair of console desks on either side of it, and along the wall were a hundred cages from which the flickery sensor lights of

SRMs blinked a dozen colours. Whak wondered how they kept the things confined, until he saw a form he recognised. A scorpion was rotating it's mandibles against the side of it's cage, but without effect. Teeth somehow drawn, Whak concluded.

Colville stopped, clasped his hands, and said in a satisfied voice "The isolation chamber."

"I saw this in Star Trek," Whak said. "How are the trilithium crystals holding up?"

Colville stared at him. "Who are you?" he asked.

"I'm a representative of Continuous Loop AI Systems, and I'm here to ask whether you are happy with your current receptionist? Consider replacing the unreliable bitch with one of our always-cheerful, never-impolite Greetings and Appointment Systems!" Whak said all this in a monotonic drone that held Colville and the nearby technicians indecisively paralysed. "Just ask one of our satisfied customers. George?"

George gave him a worried glance. "He works for PushRight Creative Media," he said, reinventing the truth a little.

"He's on the list," the young blue suit put in.

Colville looked from Whak to George to the blue suit and clearly decided that some questions were not worth asking. He turned his back and went over to talk to one of the technicians. George took a step towards the nearest console and was swiftly reprimanded by the blue suit. Whak scratched himself.

"This is exciting," he said after a minute. Then Colville came back to them and said to the blue suit that the room was now going to be sealed. The doors thudded closed.

"Wood," George noted. "Nanovirus and SRM resistant," he told Whak.

"Pity you can't made brake leads out of it, then."

"Today we're testing a new strain of nanovirus that we've just taken from the simulation stage," Colville started lecturing them. "It incorporates a completely new refocusing algorithm - mine, in fact - that will ensure that the descendent nanos trend towards the parent specification, not away from it." He looked sharply at George. "We've done several full-scale SRM tests here. We have a sample of every SRM type in these cages, or in the storage area one floor down, thanks to the Collection Project. We have too many, in fact, but it seems we have to go on collecting them. You know how single-minded Blue Suit can be." He paused, but George and Whak did not nod, in fact Whak was looking around the room as if for an exit, and George was looking at his watch. "Pay attention! George, you should be fascinated by this."

He was, but he answered otherwise. "Show me the models and I might be interested in pointing out the errors."

"Hah hah hah. Not a chance, George. The latest models are error-free. We've simulated lifecycles out to a thousand replications. Refocus on core instructions is within tolerance."

George sighed. "You must know that real-world tests show deviation from simulations, Sedric, and you know that there's no explanation for the variance, so why do you insist on treating computer tests as gospel?"

"I don't. That's why we have an isolation chamber."

"Well, I'm glad you haven't completely succumbed to hubris."

"What would happen if this blue suit here shot the isolation chamber?" Whak asked.

"I don't miss what I aim at very much," the blue suit said calmly.

"I don't fall over much, well, actually I have done once lately, but I don't walk on tightropes, either. Do you know what would happen if you broke that chamber? Lots of teeny tiny invisible machines would come out and eat you up, that 's what." Whak grinned condescendingly. "Then they'd eat everyone else, all over the world. Then they'd eat the world."

The blue suit suffered a moment of doubt. He looked at Colville.

"Absolutely wrong," Colville told him. "They don't affect organic material at all. And even if you did shoot the chamber, which I'm sure you're not going to, it is negatively pressurised. Any stray nanoviruses would be sucked into the chamber, not blown out. Don't listen to him. He's wrong."

On the wall, the flashing lights of those SRMs that possessed them seemed to blink more rapidly than before. Whak watched them uneasily. His contact with SRMs to date had been mostly at greater distance than this, except for the crocs that he had frequently surprised as they slipped away through the holes they had cut in his garage doors, bits of car dangling from their grippers. The young blue suit decided to place his faith in Colville and resumed his imperturbable calm. They must be trained to have no doubts, Whak thought. Absolute certainty can be yours by technique or predisposition. Constant uncertainty and a roller coaster ricochet ride through the infinitesimal bit of the universe that he was ever going to see, that was Whak's lot, and doubt was a piece and a price of that choice. Right now, he doubted that he was ever going to find Lino or see Jelli again.

Colville became involved in the isolation test. He went and sat down at the left hand console and gave some brief instructions to two technicians. George Assok and Whak were acutely aware of the blue suit behind them and the improbability of avoiding him long enough to get out of the isolation chamber and the wood-lined corridor beyond.

"Might as well enjoy the show," George suggested.

Colville's technicians were moving SRM cages from the back wall to the chamber. There was an airlock of sorts in the side of the tube, set up so that a cage could be placed into it and opened remotely by a little waldo. A larger waldo projected into the chamber far enough to move objects from the airlock to wherever Colville wished them to be placed.

"How can I enjoy the show? Every time I watch a magician saw his assistant in half, blood ends up on the floor." Whak looked at the neat racks of monitoring and control gear behind him. He reached over and flicked a switch up and down. The blue suit was watching the isolation chamber, and didn't notice. "Fancy equipment compared to your basement, George." He flicked it back and forth again.

"They've got funding," George said with some bitterness. "Don't touch things."

"Robot arms, yet," Whak observed.

"They're not robot arms, they're waldos. Operated by a human arm inside. Just an exoskeletal mechanism."

"They look impressive."

"It's easy to look impressive and still not know what you're doing."

"Professional jealousy, is it? You want to be the first to destroy the world. It's not the sort of thing that you want to be second at, is it?"

"Please, Puihare."

Whak fell silent as box after box of SRMs were transferred into compartments in the chamber. They were relatively quiescent, as SRMs often were - for no deducible reason - after being physically handled.

"Why are they doing that?" he asked George.

"The nanos will be released at the top of the chamber and progress downwards, I would say. Or the other way round. By stacking the SRMs, the effects can be monitored over time, as the nanos mutate."

"That other guy said that it won't mutate. Error-free, he said."

George squinted at Whak's naivete. "And you believe him?" he asked.

"I would like to."

"Test commencing in..." Colville looked at some instrument on the console. "Ten seconds," he finished. "Nine, eight, seven."

Although he assumed that similar tests had been performed here dozens or even hundreds of times, Whak was frightened and nervous.

"This is Houston," he whispered to himself. "We have lift-off. God help us."

CHAPTER 30

The Isolation test

There wasn't much to see, except for a faint yellow tinge to the air inside the chamber that deepened and spread, from the bottom, not the top, throughout, but it was never dense enough to impede vision. Men and women droned off the readings of their assorted instrumentation at the same time as the same information was displayed on Colville's console, on which his eyes were firmly focussed. What he was being told, Whak had no idea. He asked George.

"Lots of things," George told him. "Nanovirus population would be the most important one."

Inside the chamber, the cloud of nanoviruses, if that was the proper plural - Whak hoped fervently that he would survive his capture by Blue Suit and find out - was beginning to affect the SRMs. On the lowest shelf, a small scorpion turned it's cutters onto the isolation chamber wall, and Whak flinched, but there was no sign of damage to the tube, and no-one but Whak and possibly George showed any sign of alarm. The view from Whak's location showed that the tube was at thick as a man's forearm. Then the nanovirus must have done whatever adaptation was necessary for it to begin its work. The scorpion's surface, and that of the other varieties of SRM above it, behaved exactly like a fine shine of olive oil in a hot frypan into which a handflick of water has been sprayed. It burst into hundreds of minor explosions. Each explosion generated a perceptible thickening in the yellow haze that filled the tube. In seconds, the skin of the SRM became squirming yellow strands. The exposed interior immediately began to disintegrate in the same way. Within no more than thirty seconds from the moment the yellow haze was introduced into the isolation chamber, all that remained was more haze than before and a few apparently unpalatable fragments of SRM, which continued to sizzle quietly.

"Well," said Colville happily as he tapped a few keys on his keyboard. "That went entirely according to schedule. What do you think of that?" he addressed George, who was clearly impressed, if his open mouth was any indication. "I think we are on the verge of a complete answer to the SRM problem, wouldn't you say?"

"Dr Colville," said a technician.

"Yes?"

"The nanovirus population is still increasing."

"What? It can't be." Colville abandoned his one way ceremony of congratulation with George and hurried back to the console. He looked at something on the screen and grew slightly more sickly-looking than he was already.

"Replication fidelity problems?" George Assok asked sweetly, far too sweetly, Whak considered, for a man about to die. The isolation chamber was becoming visibly more full of yellow haze, and what was more worrying, Whak could see that the inside of the tube was boiling just like the skin of the unfortunate SRMs.

"It's consuming the isolation chamber! Get the deactivation agent!" Colville shouted. The crowd of technicians who until then had been scattered about the room attending to their responsibilities all jerked into action. There was obviously some disaster plan that they were trained to follow, but that plan did not have allowance for Whak, George Assok, and their captor blue suit, who became surrounded by human chaos and had to press themselves against the wall to avoid collisions. Part of the plan must have been to run backwards and forwards across the room uttering incoherent sounds, for that was what some people began to do, but there was an element that had more structured duties. Colville was showing surprising bravery by standing right next to the isolation chamber, in fact he was placing his arm into an opening in the side of the tube, the opening in which an operators hand was required to work the larger of the two waldos.

About four roughly identical technicians were all vying to remove a metal flask from a shiny steel cabinet slightly frosted with condensation that stood with other equipment against the wall between Whak and the great wooden doors. The flask was also cold and the men were using two pairs of tongs to handle it. It was elegantly shaped, a tapering cylinder that curved like a woman's hips into a neck into which a key-head stopper was sunk. Either it was very heavy, or the men were extremely concerned that it should not be dropped, because at least two sets of hands at any moment carried it from it's storage place to the airlock of the isolation tube. They left the cool cabinet doors ajar as they walked with deliberate steps across the room. Colville was flexing the waldo's fingers and shouting at them to hurry. Whak watched all of this with a odd feeling of surprise that he was calm in the face of death, not because he was prepared to die, or because he was clinging to any hope of life, but because the parts of his mind that normally dealt with hope and fear seemed to have overloaded and switched themselves off. Beside him, George Assok was pressing his back into the wall as if he might be able to travel through it by osmosis to safety.

The four struggling technicians used two and a half sets of hands to place the icy flask into the airlock and another pair to shut and seal it. The inside door opened. Immediately the large waldo, guided by Colville, plucked it out of the other side and began to unscrew the lid. But the waldo was beginning to evaporate. The thick metal fingers were hissing into gas. The guide arm sagged. Colville wrestled with failing control. With two robot fingers he turned the stopper half a turn and then half a turn more, and then the stopper fell one way as the waldo collapsed, the flask fell another.

The flask was a djinni bottle in reverse. The yellow haze that was now so dense that the interior of the tube could barely be seen quickly began to thin. Whak took his first breath for as long as he could remember as the violent disruption of the interior surface of the tube stopped and the air became clear. Colville stood motionless with his arm inside what was left of the waldo, looking whiter than white, and in the silence that had fallen said "Clean the chamber."

His voice was hardly loud enough to be heard from where Whak now stood. He continued to stand where he was while some of his staff began a well-rehearsed operation at the consoles. When preparations were ready, and his order was waited on, he swayed.

"My arm," he said, "feels odd." He pulled his arm slowly out of the waldo and as it became visible, a scream from a young man near him initiated, by infection, a brief cacophony of monkey noises around the room. Colville's arm from mid-forearm down was reduced to a shaft of shiny bone. His hand and fingers were entirely gone. Colville took one goggle-eyed look at what was left of his arm and fell heavily to the floor.

"Medic!" someone shouted. But there was no medic available in the isolation chamber room. Colville lay on the floor without even a lap on which to place his head while someone else assumed authority and the necessary steps were gone through to clean the tube. There were multiple flashes of blinding light without warning and more placing of objects in the airlock before the cleanup was complete. Then the woman who had taken charge ordered the room unsealed. The massively thick wooden doors began to creep open.

The blue suit next to Whak was staring fixedly at Colville's ulna bone, which protruded from the muscle which ceased between his elbow and wrist. The sudden discontinuity was marked by grey and unbleeding flesh. The blue suit's face was similarly grey. Except for two who were dithering around by Colville, all the technicians were now herding up to the opening doors, in haste to leave mistakes and pain behind them, and no-one was paying any attention to the two strangers and the blue suit operative. As soon as the doors gaped wide enough, the exodus began.

Whak's desire for freedom was now. He struck the invigilant blue suit as hard as he could on the back of the neck and although there was a worrying cracking noise, he was sure that it was caused by the man's nose striking the floor, and not anything more serious.

"Come on, George," he said.

"You amaze, me Puihare," George Assok said, but he jumped into action, nonetheless, and did something that Whak would never have thought of. He reached down, retrieved the blue suit's gun, and pointed it aggressively at the two technicians who were trying to make the unconscious Colville comfortable.

"Take off your coats," he ordered.

"Good scheme," Whak agreed enthusiastically. "Take off your coats," he repeated Assok's order. "This man is a desperate criminal. Don't make him mad."

With a lab coat on, George looked to be an unassuming technician, but Whak was one of those people who always look the same whether dressed in tuxedo or swimming togs, and in a lab coat he looked like a graffiti poet in a lab coat. Luckily, the other blue suit operative must have settled into an office somewhere so was not in sight, and the disaster in the isolation chamber was still occupying everyone's attention. While Colville was being carried to treatment on a stretcher, George was pushing Whak ahead of him through the maze of workstations that filled the main floor space of the station. They continued down a corridor at the far end of the complex, and up a flight of stairs.

"This must lead to the surface," he told Whak. "We might be able to escape from up there."

At the top of the stairs they exited from a door that was camouflaged behind a couple of old bus side panels, into a wide flat part of the Wasteland.

"There's some weird looking beasties out here," said Whak, looking around. There were indeed. None of the local population of SRMs that he was watching cautiously were smaller than a middle-sized dog, and they bristled with stiff wire segments and protruding mechanisms that might have been sensors or might have been weapons. While Whak and George were moving quickly across the zone, Whak saw a side panel of a large SRM open and a beam of purple light flash out, striking another, smaller machine five metres away, with a small explosion and cloud of smoke. The smaller machine burrowed with unbelievable speed and without a sound into the ragged surface, disappearing from sight in seconds. George hesitated, obviously wanting to stop and examine this latest incarnation of the meta-instructions, but he and Whak hurried on.

"They'll come after us soon," George said as they reached the glass perimeter wall. Somehow, Whak had always assumed that the wall around the Wasteland was made of glass because glass was somehow resistant to SRMs, but now he saw that at intervals there were holes of different sizes - but all perfectly round - cut through it at ground level. The wall must be a propaganda gimmick, he decided. It did nothing to protect the outside world from the strangenesses of the Wasteland, but the peculiarity and expense of it's construction made everyone think it did. It sounded like a PushRight idea to Whak. He belatedly tuned in to what George Assok had just said.

"Jelli can protect us," he said.

"Maybe," George said. "Maybe she can protect you. It's worth a try, anyway."

"How do we get over this wall?"

"Climb. It's not that tall."

Whak looked doubtful. "We can't climb glass." He noticed for the first time that George had something in his hands apart from the gun. It was a grey, brick-sized rectangular object. "What's that?"

"It's a nanoconstructor unit. It was in the isolation room, in the cool cabinet. They would have made their nanoviruses with this." He held it in front of him while he looked it over. "It's not my original one. It's got some refinements. The flask connectors are a good idea. I got a flask, as well." He patted the big pocket on the side of his coat.

"And what exactly do you intend to do with that?"

"Let's just get out of here, shall we? Look, if we can fit our toes into these SRM holes we can reach the top."

They did that. They climbed up, grabbed the top of the wall and hauled themselves over. George Assok had particular trouble because he had to maintain his grip on the purloined nanoconstructor. As soon as their feet touched the ground on the other side of the wall they ran across the street and lost themselves from sight in the ruins. When they were well away from the Wasteland they stopped at the intersection of one deserted and broken street with another.

"I'm going to go to Jelli," Whak said. "I can't find Lino if I'm going to be arrested every five minutes."

Assok was looking at the nanoconstructor with a hungry expression. He had other ideas happening in his high, narrow skull. He said that he would return to his home on West Coolio. "They don't seem to know where I live, yet. I can start looking at this."

"Why? So you too can make nanoviruses that eat human beings?"

"That shouldn't have happened. For the nanovirus to diverge from spec enough to target organic material like flesh is fantastically unlikely. And I must admit, I was surprised at the persistence of Sedric's design. It must have been up to a hundred replications. But the rate of mutation was radical enough to turn a metallotropic deconstructor into a carbohydrophage." George shook his head. "It doesn't make sense. Either it degenerates randomly, or it doesn't. To convert itself wholesale into a new, coherent form... I wonder if my meta-instruction concept is applicable to nanoviruses?"

"I don't care, George. You worry about that. I'll worry about Lino." Whak was not interested in the nanoconstructor. He had more urgent business to attend to.

Emery Reports to Sinfine

Emery returned to Sinfine's presence with mixed feelings. He was a bearer of bad tidings, and even without a classical education he knew what sort of greeting such messengers usually received.

He did it himself when nephews and other slimebags came to him with tales of overlapping patches usually resulting in deaths and retribution for deaths. He had them punished. Whether it was their fault or more likely Sinfine's that their guys and another nephew's guys had for some reason crossed territories, offered protection against each other, or raided each other's money merchants, what did that matter? They came with bad news. Off with their heads.

But he was looking forward to seeing Sinfine's face when he heard that his sexy little SRM stimulator, his hopeful ticket to Unclehood, was gone. The conflict between seeing Sinfine pop with rage like a greasy balloon and having Sinfine pour hot spleen all over him left him indecisive. He crossed from the French doors to the poolside and stood in his usual at-attention pose where Sinfine, who was having a pool girl rub his shoulders, would only see him if his peripheral vision was better than Emery believed. Today, it was warmer than usual, hot enough that Sinfine was wearing a loose cotton shirt and baggy shorts, and he had his head tilted forward as the pool girl dug her fingers into his scapula. When she moved her attention to his fifth cervical vertebra he opened his eyes and without moving his neck, said "Has that quack woken her up yet?"

"I didn't ask him," Emery replied.

"Why didn't you fucking ask him?"

"He was dead."

"What?"

"So was Horse." Emery was not a man who felt anything except caution not to leave evidence when looking over a dead body, but he had been unhappy to see Horse dead. Horse had been a harmless soft guy who had been posted to the house because he couldn't be relied upon to hurt people.

"Horse and the doctor are dead?" Sinfine repeated. "How?"

"Shot. Close range, medium calibre, I'd say." Emery was neglecting his Mr Sinfines. "Mr Sinfine," he put one in for luck, but it was too late. Sinfine jumped out of his chair, striking the pool girl's hands aside. He kicked the chair he had just climbed out of across the tiled patio. He grabbed Emery by the necktie, for Emery, despite the humidity, had to adhere to the bad guy dress code of dark suit and white shirt, and pulled him down so that Emery could clearly observe the state of Sinfine's teeth. They were rather even for a man who gave the strong impression that they should be irregular, sharp, and pointed.

"Who did it?" he said, framing each word through exaggeratedly stretched lips. "Was it another Cousin?"

"I don't know, sir," Emery said respectfully. He always felt respectful of Sinfine when the killing mood came over him. "They were just dead. And the girl was gone."

Sinfine continued to hold Emery's face within biting distance while he clouted him, not too painfully, about the side of the head. "Find - out - who - did - it - you - brain - dead - moron!" He let Emery's necktie go and Emery stumbled back, but gained his balance before ending up in the pool. He had seen Sinfine take potshots at out-of-favour individuals in the pool, and Emery was not as good at swimming underwater as some of the survivors had proven to be. Sinfine went on in a calmer tone of voice. "If it was another Cousin, I want to know which one." He slapped his forehead suddenly. "Find that Jim creep. It might have been something to do with him. He might know something. And make like the cops! Take the place apart! There has to be something there we can work with. And find the fucking girl! That's number one! Find the girl! Go and fucking do it!" He dropped back into his chair. The pool girl tentatively began work on his shoulders again. "What am I going to do about Blue Suit?" he moaned, then looked up at Emery. "Go and fucking do it, I said!" he screamed at him.

"Yes, sir."

Emery left feeling relieved that it was not his fault. He went straight to the telephone and arranged for some men to go down to the house. He would meet them there later. Then he made another call, this time to a bar in the central slums.

"Yeah," a voice answered.

"This is Emery."

"Hi man."

"I'm looking for a kid."

"Didn't know you were into kids."

"His name's Jim."

"Lot's of people named Jim," the voice said blankly.

"He's a pitfight boy for Sinfine. The other handlers will be able to describe him. He's got something he shouldn't have." Emery was a resourceful liar. "Put the word out. Sinfine wants to know where he is."

"So, if we know where he is we kill him?"

"No, just follow him. What we want to know is where the thing he stole is."

"Gotcha."

Emery rang off and started off back to the house. He was feeling pretty sanguine about finding Jim and maybe even Lino. He was good at this sort of thing.

CHAPTER 31

Jelli, drunk, collects Whak

As soon as George Assok had turned down a nameless street with an absent farewell, Whak began to reconsider his position. It had not quite penetrated previously, but he now realised that he was a fugitive, and maybe going boldly up to his own front door was not so sensible. Sure, Jelli could protect him and possibly George, but she would have to go through channels and while those channels were being gone through he could easily be recaptured or decitizened. Whak Puihare? Never heard of him. Let me check our records. Oh yes, Whak Puihare. No we don't know where he is. Sounds of screams from another room. Do you want us to put out a missing person alert? And Jelli was not going to even know about any of this until he spoke to her. Right now, he was in danger.

Whak said to himself "Telephone needed."

He remembered the days of public telephones. He had even owned a mobile, long ago when they worked, but now there were millions of mobile phone parts imbedded in SRM bodies all over the world. So he couldn't flip open a snazzy handset and call Jelli. He realised that he should have gone with George and called Jelli from his place, but it was too late now. George might have been able to sneak them both back there unnoticed, but Whak knew that being inconspicuous was not one of his talents and that he would surely draw attention to things that needed to be kept secret. With that thought he glanced all around in a suspicious manner, then marched head down in what he hoped was the direction of the city. He had a long walk ahead of him.

Jelli was drunk. She had not been drunk for fifteen years, by her memory, and that time was an accident. This time it was not an accident. She had come into her house this evening, fresh from simultaneously supplicating and dumping Blue Suit, and listened to the silence which was not due to Whak sitting paralysed by a rhyme over his work or Lino sulking over the unending injustice of being alive. Since earplugs do not keep such lack of noises out, she chose anaesthetic instead. Whisky, in fact. Somehow in Scotland they kept on making the single malt in the traditional way, and the SRMs that had thoroughly destroyed the cities over there, left them to it. Probably crossing all those kilometres of peat bog to reach an outlying malthouse, and finding only shovels, rakes, and copper kettles was insufficient reward for the endlessly fecund machines. By the end of her third triple, Jelli had devised the perfect SRM-proof city. Surrounded on all sides by peat bog, and all the citizens engaged in the manufacture of whisky. She began to see a future where islands of human civilisation endured, stone drunk, in the Highlands of Scotland, the centre of the Sahara and the Gobi, on the plateaus of the Himalaya, and on scattered South Pacific islands. Elsewhere, the self-replicating machines would rule over piles of junk until, like maggots, they consumed their supply utterly, and maybe transformed into buzzing metal bluebottles which in a great dark cloud would rise into space and fly away in search of another haunch of rotten civilisation to feed on.

She put this new idea up against the Advance Force of Alien Invasion and The Zone of Anti-Entropy theories and it was, in her opinion, just as good. Even better, because it made no assumptions about the desirability of the Earth as real estate and it broke no known physical laws. As if we know anything about physical laws beyond the horizons of our tiny brains. The Cosmic Maggots Theory. She poured herself another, slightly larger triple and dropped the bottle when the telephone rang.

After two attempts to pick up the receiver she managed to put it to her ear and said "Jelli."

"Jelli!" It was Whak.

"Whak! Where the fuck are you?"

There was a pause while Whak checked where he was. "In a police station, I think."

"You think? You think? Whak, where are you?"

"Are you all right?"

"Of course I'm all right! I want to know where you are!"

"You've been drinking, haven't you."

Jelli made an effort to enunciate a little more precisely. "I have had a little drink, yes. Where are you? Have you found Lino?"

"Yes and no. I found where she used to be."

"Wommerful." Jelli's elocution gave way to her irritation. "And where did you say you used to be?"

"I'm at a little police station somewhere near the Wasteland, it's ah... oh, thanks," he said off-phone. "It's on Dright Avenue."

"Is this your one call?"

"No, I'm not arrested, it's not the police who are after me, it's -
" his voice dropped, "Blue Suit. I've escaped from them once already."

"What? Why would Blue Suit be after you? What have you done?"

"Can you come and get me?"

"Yes. I can. I might need a coffee first."

"Good idea. Get sober first. If you die on the roads I'll, well, don't die on the roads. How long will you take?"

"I'm leaving in two minutes." Jelli was already reaching for the percolator pot with her free hand. "Bye."

She left her whisky on the bench and sucked up half a pint of strong black so fast it burnt her mouth, then proceeded on slightly irregular feet to the garage. Her plastic fantastic car, devoid of sophisticated fuel flow controls, took a few attempts to start, and then she forgot to open the doors, so she and the car bounced off them before her reflexes could swim through her spine. She got out and pushed the door up. As she did, she saw in the dim evening light a shadow up the slippery elm tree on the opposite side of the street, the familiar shadow of the blue suit operative assigned to watch her house. It was the wrong moment for such a thing. She felt a sudden rage against the prevalence of spying and detention. It had been all right when the people being observed and imprisoned or banished to the agridistricts had been the criminals, the economic underclass, and the politically incorrect. In other words, them not us, but at some unnoticed point the observation had spread to everyone regardless of position, and now, suddenly, an attempt at detention had been applied to Whak, who was not any of the above, but her husband, for what he was worth, and she was not even sure now whether she was angry because of the principle of the thing or because the victim this time was a part of her. It didn't matter which. She was angry. She left her car grumbling monoxide and stalked across the road to the slippery elm.

"You!" she shouted at the figure in the tree.

The observer pretended that he wasn't there.

"You! Up the tree! You blue suit!" Jelli screamed at him.

"I'm not authorised to hold converse," the blue suit replied eventually.

"I don't fucking care! What are you watching me for?"

"I'm not authorised to hold converse," the blue suit repeated. "I'm only authorised to tell you that I'm not authorised to hold converse."

"You horrible cretinous spy!" Jelli became more angry than before. She needed to tell Blue Suit off, and this observer was a convenient surrogate. "Come down here at once! Do you know who I am?"

"Yes, ma'am, you're Jelli Puihare, Chief Executive officer of PushRight Creative Media Incorporated. And I'm not authorised to hold converse with you."

"Get down here!"

"No, ma'am."

"Right then!" Jelli knew more than one way to get a man out of a tree. She went back and got into her car. Plastic cars, she thought, have two advantages over metal cars. They get eaten less frequently, though that was yet to be proven. And they retained their shape well after a collision. The garage doors had taken a bit of a dent, but the front of her car was unscathed. She put on her seat belt, very deliberately, and then she accelerated at top speed straight at the slippery elm.

The velocity that the car had achieved on impact was not great. The tree was only a dozen metres from the gate. But the tree swayed, and the blue suit up there, who from the moment that Jelli's car roared out of her garage had been frantically trying to reach a more secure position, rocked backwards and forwards. He did not fall. Jelli screamed out her window,

"Get down!" She reversed back a way and revved the engine loudly. The man decided that the ground was safer than the tree. He came down. Jelli drove up to where he stood on the footpath and said to him "If I see you or anyone like you again, I'll get the police to remove you. Now fuck off."

"It's my job," said the operative, shakily.

"Get another job."

As Jelli drove away, she wondered why she had bothered. The man would be back tomorrow. The police would refuse to remove him. And Blue Suit would be annoyed. Well, screw Blue Suit. She smiled faintly at the thought and wondered when that would next be, if ever. If Whak had just escaped from his clutches then the relationship might be irretrievable, which would be a relief. Jelli didn't give up on a thing just because it was hard, but Jesus Christ, being cozy with Blue Suit was harder than she had anticipated and had less reward.

Her anger had sobered her considerably, saving her from arriving at the hospital instead of the Dright Avenue Police Station. When she arrived, Whak was sitting on the low wooden bench seat which ran down the streetside wall opposite the reception desk, but he jumped up as Jelli came in. They put their arms around each other.

"I've been worried about you," Jelli said, surprised to realise that it was true.

Whak squeezed her tighter. "It's been a crazy couple of days," he said. Policemen coming and going through the same passageway gave them bleary looks and gooey stares as they hugged. They had seen a thousand men and woman touching, remaking their lives in these corridors.

"It's been three days. What happened to you?"

"I'll tell you on the way home. That blue suit isn't still watching the house, is he?"

"I think he might not be tonight. I told him to fuck off."

"You told a blue suit to fuck off? Well done, Jelli. I'll make a human being out of you yet."

He may have meant only to scratch one of the scabs that their life together had left dotted all over them, but at this moment, it was too much. Jelli exploded.

"Don't start acting like you've got the monopoly on love in this relationship! I feel all the same things you do! I believe in things! I have principles! Don't, don't you condescend to me!" She pushed Whak away. A tear rolled. He pulled her back. He was obviously shocked.

"I'm sorry," he said, studying her face closely, surprised to find that this no longer annoyed her as it always had. "I haven't seen you like this before."

"I haven't lost my daughter before!"

"I'm sorry."

"All right." It was hard to stay wild in the face of sincere regret, and Whak was a master of sincere regret. "Let's get in the car."

Whak waved to the desk officer, with whom he had developed a brief friendship, and he and Jelli took their leave. Whak took the driver's seat and held his hand out for the key.

"Why does the man always drive?" Jelli asked him, handing it over.

"Because the woman's drunk." He started the car and began to drive. "I have to tell you what happened, Jelli, it's unbelievable.

Lino was kidnapped by a Cousin named Sinfine, and Blue Suit arrested George and I when we were looking for her, and Jim found out where she was, but when we got there she was gone and there were dead bodies everywhere. Blue Suit has a big building underground in the Wasteland and they're doing experiments with nanomachines to try and wipe out SRMs, and we saw one, and it went wrong, and this guy Sedric lost his arm, and I - "

"Slow down, Whak. Slow down." Jelli was still fighting a quarter litre of Scotch. "Lino was kidnapped?"

"By a Cousin named Sinfine."

"What would a Cousin want with Lino?"

Whak was silent for a moment. "Rumour has it," he said slowly, knowing how Jelli would react, "that Lino has some kind of effect on SRMs. These SRM events that have been happening lately? She was at all of them. She goes into one of her withdrawals and the SRMs go berserk. So I'm told."

Jelli looked sceptical. "She's been going into withdrawals ever since she was a baby, and we've never had any SRMs going berserk at our house."

"Maybe it's a short-range thing. Or a new thing. Or maybe she has to be stressed. That's what Jim said. When she gets stressed. We don't usually let her get stressed."

"Not if we can help it. She's bad enough when everything's going down smooth." Jelli had her window down and the air rushing in her face was helping her think. "So this Cousin kidnapped Lino the night she went out with Jim?"

"I suppose so. He knew about it. He must have been there."

"Sneaky bastard probably set it up."

"He seems pretty worried about her. And he says Sinfine is looking for him, although we never saw anybody. We did see blue suits, though. Lots of them, all looking for us."

"And the place Lino was being held was full of dead bodies?"

"Two."

"Not Lino?" Jelli asked unnecessarily.

"Of course not. I'd have told you already if she was dead." Whak kept his eyes straight ahead. "Then we were arrested by blue suits. Jim got away. I don't know where he is now. At his apartment, maybe." Whak told Jelli what had happened at the Project Station.

"Jesus," Jelli said when he had finished. "It ate his arm?"

"Yep. George thinks Blue Suit systematically wiped out all expertise in nanomachine research except for him and that Sedric guy. Oh, and on the way out, George took a machine for making nanoviruses."

"Your friend took what?"

"He's not my friend, all right? He's an acquaintance in wartime."

"Where is he now?"

"At his place. On West Coolio, somewhere. I can find it. Do you want to go there? He's scared to death of Blue Suit. He thinks Blue Suit will kill him. He wanted to talk to you, before, but now he seems to be more interested in that thing he took."

"What about you? Why did Blue Suit pick you up? Did they know who you were?"

"They sure did. They looked me up on a list. 'He's on the list,' they said. I've noticed all these security types rely on lists a lot. They probably have a list for everything. They have to have instructions to brush their teeth. Bet they've never read a line of poetry in their lives, any of them." Now Whak was getting upset. He had always been able to turn the world he saw into an abstract microcosm. What happened in his head was more real to him than what happened in reality. But now Jelli saw by the wildness of his eyes that he was experiencing all this with vivid immediacy, without internal reruns and editing. He stopped the car at an uncontrolled intersection and tried to see if anything was coming. "All this people interaction is driving me crazy, Jelli. It's a strange world outside our house. I don't understand what motivates people like that, pointing guns at me, following instructions, checking lists, building nanoviruses. Kidnapping Lino."

"Just go, Whak."

"Without giving way? You want us to get killed? A lot of good that'll do Lino. Or George, or the whole world for that matter. God, I'm hungry. I haven't eaten for hours." A dazed expression came over him. He stared with unfocussed eyes out the driver side window.

"The way's clear, Whak. Get a move on," Jelli told him, but Whak was distracted by something approaching on his side of the car.

"What is that?" he asked, winding his window down. "Shit!" He stamped on the accelerator and stalled the car. "Ah, Jelli."

"What?"

"Get out of the car." Whak leaned across Jelli pushed her door open, and began prodding her side with his fingers. "Get out! Quick!"

They both tumbled out of the plastic fantastic automobile. At almost the same second, a dozen SRMs - peculiar, Wasteland varieties without names - pounced on it from the other side. One of them had a laser a bit like the one Whak had observed earlier in the Wasteland itself, which it used to slice the front bumper off. Another climbed in the open driver's side.

"My car!" Jelli wailed. "Not again!" She leaned on Whak, who unexpectedly sat down on the footpath, bringing her down on top of him and knocking both of them into a tangle of bodies. Whak lost his tearful look. He began to smile faintly.

"Don't get stressed, Jelli. Remember, getting stressed causes SRM events," he said. "Whenever the ambient anxiety goes up, SRMs calm their nerves by eating. That's the secret of SRM control."

He did not succeed in returning Jelli to good humour. They sat on the pavement and watched. After a few minutes, to Jelli's relief, the SRMs gave up on the car and crawled away. Perhaps the designers were right and it was too unappetising. When the creatures had gone and they both felt it was safe to approach, Whak checked the car over. They had cut off the bumper and stolen the petrol cap cover. No doubt there were other things missing.

Whak started the engine. It seemed fine. They drove quickly back to North Coolio. As they whizzed without stopping though a quiet intersection, Jelli asked if Whak had finally learned a lesson about giving way at every little corner.

"No," he said, "but we haven't got any brakes. The SRMs must have eaten the hydraulics."

"Oh."

"Don't worry the handbrake works." Whak proved it by skidding to a halt on their driveway, but he wouldn't get out of the car until Jelli had assured him that the slippery elm was empty.

Whak blames Blue Suit

When they were at last back inside their home, citadel of privacy, kingdom of protection, Jelli asked him again about his arrest.

"They had my name on a list. I'm officially wanted by Blue Suit."

"That's ridiculous. I'll call Blue Suit right now and straighten it out. He'll damn well pay attention when he knows that I know what he's doing with all those SRMs. The Consortium will have him tied to the table for this."

Whak put up a hand. "Wait a moment," he said. "I'm wondering, who might want to kidnap Lino from her kidnappers? And why?"

Jelli was stopped by the question. "I still don't understand why she was kidnapped in the first place," she said with little emotion. "Even if she does cause SRM events. What profit is there in SRM events?"

"Jim thought that Sinfine would use her to spice up his pitfights." Bitter looks.

"Ah." Jelli thought about that. "There was something in the Park the other night."

"I know, I was outside. That was Lino. Who else has an interest in SRMs?"

"No one. Everyone. Who?"

"What about the SRM Collection?"

"That's a Blue Suit project, Whak!" Jelli finally got the drift. "But Blue Suit..."

"You're very slow to catch on sometimes, Jelli."

CHAPTER 32

Jelli makes plans

Jelli was more than sober now. She was icy, focussed, and deadly. In the face of her ferocity Whak found that he had to swallow a hundred slighting references to her capacity for love that he had made over the years, but at the same time as she interrogated him further about his last few days, he was inspecting her, as if she was a delicate piece of marble statuary, for any sign of cracks. He had enough on his hands without having to worry about Jelli as well. He needed her whole. This was a switch that he had almost enough humour left to feel wry about. He had always been the half of their relationship that needed nothing but solitude, and she had been the one who brought the world home for him to study as if it was a bag of archaeological artefacts. From that thought, he realised that needing now to act upon the world and using Jelli to do it was not such a revolution. He had been using her as his own robot arm for years. He felt ashamed.

"What's the matter with you now?" Jelli demanded of him.

"I'll tell you when we're old," he replied.

"Oh, Jesus, you haven't changed."

"Neither have you, thank God."

An iota of softness came and went between them. But there was no time for reflection or sentiment. She returned to business.

"If Blue Suit has anything to do with Lino's disappearance," she said, "then it's going to be very very damn hard to either prove it, or get him to admit it, or even if he does admit it, to get her back. Unless he wants to. And I don't think he will." This would have been a good time for her to be sorry that she had ever slept with Blue Suit, but she controlled the urge. She was, however, both glad and not glad that she had cancelled their regular rendezvous. Glad, because if he was holding Lino, then he was an irredeemable bastard who could never mean anything to her again. Not glad, because it's always so disappointing to find that you have been sleeping with a louse.

"He wouldn't have taken her from Sinfine unless he had some reason to keep her," Whak agreed. "He's got you collecting SRMs for him, hasn't he? Now we know what that was about. That place in the Wasteland is where they do their experiments, and they said that they had thousands of SRMs in storage, however the hell you store SRMs, I don't know, but I didn't see Lino there. Christ, I didn't see anything there except the end of a gun and then that isolation chamber dissolving right in front of me. If Blue Suit has this," he thought about what this was, "weapon, why would he care about Lino?"

"Why don't we ask him?"

"What?"

Jelli reached for the phone. "I'll ask him around to my office. For a meeting."

"Now? At night?" Whak remembered Jelli's late night meetings. "And then?"

"Then we'll ask him whether he's got Lino."

"Forgive me, but isn't he likely to lie?"

"I can tell if he's lying."

Whak nodded. Jelli called.

"This is Jelli Puihare speaking. Put me through to Blue Suit. Yes. Yes, it's urgent. Just do it!" She drummed her fingers on the table. When she next spoke, her voice changed to a velvet smooth parody of her normal speech, as if she had switched on a microphone and begun to address the nation. Whak made a face. "Blue Suit. Hello. I need to see you. Mmmm. Well, at PushRight, of course. No, tonight. Yes, tonight. Oh, you know about that already? Your people are so efficient. Yes, it is something to do with your surveillance man. No, I don't want to talk to the Chief of Operations, I want to talk to you. In an hour?" She looked at Whak, who shrugged and felt doubtful. "That's fine. In an hour. Don't bring the Chinese army this time."

Blue Suit and Isolation Test

Telephone conversations, even when drenched with the sound of the cable along which the current flows being chewed by SRM caterpillars, have a way of meaning both more and less than words spoken face to face. When Blue Suit put down the handset after talking to Jelli, he told his secretary to organise a small contingent of bodyguards, and while that was being done, he sat at his desk and wondered what Jelli knew. He was fairly sure that he was not being invited for reasons of personal pleasure, this time. Worrying that Jelli might have found out enough from George Assok to cause him difficulty, he dialled an extension.

"Chief of Operations."

"Blue Suit. Have you got George Assok?"

"No, sir."

"Why not? Do you know where he is? What's causing the delay?"

"I was just going to report to you, sir. There's been a problem at the Project Station."

The tone of voice told him that whatever the problem was, it was not slight. Blue Suit listened while the wires squawked.

"And all this was witnessed by Assok."

"And Puihare, sir."

"Colville is an idiot."

"Yes, sir. He has lost an arm, sir."

Blue Suit said a few mild swear words.

"I don't want the project delayed. Is he able to work?"

"I don't think so, sir. He's in severe shock."

That was bad news. Blue Suit had come to rue having those scientists that he had rejected, or that had rejected him, killed outright. Now he had too many eggs in one basket. It would have been better to have confined them indefinitely, until their usefulness to him was demonstrated one way or the other. Now, circumstances dictated that he urgently needed to find George Assok. "Where are Assok and Puihare now?"

"We don't know."

"Find out. I want them both secured by morning. Your position depends on it."

The Chief of Operations knew that, and he also knew that nothing could save him but luck, which he did not believe in. "Yes, sir," he said miserably.

Blue Suit dropped the phone back on his desk. There are no coincidences. The call from Jelli, Assok's escape, and the disaster at the Station. No doubt Jelli had Assok. Her husband had witnessed nanovirus tests at the Project Station. So, she knew the whereabouts of probably the only person left in the world who knew more about nanotech than Colville, and she was obtaining potentially damaging information at an alarming rate. Something had to be done about her. He tapped a forefinger on his desk and spent a rare moment regretting the past, and the future.

Whak/Jelli meet Blue Suit

Whak realised as he wrenched on the handbrake and stopped with a jerk in the basement of the PushRight Tower that he had never been to Jelli's offices before. In all her years there, she had never invited him to her place of work. Whether that was because she didn't want him involved in that side of her life, even to such a slight degree, or whether they had unconsciously agreed that he would be spared the discomfort of watching his wife treat human beings as if they were programmable machines, was not clear. Physically, of course, he was not expecting this office block to be any different from any other. They were all concrete boxes, as far as he was concerned, and rising in elevators from ground level to the world of the high floors was an attempt to escape from the ugly reality that could only be fully appreciated when you had one foot in shit and the other poised to topple you down an open manhole. But reality and PushRight Creative Media Incorporated had always had an adversarial relationship. He wondered what kind of relationship Jelli had with Blue Suit. Not good would be good.

The floors of PushRight Tower were busy at this time of night. GOV1 was still on the air, so the studios were fully staffed, and various analysts from the Law and Order Project were running behaviour simulations on souped-up personal computers. There were the unvarying security guards on reception, and there were always a few victims of the live-to-work syndrome trying to complete some report or design for the morning. A few SRM sweepers were desultorily checking wastebaskets, water coolers, and desktop computers for unwelcome life forms.

"This is good," Whak said, looking around the office as he followed Jelli, who was walking quickly to the usual conference room. "He can't do anything hostile with all these people about."

"Don't bet on it. He doesn't care much about witnesses." Jelli paused at the door of Conference Room 6 and then turned to face Whak. "Maybe you should be out of sight," she suggested. "You're a fugitive. He might try to arrest you."

"I'm only a fugitive because Blue Suit has made me one. I haven't done anything wrong. I haven't done anything at all." Whak pushed past. "J'y ici and j'y reste." He sounded angry.

"That's j'y suis et j'y reste, Whak."

"Whatever. Homogeneity rules. Why don't you get those guards back there to protect us?"

"I hope it won't come to that."

One of the elevators at the far end of the corridor bonged. Whak stood near the glass, watching the men who came out.

"Which one's Blue Suit?" he asked.

"The tall one in grey."

"I expected him to be a dwarf in blue, apologies to dwarfs everywhere."

Of course Blue Suit had not come alone. Jelli had not expected him to. He had three men with him, his ubiquitous senior protector and two other, equally impassive and alert individuals. He showed faint signs of surprise when he looked down the corridor and saw Whak watching him with an expression of critical interest, as if he could measure Blue Suit's life from the way he walked. With one protector in front of him and two behind, he came to the open conference room door and stopped there on the threshold.

"Jelli," he said politely. "What is this?"

"This is her husband," Whak broke in before Jelli could reply, "and he is mighty pissed off."

"Whak, calm down. Come in and sit down," said Jelli. "I have some questions to ask you."

"Really, Jelli, you didn't have to ask me here at this time of the night to ask me questions." Blue Suit was annoyed. "We will be meeting during the next week. You could ask me then. By the way, according to my information, your husband has recently been trespassing in a secure government installation, and is therefore eligible for detention." He came in, but he didn't sit down. He stood by the table facing them both.

"Where's my daughter?" Whak demanded. The presence of Blue Suit had brought his last few days of dread vividly to life. His fists were clenched in front of him. "What have you done with my daughter?"

"Whak, we don't know where she is."

"Your daughter?" Blue Suit turned on an uncharacteristically vague expression, saw Jelli measuring his response, and changed tactics. "Ah, yes, Lino Puihare. I know the name. She is reputed to be the cause of several SRM riots."

"You have got her, then," Jelli said in a flat voice.

Blue Suit raised one eyebrow. "It is possible that she has been collected as part of our investigation into the increasing frequency of SRM attacks. If she has, then procedure dictates that she will be held until the investigation is complete. If she is connected with the increase in SRM violence, of course, it becomes a matter of national security."

Whak looked ready to kill him. Jelli quickly spoke.

"Give her back, you bastard."

"I'm afraid not, Jelli. It's more important for me now to find Assok, "Whak blinked, "than to cultivate PushRight. I think you know where he is. So I can't give her back to you, even if you offer to screw me on top of your very comfortable desk once again."

Whak's fists dropped to his sides. He looked to Jelli for an immediate denial, but she was glowering at Blue Suit and when she did turn to Whak, she quickly dropped her eyes.

"Jelli, no," Whak said pleadingly. He didn't expect much from Jelli in the way of fidelity, but he had hoped that she would at least show some judgement and taste. "For Christ's sake. Not with him. He's a murderer, Jelli! He doesn't have the empathy of an insect, he doesn't have enough feeling to even get pleasure out of the pain he causes, he was taught ethics by the Devil and strategy by Pol Pot! I've only known him for five minutes and I can already tell you that! He's psychotic!"

Blue Suit was not offended.

"Psychotic is a meaningless term. It refers to those who do not abide by the social compact," he said calmly, "and in these times, that applies to many."

Whak was waiting for Jelli to speak.

She knew it. She lifted her chin and said "I thought I could use him."

"No-one uses me." Blue Suit was offended now. So was Whak. His eyes turned cold with the thought that Jelli had been sharing herself, having intimate moments, doing sex with this male model Mussolini, for profit. Nothing could more belittle whatever she felt for Whak than that. Without warning, he threw himself forward and, before any of the bodyguards could intervene, punched Blue Suit with considerable force in the face. He didn't know why he had not done it before for Lino but did now for sex, and he had, anyway, always thought that it should be the woman who was punished, not the man, she having the power of choice and the man having testicular pressure against him. Old comfortable ideas like that fell dead as his fist sped. His knuckles were by accident perfectly angled for the strike. Blue Suit's mouth splashed red, his neck snapped back and he was thrown back into the glass wall, which wobbled but held. That was all Whak had time to enjoy before the protectors, who had been caught unprepared and wished to make up for it, hit him high, low and middle, throwing him on his back onto the conference table, one on each side pinioning his arms while the senior man stood between his legs, knee on groin and ugly sidearm pressed on the bridge of his nose.

"Leave him alone!" Jelli screamed, but the protectors did not move, except their eyes, which sought out Blue Suit.

He was sitting with his legs straight out in front of him and his back resting against the glass, looking dazed. Jelli screamed for PushRight security, and two guards came running down the corridor. They burst into the room and the senior protector's gun came off Whak's nose and pointed at them instead. They stopped helplessly. Jelli tried to pull the protector away from Whak, which earned her a dismissive shove into the nearest chair. The tableau held for a few seconds, then Blue Suit slowly put himself back on his feet.

"Poets," Blue Suit said in a voice made almost unrecognisable by his bleeding lips, "are dangerous." He pulled a handkerchief out of his coat pocket and pressed it gingerly into his face, looked at the amount of blood he had transferred, and did it again. "Let him up."

The protectors pulled Whak upright.

"Where's my daughter," he panted.

Blue Suit ignored him and turned to Jelli. "Don't try to do anything stupid, Jelli. I know you have George Assok. Tell me where he is."

"Stop mumbling," Whak said behind him. "We can't hear you properly."

"I don't know where he is," Jelli said quietly. "Would you let Lino go if I did?"

Blue Suit was no longer making any pretence about his having Lino, and the blow to his head had also cleared it for the moment of any lingering affection, however distorted, that he had for Jelli.

"I might. Unless I find some use for her. Think about it." He flicked a finger and two of his protectors went to pre-defend the corridor and lift. "I won't arrest your husband, yet. But," his eyes and Whak's mirrored each other briefly, "be prepared."

When the lift doors had closed and the indicator was counting broken digits down to the basement, Whak passed judgement.

"No principles. No principles at all."

The sounds of late night workers elsewhere in the office revived, slowly, as if someone was rewinding a stopped clock.

Blue Suit's car blows up

Blue Suit's lips throbbed, unreasonably, more slowly than his heart. It was also unreasonable, he thought, and furthermore pointless for Whak Puihare to hit him. If Whak had been trying to kill him, that would have been easy to understand, but this had been the wrong place and time for killing. The so-called poet apparently thought nothing of beating a man with his fists until blood poured, while he probably made cooing noises on paper about the nobility of the human spirit and the precious virtues thereof. Blue Suit abhorred hypocrisy. He was completely honest with himself, if not with others. He had even shown some truth to Jelli, from whom he still expected the whereabouts of George Assok to be revealed. That had been a mistake, obviously.

"Have the Chief of Operations place a twenty-four hour double-strength watch on both of them," he told his senior protector. "Both the Puihares. I expect that they will be trying to find Assok, if they don't already know where he is."

"Yes, sir." The protector looked a little bit worried. "Do you think they'll swap Assok for their daughter, sir?"

"Possibly. Parental emotions are powerful things. But if they don't, then instead they will try to use Assok and his knowledge to hurt me, if they can. In which case they will have to contact him. That is why I didn't have you arrest the husband. He will probably be the one to make the connection."

"Yes, sir. What do we need Assok for, sir?"

"That is not your business." Blue Suit's shredded mouth made his tone of voice less threatening than usual, but it was enough. The protector nodded quickly and turned back to face the inside of the lift doors.

As the lift slowed, he turned his head on one side, listened, and looked cautiously around. "There's something outside," he told Blue Suit. The other two protectors stepped forward with their weapons in hand. "Hold the door closer down," their leader said. He took up a martial stance and steadied his gun with both hands. The lift stopped. Blue Suit could hear the sound, now. There was a clattering and a low roaring noise outside the lift doors. Not a good position to be in. What had happened to the three protectors that were left in the basement garage? The senior protector pulled out a transceiver and pressed the call button repeatedly, but had no reply.

"Looks like we've got men down, sir."

"We can't stay in this elevator for the rest of our lives, can we? Open the doors." Blue Suit didn't even realise that he was the only man there who wasn't afraid of whatever was outside. "For Christ's sake, man, get your hand off that button."

The door closer was released. The doors remained shut. "Press the opener."

Before anyone could obey, a shrill whistling noise arose, like a worn flywheel rubbing against it's housing. The whistle grew rapidly louder, and then a circle of metal popped out of the lift door almost at the level of Blue Suit's eyes. There was a flash of metallic movement and one protector grunted as a small scorpion used one cutter to slash at his gun, taking a small slice out of his hand in the process. Another SRM, a caterpillarish thing with one grey metal eye, started sliding through the same hole.

"Open the doors," Blue Suit ordered. Using knives as levers, and stomping the two SRMs underfoot, his men pulled the doors apart. Now they could see what the roaring noise was. One of the cars they had come in had exploded, and by the look of it, the three men left behind to ensure the security of the vehicles had been standing near it at the time, because they were now lying on the floor like scattered skittles, bloodspattered and faceless, their clothes burning.

The three remaining protectors ran out into the carnage with their guns held high. In the flames of the burning car, dead SRMs were silhouetted stained with heat, sensor pods sticking up uselessly in the smoke. The faint metal footsteps of others echoed in the car park, and Blue Suit and his protectors stood alert, looking in all directions, but the footsteps faded until there was silence.

Blue Suit realised swiftly that something, probably an SRM, had activated the car's self-destruct capability. He made a mental note to have the same device removed from any other cars he might be travelling in henceforth. He stepped into the remaining vehicle and wound down the window.

"Get a team out here to clean up this mess," he ordered. "And get that watch on the Puihares in place, now."

"No principles. No principles at all." Whak repeated for at least the fourth time since Blue Suit had left.

"Snap out of it, Whak!"

"Oh, hello." His capacity for drifting off was infuriating enough when the world wasn't turning into shit around her ears.

"So he has Lino, and he'll think about giving her back if we give
him George Assok. That was predictable, wasn't it?" he said.
"If it was so predictable, why didn't you predict it?"
"Well, I expected it."
"Where is Assok?"
"Oh no. We're not going to do that. I don't care who it is.
I'm not trading a life for a life. There has to be some other
option."
"Then think of one," Jelli said exasperatedly. "And Whak?"
"Yes?"
"Good punch."

CHAPTER 33

Plotting at Home

Whak found that the only way he could feel unexposed was to sneak around his own home like a thief, staying away from windows and walking through the rooms, when night, in perfect darkness. Jelli insisted on going to PushRight each day - "At least he can't watch me there. Do you want to come?" - but Whak found the thought of sitting in an office just as disagreeable as prowling his living room and checking the slippery elm five times an hour for blue suits. Besides, he had a lot of forgiving to do. He declined to join her.

"We have to find Lino," he kept saying.

"I know that!" Jelli snarled. "But as soon as we get anywhere near her, a dozen blue suits will jump on us and we'll be worse off than we are now. He might arrest you. I can only stop him after the event, by making it difficult for him with the Consortium. I can't take any action against the largest government subcontractor on the basis of private conversations and unsubstantiated accusations. If I accused him of holding Lino with the evidence we have now, he would probably deny it, I couldn't prove anything, it would look as if I was making wild claims, and we would probably never see her again. He has the power to detain indefinitely without trial, you know. Even if we could prove that he has her, legally there isn't a thing we can do about it." She paused. "Politically might be another matter."

"Maybe if he does arrest me, then you could do something. I could make it difficult for him to deny that he had me."

"But the point is, he's allowed to, however much noise I make about it." Jelli chewed the back of her hand with violence. "What's all this about, Whak? What's really going on?"

Whak had found a pool of despair to drag his toes through. "Blue Suit's making nanoviruses. That's all we know for sure," he replied listlessly.

"Yes, but what's in it for him? By getting rid of SRMs, Blue Suit indirectly gets rid of himself, or at least, for most of the reasons that Blue Suit exists."

"Maybe the nanovirus does something else."

"Not from what you described. That chamber was full of SRMs, nothing else. If we know what he's doing, then we should know why he's doing it. And if we know why he's doing it, then we might know something useful. Something he doesn't want known."

"I didn't think he wanted any of it known." Whak thought hard, then said "The nanovirus could be a powerful weapon. Imagine if he could program it in advance to expand to a certain size and then self-destruct, or degenerate as George would probably say. Scaled from something that would destroy a room to something that would destroy a planet. If he perfected it, he could use it to destroy anything he chose. Do you think he intends to hold the country to ransom?"

"That's just mad evil genius stuff, Whak. How could he do that? He lives here."

"I don't know. The thought of Blue Suit being a hero and the saviour of the world inexplicably worries me. Suddenly, we're the bad guys, trying to stop nice Mr Blue Suit from getting rid of the terrible plague of SRMs. But nobody with honest motives could do the things he's done."

"The SRM Collection has something to do with it. He really needed those SRMs. Hundreds of thousands of them. Why? Why so many?"

"Don't know. Tests," Whak said distantly.

"But why so many?" Jelli repeated. "They must have a bitch of a time just keeping them from escaping."

"Heh. Yes. Imagine if they did. That would wreck his project station, wouldn't it?" Then Whak thought of something. The thought became words in a rush. "What if he did get rid of SRMs, except for those ones. Then he could re-introduce SRMs anywhere, anytime. That could be why he wants so many of them. He could seed them anywhere he wanted. Anywhere in the world."

"Antidote," Jelli remembered. "He said he wanted an antidote for SRMs. I think you're right. Let them wreak havoc, wait until they obliterate a country's industrial capacity, then use the nanovirus to wipe them out again. He could dictate which nations were able to recover and which collapsed into chaos. He could practically control the world," Jelli said excitedly. "Without even going across borders, just in this country, he could easily dictate to the Consortium."

"And if he can whip them into a frenzy at the same time, so much the better, That's why he's holding on to Lino."

"Right."

"Wow. Now that's real mad evil genius stuff." Whak was silent for a moment. "Do you suppose any of it's true?" The leap from his daughter being kidnapped to plans to take over the world was a bit much to believe in.

"He's capable of it. Anything is possible with that man. But let's solve one thing at a time. Get Lino back. Then we can start on his SRM project. He's not so powerful that the Consortium can't pull his plug."

So Whak stayed home and worried, while Jelli went to PushRight and did what she could, which looked, for the moment, like being nothing.

Jim on the doorstep

Whak counted blue suits through the venetian blinds in his study, one up the tree, one in a car a little way down the road, one walking every fifteen minutes past the house and around the next corner. The one on foot passed another pedestrian who, by the books under his arm and his brown plastic suit, was a Revital Church streetwalker out to bolster his self-image by comparing his spiritual self favourably with North Coolio types.

"Go away," Whak said to the window, but the evangelist turned straight up the Puihare driveway and began the long walk to the house. "Shit. This guy had better be ready to die the death of ten thousand fuck offs." He made his way to the front door so that he would be ready to pounce on the unfortunate Revitalist as soon as he knocked. Whak looked through the fisheye and saw the brown suit ascending the stairs. It was Jim. Whak waited until he was on the top step and then opened the door.

"Clever swine," he told Jim.

"Known for it," Jim agreed.

"Come in."

"That would look suspicious. You know that the street is crawling with blue suits?"

"Of course I know. Blue Suit himself has Lino."

"What? What does he want with her?" Jim showed genuine pain in his face. The consequences of what he had done to her were never-ending. "Can't you tell the police?"

"Blue Suit is beyond the reach of police," said Whak. He gave Jim a two-minute lowdown on his and George Assok's experiences in the Wasteland, including Sedric's spectacular failure and George's unexpected thievery. "Now Blue Suit wants us to give him George in return for Lino, except that he probably won't anyway, in fact he didn't even say he would, but it's a hope, except that I won't do it, I can't I mean, it's one of those uncrossable lines. For me, anyway."

"Right. You don't deal with men in suits. They'll always cut you out at the end." It was, by the way Jim said it, a piece of street lore that he had learnt from personal experience. He nodded, though, when he heard about the Project Station. "I knew they had a place in there somewhere. What about that thing George stole?"

Whak looked blank. "What about it?"

"Might be valuable."

"They'll have others," Whak said dismissively.

"Might still be valuable. Didn't you say it could destroy the world? If they know George has it, they'll get worried, I bet." Jim fished in his pocket and handed Whak a bible. "I better go before they get suspicious. I'll look for Lino. I'll find her. I'll call you," he said seriously. Before Whak could make any doubtful reply, he turned and started to go back down the steps.

"Wait," Whak stopped him. He pulled a pen out of his pocket, wrote a number on a page of notebook paper and put it in Jim's hand. "Our phone number," he said.

"OK. I'll call you," Jim repeated. He raised one hand. "May the blessings of the Lord be on you, brother."

"Hah bloody hah."

As he shut the door, Whak pretended to look at the bible. Let them think he had turned to religion. That should make them laugh. He thought about what Jim had said while he made himself another cup of coffee. He knew he might soon spin out on caffeine overdose at the rate he was downing the stuff, but when your mind has become a bursting saucepan of popcorn you must pump your body to the same jitter level or the two will part company.

Jim was right. A nanoconstructor had to be a valuable thing, especially in the hands of a man who knew how to use it. George could be making planet munchers right this minute. The thought made Whak almost want to hand him over to Blue Suit forthwith. It would frighten any sane person. Blue Suit could be excluded from the ranks of the sane, but it might even frighten him. That gave Whak a sudden idea. He went to find Jelli.

Jim searches for Lino

Jim had to visit every house in the street to avoid being suspicious, and that took quite a while. If this didn't show that he was taking his responsibility for handing Lino directly to the forces of darkness seriously, he thought, nothing would. He had never intended for all this to happen. His wasn't quite the honest intention gone awry, but his was the foolish greed that had provoked the sleeping monsters. He still felt bad, really bad. It wasn't hard to pretend to be a Revitalist expecting the sky to open up with the visitation of God in a flying saucer at any moment, lead the faithful unto, and blast the wicked with his retro rockets. Was that what they believed? Jim hadn't a clue. All he knew was that he was going to try and find Lino. He'd done it once, and he could do it again, but where to start? In the meantime, he hoped Whak would find some way to make a deal with Blue Suit. He knew that such deals happened, but that was with little blue suits spying on the drug dealers of Combine Street, and this was the man himself, who wanted and needed things for reasons Jim wasn't even going to try and understand. That stuff was Whak's territory.

By now, he had progressed around the curve of the Park until he was out of sight of the Puihare's place. He ostentatiously looked at his bare wrist as if there was a watch on it and with a comical expression of surprise at how late he was for an imaginary sermon, he went across the road, across the park, across the town and back to his mirror-glassed third floor box.

"Hate this plastic shit," he gasped as he peeled the brown suit from his skin, white and clammy with sweat beneath. "I don't care how cheap it is." It had advantages, though. It was real stretchy, so you could get it off someone who might be, say, head down in a rubbish truck at the time, which is probably where this one had come from. Jim didn't care. He had just paid for it. Now he might be able to sell it to someone else who wanted to look like a geek for their own reasons. He tossed it into the corner and sat down in his underpants and thought about this carefully.

"Guys must know how to find people," he said after a while. "What kind of guys, though?" Well, there was police. Jim wasn't going to ask them. There were the Nephews. They found people who didn't want to be found. He was sure Cousin Sinfine still wanted to find Jim. So they were not going to help, and besides, they were clearly not very good at it, because they hadn't found Jim. This wasn't very helpful. Jim made himself a cup of sood and stood with it held against his cheek while he looked down onto the street. He saw the usual sights. There were people buying stuff from the shops at street level, there were people going places. Leaning against walls and boardups were the young gang leaders who inspected the offerings stolen by their guys, then made the bags, shades, knives or keys disappear. A few old people moved around in a group. Some children were playing a sing-song game. The sky is full of crap, the sky is full of crap, they sang. A cop car was parked at the corner and a guy Jim knew to be a burglar was standing by it, talking to whoever was inside, probably about what he wanted to have stolen next. Burglary to order was a good business. Jim had nearly gone into it himself.

"Burglary," Jim said. "Hey."

He headed downstairs, went right on up to the cop car and hailed the burglar.

"Hey Go-man!" he called. The burglar's name might have been some kind of superhero joke, or it might have been genuine ethnic, Jim didn't know. He wasn't going to ask. Some people got insulted easily.

"Jim." Go-man straightened up from the cop car window and nodded casually at him. "How's things?" Go-man had no haitches in his blood. His things sounded like tings. It made him sound German, but he looked Asian. Automatically, Jim stood in the cop car's blind spot.

"Things is fine," he answered. "I was wondering if I could talk to you a minute."

Go-man probably thought that Jim wanted to order a new pair of sunglasses. He nodded and turned back to the cop car. "Gotta go," he told the cop. He and Jim together walked over to stand under a beaten-up canvas veranda that hung out in front of a grocery store.

"What do you want?" Go-man asked.

"Go-man, when someone asks you to find them something, how do you know where to look?"

"You thinking of starting some competition, Jim?" Go-man did not get excited, but neither was he pleased. He looked left and right. So did Jim. It was a habit you grew up with. "Why should I tell you that? What's your lookout?"

"I'm not trying to get any of your business. Would I come and ask you how to take over your own business?"

"You might. If you were stupid enough. Or you thought I was stupid enough."

"Hey, I'm not stupid enough."

"Neither am I."

"So you can tell me."

Go-man hadn't yet reached that conclusion. He folded his arms and leaned on the shop window. The grocer, a middle-aged guy with a gut and no hair but with big strong arms, looked across from where he was stacking fruit, but said nothing. Jim decided he had to tell Go-man some more.

"I'm trying to find a person, and I thought it might work the way you find things."

"Tell the police to find your person."

"You're joking, right?"

"People don't work with the method, Jim-boy. People go where people go."

"This person goes where she is put and stays there."

Go-man still wasn't convinced. He shook his head. "I don't need to tell you anything. Find your own person." He pushed off the glass and started scanning for someone else to talk to. Jim decided the time had come to exaggerate. Lie, even.

"OK. I'll tell Sinfine I can't find her."

"Sinfine?" Go-man's attention came back rapidly. "What's with Sinfine?"

"I was round his place in North Coolio the other day. I'm doing stuff for him."

"Yeah?"

"Yeah."

Go-man nodded. "Yeah," he said again. "You're doing stuff for Sinfine?" Jim nodded. "This is stuff for Sinfine?" Jim nodded. Go-man looked thoughtful. Small-timers had to tread a fine line between keeping a low profile with the Cousins and doing an occasional for them. It didn't do not to be in when the Cousins called. It was pointless asking Jim to prove what he said. Either he was, or he wasn't. "OK. I'll tell you the method. But if I find out you're using it to take my business, we're going to meet again, right?"

"Right."

Go-man's famous method was really designed, as he said, for finding things rather than people, and it relied on the street network to get the information, but it was clever, Jim had to admit. Scientific, Go-man called it. Once he and Jim were up in Jim's little room and Go-man had a cup of sood in his hand, he was relaxed, and Jim saw that behind the hard man act that they all had to wear outside, he was another young man like himself who was prickly all over like a porqubot, only because he was scared someone would take his job away from him. He was still looking at Jim with unveiled suspicion.

"So you've got a map of the city," Jim reiterated, "and you get the kid gangs to tell you when they see people who have got the sort of things you're looking for, and you mark on the map where they are and guess where their homes are by drawing lines from everywhere you see them 'til the lines cross a lot in one place."

"Yeah. Triangulation. Learned it from my Dad. He was a teacher, once. Saves knocking the assholes on the head while they're out. I don't go for that violent shit."

"How does that work when you're looking for something people don't carry around?"

"Shit, that's easy, man. Say you come to me and say you want something like that. Say a computer or a stereo or something like that. Anyone with one of those things is going to have to buy stuff for it. Disks and paper. Whatever. I don't even have to get the kids to lookout for me, I just go to the shops that sell disk and paper and stand round outside and follow people home."

This was good, but it didn't seem to be getting Jim any closer to finding Lino. He asked again "What if it's something they don't need to buy anything for? I'm trying to find a person, Go-man. All they have to buy her is food."

"Well, you're fucked, I guess."

"You got a map I can buy off you?"

"I got plenty. I stole a million of them. Three bucks." Go-man reached into his coat and pulled out a street map of the city. "Never go out without one," he said. Jim gave him three bucks, and they sat drinking their sood in silence.

"Could ask the kids if they've seen anyone like what you're looking for," Go-man said after a while. "Or, you know what the guys who have her look like?"

"Not really."

"Who is this female, anyway?"

"She's my girl. I think."

"Oh. Shit, man. That's kinda sad." Go-man got up and put his cup in the sink. "Gotta go. There's stuff to be stolen."

"OK, thanks."

When Go-man had gone, Jim got out the map of town and spread it out on the floor. It was an old map, but there had been no new development since the SRMs, so in fact it showed more of the city than now existed. The Wasteland was marked as a fraction of the size it had achieved before finally being walled in. Jim expected that the wall would eventually be just another Wasteland landmark, between the Old Wasteland and the New Wasteland that the surrounding slums were rapidly decaying into. He looked for and found the street where Sinfine had been holding Lino before Blue Suit got her. He wondered if Sinfine knew who it was that had crashed his hideout and killed his men. Probably not, he decided. Whak only knew because Blue Suit had admitted it to his face. Anyway, she had been there. With his finger, he drew a big circle. The slums were in the middle, Coolio Park at one edge, the city centre, Combine and Widmark Streets on the other side. Widmark reminded him of the alley party he had been to with Lino, just a week ago. And the SRM event there. With that thought, the tense, searching expression on Jim's face began to relax.

Whak sneaks out

Jelli had organised her own security to follow her everywhere, so tonight the street outside the Puihare mansion was crowded with spies and counterspies. Men up trees. Men in cars. Watching the house. Watching each other. She observed them unhappily from the kitchen window.

"You really want to do this," she said to Whak.

"It's better than doing nothing," he answered her. He was beginning to see a certain charm in being a man of action rather than words. In the last few days he had been shot at, arrested, fallen over dead bodies, held at gunpoint, and fled from nanoviral doom across the Wasteland. If experience of life is the stuff of art, then experience of death might be, too. "It's all I can think of. And it gets us something to bargain with."

"I'm not doing nothing!" Jelli's voice jumped about a foot in the air. "I'm manoeuvring!"

"Yes, I know." Whak put his hand on her shoulder. "I know that. But I have to do something, too. If I get that nanoconstructor, then you've got evidence of what Blue Suit is doing. Real evidence. He might trade for it."

"It would be better if you bring Assok in, too. We don't know for certain that Blue Suit will trade for the nanoconstructor. If we have him as well..."

"We not turning George over to him! Apart from anything else, that would give him everything he needs to complete his nanovirus project."

"I didn't say we were going to turn Assok over! But we'd have the machine, and someone technically qualified to explain it to the Consortium, that's all. There'd be no way Blue Suit could deny what it was. It would strengthen our hand."

Whak considered his wife's general demeanour carefully before he replied. It wasn't that he didn't trust her. Was it?

"All right. You speak to Blue Suit. I'll speak to George Assok. I'll try to get him to come."

"If they catch you out there, you'll disappear like Lino. Then what am I going to do?" The glare of the future was getting too bright for Jelli. She continued to stare out the window.

"I don't know," said Whak. "I don't know if anything we're doing is going to make any difference, anyway."

"I should never have tried to deal with Blue Suit in the first place."

"Yeah," Whak agreed. "Sharing a woman plays hell with my muse."

Jelli didn't show any reaction. She let it fester, instead. She picked up the phone and dialled the man who ran her security men. A few minutes after that, one of them came up the driveway and knocked at the door. When he left, he was Whak, or Whak was him. In plain view in the kitchen, while Jelli pretended to have an animated discussion with the man now wearing Whak's clothes, Whak, unmolested, climbed into one of several PushRight cars that were parked all over the street and drove away.

CHAPTER 34

Assok's new plans

Whak drove around the park until he recognised the general area of West Coolio, then he turned down the first uninhabitable looking street he saw and put the car between a collapsed building and a burned-out bus. He thought about smashing the car up a little so that it would be less conspicuous, but a deep-seated habit of conservation prevented him from having that much fun. Whak's mind, as he sidled through the shadows of shadows towards what he hoped what George's building, resembled a bee on a window pane, bashing it's ganglion out on impossibly hard and unyielding air. He desperately wanted to pull out a spray can and publicise his pain, but this was not a good time for self-expression. He walked on.

The parade of barely tenanted concrete buildings that intermittently lit the darkness with TV flicker or straining yellow electric glow began to look familiar. Whak stopped, decided on one semicollapsed doorway over another, and went in. He had chosen correctly. The disused elevator doors still stood open, and he recognised the pattern of the banisters. He went over to the metal door half-hidden at the back on the foyer and pounded on it. It boomed like a kettle drum.

George Assok never had visitors. He knew nobody, and recent history had raised his habitual paranoia to the level of mild insanity. The sound of fists beating on his door made him jump from his seat, and look for a weapon. He had one, somewhere. While he was searching his mental filing cabinet under g for gun and w for weapon, the knocking continued incessantly, regularly, neither increasing nor decreasing in volume. It was inhuman, frightening. Almost at the same time as George pulled an unloaded revolver out of the Rs, which turned out to be a drawer in the side of the electronics bench, Whak discovered that despite the uncommon number of bolts and latches he knew were on the other side of this door it was, after all that, not locked. He pushed it open to discover Assok, holding the gun by the barrel, radiating fear and guilt.

"You should lock this," he said, indicating the door.

"It's you! I thought it was the blue suits! Why didn't you tell me you were coming?"

"How? By coming around and knocking on your door? I did that. George, I need your help."

Assok recovered his equilibrium and his sarcasm with equal rapidity. "Oh you need my help, now. Your response when I needed your help was not overwhelming. I still haven't spoken with your wife."

"George, my daughter is in the hands of Blue Suit. He'll give her back in return for that nanoconstructor you stole." Whak still had no idea whether this was true, but it had to be. Everything depended upon it.

George made an angry sound. "The idea for the nanoconstructor was stolen from me, originally. If anyone is entitled to it, it should be me."

"But what's the point in your having it? It's just a piece of junk, isn't it, unless you're intending to make nanomachines with it, and..." Whak took stock of George's nonchalance and stopped short. "Oh, you're not, are you?" he asked in a frightened voice.

"I told you," George said in edgy tones. "I think I can solve the replication fidelity problem. I think I can make nanoviruses which both adapt to their conditions and retain their core characteristics." He made an expansive gesture towards a bench nearby. There was the nanoconstructor, connected to a surprisingly new-looking desktop computer by a flat, grey, tapeworm cable. An innocuous enough little box. Against the blue background of the computer screen, several different windows displayed slowly cycling or steadily progressing waveforms, possibly graphs. George put on an ingratiating smile. "Don't worry. It's quite safe."

"Quite safe like hell." Sometimes when Whak spoke to George he felt like he was trying to talk down a madman with a loaded pistol.

"I just want to do a few practical experiments," said George. "If SRMs maintain their viability through a meta-instruction set, then so can nanos. I already had all the theory worked out, but until now I never thought I'd get a chance to apply it. I've introduced a short-range communication feature into the nanoadaptive routines that will, well, potentially, allow the nanos to compare their base designs dynamically with others belonging to the same clade - that is, communicating in the same codes. The math is rather complex," he said apologetically, "but it all hangs together. Trust me, Puihare. It's fine."

The thought of George Assok here in his kitchen sink laboratory, making clouds of planet-eating nanovirus, tossing vials full of microscopic disaster over his shoulder, was so awful that Whak took a step backwards away from all this and bumped into one of the SRM enclosures that almost covered that wall. Something behind his left shoulder moved and caught his attention.

The octopede episode

It was the octopede that was moving. It was using one limb to remove another. It was twisting it's tail to attack it's own head with several tools which had appeared from a dilated metal sphincter. Arseholes with teeth, eating their own bodies.

"What's wrong with it?" Whak asked, rubbing his head. "Have you been using nanoviruses on it?"

"No." George had also noticed the unusual activity, and was staring, fascinated. "The nanoviruses are still being assembled. I only have one flask." He nodded back in the direction of the nanoconstructor and the advancing displays on the computer screen. Whak didn't know which of the two horrors to stare at. The computer bumped a progress bar along another percentage point. The octopede continued to take itself apart. One eye lens clinked and fell out. Something started to crawl out of the eye socket.

"Oh, oh." said George. He took several rapid steps away from the fish tanks and ducked down behind a table. Whak did the same.

"What's happening?" Whak asked him.

"Metamorphosis," George told him briefly.

"Does that mean we have to hide under the table?"

"After all the other SRM events that have happened lately, I think it does."

The hatching of the octopede was nearly complete. The eye socket became an egress for a stream of minute machines. Whak couldn't see them clearly from where he crouched, but he thought that they had only two front limbs. They were only a centimetre or so long. There were at least a dozen of them. As they emerged into the tank, they took to the air and flew without any visible means of propulsion, no wings, no propellers, and within a minute there was a minor tornado of the things whirling around in the enclosure. George began to stand up. As he did so, there was a sudden ear-splitting crack and the side of the tank burst, showering powdered glass across the room like snow that settled on both men's faces and shoulders. The air was filled with the glass dust and silently flying SRMs, to Whak's eyes resembling tiny deep-sea submersibles that had been in the insanely optimistic futures that once filled big and small screens alike. The flock of new variety hovered for a moment, then descended onto the nearest pieces of food, the computer and the nanoconstructor.

George Assok tried to drive them away as if they were insects, but they were not insects and ignored his hands sweeping the air. They entered the computer through the diskette drive and the fan aperture, and almost instantly the blue bar, which was reading 98%, was replaced by a bright prismatic dot in the centre of the screen, then that too disappeared and the sound of a hard disk spinning down could be heard. The small red light on the front of the nanoconstructor also went out.

"God damn!" Assok said with great feeling. Whak, on the other hand, was relieved. George turned to him angrily.

"What are you smiling about, Puihare? My work is ruined. I'll never be able to get another nanoconstructor." The flock of the flying SRMs exited the computer and reformed their hovering cloud. It seemed to Whak that there were now a few more of them than there had been a moment ago.

"Oh, no," George started to run around the room, grabbing various bits of equipment and throwing them in great haste into cupboards. The flock moved to one of the street-level windows and to the sound of another sharp explosion, broke one of the blacked-out panes. A few seconds later, they were gone. George Assok was standing with his arms outstretched behind him, defending the broom closet.

"There goes trouble," Whak said. "They're hungry." He wiped glass powder from his face. A trickle of blood appeared on his forehead. Looking suspiciously around as he crossed the room, George came back to where Whak was standing.

"Don't be so anthropomorphic," he said. "Flying like that is far too energetic to sustain for long periods. They'll probably degenerate once they're away from a supply of highly organised material."

"How can you be so optimistic when you don't know where they get their energy from? Is this a characteristic of modern science? No wonder technology has failed us."

"Technology has not failed us," George insisted. Whak imagined that he was trying to look dignified, but the effect was closer to Buster Keaton than Albert Einstein. "You just saw proof of my theory - purposeful evolution at work. The octopede had evolved into a form that, while extremely sophisticated, could not escape from the trap I had placed it in. So it deconstructed itself into simpler forms that could. Imagine a biological life-form being able to do such a thing. That SRM deliberately sacrificed whatever degree of self-awareness it possessed, in order to expand the horizons of it's species. It's quite admirable in a peculiar sort of way. This sort of thing is going on all over the world, not just in my laboratory. That's why nanovirus research is so important. It may be the only way to control them." He bent over his nanoconstructor and extracted the shiny cylinder from it. "I wonder what state this is in," he said, holding it in front of his face. "It was almost finished. Ninety-eight percent. Probably just cleaning out the constructor agents."

"What does it matter? You can't make any more." Whak and George both looked at the machine at the same time. "You could give me the nanoconstructor, now."

"Since it's completely wrecked, I suppose I could. I was going to, anyway, Puihare. Unfortunately, my research is not worth the life of a stranger." He picked up the nanoconstructor and held it out.

"Bravo." Whak smiled. "Now, there is one other thing I need from you."

"What?"

"You. Come with me."

It didn't work out that way. Try as he might, Whak couldn't prise George out of his cellar. The experiences of the last few days had taught him that to go anywhere with Whak Puihare was a life-threatening mistake.

"I'm trying to help you!" said Whak. "You said you wanted protection from Blue Suit!"

"We've only just escaped from Blue Suit, and I'm not going to let you and your wife hand me straight back, even if it does mean your daughter's freedom. My career may be worth less than the life of a stranger, but my own life isn't!"

"We're not going to hand you over to anybody!"

"It's obvious! What does Blue Suit need more than he needs a nanoconstructor? He needs someone who knows what to do with it. Sedric has obviously reached the limit of his grasp of practical nanophysics. He is gravely injured, he may be dying for all we know. Obviously, Blue Suit will be now be looking for alternatives. He will want to get his hands on me."

"You always said he wanted to kill you. Now you say he wants to use you. Which is it?"

"Either way, my life would be his, wouldn't it? I'm sorry, Puihare, but if I was Blue Suit, I wouldn't settle for a broken piece of equipment when I could get the man who invented it. I'm not going with you."

"We're not going to hand you over," Whak repeated firmly. "I wouldn't do that. Jelli's going to tell the Consortium all about nanoviruses, and that machine is evidence, and you are our expert witness. Nobody but you and I know that it's broken. If Blue Suit doesn't give Lino back then, with that and your knowledge, she can prove that Blue Suit has been exceeding his charter, his budget, and his authority. If he wants to keep nanotechnology to himself so badly that he tried to kill anybody who knew anything about it, then he's not going to want that."

"What's to stop her from doing it anyway, once you have your daughter?"

"We won't have the nanoconstructor then, so we won't be able to prove anything."

"Blue Suit could say that he's never seen this machine before in his life, which is probably true, by the way."

"So it's circumstantial evidence! People have breathed cyanide for less. Come on, George. Come with me. We need your help."

"Not a chance, Whak. I'm not going with you. You really expect me to believe that you, or your wife, wouldn't exchange me for your daughter?"

"Yes," Whak said.

George's expression grew more and more doleful as he contemplated the idiocy of that answer for a couple of seconds, then shook his head.

"I must be insane," he muttered.

Whak grabbed his hand, which was still outstretched, holding out the nanoconstructor. "Then you'll come," he said.

"No, I won't come. Not right now. You haven't the faintest idea how to keep out of sight. We'd both be arrested before we got through the park. I'll meet you at the usual tree tomorrow night."

"What about the nanoconstructor?"

"It's broken," George said sadly.

"It doesn't matter. Blue Suit doesn't know that."

"All right. I'll bring it with me. If you take it now and you're stopped, then that's the end of your far-fetched little scheme. You make sure that no-one follows you tomorrow night!"

"Oh, yes," Whak nodded and nodded. "No-one."

Jelli strikes back

It was with a painful sense of self-flagellation that Jelli had Allynn put a call through to the Blue Suit headquarters. She sat at her desk and watched the phone. It didn't ring. As she slowly boiled, Allynn appeared in the doorway.

"He's not taking your call," she said.

Jelli looked angrier than Allynn, who led a quiet life, had ever seen any person look before. Her teeth seemed to grow points. "All right, then," she said with the gasping voice of a person who is withholding a dying scream, "leave him a message. Tell him to watch the nine o'clock news."

"What's going to be on the nine o'clock news?" asked Allynn, interested.

"I don't know, yet. Something that makes Blue Suit realise that there are people better not fucked around with." She got up and stalked out into the corridor.

Allynn thought her remarks to be pure melodrama, but on the other hand, she knew Jelli. If Jelli decided to make someone jump, she was sure that she would succeed. Allynn made a mental note to be watching television at nine o'clock tonight.

This is what Whak thought of the GOV1 Nine O'clock News:

This is the news
A dying art form
Freedom of expression exists
Within carefully proscribed limits
Standard phrases are spoken clearly
From lipsticked mouths
Dripping the truth like blood
Over the subtitles for the deaf

In the Puihare relationship, disagreements were likely to be found on flyers pasted to a fence, or spray-painted on the footpath.

He had arrived back at the house after Jelli had left for work. The man who was wearing his clothes, now sort of rumpled in face and shirt, was drinking coffee in the kitchen when Whak came in.

"Real coffee," he told Whak with a jerky, caffeinated shake of the pot.

"I know," Whak told him as he stripped out of the other man's jacket and handed it over. "Thanks for being me."

"No problem."

"Where'd you sleep?" Whak studied the other man's dusty eyes.

"Mrs Puihare didn't sleep much, so I didn't either. She kept walking up and down the hallway out there. Must have been worried about you."

"It'll be a first if she was," Whak said, knowing it to be untrue.

"My boss said that you were going to be decitizened or worse." His boss was the PushRight Security Director, a man named McFee. Whak had never met him, but he had heard Jelli speaking to him on the phone. Not much of a basis for a personal judgement, but hell, Whak thought, all security wallahs are alike.

"If Blue Suit wanted to kill me, he could have done before this," he said dismissively.

"They might only just have realised that they do want to kill you. I worked for them once, grunt stuff, you know, and they're always trying to put the pressure on, scare first. It's when they can't find an angle that they get pissed off and start killing people." The coffee pot shook in the air again.

"Did you kill people?" Whak asked him.

The man nodded.

"Sure," he said. "But now I work for PushRight. I don't have to kill people any more. Now I only have to be willing to kill people."

"Great. That must be a relief for your conscience."

"You bet."

Jelli came home in the early afternoon. She couldn't go on sitting at her desk, pretending to be in control. She had to find out what was really happening. She threw herself onto the sofa with a whisky tumbler in her hand and glared at Whak.

"Where's the nanoconstructor? Where's George Assok?" she demanded.

Whak explained that George had wisely refused to be seen with him. "We're going to meet somewhere safe."

"You trust him to show up?"

"Yes," Whak nodded. "He needs your help. His lab was wrecked by one of his more evolved SRMs, last night. This smart-looking goggle-eyed thing suddenly took itself apart. Made lots of little flyers and then - "

"Spare me, Whak. I don't want to hear any more about SRMs." Jelli covered her eyes with her hand. "What about the machine?"

"He'll give it to us. The nanoconstructor was wrecked, too. Just as well, really, because he was in the middle of making nanoviruses with it."

"After what you say happened to Colville, he must be insane to do that. What did he think he was doing?"

"Proving his theories, I think. What about you? Did you speak to Blue Suit?"

"No, God damn it. I didn't speak to him." Jelli briefly shook from hands to head, a spasm of dread that she could not control. Whak knew how she felt. He felt the same. Every moment was a constant internal replay of futures in which Lino returned and Lino was all right, or Lino disappeared forever, or Lino lay alive in a hospital bed while Blue Suit's technicians took samples of her brain. Only by believing there was something that he could do to influence events was he able to retain the facade of normality, which now cracked.

"Why not?" he asked bitterly. "Does he only speak to you when you're both naked?" For the next silent moment, sharp darts poisoned with emotion stabbed them both, and then he sighed. "I'm sorry I said that. Rewind and start again. Why didn't you speak to him?"

Jelli made an obvious effort to relax. "I didn't speak to him because he wouldn't speak to me. It's just a control tactic. He's saying that he'll speak to us when he's ready, not when we are. If he refuses to talk to us, then even if we have something to offer, it doesn't matter. He's not listening."

"But how can we bargain with him if he won't talk to us?"

"I think I can make him re-open negotiations," Jelli smiled, without showing her teeth. She gulped her drink down, rolled off the sofa and went over to the television set. "Let's watch TV."

"Watch TV? Are you crazy?" Whak scratched his head. "What's on?"

CHAPTER 35

The news at nine

News At Nine

Presented by Elizabeth Furth

talking head shot

Hello, this is Elizabeth Furth with the News at Nine. Tonight, Amnesty for black economy workers wishing to register as taxpayers.

Air pollution levels reach new low.

Charter operator offers cheapest fares to Hawaii, but competitors ask, is the boat safe?

Population change set to return to positive figures this year.

And Blue Suit Security Services reveals startling new technology in the fight against SRMs.

We'll be back right after this information break.

Five minutes of Correct Management Consortium promos

Two minutes of cheap fares to Hawaii adverts

Welcome back to News at Nine. Today the Correct Management Consortium Executive in Charge of Revenue Collection, Mr Heyward, announced a new policy designed to uncriminalise the large number of citizens who are now working in the 'black' economy. We speak now with Mr Heyward on our city-to-city link.

Black and white picture of man facing camera appears right screen

Furth: Mr Heyward, why has the Correct Management Consortium taken this step? Is it because efforts to police the black economy have failed?

Heyward looks surprised and checks his script

Heyward: That isn't one of the listed questions.

Furth: Isn't it the responsibility of Blue Suit Security Services to ensure registration of every citizen and enable your department to collect the legally owing tax revenue that our economy needs in order to support the needy?

Heyward: Well, yes, it is. There seems to be some mistake with the script here.

Furth: Mr Heyward, we are on the air.

Heyward quickly assumes an expression of suave inscrutability

Heyward: The new policy, as you said a moment ago, is intended to release ordinary people who have been ensnared in the unregulated economy from their bondage and return them to government-approved employment, without there being any question that they will be punished for tax evasion.

Furth: So a large amount of tax revenue has been lost in the past due to the inability of Blue Suit to identify and register these people?

Heyward: I can't answer that question.

Furth: Will the Consortium be investigating the failure of the Tax Registration Program?

Heyward: That program is... that is a possibility, yes.

Furth: Thank you, Mr Heyward, for joining us on News at Nine. More news after this information break.

Social engineering segment: man dressed in rough clothes walks towards camera down starkly shadowed street. As he stops in front of the camera, a light turns on in a window above.

Man: The people in that apartment are watching me. They're scared that I'm here to check on their tax registration. And I might be. But am I authorised to do so?

Cut to two people passing each other on stairs. Man going up turns around, follows the man going down and as he catches up, grabs the other's shoulder. Lips move. Second man shrugs off the other's hand. First man reaches into coat and shows an ID. In close-up, the crest reads Blue Suit Security Services Inc.

Cut back to man in street.

Man: If you're not sure, ask to see Blue Suit ID. And remember, registering as a taxpayer means that fifty-five percent of your income will go to help the needy.

Cut back to Elizabeth Furth

Welcome back to News at Nine.

Air pollution segment

Hawaii charters segment

Population growth segment

And now the main story. Today, Blue Suit Security Services revealed a new weapon in the fight against SRMs. Startling new technology developed by Blue Suit under a secret research grant offers the hope that one day the reduction of industrial capacity through SRM depredation may soon be a thing of the past. GOV1 would like to be the first to congratulate Blue Suit Security Services for securing a better future for us all. From our studio in PushRight Tower, we bring you this analysis.

Pan to left, where another announcer is ready to speak. Elizabeth Furth's voice cuts in with heightened volume.

Furth: This is great! This is - *(cut off)*

Other: With us in the studio is Alan Perkle, author of 'A Dissertation on Agricultural Robotics' and a well-respected science commentator. Tell me, Alan, what has Blue Suit announced, exactly?

Perkle: It's very exciting. Blue Suit has been working on what you might call a mechanical disease. Their researchers have developed a virus, if you like, which can infect SRMs and, well, 'kill' them.

Other: And this virus is infectious, like the kind of viruses humans catch?

Perkle: It wouldn't be much use if it weren't.

Other: Is there any danger that humans could be affected?

Perkle: Oh, no. I'm sure that the developers will have been very careful on that score.

Other: But we have reports that a senior researcher on this project was exposed to this virus, and lost an arm as a result.

Perkle: If that's the case, then obviously there are some problems to be ironed out.

Other: The other question is, who owns this technology? The Correct Management Consortium? Blue Suit? Selling exterminator services may not sound very fascinating, but every country in the world will pay almost any price to get rid of SRMs within their territory. Countries that don't, will be at a terrible disadvantage against others that are SRM-free and can rebuild their industrial bases.

Perkle: Well, I suppose that's true. So far as who owns this technology, then if this was done under a grant from the Consortium, I imagine that the results belong to them.

Other: Are research grants public knowledge, or has this been developed in secret? *(slyly)*

Perkle: Both. The grant should be a matter of record, but the research was probably behind closed doors. We scientists don't like to publish until we're ready, you know *(laughs)*.

Other: Thank you, Alan Perkle. Back to Elizabeth.

Furth: Now the weather.

Whak & Jelli Discuss the News

Whak knew what the weather was going to be. Awful, as usual. He switched off the television and looked approvingly at Jelli.

"I don't know how you do that," he told her. "You told the truth while telling nothing but lies."

Jelli was pleased, but she pretended to be irritated. "That's what I do," she said.

"Exterminator services. It's a bit worse than that, isn't it?"

"Yes. This exterminator has a truckload of new pests ready to unload on anyone he doesn't like. Just a hint of that should be enough to scare the Consortium, while leaving us a bit of leverage." She was feeling confident. Her brain was ticking.

"I like that tax registration bit. I didn't know that there was a Blue Suit ID card. They don't show them while they're shooting at you."

"There is, but it doesn't look like that one. We faked one up."

That actually made Whak laugh.

"I bet there are a lot of blue suits out there right now getting the shit knocked out of them. And I'm sure Blue Suit didn't want the Consortium to know about his nanoviruses."

"With the ideas I've planted about nanotechnology being both powerful and dangerous, they'll want to have them for themselves," Jelli said with a trace of the happiness that comes from hurting thine enemies. "They'll be all over him by this time tomorrow."

"And now?"

"Now we wait for him to call us. And I'm not finished, yet."

Blue Suit Discusses the News

Blue Suit watched a video of the nine o'clock news in silence. Once again, he was impressed by Jelli Puihare. At the end of the telephone in his hand was one of the Consortium directors that he controlled, through money, secrets, and fear, but right now the director was taking a critical line.

"What have you been doing?" the director asked him. "What is all this virus crap? Why have you let the tax registration thing get this far out of hand? My enemies are scoring points with this. I've backed you on the basis that you keep control of things. What the hell is going on?"

"You've backed me because if you don't, I'll ruin you. No other reason."

The other man brushed that fact aside with the ease of a professional politician. "So what am I going to do about Heyward? He has to be seen to be doing something. He's saying that with the budget you've got, you should have had every scumsucker in the country on the books by now."

"That is ridiculous. It hasn't even been my main priority. Keeping order is my main priority, at all times." After advancing his own interests.

"What about this secret research? What's all that about? If you've been siphoning off funds for this without authorisation, you'll be up before the Funding Committee in five minutes. Machine viruses! Arms lost! Extermination services, for Christ's sake!" The director paused for a breath, and when he spoke again he was calmer. "Does it work?" he asked.

"It's a hoax," Blue Suit said flatly. He saw no reason to discontinue his policy of total-secrecy-until-he-was-ready. "There is no secret research, there is no virus. It is a hoax by PushRight."

"Why would PushRight do that?"

"Jelli Puihare wishes me harm."

"Who doesn't?"

Blue Suit ignored the jibe. "She is attacking me because I have been forced to detain her daughter, for national security reasons." He understood that the truth can serve as a lie just as well as Jelli understood that a lie can serve as the truth.

"Jelli Puihare's daughter? Jesus, you've got some nerve. What are you trying to pull there?"

"She is implicated in the destructive SRM events that have recently occurred. We are interviewing her to establish the link."

"Jelli Puihare's daughter." The director was stunned. "I hope you know what you're doing."

"Always."

When he had hung up, Blue Suit ran the tape again. Clever, he acknowledged. In one half-hour television show, Jelli had disrupted his observation operations, implied that his organisation was incompetent, and worst of all, brought the SRM Collection Program and all it stood for into the eye of the Consortium, who were not stupid and would already be asking questions. All this, without a shred of evidence, but evidence is hardly required when you are the nine o'clock news.

He drummed his fingers on the desk. He should have foreseen this, but that was then and this was now, so he turned his mind to damage control. The story that all this was a hoax would hold for a few days, possibly forever, if there was no Jelli Puihare on the scene to rub the Consortium's face in it at nine o'clock every night. That woman had suddenly made herself a serious liability. With that thought, Blue Suit turned back to the telephone and began to dial.

Allynn put the call on hold and rang Jelli. She knew that Jelli was in her office. Except for the time she had spent scripting the news yesterday, she had spent most of the previous few days sitting at her desk staring into space while her soul took a spin around guilt city, and today was following suit. Allynn found this new side of Jelli to be depressing in the extreme. She hoped for a return of the unstoppable CEO of PushRight, lurid clothes, sexual incontinence and all, as preferable to the small, unhappy woman now in the office. Perhaps this call would start something.

"Yes?" Jelli answered.

"Blue Suit is on the line. Do you want to speak to him?"

There was a moment of silence, which Allynn took to be Jelli computing her reply. In fact, it was Jelli wishing intensely that she had never been born.

"Yes. Put him on," she answered at last. There was a click and a hum as the outside line with it's baggage of static and echo connected. "Jelli," she said.

"Hello, Jelli," said Blue Suit, precisely, calmly.

"You bastard."

"Clever use of your limited powers last night."

"Limited powers? I'm going to get you audited, you asshole. I'm going to get the Consortium to replace you with Find-A-Pet. You are going to end up herding agriworkers in the desert."

"This, from the woman who a few weeks ago was sucking my penis. My, my."

"I've sucked bigger ones." Jelli forced herself to take a deep breath. "So what do you want?"

"I think the question is, what do you want, isn't it?"

"No. You're the one who wants something. Something I've got."

"George Assok," Blue Suit said quickly.

"Ah-ah. A nanoconstructor. From your place in the Wasteland. Fascinating device, isn't it? I understand that George Assok invented it. He must be a very clever man."

"I have several such devices," Blue Suit said after a short silence.

"Yes, and I have one. I think the Consortium would like to see it, don't you? It is proof that you are working with nanoviruses, isn't it?"

"Yes, I suppose it is." There was another pause. "It's a little late to try to beat me at my own game, Jelli."

"Oh, it's never too late. I might do a public presentation on GOV1. Put George Assok on to explain the details. He is a much better public speaker than Colville, I understand. I'm sure the Consortium wants to know more about nanotech, now that they have heard of it." Already, she guessed that questions would be percolating from the slimy depths of the Consortium's collective mind.

"If you do that, your daughter's safety will be jeopardised."

Jelli refused to let the images invoked by that threat affect her strategy. She said "I will do that, unless you release her immediately. How much exposure can you take? I can make your life hell. Scandals without end. Consortium scrutiny of your every move. Every time you think you've canned one issue, I'll bring up another one. I'll make sure you're a listed paedophile when you go to prison for tax evasion. Do you want that? Or do you want me to quietly bury the tax registration scandal, shut up about unauthorised nanotechnology projects, and give your nanoconstructor back?"

Unknown to her, at the other end of the line, Blue Suit was smiling with irrepressible admiration. What a partnership they could have made, if only she was not so determined to see all her opportunities in the light of a mystical greater good. He shook his head to dispel the dream. "All right. You stop attacking me in the media. Return the nanoconstructor. But you have to do more. Bring me George Assok as well. I know that you know where he is. Then I will release your daughter. Or no deal."

The phone line turned into noise.

Jelli stared at the handset with disbelief.

"You insane bastard," she told it.

After some days, Jim was fairly sure he knew where Lino was being held. Not exactly, but the general area. On his apartment wall, on the only wall that was large enough for it, the map of the city that he had bought from Go-man was pinned, and dotted all over it were dozens of little round plastic-headed board pins, red ones, and blue ones. The blue ones were reported sightings of blue suits going into or out of buildings. There were lots of those, and the spread was pretty random over the area that the kid gangs worked in, which meant most of the city centre, and the slum districts. Jim had paupered himself paying the little gougers for information. The red pins, though, were the real key. Each red pin represented a sighting of an SRM that had been acting weird, unusually aggressive, or unusually hungry. The pattern of the SRM sightings was noticeably clustered.

"It's fucking amazing what you can do with maps," Jim said to himself. He stood with his back against the opposite wall to the map and stared at it. There were three places where the red pins were more densely positioned than the average: the Wasteland, one small grouping to the north, which Jim decided to ignore, and a whole bunch of them in a circle around a small area in the city. Not, he was relieved to note, in the area of the Blue Suit office building. There were blue pins galore around that part of the map. It would have made his next steps very difficult if Lino was being held there. The circle of red he was looking at was speckled with the occasional blue. So, whatever was in that area, there were blue suits there too. For a moment, Jim allowed himself to look objectively at what he was doing. He was supposing that Lino would be mindzip plus, totally turned inside. Probably in a trance like she had been at the Wasteland the first time he saw her drive the SRMs insane. He was supposing that, in that state, she was affecting SRMs over a wide area. Some of those red pins marked happenings that the kids had been fascinated and scared of, like SRMs suddenly falling into fragments on the footpath, or a dozen different varieties congregating around a parked car and stripping it to the rubber. People in this city were learning fast that the peculiar little machines could now be dangerous.

Jim supposed also that if he found her, he would be able to get her away from the blue suits. Considering the craziness of all his other reasoning, it was odd that this was the assumption he felt worried about. He took another long look at the map and then put on his jacket. Time for some field work.

There was the usual assortment of decomposing brickwork and cold grey concrete, here and there crumbling to expose rusty reinforcing, waiting for Jim at the physical counterpart to the circle of red pins. On this block were a museum and a hospital, both long ago closed, and a line of empty retail outlets above which lived the same mixture of SHAmen and non-taxpayers that could be found in Combine Street. None of the inner city zones could be classed as desirable residential areas. Rising from the centre of the block was one tall building of two dozen floors. Jim leaned on the plywood that covered a shopfront and began to count broken windows in the tower. There were a few other people on the street and he watched them, too. He was beginning to feel like a blue suit himself, and he was feeling worried that some of the more aggro looking of the local denizens were of the same opinion. Just as a couple of big men stopped a way on, turned to each other and made meaningful looks at him over their shoulders, he found what he was looking for. On the thirteenth floor, there was a line of windows that were not broken.

Jim pushed off the plywood and began to walk, but too late, because the two big men were coming towards him. He smiled at them. Big man A, on the left, was a black guy with really short hair, and big man B, on the right, was white or Spanish, taller and lighter. So he had the longer reach. Jim kept on walking towards them with an expression of slightly stupid innocence on his face.

"Hey, you," said the taller. He took a big step, much bigger than Jim had expected, and reached out, forcing Jim to throw himself left too early. He didn't have a chance. The black man was also faster than he had guessed, and his large bony hand grabbed Jim by the biceps.

"Who're you?" the black man asked him, squeezing hard enough to stop blood.

"Jim," said Jim.

"What you doing here?" The squeeze continued. "What you up to?"

"I'm just looking around," Jim told him, showing rather more pain than he was actually feeling. "I was just going."

"You a blue suit?"

"No!"

The tall man quickly searched Jim's pockets, found his wallet (empty) and his knife. He looked in the wallet. There was still a Wasteland Tours ID in there.

"You a guide?" the tall man asked, tapping the ID with his forefinger.

"I was. I'm a pitfight handler, now," Jim replied, instantly regretting it, because no sooner were the words in flight than the tall man's eyes lit up. He turned to his black friend.

"Wasn't they looking for this guy?"

"Yeah. That's right. Jim. Pitfight handler. The Cousins want him," the black man nodded happily. "Let's take him." He shook Jim backwards and forwards a couple of times. "Stupid," he told him. "This is Nephew territory, asshole. You can't fucking sneeze here without the Cousins finding out."

Jim slumped in real despair. Sinfine would certainly kill him. He bent at the knees and moaned and as soon as the grip on his arm loosened a fraction, he struck at the lumpy black thumb joint with his free hand. The black guy grunted and let him go and he made three steps before the tall man kicked his legs out from under him and he fell onto the pavement, where the two men took turns kicking him for a minute. After that, he didn't feel like trying to escape any more. They dragged him to a car that was indistinguishable from an abandoned hulk, without doors or bonnet, but it started after a couple of chugs and while the black man kept Jim's arm twisted behind his back the tall guy drove, transmission grinding and engine beating irregularly, to a place where there were lots more Nephews coming and going.

It was a drop-off and pick-up house. There was a man there who must have been a supervisor from the Cousins. He was wearing a suit, and supervised the packaging of hallugics and stuff going out and the counting and receipting of money coming in. There were other lines of business going down, too, but Jim was too worried about the state of his ribs to pay any more attention than he had to. After the tall man had attracted the attention of the supervisor, Jim was pushed forward.

"Jim the handler man," the supervisor said. "Sinfine wants to see you." He snapped his fingers - this seemed to be a Cousin and subCousin trait - and Jim was bundled off into another vehicle, one that had doors this time, and a few minutes later he was on his way to North Coolio.

CHAPTER 36

Jim is taken to Sinfine

Sinfine stroked the leg of the pool girl next to him, under the unjudging gaze of the security maid. He had rebounded from the disappearance of Lino and the killing of his doctor - and that generally useless Horse character - but he still nursed the affront. He had kept his head down with regard to his attempted deal with Blue Suit since, and praise be, Blue Suit had apparently decided that females who played mind games with SRMs were too weird even for him, because he hadn't called. By the sound of what Sinfine heard on the news, he had bigger fish to fry.

Still, Sinfine had a business to run. He couldn't spend time grinding his molars, he thought, grinding his molars. He pushed the girl away and waved Emery over from where he stood in the shade of the house, waiting for an audience.

"What?" he demanded.

"A couple of Nephews have just turned up with Jim," Emery told him.

"Jim?" Sinfine wondered who Jim was for no more than a few seconds, then he showed his teeth. "Oh, Jim. Great. Hey, good guys come last again." Someone to bear the punishment otherwise destined for Sinfine's molars. He stood up and straightened his jacket, rubbed his hands together and sighed happily. "Where is he? Take me to him."

"Yes, sir," Emery replied. They went in through the French doors and right in the middle of the large living room there he was, with a Nephew on either side of him. The bruises on his face testified to an undiminishable desire to escape.

"Hey, Jim!" said Sinfine expansively. "How are you?" Jim did not reply. His eyes darted around the room. "Don't think about leaving, Jim. You're not leaving. You boys can, though," Sinfine told the two Nephews. "Get lost. Emery, get their names."

"Done, Mr Sinfine."

"Good. You guys had a lucky break. I'll even up with you later." The Nephews, obviously disconcerted by the lack of immediate reward, shuffled off uncertainly. When they reached the next interior door, the maid came in from the poolside.

"Show these two out," Sinfine told her. "Don't damage them."

The tall man snorted slightly at the thought that this woman could do him any damage, but they both went quietly. Sinfine had not taken his eyes off Jim. A gun had appeared in his left hand.

"Emery," he said. "Have you tortured anyone to fucking death lately?"

"No, sir."

"Don't want to lose the technique, do we?"

"No, sir." Emery always tried to agree with everything Sinfine said, when he had a weapon.

"Why?" Jim asked then in a hoarse voice.

"He can talk! I thought he could. He talked last time. I was wondering if the Nephews had cut his cock-sucking tongue out." Sinfine seemed to be playing to an audience. Emery knew from personal experience, and Jim suspected, that this was a man who struck poses at his bathroom mirror. "Because you fucked my pitfight, Jim boy. That's why. And then you didn't die when I told you to. I think you had something to do with that bitch disappearing, too. Why don't you tell me about that?" He pointed his gun at Jim's face, then let it slowly drop down until it was aiming at his foot. He pulled the trigger and Jim twitched so violently that he hopped in the air, but the hole was in the carpet and not his shoe. Sinfine looked at his gun with disgust, as if it was it's fault that he had missed, although it seemed unlikely to Emery that he had even intended to pull the trigger.

"Give me your gun," he told Emery. Emery gave him his gun. He handed the other gun back. "So, Jim," he went on as if there had been no pointless exchange of weapons. "Tell me about it. The Disappearing Bitch. Good trick, but hard on the audience. My fucking safe house is not safe and my fucking doctor is dead and I think you have something to do with it." He didn't think that Jim was the sole cause, however. "Who helped you?"

"It wasn't me!" Jim said shrilly, getting more shrill as Sinfine lined the new gun up on his foot again. "It was Blue Suit!"

Sinfine put the gun up. The enjoyment of pain that had moments ago been glowing in his eyes still smouldered, but as he often pointed out, he was not stupid. He contemplated Jim for a few fearsome seconds while he wondered whether or not to open this particular can of worms and Jim wondered whether his life was going to last more than the next few minutes, then he spoke.

"Tell me more," he said. He snapped his fingers at Emery and pointed at a chair which stood solitary at one end of the room. Emery dragged Jim over there and pushed him down into it. Sinfine didn't like looking up at people if he could avoid it, and Jim was taller than he. So was Emery, much taller, but Emery was adroit at never standing close enough to Sinfine to draw his size into consideration. Sinfine sat down on the arm of the chair and draped himself in a curiously seductive way, with one arm behind Jim's battered head and the gun still in plain view in the other, ready to blow pieces of Jim away if so things went.

Jim didn't dare to speak until he was told to. Sinfine snapped his fingers, again, in Jim's face this time.

"Talk, slimeball," he said.

"It was Blue Suit. I didn't have anything to do with it. I was looking for her, but when I found your place everybody was dead and she was gone."

"So how do you know it was Blue Suit? And, hey, you were going to steal from me, Jim. It doesn't matter that the other guy got there first. The sin is in the heart, right? Talk some more."

"I was with another guy." Jim left out the fact that the other guy was Lino's father. "He was picked up by Blue Suit and he found out then. They went and took Lino because of what happens with her and SRMs. They're doing all kinds of experiments on them." Jim spoke rapidly.

"Yeah, we know about all that SRM Project bullshit. It's on the fucking news, for Christ's sake."

Jim pretended to look surprised. "I know where they took her," he ventured.

Sinfine said nothing for a short time. Emery frowned. Surely he wasn't contemplating a revenge attack on Blue Suit. That would be risky. It would invite awesome retribution. It would be unprofitable and dangerous. It would be just like Sinfine. Emery was not particularly surprised, therefore, when Sinfine spoke.

"Where?"

"Do I get to live?" Jim asked quickly.

Sinfine gave him a look that was so cold that he thought that he had finally talked his way to death, and yet was somehow, unbelievably, amicable. Sinfine actually patted him on the shoulder as he said "As long as I like you, Jim, you get to live, and you can't get a better guarantee than that."

Both Jim and Emery thought that you probably could, but they chose not to comment.

Blue Suit sees Sedric

Sedric Linus Colville was still shocked by the fact that his right arm ended just below the elbow in a neat pinover. Shocked, and in pain. His arm ached deeply all along it's length and out to the ends of what used to be his fingers. The doctors who had tidied up the stump had been interested in what could have caused all the soft tissue of his forearm to disappear like that and leave the ends of the extensor carpi radialii cauterised as if by acid. Any chemicals that could have dissolved his flesh should have made equally short work of his bones. As the osteopath laid out his saws and his chisels beside the anaesthetised patient, he had wondered, too, at the way the connective tissues had been left completely intact. And as the spinning blade sliced and marrow squeezed out of the cut, he resolved to keep this arm for further examination. Of course, there were blue suits waiting for him outside the operating theatre who considered medical research to be a pointless endeavour, and the bony hand was shortly thereafter thrown into the hospital incinerator.

Colville had expected to be dragged up before Blue Suit about this, but not so soon. He had hoped for at least a few days of recuperation before having to grovel, but this morning one of the blue suits posted outside his room had announced that he was required at Blue Suit headquarters at ten and the summons was not to be resisted. Now, he sat outside the big wooden door to Blue Suit's office, waited, and ached. It was one minute to ten. It was thirty seconds to ten. At ten seconds to ten, Sedric Linus Colville had become fatalistic. Short of besmirching his professional reputation, which was beyond his power, or killing him, which wasn't, what could Blue Suit do to him now? So for once, it was a composed and controlled Colville who entered to office when the buzzer went at one second after ten. The painkillers helped.

"Colville." Blue Suit said politely. "Sit down."

"Thank you."

Blue Suit studied the area of the missing arm.

"Unfortunate accident," he said, "or so I have been told."

"It was not exactly an accident," Colville said honestly. "It was a mistake. The isolation test we were conducting failed disastrously, due to totally unforeseen replication divergence, and this," he also looked at his right arm, felt a little faint, but went on, "was the result."

"I am also told that you acted to prevent the nanovirus escaping and that is how you lost your arm."

This was turning out to be a session of veiled praise. Colville was surprised and encouraged by the thought. "I placed the decomposing agent, yes."

"There were witnesses from outside the project. Whak Puihare, and George Assok."

"George Assok, yes. I didn't actually note the other man's name. They were brought in by two of your men. I hoped to get some feedback from Assok on our designs, particularly on this vexing problem of replication. Perhaps there is some micro-effect we are not accounting for. An unknown long-range force. It would have to be long-range to affect nanomachine behaviour like this, I can say that much, but physics is so mechanistic, I'm afraid I've never been able to focus on the details. Mathematics is reality, and physics is just so much car paint, in my opinion, but at this stage we are forced to look for a physical explanation. We could define it by it's effects. A little like identifying planetary masses by perturbations in observed orbits, you know. Assok is excellent at that sort of thing. The best. But at any rate, the isolation test failed, and, well," Colville twitched his right arm, "I didn't see him again." He stopped, tired.

Blue Suit had listened to this monologue patiently. "Neither did anyone else," he now added.

Colville took a moment to understand, then he shrank back a little, his calm shattered. "I'm a scientist, not a jailer," he said.

"The men who let Assok escape have been punished, and I had no real need to hold Puihare. It is Assok I want, for the same reasons you do. This disaster of yours only emphasises that there are some fundamental problems in your designs. We need Assok to provide a new viewpoint." He paused and tapped his fingers lightly on the desk. Colville wisely swallowed any reaction to this slur on his abilities. "There is something else I need to talk to you about. A nanoconstructor unit was stolen from the Station when the two men escaped."

"Oh my God," Sedric groaned. "That's terrible. We only have three. They're practically irreplaceable, it could take a months to make another one, even if all the necessary parts can be obtained. Are we going to be able to get it back?"

Blue Suit looked grim. So the loss of one nanoconstructor was a serious blow, not easy to recover from. Not to mention the fact that Jelli had physical evidence that Blue Suit was performing unauthorised research. It was a difficult situation. Jelli had come close to his trust, and then thrown it away. He had had the teeth-clenching pleasure of putting his hand on her smooth stomach and knowing that soon they would be connected through the thinnest of nervous skins, and now she refused him. Now, she was screwing around with his plans. Plans were Blue Suit's life-blood. He would normally have a person killed for causing him this much trouble. On the other hand, she still had the best line on George Assok, and he knew that she was going to have to deal with him if she expected to see Lino again. So, he comforted himself with the knowledge that he had never kept his end of a bargain in his life.

"Yes. We are going to get it back," he told Colville.

CHAPTER 37

Jim bargains with Sinfine

"So you want your girlfriend back, Jim boy," Sinfine said calmly. "And Blue Suit's got her. Blue Suit's a very nasty man. Even nastier than me, I hear. All the good advice is to stay out of his way. Why should I take on all that aggravation to get back your fucking girlfriend who fucks the minds of the fucking crabs? She's no use to me. You sold me a crock, there, Jim." He cuffed Jim across the face, not lightly.

In spite of his now constant terror, Jim had a hope to hang on to. Sinfine had seemingly decided not to torture him to death. He was asking for reasons. It's always easier to talk someone around when they haven't already cut your tongue out. He had no shortage of answers.

"I know something else," he said. "I know where to get a machine that makes nanoviruses."

"You mean those things that were on the news? No shit?"

"No shit. The guy I was talking about was there when a batch of nanoviruses got away and ate some other guy's arm. They eat everything up. They're like a, a," he thought hard for a second, "like a nerve gas. One drop kills a city sort of stuff. You could have anything if you had something like that. The Consortium would do whatever you wanted." He knew that Sinfine was the last person on Earth that should have access to any nanoviruses, if what Whak had told him was true, but he was bargaining for his life now and he expected that he would never have to deliver on his promises. Besides, these nanoviruses were supposed to be for SRMs. They might not be as dangerous as Whak thought. At the moment, Jim was willing to be optimistic about the word might.

"Nanoviruses," Sinfine tried the word out. "Nanoviruses. Hey! I only needed a good excuse."

Emery and Jim Rescue Lino

Sinfine told Emery to take Jim and half a dozen of his thug ugly Nephews to where Jim had been picked up from earlier that day. It was late in the day and there were sporadic squares of light escaping from the sides of buildings wherever there were both inhabitants and electricity, but the line of unbroken windows halfway up the suspiciously unoccupied tower remained dark. Jim glanced at the faces of the Nephews and suppressed the fear that he might be mistaken. He turned to Emery, who still sat in one of the cars, leather driving gloves resting on the wheel.

"Thirteenth floor," he said.

"Lucky," Emery commented as he cast his eyes up the shadow of the tower. "OK. Let's go check it."

The Nephews hurried across the road and down the street to the main entrance of the tower, with Jim not needing any coercion. He took the lead, in fact, right up to the doors, where he stepped aside to let people with guns take the fore, a policy he had always found worked for him in the past. Two Nephews blew the lock out of the centre of the doors with shotguns and then all six moved in with surprising military efficiency. Jim now took the tail position. The fact that he was a captive and therefore unfriendly must not have been communicated as forcefully as it should, or else his enthusiasm for getting into the building had changed his status, because a large Nephew motioned with his weapon and covered him as he ran across the foyer to the elevators. He was not the first there. The call button was glowing red, itself an indication that this building was not all that it appeared. At each side of the elevator doors a Nephew stood pressed back to the wall. The floor indicator, starting with fourteen, disappeared for a minute, then began to count down. Jim watched it.

"Get under cover," said a voice behind him. He suddenly realised that whoever was in the elevator might come out shooting. Or worse, it might be empty. They were in territory that Blue Suit had had endless time to prepare against attack. Jim looked left and right. There were stairwell exits on either side of the elevators. The floor indicator said eight.

"What about them?" he asked, pointing the stairwells out to the voice behind him. At once two more Nephews took positions covering them. Jim decided that the safest place for him was behind one of the foyer pillars. As he peered out from behind, he saw another worrisome thing. There were surveillance cameras in the corners of the ceiling. He was wondering whether it was going to be better for him in the long run to point them out or keep buttoned, when Emery decided it for him.

"They know where we are," he said levelly, looking up at the corners of the ceiling.

The floor indicator said two.

The elevator doors opened and the sound of shotguns and handguns being fired more or less simultaneously filled Jim's ears. The fusillade stopped, except for a single methodical pistol sound as Emery carefully shot out the cameras. Jim noticed respectfully that he didn't miss once.

"Nobody in the elevator, boss," the Nephew who had covered Jim during their entrance said.

"No surprise there," Emery answered him. "Jacobs, check the stairs."

"We're not going up the elevator?" Jacobs asked quickly. "We could get up on top and surprise them."

"Yeah. It might come to that. Check the stairs. Take Smithy. Garrad, get the spares. Everyone else, watch the street. We won't have long." Emery beckoned Jim over and started reloading his pistol. "Looks like you were right," he said. "This place is a Blue Suit building, all right, or something like it. Doesn't mean your girlfriend is here, though. Now how much do you want to get her back?"

"Lots," Jim said instantly. For the last week he had been learning just how much. He also had a vague hope that Emery was a nicer guy than Sinfine, which seemed almost guaranteed. What was he going to suggest? The two men who had been sent to check the stairs came back and nodded meaningfully. Emery made a smile.

"I'm thinking that you can go up the elevator."

"They'll kill everybody in the elevator before the doors open!" Jim gaped at the stupidity of this idea.

"Maybe," Emery nodded. "But I bet there's another camera in the elevator. And you'll be all by yourself. They're going to want to know what's going on down here."

"And then they kill me."

"Maybe," Emery said again, treating the idea of Jim being killed with an equanimity Jim did not think it deserved. "There'll be some surprises for them."

"Like what?"

"You'll find out." Emery motioned him to the elevator by pointing with his pistol.

Jim realised that Emery was just as willing to kill without cause as Sinfine was. So were all these Nephews. There had been times before SRMs, he knew, when the vast majority of people lived quiet, peaceful and nonviolent lives, but he couldn't think of many who could say the same today, especially not himself. He looked at the elevator, which had been sitting doors opened for a sinister length of time, inviting the unwary to enter. Doors to the unknown, doors to the thirteenth floor, doors to death, they were all of these. Once again Jim had arrived at a situation where he either died or was killed. He went and stood in the elevator and looked around, trying to locate the hypothetical camera. He hoped that somewhere upstairs, it was noted that he was young and skinny and especially, unarmed.

"Good," Emery said to him. "Stairs," he said to three of the others. The three Nephews disappeared through the stairwell door. "Wait," Emery told Jim.

Jim was very happy to wait forever if it meant he would survive the next few minutes. He heard noises from above his head. Nephews climbing onto the top of the elevator. He imagined them crashing through the access trap one at a time to fall dead over the top of his bleeding body.

"OK," Emery said. "Go find your girlfriend."

Jim pressed the button for the thirteenth floor.

Jim goes to the 13th Floor

The ride from the foyer took no great length of time, except inside Jim's head, where each time the floor indicator mounted above the emergency telephone cabinet changed he felt his heart beat in his throat. When the twelve light pulsed out, he pressed himself against the wall, as far to the back and left as he could go.

The doors opened, and facing him were two nervous looking men with guns in their hands.

"Hands up!" said one of them harshly. "Up! Up!"

Jim put his hands up. Things were going much better than he had expected. He was still alive. He was so pleased that he grinned inanely and said in an incongruously cheerful voice "Hi!"

"We know there are more of you," the talking one said. The other one looked around the inside of the lift as if he expected six full-grown men to emerge from the carpet. "Why did they send you up?"

Jim flinched violently as the one in the lift fired a few shots into the ceiling of the elevator. "I'm looking for my girlfriend," he said, choosing truth. "Lino Puihare. Is she here?"

"You are not authorised to receive that information." The blue suit edged his way over to a window and looked down onto

the street. "Help will be here soon," he said, half to himself and
half to the other blue suit. "Tie this guy up."

Jim was dragged out of the lift, into a nearby room, and made
to sit in a chair while his hands were bound. He wondered where
the Nephews were. He wondered what they were going to do
when they arrived.

"Can I see Lino?" he asked hopefully.

"You can see her, but she can't see you," the man who was
tying his hands said. "Stupid woman's never awake."

The other immediately snarled at him about information,
authorisation, and need to know, but Jim felt a double sense of
relief. He was right, Lino was here. That meant not only that he
had a chance of rescuing her, but also that Emery and his men
would not kill him for wasting their time. As he was
congratulating himself on his survival, there was a fantastic noise
and the ceiling fell in.

The noise must have been an explosion, Jim realised
afterwards. The room was filled instantly with dust and smoke
and pieces of rafter, and the two blue suits were all but knocked
over by the blast. After that, the big Nephew named Jacobs
suddenly appeared at the door and shot the man who had been
tying Jim's hands and feet. Everything was happening a long way
away, it seemed, through the air clogged with debris and without
sound. The other blue suit jumped behind Jim and shot back. Jim
wished he hadn't done that, because Jacobs lined up his weapon
apparently on Jim's head and returned fire. In panic, Jim threw
his weight sideways and succeeded in knocking over his chair and
Jacobs immediately shot the blue suit through the thigh and
shoulder.

Jim was left lying on the floor for a long time, during which
he mentally checked through his body parts. Except for his ears,
which felt as if they were filled with water, everything else he
could wiggle or twitch worked. He could see the blue suit that
remained alive lying near him, and he could see his mouth
moving, but so far all he could hear was a crackling interference
noise. But then he was picked up and untied by a Nephew.
Emery appeared and said something to him, and he shook his
head and pointed at his ears.

"I can't hear a thing," he said. He pointed at the blue suit.
"He said help was on the way. Where's Lino?"

Emery looked at the blue suit, and spoke again, looked at his
watch, and jerked a thumb towards the window. A faint, shrill

noise arose. Jim figured he wasn't going to be deaf for very long.
He wondered what the noise was. When the blue suit was picked
up by the Nephews, the sound increased in pitch and frequency.
Jim realised that it was the blue suit, screaming. They took him to
the window and while Jim watched with utter horror, threw the
wounded man out. They didn't even open the window. Broken
glass followed him into the air.

"Jesus," Jim said, "you didn't have to do that! You could
have shot him at least." He had the notion that being shot was
more a humane and maybe even painless way to die, but choice of
death is a personal thing, and it is not the dying itself but the
painful and fearful moment between cause and effect that
everyone wants to avoid. Instantaneous evaporation in the core of
a thermonuclear explosion seems best. Falling thirteen floors is
no good. It allows just too much time for knowing that this is the
end. Jim couldn't help himself. He went to the window and
leaned out just far enough to see the blue mark on the pavement.
And the imminent arrival of several large black cars.

"Help is here," he said.

Emery's voice was almost audible. He said something that
buzzed to the men around him. They walked quickly from the
room. Jim followed Emery to another room and there was Lino
lying on a bed, apparently asleep, although Jim and Emery knew
better. When a Nephew tried to wake her by giving her a shake,
Emery pushed him away. Jim went to the bed and ran his hand
lightly over her forehead.

"Lino," he said, much more loudly than he had intended. His
hearing was improving rapidly, but there was still a shrill
screaming buzz of damaged nerves, constantly ringing as if at the
end of a long metal tube stuck in the side of his head.

"Pick her up and let's go," Emery ordered. "We're going to
have to fight our way out of here as it is. Shit. Make sure that lift
goes nowhere. We'll go out the basement. If there is a way out of
the basement. Go go go go go!"

Jim took Lino's top end and Smithy took her legs and they
ran, staggered and bumped to the elevator. The doors were
jammed open with a plaster-crusted piece of wood that must have
come out of the ceiling when Emery's men blew a hole in it. A
Nephew stood in the open stairwell door, pointing a complicated-
looking short-barrelled shotgun down the stairs.

"What do we do now?" Jim asked, feeling strangely confident
that Emery would know the answer. When it came to mayhem

and killing, this guy was good. He couldn't have become so good
without a talent for escaping from the scene of the crime.

"They'll be coming up the stairs, unless they weren't
expecting serious killing, in which case they'll be sitting in their
cars calling for more firepower. There's two stairwells. All of us
go down the same one and keep going. Got the other bomb?" he
asked a man behind him, who brandished a square package.
"Fucking home made plastic is not too stable. Don't let it get shot.
If things get bad, blow someone up." He thought for a moment.
"Unless we're still on the stairs. Then wait till I tell you."

They started down. Jim took the high position and Smithy
took the low, with Lino slung between them like a hammock, and
every time Smithy turned the corner at a landing he bashed Lino's
hips against the wall. Jim did his best to compensate. It was a
long way down and his arms were pulsating with cramp. As they
reached the ground level, his skin crawled with the anticipation of
the stairwell door crashing inwards and more bullets and
bloodshed following. But there was nothing except a thumping
noise which had become gradually louder as they descended, and
when he could see the door, Jim realised why. It was securely
jammed from the stair side by a spare tyre, from one of the cars
they had come in he guessed. The door had once been a fire door
and was solidly built, probably steel-lined. Jim could see it
bouncing slightly inwards as attempts were made to break the
door down, but the tyre, acting as a shock absorber, was making it
an impossible task.

"They'll climb the outside and come down the stairs after us
in a minute," Jim heard Emery saying ahead of him. "Hurry up.
You two at the back! Faster! Jacobs, go back and cover them."

Jacobs came back up, pushed past Smithy and Jim, and took
the rear. Jim wondered how men like this could, without any sign
of concern, stand at the bad news end like that. Then the
basement door was in front of him and he followed Lino's hips -
bump - and body through it.

"All here? OK, find a safe way out. Jacobs? Good. Look
over there. Garrad over there. You," Emery said to Jim, "stay
here. Under cover. Get behind that whatever-the-fuck-it-is
there." He pointed at an air-conditioning fan unit, the size of a
truck, that occupied the back wall of the basement. "Stay there
until I tell you. Try to wake the girl up." He turned away. The
now-familiar sound of gunfire sounded briefly to the left. "Shit.
Do as I told you!" Emery ran off. Jim dragged Lino to where he

had been told and, sitting in the shadow of the great machine, he whispered in her ear, rubbed her forehead, and at last hugged her to his face, as more gunshots and more gunshots sounded.

After a minute or two, he felt a change of state coming on. Until they had found Lino, he had been a part of Emery's team, accepting his orders and doing his utmost to make their mission a success, for Emery's objectives then had been his objectives too. He had even felt camaraderie with the repugnant and homicidal Nephews, but all that was rapidly slipping away. He had Lino lying across his lap. He had what he had come for. He owed Emery and the others nothing. A new objective was calling him. He should be thinking about getting out of here.

Several more gunshots and an explosion made up his mind. He picked himself up, with Lino swaying against him like many an OD girl he had helped home, and inspected his surroundings. He was at the back wall of an underground car park. By the increased light ahead he guessed that in that direction there was a big opening, probably the in and out ramps, and to his left were the lifts and the stairwells, and in that direction he could see a man with a gun prowling. He drew back behind the fan unit and wished momentarily that he too had a gun. Not that he had ever really used one in anger, but fear wants little practice. It quickly occurred to him, however, that a weapon would be a comfort only up to the moment that Emery shot him accurately between the eyes. He was totally outclassed here so far as violence was concerned.

To his right, a huge, dull-red air shaft came out of the fan unit and curved up to the ceiling, where it hung from threaded steel rods that were screwed into fittings in the concrete. The shaft intersected another that made a long run through the car park, went right and bent upwards again to disappear from sight. Jim had an idea. He had never seen a late-twentieth century action movie, so he thought it was original. The problem was Lino. He wished fervently that she would wake up, and when she didn't, he re-rated his chances of success down to zero, but he nonetheless managed to swing her over his back in perfect silence and began to climb up onto the top of the red shaft.

CHAPTER 38

Assok picks up the canister

George Assok was feeling despondent. His laboratory was damaged, his most compelling evidence of SRM meta-instructions had purposefully evolved into Houdinis and escaped, and his prospects of further nanotechnology development, and perhaps the future of human civilisation seemed now to hang on his association with an erratic graffiti poet and his invisible wife. The future looked dangerous and bleak.

George was also furious with himself for not capturing one of the octopede offspring. Who would have thought that any life form, no matter how strange, would deliberately opt for decreased intelligence and loss of discrete consciousness rather than continued freedom? A hypothetical question, perhaps, since he had never been able to communicate with the octopede and no measurement of intelligence was truly possible without communication, but George still shook his head in frustration. If he had been less busy futilely defending his equipment against the flock of voracious houdinis (he had found a name) then he might have at least had one to study. He looked around his lab. Study with what? Unless he could reach up out of this hole of a place and get Jelli Puihare to fund his work, then he might as well go back to teaching or some equally awful profession. That fact was more than enough to force him out the street again, even after the awful experiences of his last outing.

Looking up, he judged the time of day to be just before dusk. He had several hours to kill before he was due to meet Whak, so, pointlessly, he began to tidy the shambles that the houdinis had made of his lab. The computer was still crackling and fizzing, and the smell of an overheated power supply came from it. He turned it off. Beside it on the table was the graceful, silver bottle, smooth as glass and dusted inside, he knew, with a metallic carbon allotrope, an agent which prevented the nanos from commencing their short and startling lives.

He reached across and picked up his canister of nanovirus. Ninety-eight percent finished. Ninety-eight percent perfect. It would be useful to know what the missing two percent comprised. He tossed it lightly in his hands, then put it in his pocket.

McFee appears

"So," Jelli said in conference-presentation fashion, "the deal
we have is this. One, we stop the news story about the Blue Suit
tax registration scandal. Two, we withdraw all allegations about
nanomachine projects, lost arms, exterminator services, and all the
less solid and more juicy rumours that my people in Attitude
Adjustment have been able to come up with. Three, we return the
nanoconstructor to Blue Suit."

"And he releases Lino." Whak was dogged on that point.

"That's what we're talking about," Jelli said. "That has always
been what we're talking about. Of course, then he releases Lino,
unharmed."

"And if he doesn't?"

"All right, we'll do a swap. We'll meet, hand over the
nanoconstructor, and he can release Lino, right there. We won't
stop the media bombing until afterwards. That way, we still have
some extra knives to stick in, should they be needed."

Whak didn't like that option much, either, but he didn't see
many alternatives. "Okay," he said grudgingly. "That sounds
better."

"So when, and where, is George delivering the
nanoconstructor?" Jelli asked with keen interest. Whak looked
out the window at the sky.

"Tonight, in the park," he replied.

"Then we'd better get organised."

Whak couldn't pretend to be a security guard again. Making
fools of the blue suits was undoubtedly satisfying, but Mr McFee,
PushRight's Director of Security, insisted that it had been foolish
and risky. Jelli had asked him to come to the house that
afternoon, and here he was, exuding an air of preparedness that
Whak found particularly offensive. Now that he was involved, he
said, there was to be no more of this amateur bullshit.

Whak had never been comfortable with experts, from garage
mechanics to publishing and marketing consultants. He preferred
to make his own choices rather than trust to the well-worn tracks
of people with years of experience but without an original
thought, but this once, the probably false security of being told
what to do by someone who was being paid to sound convincing
lulled him.

McFee was about the same age as Whak, but in sparkling physical condition. No slight flabbiness of the belly for McFee. Tight cheeks at both ends, firm biceps and catlike walk were signs that this man took physical danger seriously. Whak wondered, for no more than the time it took to develop a prickly dislike, whether Jelli had ever slept with him.

"You could sneak out over the back wall," Jelli suggested.

"There are blue suits watching the back wall," McFee advised her complacently.

"Then you could turn invisible!" Jelli screeched. "You could dig a tunnel! I don't know! This is all your fault, Whak! Why didn't you just drag him back here by his neck?"

"It's not all my fault," Whak snapped. "It wasn't me who dragged Blue Suit into this by screwing him senseless." He drew a black cloud over his head and fell silent. Jelli treated him to a rare apologetic toss of her hands. That was as much as she could afford to be sorry at present.

"Why do you suppose Blue Suit has you under observation?" said the security director. He adjusted his shoulder holster further out of sight. "He is accomplishing nothing, on the face of it, except for your discomfort. He doesn't stop you," he addressed Jelli, "from going to PushRight each day. He doesn't try to stop any of my men from coming and going."

"So, your point exactly?" Jelli asked.

"Its obvious," McFee went on. Whak bristled. He hated being told things were obvious. "He's watching you so that if you contact this George Assok, or anyone else involved in this mess, or if you try to move this hypothetical nanoconstructor -" He looked at Whak. "No offence, but I haven't seen it. If you try to move this thing, then he will take some action."

"I haven't heard the point, yet," Jelli said patiently.

"The point is I think your husband can leave through the front door. There are no formal charges against him. They won't jump on him and arrest him. If they were going to do that they'd be knocking on the door right now. They'll follow him, of course, but with my help he can evade them."

"I'm actually here in the room," Whak pointed out, "and may be spoken to directly, thank you."

"Sorry."

"Politeness is a virtue," Whak added.

"Certainly," replied McFee, but with obvious concern for Whak's sanity. Jelli, though, was used to the meanderings of her husband's mind and stuck to the point.

"So Whak just walks out the front gates, they follow him, then what?" she demanded.

"We cause a diversion and he makes himself scarce. It's unlikely that the blue suits will expect the meet to be right across the road in the park," said McFee. "It just might be the last place they'll think to have watched."

Whak had to admit that it sounded if not sensible, then possible. He gave a little shrug and nod. Jelli agreed.

"Sounds good to me. Let's do it."

"I think I'll pack some spray cans," said Whak. "I may want to say something."

"Fine, Whak," Jelli said. "Spray your words, but first, find Assok. You clear on what has to be done?" she asked McFee.

"Clear," McFee nodded.

"So I just stroll out the front, stark naked, swinging my bag full of spray cans."

"That's it," McFee agreed. "Nakedness is optional. I'll have a couple of guys tailing you. They'll play interference if any blue suits show up. Bring Assok to the park gates. I'll be waiting."

"All organised, then."

"Yes."

"Get on with it, Whak!"

Whak goes to find George

"All right, all right. I'm going." He went to his study and collected his satchel. On the way out he stopped by the living room door and beckoned Jelli over.

"What is it?" she asked abruptly as soon as he had her in the hall.

"I'm going out. I may be some time. Good-bye," Whak told her, and before she could make any response he kissed her lightly on the mouth.

"God damn you, Whak," Jelli said. "Don't disturb my concentration."

"Sorry."

"And be careful."

"I will. Thanks."

He went down the driveway and out the gate. He knew well where all the observers were positioned from many an hour staring down binoculars in his kitchen, but none of them were visible in this light or from this angle. In spite of that, his skin prickled with the sensation of a dozen eyes watching his every move. He often felt that sensation, anyway, even when he was shut in his study on a wintery day, in fact especially when he was shut in his office on a wintery day. He had wondered now and then whether invisible time-travellers liked to see The Famous Whak Puihare in Winter, or a civilisation of cold-climate aliens was using him as a conduit for the creation of a new order through semantics, but after some thought he was pretty sure that he had read both those ideas in a comic. Even so, he hated to think that it could be anything as mundane as thwarted self-protection mechanisms. He crossed the street and, still prickling, proceeded to the path that ran between the Enright and Yang estates. When he reached the entrance to Coolio Park at the end of the path, his sensation of being watched was displaced abruptly by the sound of footsteps behind him. He looked back. The dark outlines of two men were coming down the path.

Now, it is a true fact that all security guards look alike, and whether they work for Blue Suit or for PushRight Creative Media Inc is not apparent at a glance. Blue suits do not always wear blue suits. In the dark, it was difficult to tell either way. Not knowing whether this was McFee or not, Whak decided to wait and see. When the approaching men saw Whak waiting for them, they doubled their pace and put on aggressive expressions. Blue suits, then.

"Mr Puihare, please submit to physical search."

"Sure," Whak agreed. He held out his satchel. "There's a bomb in this. Shall I take my clothes off?"

The two men eyed each other in the way that Whak knew to indicate incomprehension. He saw that look a lot. He continued to hold the satchel out at arm's length. "Don't you want to look in the bag?"

After a moment spent unbelieving Whak's statement about a bomb, the men took the satchel from him and looked inside.

"It's not here," one said. "Mr Puihare, we're looking for a device stolen from a Blue Suit research station. We have reason to believe that you are in possession of that object. If you do not immediately give us information as to it's whereabouts, we will have to arrest you."

"You are just robots, aren't you?" Whak puzzled aloud. "What kind of device?"

"No, we are not robots, and we are not in possession of that information. Do you have the device?"

"I don't have any such thing and I don't know where it is."

"Then do you know where an individual named George Assok is located?"

"Not a clue."

"Then we will have to place you under arrest. Please come with oof."

Oof, and fall down. McFee and another PushRight security man stood over the unconscious blue suits.

"Poor field skills," McFee commented. "I would have heard us coming."

"I didn't," Whak assured him, feeling much more positively inclined towards McFee than before.

"It will be best if we shadow you at a distance. Can you point out the tree you're meeting under?"

"Not from here. It's across the park. West Coolio."

He looked in that direction and when he looked back, McFee and his offsider were gone, disappeared back into the shadows. So with a shrug of his shoulders and a pat of his bag, he followed his feet. It gave him an unusual sense of invulnerability to know that Jelli's professional security men were somewhere in the night, watching and protecting him. He could see the telltale corona of the pitfight arena in the sky ahead of him. Obviously Sinfine was back in business, there was a pitfight on tonight. He detoured around the back of the arena, where it was relatively deserted, and a minute later was standing underneath the well-climbed oak.

"Hey George!" he whispered as loudly as the leaves rustled. "George! You up there?"

There was silence, which was much what he expected. But he refrained from immediately climbing into the tree, disappearing from his protective shadows, maybe attracting unwanted attention from the pitfight fans. It was only a few days, or was it a week? He couldn't remember anymore, his routine by which he counted the days was shattered, but however long it was since this very arena had seen death by unpredicted SRM attack, the crowd seemed as numerous as ever. Whak walked around to the other side of the tree and tried to recognise the lower limbs. This was hopeless. He could have been looking into the wrong tree for all the pattern of the branches told him.

"George," he said in a low voice, "if you're up there, please listen. Blue Suit will do a deal for the nanoconstructor. We have to get you and it to a safe place. Can you hear me?"

"Perfectly," said George from behind his left ear. Whak spun around. George was standing right beside him, looking up into the branches.

"Have you got the nanoconstructor with you?" Whak asked him.

George looked shifty-eyed, an expression that was totally incongruous on his usually tight, analytical face. Hanging at the end of one arm was his usual aluminium carrycase. He pulled it forward and put his free hand down as if to open it, but before he could, shadows surrounded him. The shadows grew arms. The arms grabbed George from either side.

"What the hell is this, Puihare?" George shouted angrily, looking at the powerful hands that were holding him.

"I don't know!" Whak shouted back. Funny how everyone shouts in tense situations.

"They're mine," said another voice, as McFee stepped up from behind Whak. "Jelli wants to be sure this man doesn't escape."

"Escape? What are you talking about? He's coming with us voluntarily!"

"I have my instructions. He might change his mind, and he is a necessary part of the deal."

Whak and McFee locked eyes. "You mean, Jelli has agreed to give him up for Lino," Whak spoke disbelievingly. "The miserable slimy two-timing bitch."

"I'd guess you must know your wife pretty well," McFee said briefly. He stepped closer to George, who stood motionless, making no effort to escape the grasps. "You're not going to cause us any trouble, are you?"

"I never cause trouble," George told him shortly. He scowled darkly at Whak.

"No, he doesn't," Whak said, stepping forward. "I do." In each of his hands appeared a fluorescent spray can. He swung them up to face level and let the men on either side of George have facefuls of paint. They rolled backwards, trying to wipe their eyes clean, and in an instant, George was off and running away into the shadow of the oak.

George's sudden departure triggered a flurry of actions. From nearby gardens two men stood up and sprinted after George, while McFee grabbed Whak by the arm and held him still.

"Hey!" he jerked forward and the grip loosened enough that he could turn. "Jelli has no right to do this!" he shouted at McFee. His total lack of resistance to curiosity made him quieten down a little to ask, "Who are those guys?"

"They're mine as well," McFee said calmly. "He won't get away."

"He has gotten away!" Whak pointed out loudly.

"My men will catch him. Has he got the nanoconstructor?"

Whak didn't answer, but instead reached down and seized the handle of George's ubiquitous aluminium carrycase. He opened it and felt around inside, looked in, and closed it again. "I've got it," he said. "No thanks to your stupid tricks. I promised George that he would be safe with us, and now, now he'll never trust us. We'll never be able to get him back."

McFee pulled out a transceiver and spoke into it in snappy paramilitary jargon. Becoming concerned of face, he mumbled into it some more. "Jesus," he said at last, looking up. "They lost him."

"He's avoided better men than you."

McFee responded with a grunt. He offered his handkerchief to one of the graspers, both of whom were still staggering around saying, ow, God, Jesus, shit, what is this stuff, argh. Rubbing his eyes empathetically, Whak was filled with an urge to fall asleep until this was all over.

"Back home, then," he said, hoisting the carrycase. "At least I got the nanoconstructor, but Jelli is not going to be happy."

"I'm just doing my job," said McFee. "My conscience is clear. Is yours?"

"Never."

CHAPTER 39

Jelli decides to bluff

"You lost him," Jelli said in a disbelieving voice. "You lost him. You lost the only thing that we've got that Blue Suit really wants. God, McFee. How did you let this happen?"

"He caused it to happen," Whak broke in. "George wouldn't have run off if I'd been alone. He trusted me. He was going to come with me. Jelli, how could you think of handing him over to Blue Suit?"

"I don't know him, Whak. I don't care about him. I'm only thinking of Lino."

"You don't give a fuck whether he lives or dies, you mean."

"Well, all right, I don't! This is no time to debate morality! We're trying to rescue Lino, damn it!"

"I know that! But you told me that George was not part of the deal!"

"I didn't want to confuse things. You confuse things enough without any help from me. Do you care more about George than your own daughter?"

"No! Of course not!"

"Anyway," Jelli said more calmly, "there's no reason to expect him to be harmed by Blue Suit. Isn't he the great nanotechnology expert? Blue Suit will treat him like royalty. He is in no danger!"

"Yes, fine, but what happens when George refuses to co-operate? He will do."

"That's his problem. Our problem is to get Lino back."

"I'm completely confused now as to who the good guys are," Whak muttered.

Jelli grimaced at him. "We are," she said definitively. She turned to McFee, who was talking the transceiver. "Just tell me that he hasn't been picked up by anybody else."

"No indication of that," McFee answered. "All blue suit operatives in the area are still at their stations. No unusual activity."

Jelli gave a relieved sigh. "Good. At least Blue Suit doesn't have him already."

"But neither do we," McFee pointed out. "And according to your husband, this guy is capable of disappearing for years on end."

"So now what do we do? We have the nanoconstructor, but Blue Suit is expecting us to have George as well," Whak said, his eyes staring unfocussed into the maelstrom of chaos that fills the universe. "But does that matter?"

"No, it doesn't," said Jelli decisively. "We have nothing to lose that we haven't already lost. We bluff."

Jim and Lino in the Riot

Emery came back to where he had left Jim and Lino, reloading his gun and looking carefully around, stopped when he saw the absence of his charges and swore.

"Jacobs! Get over here!" he called. Unlike Jim, Emery was old enough to recall, albeit vaguely, the way ventilation shafts had starred in many films of his youth. He pointed up the length of curving red.

"Find a way into that," he said, "and see if the slippery little bastard is in there." Professional criminals had proven to be more than a match for the first contingent of blue suits, but Emery figured that he had only a few minutes before more serious opposition arrived. Jacobs climbed up and pried at a cover plate, but it was securely screwed down from the outside. He shook his head at Emery. "No way he got in here," he called.

"Shit." Emery looked at his watch. "Any other way in?" He walked underneath the shaft until it disappeared upwards, but he could see no other entrances. He looked at his watch again. "All right, let's get out of here," he decided. "We'll track the little shit down later. He can't move very fast with a limp female on his back. Come on, let's go."

Emery and his collection of Nephews reassembled near the elevators, took the stairs back to the ground floor, and shortly thereafter the sound of engines told of their departure. Jim pushed his face to the edge and looked out from on the top of the ventilation shaft, where it ran across the car park beside a ceiling beam. It was a position that was unobservable from anywhere below. He and Lino had been lying there for the past fifteen minutes, while he stroked her hair and whispered to her, and now she was starting to tremble. Jim didn't know whether that was good or bad, but it was a change. He started to drag her along to the end of the shaft that lead down to the fan unit.

"Ow," she said. Then, "I'm cold."

"Thank God," Jim sighed in relief, for he was tired of carrying her around. "You're awake".

"I know that," Lino said tartly. "And I'm cold." She felt the metal that she was lying on and said querulously "Where are we?" She blinked hard a couple of times and then her face darkened with memories. "I've been kidnapped. By that horrible man you took me to. Where is he? Are you taking me to him?" She pulled herself away from Jim and lodged against the wall. Her voice started to rise. "Why are you doing this to me? Who were all those men with guns? Where are we now?"

"That was days ago, Lino." Jim tried to calm her down, at the same time watching for any movements nearby. "You've been around. Blue Suit stole you from Sinfine."

"And you're stealing me back, is that it?"

"No! I'm trying to get you away from both of them! Now keep quiet and follow me!"

Lino remained wedged against the concrete and didn't move. "I'm not moving," she said tearfully.

She obviously no longer trusted Jim, a conclusion he couldn't find grounds to argue with. He stopped crawling down the shaft and with a series of twists and grunts, he turned himself so that he could look at her without twisting his head around in a circle. He wanted to tell her that he had made a stupid, selfish decision to trade her strange talent of SRM mayhem for money when he had been two weeks and twenty years younger, and that his every organ from the stomach to the brain had ached with regret ever since, and that he thought he loved her, and that he had risked his life over and over to get her back, but as he stared into her eyes none of these words made it.

"If you stay here you'll probably be killed. Or locked up again, and this time I won't be able to find you. I won't take you to Sinfine. I promise. Please come with me," he said instead.

She did. But it was a strange trip back to Jim's apartment. Whatever it was about Lino that turned stress into SRM activity, it was now fully-developed and broadcasting continuously. As soon as they emerged from the basement garage onto the street, a group of nine or ten scorpions scurried into sight out of unseen openings from their world to this and with their front pincers clacking, followed Lino down the footpath at a respectful distance.

"I like your bodyguard," Jim told her lightly. A mistake, because almost before her angry response had left Lino's lips, the scorpions converged on the nearest manufactured object, in this case the shell of an abandoned taxi, and drilled it so full, if that is the term, of perfectly round holes, that it seemed to be polka-dotted with glimpses of reality. Jim hurried on, dragging Lino as much as he dared. The scorpions continued to cut the car into pieces, but later Jim looked back and they were following again. A few pocket calculators and some crocodiles spilled out of a side street, tearing each other apart as they travelled and rebuilding almost as quickly from whatever was at hand or claw. Now that they were in the more populated blocks of the inner city, there were other people about, and one fat woman carrying two cane baskets screamed at the sight of this rotating mechanical reincarnation, but screams counted for little attention on the city streets. Some other heads turned and scowled. SRM fucking madness. Where will it end?

Jim pulled Lino past a piece of barricading that spoke with Whak's words.

the planet has a strange infection
pits of pus, scabs and pockmarks
appear on it's perfect skin
childhood diseases must be endured
long-term effects are not predicted

Jim wondered whether Whak thought the infection to be SRMs, or human beings. Maybe that was what the impossible machines were. Antibodies, come to clean off a bad case of mange. Then he saw ahead people running towards them. He instinctively slid against the wall, his arms around Lino's waist, which felt cool and smooth under her dress. There were about a dozen men and women and a couple of children fleeing from something. He could guess what. A metallic crash confirmed his thoughts. Edging forward to the corner he saw a street alive with SRMs of inconceivable variety, engaged in the same asystematic disassembly and reassembly of themselves and everything within range that could be made into themselves, as the smaller group following Lino from the other direction.

"Shit, you are driving the bugs crazy," Jim told Lino briefly, scratching the side of his face and looking up and down the street. The people who had fled were all cowering now on the steps of a building across the street. There didn't seem to be anywhere to go. Lino shook her head violently from left to right and from right to left, not answering Jim's remark but looking for escape from the creatures she hated so much. When Jim tried to take another step, her arm held him back. She had become totally rigid.

"Oh, God." He waved his hand in front of her face. Her eyes were open but they did not follow the movement of his fingers. "Hello, Lino, goodbye." He pulled her and she fell against him. In this position, he was able to half-walk, half-drag her along, and he began to search for a route through the SRM riot.

The riot was relatively stationary, at least. He edged around it, shuffling slowly so as not to let Lino drop like a stone to the ground, which he felt sure she would if he removed her support for an instant. There were a couple of people lying face down, or up, it was no longer possible to tell which, in the middle of the riot, their bodies covered with tiny SRMs which as Jim watched suddenly swarmed into the air and descended upon a massive buzzhead type which stood there stoically as it was nibbled to pieces at high speed.

"How the blue fuck do we get though this?" Jim asked. Maybe go back the way they had come, he thought. But there was screaming behind him. Lino's 'bodyguard' had caught up with them. A man wearing a wristwatch took it off and threw it at the SRMs, but that did not save him from having his hidden gun removed from under his coat by a scuttlebug, a thin slice being taken from his intercostal muscles in the process. He pressed himself into the wall while blood dripped down his chest. Beside him a woman tried to calm the two young children whose eyes were flat with terror, reminiscent of Lino's.

"No way back, either," Jim went on talking to Lino as if she could hear him, which, who knows, maybe she could. Back where the children were, three enormous black cars arrived. Men, clearly blue suits, jumped out, guns in their hands, and without making any effort to help the trapped bystanders, called out "You there! With the girl! Come back here! You're under arrest!"

Obviously it was not only Jim that could trace Lino by unusual SRM activity. He looked at the chaos in front of him. The small flying SRMs were in the air once again, and now there were about twice as many. He had never seen anything like them before. In a small cloud they moved towards him.

"Rather you than the blue suits," he said. Still shuffling Lino step by step, he moved in the opposite direction to the man who was yelling at him to stop. Glancing over his shoulder he saw the blue suit point his gun. Then his gun was gone, and blood was pouring from his fingers. The man shrieked and fell to his knees, clutching his hand, and a few seconds later he was knocked on his back by a drillhead's startling aerial pounce. The other blue suits hesitated, turned, and ran back to their cars, leaving the people trapped on the steps behind.

"Damn it!" Jim shouted. "You bastards!" He took another step into the riot, but he already knew that he had to go back. There were children back there, and the protection of innocence was an instruction that he couldn't ignore. Jim liked children too much to leave them in fear. But he couldn't leave Lino behind, either. "Come on, Lino. God, you don't look this heavy."

He dragged her back a couple of metres. It was only then that he saw the obvious. Neither he nor Lino were being attacked by any SRMs whatsoever. Jim never wore any metal, a habit he had collected when he was A Wasteland Tours guide, but Lino's dress sported a large decorative buckle, prime SRM fodder, and yet she was not approached. The people on the step, on the other hand, were kicking and pushing SRMs away as the insatiable things tried to remove all sorts of bits from their clothes and pockets. One older woman, hiding behind the others, was screaming "Don't let them near me! Don't let them near me! I have a pacemaker! I have a pacemaker!" It was impossible to think too hard about what might be going to happen to her unless Jim's theory was right.

Jim pushed Lino forward right through a dense knot of half-dismantled, half-dismantling crocodiles and hosenoses that were involved in a perpetual motion competition that neither looked to be winning. The conflict paused as Lino passed. The SRMs climbed off the backs of their prey and waddled aimlessly around, then, as Jim moved Lino on further, the war was continued. Jim was delighted. This meant they could rescue these people without losing any limbs.

"You're an SRM remote control, Lino, wonder what channel you're on. Wish I knew where your standby button is," he burbled nervously. They arrived at the steps. Immediately the SRMs that were crowding around and climbing over each other to get to their breakfast stopped doing so. They lost any co-ordinated motivation and drifted back into the overall insanity of the riot.

"Gee, look, they're leaving," Jim said cheerfully.

The man with the sliced ribs looked at him and Lino dubiously. The streetfull of SRMs resumed some overall direction and after another five minutes, there was a gap between the two crowds, which interestingly enough had maintained their own identity more or less as they passed through each other. Five minutes after that, the riot was over and the SRMs were gone. Only the three human bodies lying in the road, maybe alive, maybe dead, remained.

"What's wrong with her?" asked the sliced-ribs man.

"Tired," Jim said as he carried her away. He had scarcely rounded the corner from the riot scene and entered a street busy with speculation and rubberneckers when more blue suit cars zoomed past, but he and Lino were lost to sight.

Jim wanted to get Lino to her home and then step back and wait. Maybe when the memory of all this had decided where in her history it belonged, he could get her into bed and find if there was any other way into her heart than through an argument. His first stop was his apartment on Combine, where he had left the scrap of paper that had Whak's phone number on it. The distance between himself and Whak Puihare was all symbolised that that single fact. Whak had a telephone number, and Jim didn't. Whak was famous, in a faceless way, through the words he scattered around the city, and Jim wasn't. Jim leaned Lino against a street light pole and took a breather.

"Where are we?" she asked.

She was like that. She was gone, or she was here.

"Nearly my place."

"Why?"

"I want to call Whak. You know your number?"

She did, but they still had to go to Jim's place. She needed to pee. All she could remember of the last days was the inside of a toilet. They reached his apartment. Lino stumbled past him and gave the tiny box of a room a scathing stare.

"Where's the bathroom?" she asked in an angry, shaky voice. Jim pointed to the door that led to what the landlord called the en suite. She went there and before the door closed, Jim heard her say, oh my God, in a resigned way which was not far from what he felt every time he used his own toilet. He looked out the window, unable to stop himself scanning for blue suits, Cousins, or any other kind of goons, until she came back out. She looked wet-eyed and soft-lipped. He wanted to wrap her in his body right then and there.

"What happened?" she asked, choking slightly. "Why do those horrible things keep following me? What's wrong with me?"

"Nothing," Jim said quickly. "You faint at the sight of SRMs. Lots of people do it."

"Don't bullshit me!" She flashed a little bit of the Lino he had taken to the street party, the arrogant young bitch Lino. He liked her, too. "I didn't faint. I know the difference. I turned cataleptic, didn't I? I froze. I stopped blinking."

"Yeah. You did. I think you've been out of it most of the time you were kidnapped, too. And every time it happens to you, SRMs go insane." He decided to tell her the worst. "They killed three people around you today."

"Oh. Oh." She didn't deny it anymore. She sat down heavily on the edge of the bed and a pair of tears, quickly wiped away, spilled from her eyes. "Why is this happening to me?"

"It's not happening to you, it's happening to other people," Jim tried to be upbeat. "You miss all the bad bits." He saw her reaction starting to boil and he went on before she could cut him dead. "Let's ring your father."

The nearest phone was in the alley Sood Shop they had visited once before, weeks full of fear ago. Whak did not answer his phone. No-one did.

"Nobody there," Jim said as he hung up.

"Why don't you just take me home?" said Lino. She had repaired herself, at least on the outside. She wore the aloof expression that usually characterised her. But it was easy now for Jim to recognise that she had always been a bird in very brittle cage.

"Your home is being watched by blue suits," he told her, "and since I just got you away from them I don't think it would be a good idea go anywhere near your house right now."

"Then how am I going to get home?" Her little flare of panic said that she wanted to go home, badly. Her eyes started to look white. Jim was getting to know the signs. Calm her down, cool her out, avoid nastiness. He wasted no time in rushing her back to his apartment while she was still mobile and before Combine Street became the next SRM epicentre, arriving he reckoned not a moment too soon.

He pushed open his door and as soon as the view into his
room opened up, he saw that there was a man sitting on his bed.
All news is bad news. He threw himself away from the doorway,
knocking Lino flying, and landing half on top of her in the
corridor. Feeling his terror, she pulled herself further along the
bare wooden boards, while he tried to get to his feet, search for a
weapon, and help Lino up all at once. They were framed there, a
man pulling a woman to her feet, when a shadow stepped out of
Jim's doorway and spoke.

"Sorry to let myself in," said George Assok, "but I didn't
know when you'd be back."

CHAPTER 40

The meeting is arranged

Blue Suit was ready to believe that bad things come in fives. The spectacular instability and failure of Colville's SRM designs, the capture and then the loss of George Assok, the loss of the nanoconstructor, Jelli's media attack, and now this.

"Where was she held?" he asked his Chief of Operations.

"In a local safe house. The thirteenth floor of the old Ambank Building," the man said glumly. His tone of voice suggested that he already considered himself to be well advanced on the slippery road to hell, and that nothing he could do or say would now save him from a manual role in the maize farms, if he was lucky. Blue Suit noted this with approval. Such a mood overtakes one with honesty. Blue Suit always wished for honesty.

"How many guards?" he asked.

"Two. I had no reason to expect more would be necessary."

"You had no reason to expect more would be necessary. This is the daughter of one the most powerful women in subgovernment. Held against her will. Part of negotiations with Jelli Puihare to recover George Assok, who is critical to the SRM Project. This girl was key." He turned away by rotating his chair to face the window. "And since the attack, has she been sighted?"

"No, sir. But there have been violent SRM events in the city."

"Which you connect with Lino Puihare?"

"Possibly, sir. There was a noticeable increase in SRM activity around the building where she was held."

"So, she performs as advertised. Very interesting. I wonder if the effect is genetic. Have you investigated them?"

"Yes sir. We lost an operative at one location when he drew his weapon. There were a number of people present, including a young woman."

"Then search that area! Door to door if necessary!"

The Chief of Operations was delighted that he was still being given things to do. He jumped to his feet and visibly resisted a powerful urge to salute.

"Yes, sir!" he shouted, and rushed from the room.

Blue Suit pondered on why senior-ranking members of his organisation were such fools, then he buzzed his secretary.

"Send Colville in here," he said.

While he waited for the slinking squirming Sedric to arrive, he thought about his options. He could recapture Lino. That was desirable, but unlikely. Whoever had so efficiently located the safe house and removed her with violence would be careful to avoid the same fate. He could reject the entire Jelli Puihare deal, the whereabouts of George Assok, and incidentally the nanoconstructor, for her daughter. Blue Suit disliked that choice, also, since he had convinced himself that Assok would be able to turn Colville's failures into successes, and without a nanoviral agent that could control SRMs, there was no grand plan. No lever for domination of the Consortium.

Which left him with the possibility that Jelli did not know what had happened. He would know the likelihood of that the next time she had her obscure PA arrange a telephone call.

He didn't have to wait very long for that. Colville had hardly brought his empty sleeve and his eyes burning with bruised scientific ego into the office when the desk phone buzzed twice.

"Sit down," he told Colville as he answered it.

"Mrs Puihare for you, sir," said his secretary.

"Connect her."

"Blue Suit?" Jelli asked.

"Jelli," Blue Suit said. There was nothing in his voice to show any change in his situation. It was the deep but subtly toneless organ it always had been. "How are you?"

"Oh for Christ's sake," Jelli snapped. "Save the etiquette for your mechanical bride." There was the sound of male voices in the background. "You shut up, too," Jelli went on. "I don't care who invented the expression. Blue Suit. We have the nanoconstructor."

"Good," Blue Suit replied without noticeable enthusiasm. "And you also have George Assok?"

"Yes," Jelli said firmly.

"Is he with you now?"

"No, of course not. If I had him here you'd just charge in and take everything you want. They're both where I can get them."

"Of course, Jelli. You are a very clear-thinking woman. I like that."

"I don't care what you like," Jelli replied. The male voice in the background began asking insistent questions. "Whak! Will you let me get on with it?"

"Ah, your husband is with you. A man with principles." Blue Suit actually laughed. "Tell him that my teeth are still straight."

"Where are we going to meet?" Jelli was ignoring anything not on the straight line between her and having her daughter back. She cast a withering look at Whak for some internal-compulsion reason that she couldn't explain.

"What are you looking at me like that for?" Whak asked her. Jelli hesitated, then put her hand over the mouthpiece.

"For having principles," she replied. She uncovered the mouthpiece and spoke to Blue Suit again.

"Can we keep this to one conversation at a time," said Blue Suit impatiently, "or is there something else more important that you want to deal with first?"

"No," Jelli said. "Where will we meet?"

"I have an excellent office."

"So do I," Jelli came back with withering sarcasm. Blue Suit failed to be withered.

He said "Since obviously neither of those places are going to be agreeable, why not somewhere neutral?" He rolled the phone cord around in his fingers. The location he had met that noxious Cousin Sinfine had been surprisingly secure and private. "Let's make it the Wasteland, shall we?"

"The Wasteland?" Jelli shot a look at Whak, who looked concerned.

"Dangerous," he mouthed. Jelli nodded.

"Not anywhere near your project station or whatever you call it. This has to be no goons and no guns," she said into the phone.

"Of course."

Jelli didn't believe him, but she would deal with that later. "All right. At the Wasteland."

"When?"

"Tomorrow morning. Eleven o'clock."

"I'll have a man waiting for you at the Wasteland Tours building."

"All right." Jelli put the phone down and turned to Whak. "Tomorrow morning at eleven o'clock," she said, and the nearness of it made her blink rapidly in the way she always did when she was trying by willpower alone to make dice roll in her favour. "At Wasteland Tours."

"I heard." Whak discovered that he almost forgave her for fucking Blue Suit and using him as bait to catch George Assok. There's no honesty so touching as the lie that cannot hide. "Don't worry. We'll get her back if it kills me," he said.

"Don't say that, Whak. Things you say are too often true."

Colville must be there

Colville was tired. It was late at night, and he was sliding down the steep side of a cloud of narcotic analgesics. He waited until Blue Suit had replaced the phone on his desk and then spoke.

"You wanted to see me," he said. His arm, or lack of it, hurt continuously. At least that, and the painkillers, dulled the fear he suffered whenever he came to this office.

"Yes. We may be recovering the nanoconstructor. Tomorrow morning, as it happens." Blue Suit nodded at the phone.

"Oh, good."

"I think it would be useful if you were there to verify that that the machine is untampered-with."

"Does it matter?"

"Not in itself, no, but I am also hoping to obtain George Assok tomorrow, or at least discover his whereabouts. I want you there to confirm his identify for me."

Sedric shrugged his shoulders. So he was to confirm the identity of his replacement. And after that, what?

"All right," he said.

Goons and guns were to be met with more goons and guns. Whak disapproved.

"If both sides have guns, it's fifteen thousand times more likely that someone will get killed," he argued.

"It's a hundred percent likely that someone will get killed, if we don't," said McFee. "Since you don't have what Blue Suit wants, I'd say that having my men protecting you is all that stands between yourselves and a shallow grave. That and these bullet-proof vests."

"The gunfire is going to be deafening," said Whak. "Twice as deafening."

"I'm not going to let you go in without armed backup. That's final."

"Don't argue, Whak. This is the way it has to be. Blue Suit might just march us all off to indefinite detention if we try to go in without McFee. That reminds me, I have some more pain I want to inflict on him, first. I have to talk to Allynn."

Whak stared out the window while Jelli took the phone from the breakfast bar and trailed the cord to the dining table, where she sat and dialled. It was the best part of the morning. The sky was bright. Grey, but bright. The neutral light of winter was combined with heat, leaf and green. The reduction of weather to a constant was another reminder that life resides on the edge between order and chaos. Thoughts of Persephone and Pluto came irresistibly to him. In his ears was Jelli's rapid, decisive voice.

"So you have all that? We're on our way to the Wasteland. Be ready on my call to run the rest of the Blue Suit material. If I don't get Lino back, then I want him nailed to the Consortium's toilet door." She listened. "Yes, it does say he's a child molester. What would you call what he's done to my daughter? Right. And if all goes well, you can run the apology piece. Right? All right." She hung up and smiled like it hurt her teeth. "Right," she said again.

She opened George's carrycase, which was near her on the table, and took from it a dark grey object.

"This is it?" she asked.

"That's the thing George stole."

"Well, I hope it's as valuable as you think, or we're going to have to tell Blue Suit that we don't know where George Assok is even earlier than I think we are."

"How early do you envisage?"

"Before we get Lino."

"At which time he gets in a temper with us," Whak murmured quietly.

"On the other hand, if we can get him to hand over Lino before we show him Assok, then all we have to do is walk off. He won't shoot the CEO of PushRight Creative Media, Whak. Too many repercussions. Here, put this inside your coat."

They went out the front door. Whak, Jelli, and McFee all studied the street and the trees. The blue suits were gone. That was somehow expected, and none of them made any comment on it.

Whak and Jelli got into the car McFee indicated and let him make like a chauffeur all the way to the Wasteland. Another car containing two young monsters from PushRight Security followed.

They didn't go directly to the Tours building, though. It was too early for one thing, and for another thing McFee wanted to set his men up somewhere high. He had insisted that sharpshooters were their best chance of escaping any unpleasantness.

"Too many men on the ground just makes for more itchy fingers," he said. "From above, two men with rifles can pick their targets and cause a lot of confusion and fear."

Whak knew that they could get up high across the road, because he had that little episode with Jim and George to call upon. It had created a bond, that couple of days, which had forced Whak to help George escape from the Jellipolice, even though it put his daughter's life at risk. Whak hated himself, and George, for that, but hate was not something that he felt very strongly.

He followed Jelli, McFee, and the two security men up the dilapidated fire escape stairs that they had chosen as the best route to the top of the building. Climbing stairs is a good time to think. It is a time when you are no longer where you were and not yet where you're going. Whak thought about Jelli. She fascinated him, just as she had when they first met. To her, results were everything, even more important than her own happiness. Living with her for the last twenty years had been an important part of Whak's development as a poet. She was a motivational magnifying glass. Whak had grown from assuming that everybody was the same as him to realising that two people in the same situation would inevitably react in different ways, to the further realisation that he might never understand why. He loved Jelli for that.

"There it is," he said breathlessly as he pulled himself up the last steps. "The Wasteland."

"It's well named." Jelli was already sitting on the inside of the pelmet, also panting, surveying the indeterminate contours of the SRM jungle. McFee was further along the roof discussing signals with his men, who were unpacking sophisticated-looking rifles from neat black cases.

"That must be the Tours building," Jelli pointed.

"Must be." At the outskirts of the Wasteland there was a single complete building, forming a bridge from the outside world to the intestinal insides. Beyond that, piles of mechanoid garbage and military-industrial shit buried the earth and undulated irregularly into the haze of distance. "Do you think we're going to get Lino back?"

"Yes." Jelli had no doubts. "There's nothing going on here that Blue Suit can think worth the pain I'll cause him if he goes on holding her. I'll give everything to send him down. He has no idea what I can do."

"Neither have I," Whak said. "What can you do, without losing your job?"

Jelli stood up. She looked fierce.

"I'll think of something," she said. Her fierceness lasted only a moment. Her eyes blinked, not as before, but the irregular blink that holds back tears. "I hope I don't have to."

Whak put his hand out. He took her hand, carefully as if she was a frail thing of failed hope. "We'd never have had a chance of getting her back if it wasn't for you." But his words must have struck a cyst of doubt inside her that surged with puss and vibrated at the edge of explosion, because she shut her eyes tightly and swayed in the altitude breeze. She looked a lot like Lino. Then she spoke.

"She wouldn't be wherever she is now if it wasn't for me."

It had been a long time since Jelli showed uncertainty. Unless Whak plugged her wounded confidence right now, she would certainly burst with the accumulated fears of a dozen years. He pulled her over so that they were touching and told her the truth, because that was all he ever told her, and if the truth didn't serve then there was nothing else on the menu.

"Something about her makes SRMs insane," he said. "That's why she's been taken. If she was the daughter of anybody else she would have been killed by now." Maybe that is what has happened. "The power you have is protecting her. If we're right and Blue Suit is planning to blackmail whole countries with his nanovirus, then he doesn't want any other way of influencing SRMs to be on the loose. If he wasn't worried about what you'd do, he'd - " Whak didn't want to dwell anymore on what Blue Suit might or might not have done. "Look." He pointed. "They're coming."

There were grubby reflections in the glass wall of a line of blue cars rolling slowly along the side of the Wasteland. Jelli pulled away from Whak and looked over the pelmet again. When she looked back, she had sealed her fear away.

"Do you know what to do?" she asked.

"I think so."

"It would have been better - " Jelli bit off her words.

"If we had George Assok, I know."

"Principles are bullshit, Whak."

"Yeah. I used to think that."

Five men got out of the two front cars and took up defensive positions around the third, with practised grace, like big ugly ballet dancers with guns.

"He brought force," McFee said. He had been taking views of the scene, through circled finger and thumb. "Lots of it."

"He always brings force," Jelli repeated, but she was worried, and looked it.

The Wasteland Tours building was deserted, of course. Everything of value had been removed when the tour business closed. Everything not of value had since been scavenged and removed either by SRMs, or by the humans who had broken into this cold, spare place in order to make off with pipeform chairs and pencil sharpeners. Whak felt serious fear as they walked past the blue cars, parked neatly side by side as if there had been no other spaces free in the big Tours car park. People who parked like that were people to be scared of. The gate was wide open, and none of the men they had watched pile out of the cars had been left at the door. McFee gave final instructions.

"I'll take the front until we see Blue Suit. Then Jelli, you move up beside me. Whak, keep behind me unless I say so." He made loose circling motions near his shoulder with his index finger and looked up at the snipers' position. "Everything's under control. There'll be no shooting unless I give the sign."

"No shooting unless I give the word," Jelli contradicted.

"Whatever," said McFee. "We're outnumbered. Everyone remember that."

When they went inside, there were no men there either. The doors to the ramp that lead into the Wasteland itself were open. A single tentacular SRM tip-toed across their path. A Wasteland Special.

The floor made a distinctly hollow sound as Jelli's heels clacked against it. They went across the room and looked down the ramp. A glass wall, open at the centre where a sliding gate of the same material was missing, separated them from a flat area at the foot of the ramp, merging into holes in the surface and hills of mixed TV screens and plastic, and then cliffs of broken reinforced concrete, bus bodies, and power pylons. Out there, a blue suit was standing near the edge of the clearing with his arms crossed.

A big blue baboon. Whak found those words very difficult not to say aloud. As they walked across the irregular surface, Jelli very unsteady in her fashionably pointy heels, he mumbled under his breath.

"What are you muttering about?" Jelli snapped at him.

"Don't say big blue baboon," Whak said just as they came within earshot of the blue suit. The man's eyes flashed. No doubt behind his muscles, his gun and his employment with the earthly representative of Satan, he was a sensitive lad who suffered wounding remarks with deep hurt. Whak smiled weakly at him. A hated reflex. McFee didn't smile. He scratched his face ostentatiously instead. Marking him for later, Whak imagined.

"Where's Blue Suit?" Jelli asked, her voice reverberating with authority.

The man pointed through a gap in the jungle. A section of concrete wall faced with brick and hanging together by strands of rusty reinforcing steel formed one side of the passage, a mound of unrecognisable electronic chassis formed the other. Jelli gave up and took off her shoes, then limped on.

The next area looked familiar. Whak stopped at the edge and took it in. Directly ahead there was a train carriage with one corner missing sticking vertically out of the ground and leaning at a distinct angle to the north. There was a large hill, which looked to be made entirely out of aluminium cans filling the view to the left. Girders, poles and the limbs of unknown machines protruded above the ground like fenceposts bordering a field of flat metal sheets, car doors, and the tops of buried trucks. Scattered across all of it was a screed of smaller, unpredictable objects.

"The leaning carriage," Whak said. He remembered Jim's description of this place. "This is where it started."

"Then this is where it's going to finish," Jelli breathed.

CHAPTER 41

Blue Suit at Can Hill

Blue Suit was standing at the foot of Can Hill. Four men were posed around him as if for a publicity shoot, right elbows crooked across their hips and hands hidden under their coats.

Jelli walked unsteadily but purposefully to what she thought to be the counterspot to Blue Suit, about fifteen metres from him in front of the top of what looked like a petrol tanker that protruded obliquely a metre above the ground and skewed away to nothing. A good place to hide from bullets, Whak noted. He resisted the urge to pat the nanoconstructor where it resided in his coat pocket. Instead, he pressed his knuckles into the fabric of his bullet-proof vest.

"Where's my daughter?" Jelli shouted across the clearing.

"I have her," Blue Suit called back. "Do we have to shout at each other at such a distance?"

"If you came any closer, I'd have to punch you in the face again," Whak broke in. He felt stupid as soon as he had said it. Here they were with hostages and world domination and firepower, the Blue Suit himself and the PushRight CEO playing out a drama that would surely take one of them down before it ended, and he had no more to contribute than a smack in the head. Suddenly, poetry was the intellectual plaything of the leisured. Words, usually his allies, seemed very weak now.

"Really?" Blue Suit replied. "Very well, then." He raised a hand and from a fold in Can Hill behind him, Colville came out, staggering slightly across the junk beneath his feet.

"Let's start with the simple things," Blue Suit suggested. "The nanoconstructor."

Whak took the nanoconstructor out of his inside coat pocket. He hoped and wished that Lino would be handed over before Jelli had to admit that she didn't know where George Assok was. "Send someone over to get it," Jelli said. More quietly "Give it to McFee, Whak. He'll take it over."

But Whak couldn't. He could not be a spectator. He shook his head at McFee, who scowled at his disobedience. Under Jelli's non-communicating gaze, he walked out to the halfway place and handed the little grey box over to a disinterested-looking giant.

What did it matter where he was? It was pretty clear to Whak that at any time, Blue Suit could order them seized, overpower them by force of numbers, have them dragged over to his side of the clearing and conduct the whole affair without having to raise his voice. What would McFee's sharpshooters do then? But luckily, he was accepting the conventions of the showdown. The giant went back and handed the nanoconstructor over to Sedric, who took it awkwardly with his one hand.

"Where's Lino?" Jelli demanded again.

"Where's George Assok?" Blue Suit responded quickly. "I don't see him."

"Do you think I'd bring him with me? I'll tell you where he is when you hand over Lino."

"Who obviously isn't here, either," Whak pointed out to her.

She jerked her gaze from Blue Suit to Whak, and back to Blue Suit, who was tipping his head slightly from side to side as he observed them.

"Is Lino here?" she shouted. "Answer me!"

But before Blue Suit could compose a reasonable sounding lie, he was interrupted. When he had received the nanoconstructor, Sedric had sat down on the side of a polycarbonate waste drum hopefully not bubbling inside with bioactive goo, and inspected the thing. Without looking up, he groaned loudly.

"It's broken," he said. "It's useless."

Jim, George and Lino realise

It took Jim several minutes to flush the overdose of adrenaline he had just received from his well-meaning glands from his body. It was going to take Lino longer than that to return from wherever she went to at times like this. Jim laid her down on his bed and pulled his ineffective curtains and put both his blankets over her, for she felt as cold as ice, and when he had done that he sat down at the tiny square of plasticised wood which he called the dining table and stared at George expectantly.

"I had nowhere else to go," George said. "My lab is wrecked. And it's being watched. I needed somewhere safe to think."

"Why not Whak's place? He's got a bit more room than I have," Jim said sarcastically.

"It's Whak I'm running away from. Well, his wife. She was scheming to hand me over to Blue Suit, to get Lino back."

George, who had never seen Lino before, looked at her curiously. "Who's the girl?" he asked.

"That's Lino." Jim smiled a little self-consciously. "I rescued her."

George looked puzzled and concerned.

"If you've got Lino," he said, "why should Jelli Puihare want to exchange me for her? That hardly makes sense."

"Well, she wouldn't have known. I only just got her."

"Of course," George agreed. He relaxed and after a moment in which they both sat there nodding to themselves and looking thoughtful, asked if there was any coffee.

"Sood," Jim said briefly. "I don't have real coffee." He got up and poured a pot of water, found a near-empty jar of Sood in the cupboard and prepared two cups, then as an afterthought, three cups in case Lino woke up.

As he placed them on the table, George said "So what are you going to do now?"

"I'm waiting a while, then I'll try and call Whak again."

"Oh, so you have called him."

"He was out."

"Really." George gulped some Sood and made the obligatory shiver of disgust. "Look, she's waking up." Jim jumped over to the bed and pulled her into a sitting position. "It's all right, Lino," he told her as he rubbed her hands, "it was only George. Oh, you don't know George. He's a friend of your father's."

Lino pulled her hands away. "I am not a goddamned old woman, thank you," she growled. Jim accepted her anger as her usual way of recovering herself after one of her episodes, rebuilding her self-esteem or something, he supposed. He didn't take it personally. If she thought that throwing a fit was a sign of weakness to be hidden behind constant anger, that was her business.

"Who did he say you were?" Lino spoke to George as she swung her legs off the bed. She looked weary. The effect of these SRM panics on her insides was beginning to show. "A friend of Whak's? Do you know where he is?"

"Last time I saw him he was in Coolio Park, but that was last night." He looked at Jim, who was hovering behind Lino as if he expected her to keel over again at any time. "But he's not at home, Jim tells me. I was just saying that your mother was going to trade me to Blue Suit today for your safe return."

Lino narrowed her eyes. "That sounds like my mother. What do you have that Blue Suit wants?"

"I'm the world's leading expert on nanotechnology," George said unhappily. "Blue Suit wants me to work for him."

Lino gave him an appraising stare that ended with a dismissive shrug. She cared nothing for George's credentials. "So, Blue Suit is going to trade me for you."

"Well, not now, of course, because you're here. And so's George," Jim put in.

"Do Blue Suit and my mother know that?"

"Blue Suit knows that you've escaped. He must do, by now," said Jim.

"Your father helped me to escape from your mother's security men," George added. "His impetuousness can be useful at times."

"So they both know that they can't keep their end of the bargain, but they don't know that the other can't either. Blue Suit still thinks he can have you, and Jelli still thinks she can get me back. When did you say they were going to do this?"

"I don't know," George said, starting to catch up. "Soon, I would estimate."

Through all their minds a short movie ran, out-takes from the Lino trail. Dead bodies and bullets, explosions and fear. Lino turned to Jim, whose mouth was hanging open as he whispered oh shit, and fuck, and damn.

"If Blue Suit hurts my parents," she told him, "I'm not going to let you forget it. Ever."

Jim was already putting his leather jacket back on.

"Let's go," he said.

Reduced economic circumstances, by reducing the quality of a man's life, reduce in his eyes the value of everyone else's lives, so life was as cheap as it had ever been. One man who considered his life practically worthless was the number man who hustled Combine Street, who had first mentioned to Jim the name of Sinfine, and who was hurting for cash real bad because the pitfights were stealing all his business. Now, Jim was a nice kid and he still bought a number now and then even though he never won a damned thing, but there was important people who wanted to know a thing or two about him, like where exactly he lived, and for a wise call these important people was offering more funds than he could make selling Jim a thousand numbers. Easy arithmetic, sorry Jim. The number man watched Jim leaving his building with a beautiful fucking woman and a geeky looking older guy in tow. The group cut straight across the street and headed down the alley to the Sood Shop. The street was pretty busy, so the number man just strolled on after them as if that's where he was headed, too, and then he stood bored-like against the damp bricks outside the shop, waiting to see what was what.

Jim wondered whether telephones ever worked. Lack of pick-up at the other end, the failure of person-to-person communication as a concept, was the fault of the heavy, ugly block of yellow metal hanging on the Sood Shop wall. Lots of other people must have felt the same, because the phone was dented and scratched in a lot of interesting ways. A trained eye could have read of the personal weapons inventory of the whole of Combine Street from the score marks on this phone.

Jim hung up gently and with restraint, not wanting to upset Lino, and said "Still no-one there. They're out."

"Get out of the way," Lino ordered. She elbowed Jim aside and held out a hand. "Money," she said impatiently.

"Who are you calling now?" Jim asked, digging in his pockets for nonexistent coins. When he came up empty, George quickly reached over with a handful. "Thanks. Lino? Who you calling?"

"PushRight. Be quiet." Lino punched the buttons fluently and waited. "Hello? Jelli Puihare, please." Looking vacantly in Jim and George's direction, she drummed her fingers on the top of the phone.

"Allynn? It's Lino." Lino's voice dropped. "Yes, I'm all right. Sort of. I know! I know! Where's Jelli?" She shut her eyes. She wilted a little against the wall. "Oh, God. When did they go? All right, we're going too. Shut up! Shut up! It doesn't matter! I don't care! We're going! Oh, Jesus Christ, Allynn, it would take too long. Goodbye."

"So where are they?" George asked.

"They've gone to meet Blue Suit. At the Wasteland."

"Hope the car starts," said Jim.

"You've got a car?"

"Yeah. Come on."

The number man stepped out from the wall and collided heavily with Jim, who was paying more attention to exhorting his companions than to watching where he was headed.

"Hey, sorry Jim," said the number man, catching him by the shoulders. He was a lot longer than Jim, and with his arms out he barred the way.

"Oh hi," Jim said. "Gotta go, gotta go. Be seeing you." He pushed past.

"Where you headed in such a rush?"

"The Wasteland. Meeting someone."

They hurried off. The number man waited patiently until they had turned out of sight onto Combine, then he hurried off, too, but in a different direction. Straight into the Sood Shop.

Meantime, Jim hurried the other two along the footpath until they reached a car park building.

"Well, shit, where else was I supposed to keep it?" Jim asked when George made a sarcastic remark. "On the street? At least in here there's twenty other cars that look like they might go better than this one." He stopped beside the old Fairlane. Lino wrinkled her nose. "You'd rather walk?" he asked her, and opened the door.

"No," she answered. "How fast does this thing go?"

"We're going to find out. Get in."

As he drove the car as rapidly as total accelerator depression could achieve, he stole a look at Lino, who sat beside him, catlike calm her mood for this moment.

"What the hell are we going to do once we get there?' he asked her, but it was George who leaned over from the back seat and answered.

"I have a suggestion," he said, surprising even himself.

When they arrived at the Tours building, there was a line of the customary big black monsters parked with anal precision alongside the Glass Wall, but no blue suits in sight. Jim, Lino and George pressed themselves against the wall and watched the Tours entrance for a minute.

"Can you see anyone?" George asked.

"No," Jim replied.

"Why are we hiding beside a glass wall?" Lino asked peevishly. "Look over there." She faced the wall and pointed. A man stood on an elevated point, his back to them. "That's a blue suit."

"That's a blue suit," Jim agreed. "So they're in there. That's near the leaning carriage." He gave Lino a sympathetic smile. "So what are we going to do, George? What the hell is that?"

George had in his hand a shiny metallic cylinder, which on closer examination was made from some kind of glass or plastic. It was sealed at one end by a slightly bulging plug of the same material.

"This is a nanovirus sample," George said, holding it with both hands. "I made it with the nanoconstructor, before it was destroyed. This is a metallotropic deconstructor with a high degree of adaptive capacity, and in an attempt to overcome the problems that wrecked the isolation chamber at the Project Centre, I have designed in short-range communication capabilities so that the internal specifications of any single nanomachine replicant are a composite of the surrounding monads."

"Neat," said Lino.

"The intermachine communications should maintain replication fidelity almost perfectly," George added, "but Blue Suit doesn't know that."

"Should?" Jim wanted to make sure he understood what this bullshit actually meant. "What do you mean, should?"

George rubbed his nose violently. "I mean that one, there's a breakdown in theory versus actual when it comes to machine behaviour at this level, which might be related to whatever created SRMs. You know, the Sphere of Anti-Entropy theory. And two, my nanoconstructor was eaten by houdinis before the stabilisation phase was complete, so there may be some unpredictable factors."

"Houdinis?" Jim couldn't help but ask.

"That's what I call them. They evolved in my lab out of a semi-intelligent octopedal SRM and escaped."

"Cool," Lino said in the same impatient tone as before.

"So I thought that I'd give myself up to Blue Suit."

"You what? You're terrified of Blue Suit! You've spent the last however many years running away from him!"

"Yes, but as soon as Puihare and his wife are safe, I'll threaten to crack the cylinder unless Blue Suit lets me go," George went on with diminishing enthusiasm.

He held up a small screwdriver. Jim stared at it.

"Well, that's very, er, very whatever it is, George, but you're a bloody fool. The first thing they'll do is shoot you if you blink too fast. You'll never get a chance to make threats, let alone prise that tube open. These sort of people are killers."

"They won't shoot me now that I'm the only nanotechnologist left in one piece. They need me. I think." George put the screwdriver back in his pocket.

"You're not usually a hero."

"It's not my preference, no. Have you got any other ideas?" George said hopefully.

"No." Jim tried to think of some. Nothing happened. "Okay. Okay. Why not? Shit, we've got to do something." Jim stopped. Lino was walking quickly away, towards the Tours entrance. "Lino! Where the fuck are you going now?" Without another word to George, Jim hurried after her. George followed them, still clutching the cylinder of nanovirus in his hand.

Shoot everyone

"Useless, you say," Blue Suit said to Sedric.
"That's right. Completely wrecked. The wafer is missing. He must have transplanted the protonanos." He stared at the box. "Why would he do that? I don't understand."
Blue Suit didn't really care about the nanoconstructor, important though it was. It was just a start point for the main event, being the acquisition of George Assok. But if the nanoconstructor was a feint, then so might be the rest of this circus. He raised his voice.
"The nanoconstructor has been tampered with," he shouted, "as I'm sure you are well aware. That part of our arrangement is void. Do you have George Assok or don't you?"
"Do you have Lino or don't you?" Jelli shouted back.
"I'll take that as a no," Blue Suit declared, and turned to face his protectors, who were poised to do some protection at his order.
"Start moving back slowly," McFee said quietly, himself stepping forward with one hand signalling behind his back. "Keep talking."
"We're in trouble," Whak said, grabbing Jelli by the arm. The corner of the petrol tanker was a few metres behind them. He pulled Jelli in that direction, she crying out "Answer me! Where's Lino, you limp-dicked megalomaniac!" and he registering any movement of Blue Suit's protectors as the signal to run for their lives. For the briefest of instants he took a sighting on where he was heading and that was when he saw someone emerge from the Tours building side of the clearing.
At the same time, one of the protectors drew Blue Suit's attention to this latest development. Blue Suit turned around and squinted into the afternoon sun.
"And who are these people?" he demanded of the air, but he had already identified one of them. It was Lino Puihare. He knew what she looked like, but he would have recognised her

even if he had not spent time studying her file. She was unmistakably the offspring of Jelli.

"Lino!" It was Whak calling. "Lino! Get out of here!"

As Blue Suit reconsidered his intentions, another person appeared. This place was proving to be like a railway station, particularly busy places since trains had become the only halfway reliable means of long-distance travel. Blue Suit felt a minor sense of irritation at the untidiness of a universe where unplanned witnesses could clutter up his private rendezvous and interrupt his negotiations with Jelli, even if so far the effect was entirely in his favour. He glared at the third arrival and was surprised to see him raise his hand in the air, holding a shiny cylinder, which glittered bright as it caught an uncommon shaft of sunlight. Blue Suit wondered if it was an explosive device. He indicated that his nearest goony bird should stand ready.

"Who is that?" he asked tetchily.

"George Assok," Sedric told him.

"Ah," said Blue Suit. Fortune smiles on the pure of heart. He smiled. "Good." He nodded slowly to himself in the manner of a man who has been struck by an idea. Jelli was still shouting at him as her husband pulled her away. He pointed at George Assok.

"Don't hurt that one," he told his goony birds, looking directly, and rather sadly, at Jelli. "Kill everyone else."

CHAPTER 42

Lino is shot

When Whak started shouting at her, Lino at first took an automatic step back the way she had come, but that step bumped her into Jim, who was just catching his breath after telling her unceasingly all the way from the gate that she was insane to be crashing this get-together and that if she was going to, she had better have some plan for how to at least survive it. She changed her mind, then, and took another step towards Whak and Jelli, Jelli who had both hands out and was also calling her name, while Whak went on shouting at her to go away, that it was dangerous, to run, and he was grabbing Jelli by the sleeve, too, saying something to her that Lino couldn't hear. She couldn't hear Jim, anymore, either.

Beside Jim there was George the strange man, holding his silver tube above his head, and he was also shouting, and she couldn't hear him, either, and then the ground three centimetres in front of her feet exploded. A brief feeling of nearby wind passed her head. A big man standing near Jelli and Whak pointed at one of the blue suits, who immediately fell dead, and then several shots hit him at once and he fell.

"Oh Jesus Christ, more shooting," said Jim. He glanced behind. They would be cut down long before they reached the Tours building if they went that way. With impeccably correct choice of strategy he decided that the safest direction to flee in was towards the enemy, more or less. He shoved Lino in the direction of the three-quarter-buried petrol tanker that Whak and Jelli had already picked as their refuge, so hard that she almost left the ground, and with her hand clenched immovably in his, he ran across the clearing. George Assok had somehow managed to get ahead of them, running in his peculiar Groucho Marx fashion through the debris faster than Jim could keep up, still holding his canister of nanovirus high. More bullets struck near Jim's feet. He pulled harder on Lino's arm, but she resisted. He looked back. Her eyes were endlessly black. Blood was pumping from a bullet wound in her side. Jim had only time to feel an awful fear burst in his heart before she was hit by another bullet. With her hand still gripped tightly by his, she fell down and lay like death on the coke cans.

Jim let go of her hand when Blue Suit's protectors let another series of shots loose at him, one of which whistled so sweetly in his ear that for just that moment he wished that it had come a little closer. Then he ran. He reached the shield of metal that was his target and threw himself over the top of it, landing on his face. Ricochets sounded on the strong steel wall. And there was another sound that Jim recognised. The sound of things coming up from beneath the surface. The sound of SRMs. His ears were buried in the sound, then without warning his head was lifted up and another face was pressed up to his. Whak.

"Where's Lino?" Whak was holding him by the neck and banging his head on the ground. He didn't even know he was doing it. "Where's Lino?"

"Out there," Jim managed to squeeze past Whak's grip on his windpipe. "She's been shot."

Whak's face froze. He stopped banging Jim's head on the ground, stood up, and ran back the way Jim had just come, out into the field of gunfire.

"Whaaaaak!" Jelli screamed.

McFee was crawling from where he had fallen towards the tanker. Another long-range bullet popped into a blue suit's chest, and the remaining men, not knowing where the shots were coming from, let loose a barrage of return fire at McFee before making for cover. He gave up crawling, staggered to his feet and ran stiff-legged towards Jelli.

"What is he doing?" he shouted at her as soon as he was behind the tanker. Jelli didn't answer. He grunted and pointed his gun around the side of the tanker, let loose a few shots, and then paid some attention to his leg, which was bleeding freely. "Who are the uninvited guests?" He glanced around the corner again.

"My daughter," said Jelli.

The surfacing sound was getting louder. While Whak was running across the line of fire and the blue suits should have been training their guns on him, they were instead looking nervously at their feet. Blue Suit himself snatched a weapon from inside his coat and pointed it, but he was to wish he had not, because from somewhere to his right, a flashing strip of wire shot out and wrapped itself around both the gun and his wrist. He stared at the other end of the wire, which was protruding from an opening in the front of a machine with four limbs and two wheels, about the size of a cat, which was emerging from the ground. It glistened with mechanical perfection. Now it did the exact opposite of what Blue Suit was expecting. Instead of trying to reel him in (against which he was already bracing himself), it came flying through the air, drawing on the wire as it did so, and before he could move it was latched firmly onto his arm by three of it's four grasping arms. The other arm produced a sparkling electrical arc, neatly sliced the end off the gun barrel, caught the metal section before it could fall, and passed it to another arm to hold while the first arm raised itself for another cut.

"Help me!" Blue Suit shouted to his protectors, but they had their own problems. From her position behind the tanker, Jelli saw a swarm of unknown SRMs only slightly larger than insects sweep over a blue suit, leaving naked skin where they passed. A larger contraption with dozens of projecting spikes, antennae, or feelers, or something, had grabbed the shoes of another blue suit, throwing their occupant to the ground, and was now cutting the shoes off, to the accompaniment of unusually shrill cries. Then the cries were silenced by another shot from the far rooftop.

And Whak had reached Lino. Jelli saw him pick her up. Jelli saw Blue Suit beat the thing on his arm off, using another gun as a club. Blood ran down the sleeve of his light grey suit. Then he pointed his new weapon at Whak.

George Assok was sitting with his back to the tanker, gasping for air that he no sooner breathed in than panted out again in his panic. Beside him was the silver cylinder. It looked reasonably heavy. Jelli grabbed it and hurled it with all her strength at Blue Suit.

"Oh, shit," said Jim.

It didn't hit Blue Suit, but it did fall across his line of sight and cause him to lower his aim. Perhaps his judgement was a little frayed after the experience of having a robot frog try to cut his hand off, but for whatever reason, he turned his gun from Whak's head and instead fired one off at the canister. It was a good shot. It drilled a neat hole in the centre. A cloud of yellowness poured out of the hole and expanded evenly in all directions in the lack of breeze.

"Somebody kill them!" Blue Suit cried, but one of his remaining protectors was busy beating away a spiky machine which was tearing his bulletproof jacket from his back, and the other was face down and had a pair of flat ellipses joined by a thin flexible band, latched barnacle-like to his back. By the sounds he was making, they, or it, were trying to obtain his gun holster by drilling through his chest for it. Another sniper round hummed close to Blue Suit and he moved quickly to the shade of the leaning carriage.

Behind the tanker it was relatively quiet. A few scorpions and a snakelike tube marched through, but only Jelli was wearing any metal objects and she was ignored. There were richer pickings elsewhere. The yellow cloud had reached a diameter of about five metres. Whak was unsteadily running back with Lino cradled in his arms.

George yelled "Whak! Watch out! Don't go through there!"

But Whak passed through the edges of the cloud. Blue Suit fired at him, missed, made a growling sound of annoyance, and raised the gun again. He was determined to finish what he had begun, apparently oblivious to the state of affairs around him and the condition of his protectors. McFee sent two bullets boring into Can Hill behind him. Then a drillhead plummeted from somewhere above and landed on Blue Suit's head.

Blue Suit loses his jaw

It seemed that his perfect teeth were held in place by steel pegs. The SRM suddenly took on an uncanny resemblance to a dentist's drill. It began to remove his shiny whites, through the side of his face where necessary. A few seconds later, when Whak reached the tanker, the drillhead had extracted Blue Suit's entire lower jawbone and was undoing the stainless steel nuts where they protruded through the blood and attached muscle. As Whak lowered Lino to the ground, Jelli turned fascinated eyes from the distant sight of Blue Suit twitching and bleeding and stared at the holes in Lino's side and chest. Lino's face was strangely calm and relaxed.

"Oh, Whak," Jelli said, dropping to her knees beside her. She curled her fingers like claws. "What are we going to do?"

"Stop the bleeding," McFee suggested. He looked critically at the wounds. "Quickly," he added. Whak stripped off his tee-shirt and McFee wadded it up and applied it to the large chest injury. The cloth immediately turned deep red under his hands.

George was watching Whak closely, studying him from head to foot.

"Are you all right?" he asked.

Whak looked up for just long enough that George could see the spiralling pits of his eyes. "No," he said briefly, loudly.

"I mean, are you injured?"

"No!"

Jelli took over holding the cloth against the flow of blood while Whak checked her other wound. Whak put his hand out to her face. He couldn't tell if she was breathing. He ran his fingers over her forehead and made a gasping sob.

"You passed through the nanovirus cloud," George mumbled. He could not help turning towards the faint yellow smudge that hung in the air at the centre of the clearing. Within the cloud, at ground level, all that could be seen was a blur as the surface was torn apart by the piranha mouths of voracious molecules.

"We need a doctor," McFee said urgently. Blood was still running freely from his thigh and his face was white. He turned to George. "You. Go tell my men. Go out the front and put your hands on your head, like this. They'll come down." His eyes rolled up and he panted rapidly.

"Get help, George! Get help!" Whak pleaded. George hesitated a moment longer, torn between observing the yellow cloud and the need to save a life, and then he nodded and went.

Jim tried to look at Lino, but he couldn't. He stared instead across the animated junkpile that comprised the floor of the Jungle at this instant, at where Blue Suit's twitching grew steadily less. Jelli was making constant moaning noises and exhorting Whak to give Lino CPR, or mouth-to-mouth, or something, and Whak did those somethings, but Jim watched the SRM orgy of reproduction and destruction and was therefore the first to notice Sedric Linus Colville getting unsteadily up from a place of hiding, still with the nanoconstructor clutched against his chest, and look around him. When he saw what remained of Blue Suit, he gave a little shriek, staggered backwards, and was immediately set upon by a common scorpion. Sedric batted it away, but realising his danger he began to run towards Jim and the Puihares.

He was over halfway when he saw the slowly expanding yellow cloud of nanovirus in front of him, which for good personal reasons filled him with paralysing fear. A number of SRMs that had wandered under the shadow of the cloud were shuddering and ceasing to move as their metal skins boiled into darker yellow vapour that fed the whole. The cloud seethed and writhed. Sedric stopped at the sight, shook violently from head to foot and made several uncompleted lunges to the left and right, looking for a way around, too terrified to actually move. Jim found something he could do that didn't involve hearing the sobbing of Jelli and the silence of Whak and the imagined slowing heartbeat of Lino. He crossed over to Sedric, taking a wide berth around the nanovirus. He had a vague idea that this was not a wise thing to do, the yellow cloud was dangerous, that it could without warning extend an immaterial arm and gather Sedric and himself up, but it no longer mattered much. He reached Sedric and tugged on his jacket.

It started to rain.

"This way," he said in a neutral voice. The cloud was becoming more transparent. Sedric went with him, never taking his eyes away from it. Just before they had a clear path back to the horror of Lino's blood draining into Whak and Jelli's hands, Jim saw the nanovirus canister lying in front of him, meaningless and empty now. For no good reason, Jim bent and picked it up.

"Well, hi there, Jim!" called a voice. Jim's head swung around. He had a weary feeling that the bad times were never going to end. Sinfine was entering the area, with Emery as usual at his heels and a pair of Nephews, Jacobs and Smithy if Jim's memory served him right. Smiling teeth and guns at the ready. He hoped that they had not bumped into George. Sedric gave another of his high-pitched squeaks and crabwalked in the direction of the petrol tanker. Emery glanced at him, measured the risk, and let him go.

"Jim," Sinfine repeated. "Imagine meeting you here." He put away the false humour and his face turned evil. But before he could breathe that evil into life, he heard a sound from his right and went over there to look down on Blue Suit, who was still alive. He studied him critically for a few seconds.

"This guy looks familiar," he said at last. "Had a little SRM party, have you Jim? Your fucking girlfriend sure kills them dead. Where is she?" Without waiting for an answer, he pulled Blue Suit's wallet out of his jacket and studied the ID. "I thought I recognised you," he said to the bloodily bubbling half-face on the ground. "You don't look half so dangerous any more. I think it'd be safe to do this now." He pointed his pistol down and pulled the trigger twice. Blue Suit jerked like a stuck flounder and lay still. "Jesus, that felt good," Sinfine said happily. He pointed his gun again as if planning to shoot the corpse a few more times, but thought the better of it. He turned back to Jim.

"Now, you had a deal with me, you little shit. Your fucking girlfriend for this goddamned virus thing. But you took off. Good skills, but stupid. Everyone's an informer. You can't hide from me."

"I wasn't exactly hiding," Jim said. "I was just trying to get Lino somewhere safe." He squeezed his eyes into wet slits. He had not got Lino somewhere safe. He glanced towards the tanker. Whak was standing up, watching, bare to the waist, his tortured face almost unrecognisable.

"She's over there, is she?" said Sinfine. He waved a hand. "I don't want her, anyway. She's too much trouble. What's that in your hand, Jim?"

Jim held up the nanovirus canister. He had a flash of hope. "This is it," he said, holding it up. "The nanovirus. I just got it for you."

"Ah hah." Sinfine walked a few steps closer. "Sure you did." He wiped the drizzling rain from his face. "So give it here."

Jim had other ideas. He tossed the canister once in the air, and then he said,

"You fetch it." He hurled the object away. It traced the glittering arc through the air and bounced to a stop in the mouth of a huge rusty pipe that receded gradually under the surface, a connection between the outside of the Wasteland and whatever mechanical ecosystem existed beneath.

Sinfine shook his head sadly.

"Stupid, Jim," he said. "I'm not a guy you want to piss off," and with those words, he put his gun up to shoulder level and shot Jim in the chest. Jim felt a colossal impact and fell flat on his back. The smooth grey sky filled his eyes. He felt very, very tired, so tired that he didn't even want to stay awake. Light filled his closed eyelids. Insert your favourite religious interpretation. I have none.

Whak saw. He saw Sinfine point his gun at Jim and heard the sharp sound of the bullet. He saw Sinfine pocket his weapon, with a brief glance in his direction, and tread carefully in his shiny black shoes across the clearing, avoiding the sharp objects which threatened his leather at every step. Whak saw him stop at the mouth of the tunnel to the underworld. Whak didn't care about any of it. Tears were running down his cheeks.

Sinfine peered into the pipe. Hanging across its mouth and visibly beaded with moisture by the fine misty rain, were fine lines of watery whiteness. The canister had bounced about a metre down the pipe.

"Fucking smart-ass kid," Sinfine said to himself, his voice collecting somewhere deep below and echoing back at him with unexpected volume and disconcerting offset. "Fetch it yourself. Well, you're fucked now, Jim." He stepped forward, wiping away the webs with his gun arm, and was surprised to see his arm from the elbow slide neatly off the rest of his body and strike the bottom of the pipe with a dull thud. Blood was pumping out of the stump. He stepped sideways, away from whatever had done this to him, a scream almost in his mouth, and the lattice of monomolecular threads that hung on that side efficiently separated his head from his body, and his body into several irregularly sized pieces, all of which abandoned the whole and joined his arm where it had fallen.

After a few seconds, Emery told the two Nephews to stay where they were and went over to see what was keeping Sinfine. He stood at the end of the pipe for a short time, but unlike Sinfine, he had once done the Wasteland Tour and knew about Spiders. He did not try to retrieve any of Sinfine's bodyparts, or the silver canister. He tilted his head and perked his ears at the sounds of McFee's men approaching with much noise and speed, then, having evaluated the situation, he went back to the Nephews and signalled them to vanish. He had no further commitment to being here, and there were dead people all over the place. Time to leave. He took a stop and looked at Jim as he passed him, and then he and his men disappeared over Can Hill into oblivion.

> *Good guys are dead*
> *Bad guys are dead*
> *The live ones stand up from their cover*
> *In a television show they say*
> *Beam me up Scotty*
> *Wake me up, someone*
> *Turn my life into pictures*
> *Don't let it be real.*

Whak looked down at Jelli, who was still pressing his wadded tee-shirt into the holes in Lino's chest.

"Jelli," he spoke in a whisper. "I think she's dead."

Seconds of reality grow stronger as they pass.

CHAPTER 43

Whak writes a poem about it

Change defeats us
The gods of change
Before cause and effect
There was love and hate
There is no power that cannot be measured
But I left my ruler someplace else

Whak turned his eyes from the computer screen to the window and beyond, to the slippery elm, now empty of blue suits. He tested the edges of his mind and they were still unfit for him to leave his study, so he added more words to his telling.

The freezer at the morgue is broken
Wrapped in their odour lie last week's stories
Waiting for a man who feels no sorrow
To put hearts in a jar
And write down reasons
There's no love for the dead
Love takes life

Whak had wanted to be there for the autopsy, when Lino was dissected as he couldn't help but call it. The powerful dead are routinely desecrated by the law. He couldn't say whether he had wanted to be there to receive this punishment in person, or as a mark of respect and a final goodbye, but Jelli had forbidden it, wisely, he was sure. The hole she had left was too deep to fill with gestures.

Jelli was doing just the same thing as Whak, working. She was on the telephone, static permitting, to her office, ordering Allyn to pull the anti-Blue Suit campaign and drop the SRM Collection ads, and concerning herself far too minutely with the state of the Law and Order Project. She came out of her office even less frequently than Whak came out of his. There wasn't much to come out for. Every time they met in the hall, they parted with tears on their faces.

Whak finally decided that he was able to leave the computer when the screen contrast suddenly died and greyness ensued. An ordinary hardware failure, of the type that happened more and more as the lack of new equipment increased the need to repair and reuse. He came upon George Assok in the living room. George had nowhere else to go so Whak had invited him home. He was a welcome distraction from the end of a life.

"My nanovirus seems to be a complete success, wouldn't you say?" George said for at least the fourth time that day. "It quelled that SRM event in quick order, and dissipated with no further effects. Completely according to spec."

"And it didn't eat me alive, for which I am grateful," Whak agreed. He stood with his hands in his pockets, an unusual pose for him, and sighed the wishing sigh. "I think."

"I'm sorry about your daughter," George said sincerely, for the ninth time. "I fetched help as fast as I could."

"I know that. I know that," Whak said with a painful effort.

They both stood silent for a minute, then George struggled with his politeness and won. He asked "Do you think Jelli will be able to arrange funding for my research? We have the secret of SRM population control in our grasp, Whak! We can both recover our industrial capacity, and uncover whatever new laws the SRMs represent. It's a new beginning."

You had to credit George with honest motives, Whak admitted. George thought that all the problems of the world could be systematically eliminated by correct use of the fortunate fact that the laws of physics were within the scope of human comprehension. It was an optimistic outlook that Whak did not share.

"Yes, I know," he nodded disinterestedly. "We have the secret of everything control in our grasp. But listen, George. Lino communicated with SRMs. You think about that."

"Possibly they reacted to something Lino did or produced, and that is extremely interesting, but difficult to study now that the subject is - "

"Dead," Whak said for him. He could say things like that where those less directly affected couldn't.

"Yes."

"I could propose that it was coincidental," George continued carefully.

"How likely is that?"

"How likely is it that your daughter happened to emanate something, only when she was on the verge of one of her breakdowns, that was intelligible to SRMs? Human beings emit electromagnetic signals at extraordinarily low amplitude. SRMs have no apparent way of receiving such signals."

"But we saw. Jim saw. It happened. You can't deny the facts just because you don't' have a convenient theory to explain them."

George stopped at that remark and stared into space. "Perhaps there are some basic assumptions that need to be questioned before we find the answer to this."

"Basic assumptions always need to be questioned." Whak was not trying to make suggestions for George's research. He was trying to say that there was much that was not known. He was trying to say that SRMs were more than they appeared. He was trying to say that it is in the soul of the man that life and death are made and the balance had shifted sharply to death. He let George go on about communications and probability theory, while his ghost sat silent.

Jim had been dead on arrival, but was revived by an emergency room doctor and a few ccs of heart stimulant. He didn't know it yet. He might never find out. In the same hospital where Lino was now lying white on a stainless steel trolley, Jim was tubing a bag of blood and a pipe of oxygen into his failing body, while a grotesquely thick drainpipe dribbled what leaked out through the hole in his lung into a bottle on the floor.

The morgue was at the opposite end of the building, well removed from the patients. This had once been a private hospital, before all the insurance companies in the world went broke (there is some good in everything), and in the old days, being wealthy meant never having to see the dead. The corpses of loved ones were trolleyed away, under sheets. Some people lived their whole lives and never saw a dead body. It was an unhealthy thing. Fortunately, those days were over. Everybody now got to see more death than they wished. Especially the morgue attendants, who had a lot more bodies to deal with most of the time than there were slots in the wall, and much less time to deal with dearly departed meat since the morgue refrigeration had failed two years previously and parts from Sweden were unobtainable. It was, therefore, important to get the cadavers post-mortemed and embalmed. The attendants made a point of walking the wards in their quieter moments, predicting the body count for the next shift. Jim was down as a probable.

Kutters Returns

At much the same time as Whak was watching the slippery elm instead of listening to George prattle about thermodynamic arrows, Elder Kutters was approaching the Puihare house. As usual, it was humid, his skin was rubbing unpleasantly inside his clothes, and he had to wipe his upper lip of sweat periodically to prevent it dripping onto his chin. But Elder Kutters had never been prevented from his duty to proselytise by such things, and today he would not be prevented from saying what had to be said. He was regretful that he could have no other fellows of the Church with him, or devotees at least, for this was going to be a great moment for the Church of the Revital God, and a few malleable witnesses would be useful, but he knew that only he alone would be able to enter into the house. A crowd of dribbling fools would not gain him entrance.

It had taken a long search of his soul before Kutters had come to terms with the events of that day in the Wasteland. A long search of his soul, and extensive use of the wide-flung network of the Church to gather unto him every iota of information about the subsequent SRM events. Now Kutters knew that Lino was suspected to be involved in every single spasm of SRM violence that had occurred.

SRMs were central to the Revital faith. They were indisputable evidence that the will of God was alive in the world. Anyone who had such a close connection to SRMs as Lino evinced must also have a close connection to God. It had taken Kutters a long time to come up with theological viewpoint that matched the facts. He had finally realised Lino's significance only upon hearing from one of his better-placed acolytes of her death. He was convinced that this eccentric young woman would in time be recognised as the first prophet of the Revital Church. It didn't matter that she had never actually prophesied anything. Kutters, who in spite of the belief of his followers had never felt a touch of grace in his entire life, nonetheless understood the mechanics of religion extremely well, and he knew that for every prophet there must be a corresponding disciple to bring the story to the people. He knew very well, if he had the choice, which he would rather be. Not Jesus Christ, nailed up and dead, but Paul, the Patriarch of Rome. It was the record keepers who had the power to make and unmake history. He hurried his stride. There was a legend to be born.

In the three days since the meeting in the Wasteland, Jelli felt that the world had redoubled the rate at which it decayed. She gave up yelling down a phone that sometimes worked and sometimes didn't. It was a thoroughly unsatisfying business, anyway, even when she could hear the other half of the conversation. Instead, she sat in the kitchen and listened with no great interest to the sound of Whak and that man Assok, arguing mildly in the living room. She didn't know what they were arguing about. She didn't care. Whatever it was, it wasn't going to take away the responsibility that she was carrying for Lino's death, which had taken up residence dead centre of her brain so that no thought or emotion could travel from any point without passing through it and arousing the dragon that lived there. She made herself busy with the coffee percolator. Familiar physical tasks were supposed to be soothing, she had heard. While she was rinsing the old grounds down the wastepipe, she heard knocking at the front door, and, still operating by simple repetitive actions, she dried her hands and went to answer it.

The opened door had an over-weight, over-middle-aged, plastic-suited man behind it, with pronounced jowls, a large gut, and repellently soft eyes. Jelli disliked him on sight. It was a measure of her despair that she didn't simply slam the door immediately in his face, as she might have done mere days ago if visited by such an apparition. Instead, she held the door open and waited for him to speak.

"Good afternoon," said the man. "I am the Elder Kutters."

"And exactly who is that?" Jelli said with distaste.

Kutters raised his eyebrows as if he had not met with such a reaction before. "I am an Elder of the Church of the Revital God," he explained. "I knew your daughter."

"What do you know about my daughter?"

"I know that she has passed into the care of the Lord," Kutters said solemnly.

"How? How do you know?" Jelli cared for none of this. Her tongue bit the visitor without her heart being involved.

"I have a television."

Jelli felt that she would like to argue with that bland assumption that television carried all news to all corners. It was pointless, though. She had issued no specific instructions to GOV1, and it was quite likely that the death of the PushRight

CEO's daughter had been on the news. She would have been seriously disappointed in the news team, she supposed, it had not.

"What do you want?" she asked instead.

"I want only to offer you the support of all my people at this time," Kutters told her, stepping irresistibly over the threshold as he spoke. "Your daughter was a rare individual, Mrs Puihare. She was touched by greatness. She was under the guidance of the Lord." He quietly closed the door behind him. "Can we speak?"

The presence of Kutters in her hallway angered Jelli, but where once she would have threatened an intruder with punishments designed to seek and destroy the ego of the man, today she couldn't find the well of spleen that used to serve her. Through slitted eyes, she looked not at Kutters, but at herself standing in the hallway looking at Kutters.

"Oh fuck it," she said, and turned on her heel and marched back to the kitchen.

Kutters had not been expecting that reaction. He was used to being thrown off doorsteps and discharged from living rooms, but to be ignored was a new experience. He gave his head a slightly bewildered shake and followed Jelli down the hall.

Whak left George alone in the living room, trying to fix the TV remote that had not worked for five years. They had talked for half an hour, but George was no closer to understanding what Whak was saying than when they had started. He lived in a mechanical world, where every push resulted in a shove and there was an unbroken line of causality from event to event. Whak believed that, too, but he also believed that the cause and effect could be connected in ways that human beings were not yet equipped to understand. He had a weakness for the Advance Force theory. Maybe SRMs were the incalculable workings and triggers of a plan conceived by an alien mind. But Lino's connection with whatever force motivated the moving metal objects was incomprehensible.

Whak came into the kitchen mumbling "Giant mechanical brain in the bowels of the earth, that's what it is. Antlike queen of the mobile hands."

"Mr Puihare," Kutters said smoothly. "My condolences for the terrible experience you have undergone."

"Thank you," Whak said politely. He looked closely at Kutter's face. "You're that religious doorknocker," he realised. "Jelli, what is he doing here?"

"He let himself in," Jelli said tiredly. She pushed a button on the coffee percolator, which immediately made a sharp noise and spat an overpowerful jet of steam into the filter. Jelli went to the cupboard and took out a cup.

"You can go away," Whak suggested to Kutters. "We don't believe what you do."

"How can you disbelieve in the power of creation?" Kutters demanded forcefully. "How can you disbelieve, when your own daughter was part of the Lord's plan? I have seen with my own eyes, Mr Puihare, that the voice of the Lord spoke through your daughter and to his new children. She was a conduit between this world and God!"

"Oh, please go away." This was a terrifying threat to Whak's sanity that he didn't want to deal with. "Whatever Lino did to SRMs has nothing to do with religion, or God, or anything like it," he said firmly. "So, please get out of my house."

Kutters was not an easy man to dismiss. Instead of leaving, he sat down on a stool by the bar.

"The Revital Church has two million members," he announced. "It is the fastest growing church in the country. I am not mistaken, Mr Puihare."

"I think your rate of growth has very little connection with how mistaken you are," Whak snapped, losing his temper. "Get out of here! We don't want your self-serving sympathy and posturing! What do you want to do, make Lino a fucking saint or something?" As his voice increased in volume, he stepped closer to Kutters and towered over him threateningly.

"We do not hold with the concept of saints," said Kutters. "We - "

"The best voice of the Lord is a dead voice of the Lord, is that it?"

"Let him talk," Jelli broke in, uncharacteristically tolerant. "He came here for something. Let's hear what it is. Then you can throw him out." She poured her coffee. Whak gaped at her, astonished.

"Thank you, Mrs Puihare." Kutters shifted into a sermonising tone that grated severely on Whak's patience. "We believe that God has afflicted the world with SRMs, not as a punishment, but as a sign that His power to create is far from ended. We believe that a millennium is coming, and that God will speak to us directly as he did in the days of our youth."

"You missed the millennium by a decade or two," Whak pointed out, but Kutters went on without heed.

"So we know that the machine creatures called SRMs are directly motivated by God's will. Science cannot explain their life. There is no energy source, they say, to power them, no engine within them, no explanation for what they are or what they do. But we know the answer. Every movement, every action of the SRMs is a direct result of God's will."

"This is crap," Whak moaned to Jelli.

"It's not that far from what's been said in some of the science journals and papers I have summarised at work," Jelli replied.

"Some have glimmers of the truth," Kutters nodded. "I was at the Wasteland the day that your daughter caused the first of the SRM events, as they have come to be known." His face and voice remained smooth, but there was a faint shadow of guilt hovering over him. It does not do for an Elder of the Church to touch the breasts of a prophet. Kutters broke from his momentary and unnecessary fear that punishment was due him. "This was the first speaking of the Lord." A theatrical resonance in his tone suggested that he was winding up for a humdinger of a sermon.

"What was he saying, exactly?" Whak asked sarcastically.

"Hey!" George's voice came from the living room. "Hey! Whak! Jelli! Come here!" He sounded frantic, if anyone could imagine such a thing. Whak and Jelli both tilted their heads. He called again.

"All right!" Whak called back. Anything to escape from Kutters. He and Jelli both left the kitchen.

Kutters was vexed. It was hard to teach the gospel to these people. He followed.

CHAPTER 44

What with all the SRM events lately, on top of the usual random shootings, things were getting behind at the morgue. It was depressing to come to work each day and find mostly the same old bodies lying there waiting for you. To add to the malaise, diagnosing the cause of death became pointless when there can be nothing to gain from it. Murderers were not punished, epidemics were not treated, and patterns were not analysed.

The coroner was late, and there were a lot of cases that had to be dealt to today. The duty attendant knew what that meant. After a small random sample, the less interesting corpses would be tagged and bagged and dispatched for disposal, and the coroner would file a pile of identical reports. All the Joes and Janes went that way. But there were also a couple of real people here, and real people had relatives and friends waiting for the body. The duty attendant, despite everything a human being, always pushed those ones through first. He took his list and began to search the room for Puihare, Lino.

He found her on a rack in the corner. The attendant rolled her out through the flapping swing doors, into the cold and empty theatre. He switched on the lights and went out to find his assistant. When he and his assistant returned, the coroner had arrived and was picking up his instruments one by one, studying the blades and saws, and with an occasional tutting sound, putting them down again. He said hello.

"Hello," said the duty attendant. "Ready to have her on the table?" He had a habit of making sexual innuendoes about the dead. It was standard mortuary humour and made them feel less like bags of organs and more like people, however deceased.

He unzipped the bag. Lino was white and cold and dead and naked. They took her by her shoulders and feet and placed her under the glare of the lamps. The assistant attendant went back to the dead room to detail the next corpse.

"What's the story of this one?" asked the coroner. He had moved over to the sink and was scrubbing his hands, a procedure the attendant had never understood. He wasn't going to infect anybody. Death is the ultimate antibody.

"Shot, two times, bled to death before help arrived. Name," he checked the bagtag again to be sure. "Puihare, Lino."

"Oh, that one. Daughter of the PushRight woman. Even the rich and famous end up under the lights, don't they?" The attendant made no comment. What could he say? The truth can be too banal for serious discussion. "Well, let's get started. We'd better do her thoroughly. We'll get the bullets out first." He came back to the table, picked up a scalpel and inspected Lino's torso for holes.

"Two bullet wounds," he commented, "fatal wound is to thoracic cavity. Probably severing the subclavian vein." He bent and eyed the bullet entrance carefully. "There's some yellow material in the opening." He took up forceps and began to probe. Almost as soon as he touched the yellow, he jerked back. "Ow," he said forcefully.

"What's the matter?"

"Something tingled me. The forceps. Got a bit of an electric shock." The coroner shook his fingers, and made to probe the wound again. "Damn!" he said, pulling back. "It's doing it again!"

The attendant had seen a faint yellowness arise around the forceps as they entered. "There's some kind of gas coming out," he observed. "Yellow gas."

"Decomposition is not that advanced," said the coroner. "In fact, there's little sign of it." He looked curiously at the ends of his forceps and his eyes widened. "The ends of these have been dissolved," he said urgently. "Evacuate the room, quick!"

Biohazard was not a situation that the morgue was designed to cope with. There were no airtight doors or positive air pressure areas here. The room had once been a storeroom for biomedical equipment parts. The two attendants and the coroner stood outside the theatre doors, faces pressed against the fuzzy plastic windows as from Lino's body the yellow cloud slowly expanded.

"Go and tell someone what's happening," the coroner ordered. As the assistant gratefully ran off, the duty attendant saw Lino begin to move. She rolled her head to the side and looked straight at the window behind which the two men were cowering.

"Oh my God," he shouted," oh my God, oh my God! She's alive!" He fell back from the window, aghast, and pawed at the arm of the other man. "She's alive! She's alive!"

"Shut up!" the coroner shouted back at him. "She's not alive. A reaction of some kind to that yellow cloud, or an electrical effect. Of course she's not alive."

"Of course she's not alive," the attendant echoed instantly, nodding furiously in agreement. "Of course she's not alive." He bravely put his face to the window again.

Lino swung her legs to the side of the operating table and sat up. She continued to stare at the doors. It was a nightmare come true for the duty attendant. For years he had deliberately deadened his reaction to working in rooms full of dead bodies, by treating them lightheartedly as if they still possessed the spark of life, however faint. He talked to them, slapped their faces, and smiled into their unseeing eyes. Trivialised, the physical remains of death had lost the ability to disturb him. But he was disturbed now. That woman was dead. She couldn't be getting off the table and walking naked towards him, hard nipples almost black against her breasts, her body surrounded by a faint yellow haze. He panted in panic and whimpered involuntarily with every step she took. Before she had crossed half the distance to the doors of the morgue, he had given in to his fear. He ran as if for his life down the corridor that led to the admitting desk.

The coroner was not so quick to flee. He waited until she was pushing the doors open and her halo was in his face before he retreated slowly down the corridor, avoiding her shining touch.

The great days of newscasting were over. News was what PushRight Creative Media said it was, not what was actually happening, and the power of individuals to affect events was a myth, but the story of a woman rising from the dead was too good to miss. A GOV1 news team was set up at the front of the hospital within a few minutes of the story coming out. They had already interviewed the coroner, who in a rather clipped medical manner had described the events leading up to this phenomenon. If he had been reciting his findings as he sawed the top off someone's cranium he could not have been more controlled. For contrast, the mikeman lined up the morgue duty attendant, who gibbered in a much more satisfying way that the corpse had come alive before his eyes, and stood up, and walked. It had been he who had called GOV1.

"So is there in fact a walking corpse at large in Central Hospital? These two men seem to think so. We're approaching the main entrance now. Here comes someone who must have seen this woman. Excuse me!"

The nurse he called to never even looked his way. Instead, she made haste down the ramp and away along the street. The mikeman beckoned his cameraman onwards. "Missed her chance of fame," he said. "We'll go inside and see this shining woman for ourselves."

"OK," said the cameraman. He was a man of little imagination who was allowed to drive a camera mainly because he had the technical knowhow to keep it functional. If he lost the camera, he lost his job. He was, therefore, acutely concerned about SRM populations. "But, er, Gene, there's some SRMs around, look there." There, was a teddy bear climbing slowly up the brickwork towards a window. And there was a croc in the gutter, travelling in smooth silence from it's last hydraulic meal to it's next.

"Shit on that," said Gene. "This could be the most interesting story I've ever covered and I'm not going to walk out of here because of a couple of metal mice. Come on."

"OK," said the cameraman again, uncertainly. An ambulance pulled in behind them, half the lights flashing and the siren silent. The croc changed direction and crawled underneath it. The news team continued up the ramp and went in the emergency admittance doors. There was a wide long corridor leading to the admitting desk, where rows of wooden seats like pews were occupied by dozens of people waiting for attention. Hospital staff were milling around in the space behind the desk, in front of the wall of venetian blinds that separated the admitting area from the consulting rooms. Incandescent light gave the room an old and yellow appearance. Gene went up and attracted the attention of a nurse, an easy thing to do when there is a large man behind you pointing an enormous video camera over your shoulder.

"Excuse me! Where is the walking corpse?" Gene had already developed what he thought was a neat and newsworthy appellation. The nurse gave him a stern look.

"Are you a doctor?" she asked unnecessarily.

"No, I'm from GOV1," said Gene, flashing a smile. "I've just interviewed the coroner and the morgue attendant. I know that there's a woman strolling around in here who's supposed to be dead. So where is she?" He waved his hand mike in front of the nurse. "I want to interview her." The video camera whirred softly by his ear.

The nurse decided to get busy with a dosage schedule. From the group of white-coated men and woman near the venetians, a grey-haired man looked up and saw the video camera nosing around. He came straight over and spoke to Gene in the calm and authoritative manner which usually means lies are being told.

"If you're here about the woman in the morgue, I'm afraid you've wasted your time. It's all just a practical joke, and when I find out who started this ridiculous story, I'll..."

He was interrupted by another doctor, who banged down a telephone handset and said loudly "Jesus Christ! She's heading for intensive care!"

The words had only just hit the air when Gene looked up at the department signs that hung over every door. The mikeman and his camera wasted no more time with the official apologist. Neither did the group behind the desk reciprocate. With the exception of the nurse that Gene first spoke to, they all moved off at speed in the direction of intensive care.

Jim was not aware. He was not even dreaming. It's a non-state, dying, that indicates how peripheral the mind is to the important business of being alive. The mind is switched off when it is uneconomic to run it. What further evidence is required that the soul dies with the body?

Lino's body had died, but now Lino's body was alive. She stood at the end of Jim's bed, from time to time turning her head as if listening. Her cloud swirled in varying densities around her.

Gene had succeeded in reaching the ward before anybody else. With his cameraman glued to his shoulder, he ran into the room.

"There she is!" he said excitedly. "Oh, this is going to be great! She's got no clothes on! Justifiable news time nudity! Excuse me! Shit, what's her damn name?"

"Lino Puihare," supplied the cameraman, who had been listening to the doctors who were quickly arriving behind them. "Jelli Puihare's daughter. Jesus, look at the holes in her chest."

"Lino Puihare! She was killed in some big business confrontation a couple of days ago. Terrific! Daughter of PushRight CEO Rises from the Dead! And it's for real! And it's my shift! Hey!" Gene went straight across the room and stuck his mike into Lino's aura. "Can you tell us how you feel?"

The crowd of doctors, nurse, and porters which had been slightly less swift than GOV1's finest, all arrived at the moment that Gene dropped his microphone. With a loud exclamation, he started back away from the girl, shaking his hand. Her aura glowed and several objects nearby, including the dropped microphone, deliquesced vigorously, adding colour to yellow gas, only faintly visible under the lights, that surrounded her. Her face was easily visible through the cloud, but there was nothing to be read there. Her eyes stared and her mouth hung slightly open. Gene's disturbance turned her away from Jim's deathbed. She walked to the door, scattering the assembly there in confusion, and went out.

"Did you get that?" Gene shouted at his cameraman.

"I, uh, yeah, I think so. Look, you can get another mike but I can't get another camera. Let's, like, not get right up in her face, you know? Who knows what she might do next time?" He picked up the remains of the microphone, which weighed half what it had a few moments before, and handed it back to Gene, who looked at it with a thoughtful expression.

"Yeah, whatever," he said at last. "Let's feed what we got through the truck."

"Right," said the cameraman, relieved.

Going back to their vehicle, they followed a path of some chaos. Wherever Lino had passed, there were frightened faces and a general meltdown of equipment, and when the two newsmen came out onto the street, there was a new factor to the situation. Lino was walking slowly down the footpath, glowing slightly under the moon-illumed clouds, and from the gutters and the potholes, the drainpipes and the derelict trucks and cars that lined every street of the city, SRMs were emerging. They surrounded Lino, another cloud, this one of path-clattering legs and silently swivelling sensor pods. Not a woman, anymore, but a collection of things. Lino, her cloud, her remote biomechanical parts, together progressing towards who knows what. When she moved, they moved. When, with a gulp of nanoviretic hunger the surface of a nearby car or the contents of a shopfront window hissed into gas, the SRMs expanded their range from her body, taking the more mechanical parts of the environment to pieces. Most people had already cleared off the street, but one man who had just arrived on the scene was being chased from her way by at least twenty SRMs that were only satisfied when his buckles were their dinner and his wristwatch their dessert. A formation of small flying objects wheeled into view and hovered a few metres above Lino's head.

"I'm going to lose my camera for sure," moaned the cameraman.

"Stop whining! You're going to be able to buy a hundred cameras," Gene told him. "Go plug into the truck. Let's get this story on the air."

"This is Elizabeth Furth with a special interest bulletin."

"She's a Revitalist," Jelli said irrelevantly, studying her face. She, Whak and George all looked at Kutters, then back at the screen. Static flickered around Elizabeth Furth's face as the light-drama news-tone theme played.

"What did you call us for, George?" Whak asked.

"They said that..." George stopped. "Well, you'll see."

"God damn it, George, what did you call us for!" Whak said angrily, but the picture on the TV screen stopped him from further comment. Large behind Elizabeth Furth, Central Hospital appeared, and outside it a crowd of people. The camera drew back and panned left onto a man holding a microphone in the face of another. At the bottom of the screen, the byline read 'Gene Weldon at Central Hospital'. Elizabeth Furth faded out and voiceover began.

"Startling events unfolded this evening at the Central Hospital when a recently deceased body allegedly came to life during an autopsy procedure and walked around in the hospital. We interviewed the eyewitnesses at the scene."

"Central Hospital," Whak said.

"Lino," said Jelli, swallowing hard. "Lino's there."

The text on the screen told them that the man now speaking was the second senior city coroner. In a controlled voice he described the rising of the corpse. "There is some sort of atmospheric effect around her," he finished. "A yellow glow surrounding her body. I received a slight electric shock when I came into contact with it."

Whak put George's shoulder in a fierce grip. He needed no further identification. "What's happened to her?" he asked in fear.

The frame cut to another man, a smaller, more excited person who spoke twice as fast as the other.

"Everything she gets near is just vapourised, you know, just woosh! Boiling yellow stuff! I just ran down to the desk and told everyone we had a class A biohazard, but really, I don't know what the shit it is. She melted the ends of the doc's forceps. I don't know where she is in there, but I'm not going to try and find out, no way. She can go wherever she likes."

The voiceover resumed, while the camera angle took a crazy walk through hospital corridors. People's faces. Doors swinging open and closed. White-coated men and women avoiding the eye of the news.

"Latest on this amazing event. The identity of the woman allegedly returned from the dead is Lino Puihare, daughter of the well-known Government subcontractor Jelli Puihare, Chief Executive of PushRight Creative Media Ltd." The voice doing the voiceover sounded surprised even as it read out the words. Quickly recovering the impersonal language of the media, it went on "Live footage now on your screens!"

The picture grew dark. There was a streetlamp glowing at the end of the hospital drive. Gene Weldon appeared left of centre, following the luminous figure of Lino Puihare as she walked, slowly and without a glance around her, away from the camera.

"As you can see," he said breathlessly, "the woman is totally naked, and there you can see the two horrific wounds which caused her supposed death. She is literally glowing in the dark, but we are informed by the hospital biohazard team that there is no indication of radioactivity in the morgue, where she has been lying for the past three days. Less obvious to you at home, perhaps, is the retinue of SRMs that are following Lino Puihare down the street. There are some types I have never seen before. Some are actually flying just above us, and there are all manner of ground varieties, surrounding her. Outside the circle of SRMs I see that people are starting to gather at the sides of the street to witness this extraordinary event. We'll try to get in front of her and ask her some questions."

The camera jerked around. From distant to the mike came a worried announcement.

"I'm not getting any closer. I don't want to lose my camera."

Gene's hand took up the screen, pulling the lens back to where he wanted it, on him. His face was angry. "Are you crazy? This is a goddamned once-in-a-lifetime piece of news, you dummy. Come on!" Towing the cameraman, he ran ahead of the mixture of Lino, cloud, and machine, circled around. Briefly the gathering crowd flashed by, then Lino's face appeared. Pale, cold, and glassy.

"Where are you going, Lino Puihare?" Gene asked.

The camera zoomed up to a close head shot. As it did so, a faint trace of awareness phased into view.

"Home," she replied, and then there was a shrill screaming sound and the picture cut off.

Jelli whimpered.

"She is the Return of God," Kutters said, awestruck. It was one thing to devise a plausible story of Saint Lino of the Wasteland, and quite another for her to rise from the dead. "She is the Return of God to our world!" He looked terribly, terribly frightened as he thought about the possible penalties for trying to touch God's breasts. And all his other weaknesses and sins. He fell to his knees and put his hands together. His frantic murmuring prayers sounded like a small animal in pain.

Whak spent a distant moment contemplating the possibility that Lino was indeed, as this fool next to him said, the Second Coming. He had just about finished this purely intellectual exercise when Elizabeth Furth's head and shoulders, in the studio, came back onscreen. She was smiling widely. Her hair was disarrayed.

"Oh, rejoice!" she said happily. Whatever else she might have planned was interrupted. She was roughly pushed out of the way by another presenter.

"We regret that the preceding news item has been found to be a hoax by a freelance news team," this man began. Elizabeth Furth's hands came from right screen and scratched him bloodily down his cheek.

"Lies!" she screamed. "It is the Coming!"

"We'll be back after this commercial message," said the bloody-cheeked man as the lashing hands continued to attack him. The news studio disappeared. So did everything else. GOV1 was off the air.

Kutters was chanting a hymn to the greatness of God.

George stood up and nodded firmly.

"Nanoviral effects," he said confidently. "It must have, er, repaired her, somehow. And whatever she does that affects SRMs, the nanovirus has obviously enhanced it significantly. It looks as if the effect of intercommunication among the nanomachines has produced a whole that is infinitely more powerful than it's parts. It may be acting as a neural network."

"Is it still her?" Whak asked quietly.

"I don't think we'll know the answer to that question until she gets here," George said carefully. "We'll have to get some equipment organised." He looked expectantly at Jelli. "Mrs Puihare?"

She was still staring at the television. Whak took her hand.
"Jelli," he said.
"What have I done to her?" she whispered.
"It's not your fault, Jelli." Whak pulled her to the window.

People were starting to collect on the street, people wanting to see the home of the woman who had risen from the dead.
In the distant sky, Whak thought he saw a group of spinning lights.
The alien force is here.
God is alive.
Nanomachines mutate out of control.
It didn't matter what the truth was. From this moment forward, history would take over from truth.
Whak held Jelli, but then, important words came to him. Gently, he let go of the woman he loved and went for his satchel. The living room wall was a large blank space that he had never, until now, wanted to write on. He took out a spray can and went over to it.

W E L C O M E   H O M E

THE END